DEATH REGISTER

For my son, Julian Ryo,
I truly hope you find your place in this world

DWIGHT THOMPSON

DEATH REGISTER

PEEPAL TREE

First published in Great Britain in 2018
Peepal Tree Press Ltd
17 King's Avenue
Leeds LS6 1QS
England

ISBN13: 9781845234072

Supported using public funding by
ARTS COUNCIL
ENGLAND

PART I

DEPARTURE

I sat at the kitchen table watching Mama make duckanoo. I had cut banana leaves that morning and was stripping the husk into long thin strands for her to tie the parcels with, before she dropped them into boiling water to cook.

Recipe for Revenge: Ingredients

225g cassava flour
125g coconut (dried or shredded)
300ml fresh milk
55g raisins
30g melted butter (avoid margarine!)
60g brown sugar
4-5 tablespoons water
¼ teaspoon grated nutmeg
½ teaspoon cinnamon
1 teaspoon vanilla extract

Mama made her duckanoo with cassava flour rather than plain flour; that way it was more glutinous, more pudding than cake. As it boiled, the sugar would leave the jellied centre to combine with the natural sugar of the cassava, then rise to the surface of the glazed skin, absorbing a tinge of bitterness from the banana leaves that balanced the flavour and provided a distinct fragrance. It was so succulent that even fresh out of the pot, when the steaming mixture stuck to the roof of your mouth and felt as if it would melt your gums, you tolerated the pain just to savour the unadulterated sweetness before the cake cooled and solidified.

After blending the coconut and milk till smooth, she combined it with the flour and stirred in the other ingredients. Then, she spooned the mixture onto banana-leaf squares (made pliable by dipping them into boiling water), tied them snugly with the husk strips, and dropped them into the pot. Preparation Time: 40-60 mins. Servings: 5-6. Serve warm.

"The raisins, Mama. You forgot the raisins!"

"It's sweet enough!" she snapped. "You tryin' to sick yourself?"

"Then why you make me buy them?"

She ignored me. I sighed, but I couldn't be angry, not when my feelings for her were so acute. But was it fear of leaving behind a familiar life rather than just leaving her protection?

"You lucky," she said, her back turned to me at the stove. "Let's see who goin' to fuss over you when you go to Kingston. Them don't know the meaning of sincerity. If you ask for a drink o' water they serve you in a plastic cup, smile in your face, then throw it away. That's what passes for hospitality. An' they consider them-selves civilised."

She said the word 'civilised' so that it came out as a long contemptuous hiss.

"I don't know," I said. "Maybe I'd rather drink from a plastic cup than from a glass everybody else spit in. An' at least they pay you the courtesy of a smile."

She took my bait, thumping the kitchen counter in exaspera-tion. "Chauncey, that's not the point. If you keep givin' people fake smiles all your life is whose jaws hurting? Who plays the hypocrite is the same one who suffers, nobody else."

She spoke to the pot as she stirred. "...They don't go to the beach to swim, they go to 'lime' – 'cause everybody speakin' like Trinidadians these days. They don't eat bulla cake with avocado they eat it with cheddar cheese..."

"How you know so much 'bout Kingstonians?"

"Don't worry yourself 'bout that. An' you won't believe what Sheila tell me the other day."

"No," I said. "I don't think I will."

"You remember that gentleman who promise to rent him the

shop space downtown? Well, he's a Kingstonian. He told Sheila that before he start sellin' property, he used to sell crockery. An' he had a motto for his store: If you break it, you buy it. A man impregnate his teenage daughter, an' when she tell him who the father was he pack her bags an' march her straight to the man's house an' drop her off on his doorstep. He tell the man: 'If you break it, you buy it,' then left. Now you tell me if those people normal. Cold even to their own kin."

I laughed, flipping through the pages of an old notebook as I sorted through a box I was packing.

"You free to shop around," she said. "You can look, you can touch, you can even sample. But anyone you break, make sure she worth buyin.' You hear me, bwoy?"

I feigned deafness.

"You hear me?" she said louder.

"Yes, ma'am. But if I break anybody I can't afford, can I send you the bill?"

"Don't get saucy."

Then she asked, "Harry serious 'bout that girl?"

"Harry…? Harry says she's pregnant. But then the next word out of his mouth was 'paternity test'."

Mama said, "Ugh!" and shook her head. "You jus' watch yourself… dem college girls experienced."

(She meant they were sex-crazed).

"Dem family rich, yours isn't. You mess up an' you lan' right back in Mobay on your backside; no second chance!"

"You don't have to worry 'bout girl makin' baby." I wasn't coming back.

She gave me a strange look. "What you mean by that?"

I shrugged.

This was the closest we'd ever come to discussing the birds and the bees. I wish I'd provoked her more but my concentration was divided. I was looking through the notebook. Yet I wanted to talk, wanted her to know what I felt, and my yearning for her sharpened when she bent over me to give me a glass of prune juice. I wanted to catch the end of her skirt, the way I would as a child, sitting on the sofa sucking my lip and playing with my belly-button.

"How Sanjay gettin' on?"

I was glad for the question because I had a joke to share. "He workin' by the city centre in his family's shop. Harry said when he start workin' by the courthouse, he and Sanjay used to meet for lunch everyday. At first when he went by the shop, Sanjay's uncle would smile an' slap his back an' say, 'Harry... that's a Hindu name, you know. Say hi to Vice-Principal Glenn for me.' But by the secon' week, his uncles started showin' Harry bad face. Sanjay start actin' sulky. Then Harry realise that goin' out for lunch was a foreign concept to them. They work right roun' the clock. Monday, when Harry call on him, Sanjay say, 'Harry, what you want?' The Tuesday he say, 'Harry, what you want to buy?'"

"Kiss me neck!" Mama exclaimed softly, and turned her face away and laughed. "Is lie you tellin' on de poor bwoy. You been to see him before he goes back to Miami?"

"I went to his house yesterday. He said he's had enough of college, he not goin' back, his place is in the duty-free shop. Him already gettin' that money-hungry Hindu look in his face – with the black teabags under his eyes an' the long nasty nose hairs."

"Chauncey, you take it too far." Her tone had hardened. "Sanjay should know. He was always de level-headed one. You an' Harry now... mercy... when de two o' you lick head, what oonuh won't do, Diego Tobago ain't invent. So all t'ings considered, I glad both o' you separatin', an dis is a fair warnin'. I takin' dis las' chance to try an' call yuh to yuh senses. Foolish dawg grin him teet' at bulldog an' bark after flyin' bird, an' if yuh play de foolish dawg when yuh leave here, kindly remember – yuh don't have a kennel to come back to." She started juicing the soursop, the milk flowing through her thin brown fingers.

"This prune juice is very good." She seemed pleased to hear it. I smiled and smacked my lips. When she turned her attention back to juicing, I said, "Mama..."

"Yes, dear."

"Why yuh leggo dat gardener so quickly? Him do somet'ing wrong?"

"Is a funny t'ing; he was so nice an' polite in de beginnin', then Tuesday I serve him lunch on de verandah an' I ask what him like to do – you know – jus' makin' small talk. Him say fishin.' Fair enough. Then de next day him say him have an album to show me. I say fine, 'cause I feel it mus' be an album wid pictures of his family. Only fe de man show me dis album full o' dead fish!"

I did a spit-take, the juice spilling through the gap in my front teeth. Mama's surprise at the unexpected grimness still animated her face. She looked at me and I could see she wanted to laugh too, but didn't. "Yuh laughin', Chauncey, but it ain't funny. Wha' kinda man keeps an album of fish him catch? Not someone wid all dem screws in place you hear me. I get de feelin' right there I had to fire him."

"A death register," I said, "That's what that album was… Writing about Tristan often feels like that."

She ignored my comment, pressing her thin fingers through the foaming white soursop pulp. It was still too hard for her to talk about him. No matter how much I tried to coax her into conversation to court her comfort, she denied it. "You can resist talkin' 'bout Tristan all yuh want, but I'll keep sendin' down my bucket till something comes up!" Sometimes, when I spoke to her without thinking, she would give me a strange look as if I weren't her own. I knew it was my corruption she saw, but pretended otherwise. Her shoulders jerked, but she didn't respond.

She must have felt my eyes lingering on her, on her long hair bundled under a yam-yellow head-wrap. All the children had her hair, though not as straight; theirs was a wavy strain, but they all had her large, deep-set eyes and prominent brow bone. Aunt Girlie had her pale brown skin. Ma turned and caught the look of longing in my face and it pleased her. I dropped my eyes, embarrassed. Her powers renewed, she said casually, "I go pack some goggle-eye fish so you can have something to eat on your first night."

"But Mama, it will smell! And why you put that plaque of Barnett Estate in me bag? Saul Marzouca don't know me any different from his horses, yet I suppose to hang a picture of his mansion and estate…"

"Shut your face! What so wrong if I put few souvenirs in your bag?" This quiet aggressiveness would strike fear in us as children –Tristan and I – because it signalled the start of a beating, but now I knew it was because of her sorrow over my leaving. She raised her voice for the neighbours' benefit. "Ever since you know you leavin', you fulla big chat, as if you already out the door, but as long as you under this roof, you're *my* child. I don't care how old you be, I don't care what you doin' outta street either, you hear me? An' don't mind what dem others doin' too; you ain't man yet! You start smellin' yourself – I know – but don't pass your place with me – don't do it! – an' you kindly tell your combolo that once I'm alive you have to respect me! You know I don't take backchat from pitney, an' when you see dem formin' fool or playin' man, tell them no. Sorry, you can't play that game with me 'cause I ain't that sorta woman no how, you hear me? You not out the door yet! You have to treat me with respect! An' don't think you too tall for me to drag your pants down an' give you a good soundin' out."

I couldn't help smiling at the prospect of her attempting to beat me; it had been so long since she threatened to do this, and her euphemism – "soundin' out" – struck an absurd note. She caught the amusement in my face.

"What yuh smilin' for? You think I makin' fun?"

"I know you not makin' fun, Mama."

She sighed and tossed her head. "But what you really take me for though, eh?" *This* question, I knew better than to answer. I closed the notebook and kept my eyes on her, never sure she wouldn't reach for something to fling at my head. "You think I would allow you to leave here without packing your supper – never mind souvenirs – but without *supper,* your first night in a strange place? You were always a cold, unfeelin' child, Chauncey, never thinkin' one tot 'bout anybody but yourself. How yuh come so? Who yuh take dat coldness from?"

"I *feel* all right… I feel enough."

"Wha' kinda writer you goin' to be when you so selfish, when you never take into account other people's feelings? That girl Marzipan told me that you so strange you refuse to even take her to the cinema when you go to see a film."

"I don't read a book with anyone, so why should I watch a movie with anyone. It's difficult to find the concentration and quiet I need to figure out why the picture is affecting me."

"That's it right there! That tone – that self-serving tone! An' you treat your family no different! If me or Girlie clean your room and misplace anyt'ing you writin', you act as cold as ice to everybody in de house for days. An' every time you writin' and I call you for dinner, you t'ink I don't hear you suckin' your teeth. You ever t'ink how it make me feel to hear that? When all I tryin' to do is feed you, yet have to endure your scornful nature, as if I deprivin' you of somethin', as if I drivin' a wedge between you an' your…"

This was too much. My head was so hot I could see her lips moving but couldn't hear the words anymore. I said, "Why you puttin' all this on me? You never know how much it hurt to be always worrying 'bout how what I say or do will make you feel. Is like I wearin' a pair of shoes that always squeezin' but can never take them off."

"Is what you not saying? Tell me more."

I was dying to say a lot more, but I didn't trust myself to speak because I feared I would lose control and say something cutting, but the words tumbled out anyway. "When I writing…" I began, but stopped. "When I'm writing – is the only time I get to be myself! Why you tryin' to make me feel bad about it?"

Now she watched me with a mute restraint I couldn't bear.

"It's a pity," she said dolefully, "that's probably your best self…"

Fire and ice were inside me. The tears slipped down my face. I was powerless to stop them. "I love you, Mama… don't you know?"

She watched me warily. "You've spoken the truth and let's leave it at that. Don't spoil it by pretendin' those tears are for me."

I went back to my reading. In the silence the tension between us eased. I was looking over some of my older stories, reading with tightness in my stomach. In some I'd placed myself at a safe distance from what I wrote, as if afraid that if I got too close I would touch my true self buried beneath the words. At the back of the book, I saw the draft I'd jotted that day after coming home from Sugar Navel and quarrelling with Tristan. I reread the working title: *A release is coming! The stone is being rolled away.* I put the notebook aside, I didn't have to read beyond that; the story came quickly to memory, as did his face. I got up and went to the fridge for ice cubes for my glass. "Mama, how long before the cakes finish?"

"'Bout twenty minutes, love."

Everyone else was at work and the house was quiet, save for the gurgling of the pot on the stove and the yard fowls making a racket on the water tank outside, fighting over hog plums that dropped like hard little green stones onto the tank's roof. The fowls had a clever method of consuming them; they pecked at the unyielding flesh, then left the bruised fruit to spoil from exposure; later they returned to reap the worms from the rotting pulp.

Looking through the window, Mama said, "Those fowls don't scratch dirt anymore like normal birds, but gone all the way up on the tank."

"They don't roost in trees anymore either," I said. "They sleepin' in Papa's old couch in the garage. The whole room stink o' fowl mess. Sheila should take them to the farm." I sat back at the table, passing a hand over the notebook's back page, yellowed and curling, its ink fading, yet the words still disturbing. Where *was* my release from the demons of the past. I knew now, more than ever, that leaving everything behind wasn't progress. Walking away wasn't freedom. I'd always carry the past inside me, my affairs far from settled.

Mama opened the pot and tested the duckanoos with the aluminium spoon. "Won't be long now. You think they know how to turn a good duckanoo in Kingston, Chauncey?"

"I suppose they manage."

"Manage?"

Aunt Girlie had walked in and winked at me. "What Chauncey means, Mama, is the men there don't mind their women baking right off the back of a cake box."

"Ugh!"

I went out on the porch and opened a more recent notebook.

Red Dragon

I ordered two prostitutes. I told the manager I was going away and wanted a last hoorah. He said, "You always goin' off. Last week it was the army, the week before it was Canada, and the week before that it was to heaven." He seized my hand and shook it vigorously while eying my pool-cue case. "Don't take it so serious, man, is likkle joke I runnin'. Yuh cock tough like a wall in your pants tonight, eh. No worries. We soon tek care o' dat. But you see, I don't want any Missa

Man comin' in here thinkin' he can order me around jus' because we have a passin' acquaintance."

"Familiarity breeds contempt," I said. "I suppose this time when I leave I should stay away for good."

He ignored this and said, "I have the perfect girl for you. They call her Forget-me-not." He beckoned behind him with his fat black fingers, but the girls were already traipsing round the lounge in their nightgowns and stilettos to see who had come in.

I rubbed my palms together. "Now it's time for bartering, that tug-o-war I can never seem to win. For the umpteenth time, when you goin' to have a discount day? You know… like they do at the cineplex: Monday is Couples Day, Tuesdays Ladies' Day and Fridays Mens' Day and 30% percent off."

He replied as if scandalised: "But see here! Every day is Mens' Day here. I jus' too modest to advertise the discount." He clapped his hands and called, "Forget-me-not!" A slender, sweet-faced girl with long curls stepped from behind a beige partition, tall and shapely, with bow legs and a thigh gap that stretched the sheer fabric of her nightie over her wide hips. She held her hands behind her as she sauntered up the steps, as shiny as a new penny. The other girls dawdled back to the velvet settees and pool tables.

He said out of the side of his mouth, "You see how she walks on the outsides of her feet? Never marry a girl like that; she'll ruin a pair of shoes every month." Then he looked me in the eye. "Now that's the glow I like to see on a man's face. It give me a great feeling, bwoy. Have fun."

The girl was smiling invitingly, with the lush light of the neon RED STRIPE BEER sign shining through the window behind her and falling on her head and shoulders. We made our way down the steps to a room of her choice. She slipped out of her nightgown, lit me a Matterhorn, and lay on my arm while I smoked, staring at the ceiling. "How do you like it here?" I said. She said quietly, "I live in St James before – I'm no stranger to this place. But I spend most o' me life in St Ann. I only come back here two weeks ago to start workin.' I lef' me daughter with me family, an' told me mother I goin' to the Caymans to work in the service industry." She smiled at her joke and snuggled up to my chest. When I laughed, she looked up and said, "What's so funny?" "You wouldn't want to hear." "Try me." I put out the cigarette and eased up on my elbow. "OK, when Vidia Naipaul, my favourite writer, was *young, looking for a room to rent in London, he rang at a house advertising a vacancy and a woman said over the intercom, 'Are you black?' And Naipaul answered, 'Hopelessly.'* I watched her face for a response. "See, now you've embarrassed me by making me tell you an unfunny joke." She said quickly, "No no – I like it." Her manner was calm and graceful. I placed my hand along the gentle rise of her hip then stroked her cheek and held her chin and stared into her eyes. The smile came very easily to her face. I kissed her forehead: "Now ask me." "Ask you what?" "If I'm black." "But I can see that you are." "Yes, but can you really see me?" "What do you mean?" "Just as I said, can you really see me?" "You're lying right beside me." "Yes, but can you see me?" She started getting up. I grabbed her wrist. She flounced and snapped, "Leggo me bloodclaat hand! Me nuh ina de kinky fuckery wid yuh today."

She got up and pulled on her nightgown, her eyes flat and dark, her mouth jutting with hostility. I jumped up and said to her as she stood at the door, "You know what I want, and I'll pay good money for it." She looked at my fingernail prints in her wrist. I could see her considering, hesitating. I hurried over to her and held her slender smooth elbow and gently led her back to the bed. As she undressed, I opened the pool-cue case and took out the cane. She flinched at the sight, before she started acting lively and curious. Grinning, she took it from me and flexed it. She smiled wryly at the inscription: The Meat Inspector. She narrowed her eyes in sly amusement. "So you come to the meat shop, nuh true?" "I didn't write that." Still looking it over, she asked, "Who's Oswald Harding?" "My old master. This is a memento, the masters traditionally break their canes and offer the pieces to their favourite students after graduation as a parting gift. Either I was the only student he ever fancied or I suspect he knew I needed this one whole." She looked up at me. "You're a Chester boy aren't you? You missing it?" "No. Today you're the student and I'm the master. Take off your panties and lie on your stomach." She hesitated, looked at the other side of the cane, at the fresh inscription I had written only that morning. The Red Dragon. She seemed on the verge of comment but thought better of it. Instead, she took off her panties and sat with her arms back and her legs open, in a last ditch effort to entice me away from my intentions; her pubic hair was waxed to a landing strip above her neat pink slit, the centre wet and shiny. She held my gaze and parted her legs more, but

16

I insisted firmly, "On your stomach." She obeyed reluctantly. I said, "Well, since you're freshly returned to St James, let's have a civics test." She turned her head to one side. "What's the passing grade?" "Six out of ten questions. And for every wrong answer, there's a penalty." With the first strike she made a brief howl like an animal that had had its throat slit, with the second wrong answer, and the second strike, she whimpered and bit the pillow and blood flushed her shapely buttocks, the flesh quivering with her slight shudders. "Next question, who's the patron saint of Montego Bay?" But instead of answering, she spoke to herself in a faraway voice, as if defying me, "Yes, Peaches girl…" With the third strike she made a sharp intake of breath and clenched her buttocks, when she released them, exhaling tremulously, there was a gush and dark wetness spread on the sheet below her thighs. "Yes Peaches…" she said again after the fourth strike, clutching the sheets and speaking in the same detached voice, "Mommy earnin' har money girl…" She wiped her eyes with the heel of her hand after the fifth wrong answer, and the remark that rose to my lips was the same one the good deacon had used when I watched him punishing Tristan that afternoon with the fan-belt. "You coulda cry till your tears touch the sea…" I spat it out like poison, like the Red Dragon's venom, and the cane came down.

I closed the notebook, went back in and said, "Mama, how Brother Mac doin' these days?"

"Not so good," she said. "They stabilise the sugar, but he lost the left foot. They release him from the hospital, though. He's at home resting. But they have to keep an eye on his circulation. Poor soul. Tess beside herself 'cause he won't eat a thing. I made de prune juice for Deacon Mac. It's good for the sugar. Would you mind takin' it over to the house."

As Mama spoke, her hands made aimless circles across her apron. I knew she was thinking of Papa. She tested the duckanoos again and this time was satisfied they were ready. Lifting them carefully from the pot with the spoon, she laid them out in a wooden basin on the table. The steam rose thick and watered my eyes. The banana leaves, moist, dark and soft from simmering, were murderously hot. I was eager to tear them open and ravage the deep-blue sweetness they protected. But I'd wait. "Yes," I said. "I'll take it over to the house."

"You're a dear," she said, smiling at me. "I'll keep the duckanoos warm in the oven till you get back."

"I think I'll take some with me to eat on the way. I too hungry to wait."

"All right, I'll put a few in the bag with the juice jug."

It was almost noon. The day was cool despite the sun's glare. The fowls kept up their racket but the falling fruit had been forgotten; now they squawked and fought senselessly. Mama shaded her eyes to look at them. "You know," she said. "It's a bad thing to say, but I wish the concrete slab would get hot enough to scorch their little feet so they would remember themselves. God forgive me."

"Don't worry," I said, "I think we're allowed at least one evil thought per day. It feels good to break a rule every now and then."

"Don't be too late in comin' back." If I were still a child, she would have finished with: "'Cause the Devil makes his soup from children's bones." But she didn't have to worry anymore. I had watched the Devil make his soup, and drank it.

Serving 1

When I got to their house, Sister Mac was sweeping the verandah. She looked hard before she recognised me, then mumbled for me to enter. It had been over ten years since I'd last visited. Whenever Papa needed sawdust, I'd find some excuse to get out of the errand. But the yard was the same as I'd remembered – flat, treeless, hot – except the woodwork shop at the side of the house had been torn down. I climbed the steps, smelling the wax on the red verandah tiles. Sister Mac held a mop and had a red handkerchief tied over her nose. She was a small, sad-looking woman, undemonstrative, drawing neither attention nor concern. But did she now wear the handkerchief to mask her grief? She acknowledged my greeting, took the bag and thanked me, then led me through the dimly-lit house, asking after my family. My heart hammered as I approached the door. The homily above it said:

WE'RE ALL PUTTY IN THE MASTER'S HANDS

We entered a large, well-ventilated back room that had been converted into a sickroom. His bed was positioned near a double-sided jalousie window. He had heard us coming and was sitting up in bed, with a pretence of jauntiness. He looked weak and wasted, his body swallowed up by his pyjamas, a tangle of sheets covering him from the waist down. He had lost most of his hair and handsomeness; his eyes looked big and bright in his emaciated face; they still had their cunning energy. There was a half-filled glass of pulpy liquid that looked like coconut water on the bedside table. I stood at the foot of the bed, waiting for him to recognise me. The odour of dried sweat and stale urine sharpened; a chamber pot peeping out from under the bed needed emptying. I wished I could see the amputated foot. He caught my eyes moving over his body. I offered a vague smile. He wagged his head and grinned, his lips loose and wet. "Chauncey, you come to look at the half-dead." His wife winced when he said this; she fussed with the window slats, regulating the sunlight falling across the bed.

"Miss Phyllis made prune juice for you," she said, her voice sullen and strange below the handkerchief. "Chauncey was kind enough to bring it." I had taken the duckanoos from the bag and stashed them in my pockets.

"Was he?" Brother Mac said, watching my face. "And how is your grandmother, son?"

"Fine, Deacon Mac. She sends her love. And said to tell you you're always in her prayers."

"She's too kind. Tell her I appreciate that."

Sister Mac brightened, pleased at his change in tone. She removed her handkerchief and used it to dab the perspiration on his forehead. "Chauncey leavin' soon for college, Delroy. Next time you see him he'll be a big shot lawyer."

Brother Mac's eyes popped. "What yuh saying! Congrats, man." He jerked back in annoyance from his wife's touch and swivelled his head towards the bedside table; the papery skin over his neck looked as if it would snap with the effort. "Tess, where my glasses? Why you keep mislayin' me t'ings, woman? Why your hands so light?"

Sister Mac searched while he kept up a steady stream of nagging, contempt curling his lips. She found the glasses behind his pillow. He snatched them from her hands, put them on and leaned against the headboard. "There," he said smiling, "now let me take a good look at Lawyer Knuckle before he leaves Anchovy. The likes of us may never see you again after you open your big firm in Kingston, eh. Mas' Clarence would be proud. He had such high hopes for you. And what a strapping young man you've become."

"You want anything to drink, Chauncey?"

"No thanks, Sister Mac."

"Get him something all the same," he barked.

"No," I said. "I'm really quite all right."

Sister Mac re-tied the handkerchief over her face and gently lifted the chamber pot. The stench swirled. He scowled at her retreat. "You clean this house top to bottom, from mornin' to night, and the dust killin' me faster than this damn diabetes." He reached for the coconut water on the bedside table, but when he lifted the glass he grimaced. "I go ask a favour of you, son. Can you buy me a small bottle of Gilbey's down Reds's supermarket." He rubbed his wrist and groaned. "When the joints get stiff and sore like this, only a little gin can soothe them. Can you do that for an old man?"

"Mind you fixin' to make yourself a cocktail eh, nuh, Deacon Mac."

He appreciated the joke. He laughed and hummed the calypso, *'Gin and coconut water… cannot get in America',* and raised his glass. "Who knows?" he said. "I might get careless and add a few drops. Could you blame me? A man in my position deserves some indulgence." The cunning energy was bringing the colour back to his face. "And what's that smellin' to high heaven since you come into the room?"

"Oh, just some duckanoos," I said. "Mama baked a batch this morning." I took a cake from my pocket. He stared. "I'd share with you," I said good-naturedly, "but you have to watch the sugar." I unwrapped the banana leaf, took a bite and chewed.

"They still warm."

"They smell good, too." He watched me intently, his mouth half-open. "You can't mind this sugar too much," he said. "Some day it up, some day it down. I'm not going to park my life like bus just to please it. No, sah. You can't live your life for sickness. I had a plumbing partner named Afoo Dayday; we went to trade school together and used to go on contracts together. Sickness chop him down a few months back. He never agree with the doctor's warning if he didn't take his meds. Last week the fool fully agree and he drop dead. Ask me how him die?"

I humoured him. "How he die?"

"Son of a bitch catch a pleurisy and dead."

We heard Sister Mac sweeping the yard.

I offered him a cake. He undid the bundle with his teeth, spitting bits of husk into his palm. "*Wooh*," he cooed, savouring each mouthful and working his bony jaws, "I never miss your granny's bake sale at church." He winked at me. "And you know I always had a weakness for sweetness." That was Renee, his secretary at work. We ate in silence. He asked for another cake, a self-pitying look on his face. "This was always my problem. No self-control." Now heady with the pleasure of the unexpected treat, he became chatty and jovial. "You know, I was certain you'd become a famous writer. I remember you spent all that summer with your nose in a book. I couldn't find you to do anything round the shop. What happen, you still do the writing?" When he opened his mouth blue bits of cake filled the caves of his teeth. The sight made me sick. I thought of yard fowls with black worms wriggling in their beaks.

"I still write from time to time," I said.

He half-closed his eyes and said in a confidential tone, "You know, my favourite story is one my technical drawing instructor told us at trade school. You want to hear it?"

I nodded.

The story was about a village lunatic who stole upon a woman washing clothes by a river, overpowered her, raped her, and fled the scene. He told it with jovial abandon. It was a joke after all, the punchline being the newspaper headline: *Nut Screws Washer And Bolts*.

I'd heard it before but laughed anyway. I wondered if he thought he'd got away with his crime, cornered and weak as he was, but obviously content. I said, "I have one too. In fact I wrote it only recently. You want to hear it?"

"Please, be my guest. I have nowhere going."

I leaned forward and took a deep breath. "This story takes place during Market Week, just before Christmas. A vendor goes to Cayman for a few days to buy stock for her store, and leaves her teenage daughter home alone. A man breaks into the house while the girl is asleep and rapes her brutally, over and over again…"

When I was finished, he cocked his head like a bemused mutt. "That's a helluva story. Not jokey like mine. Makes you think 'bout all the suffering in this world."

"Yes," I said. "I suppose it does."

He cleaned his teeth noisily with his tongue. He'd eaten five cakes while I spoke. "These things really happening."

"Yes. I suppose they are."

"As much as you think you have it bad, someone always have it worse. But anyone who causes another suffering will have to answer for it."

I looked at him. "You think so?"

"But of course. God not sleeping. No sin going unpunished."

"God has nothing to do with this." I said this sharply and he looked bewildered by my outburst. I couldn't bear to hear him speak anymore. I got up to leave. "I'll bring the gin tomorrow."

"Thank you," he said. "Pass me that wallet on the table. And bring more duckanoos if you can."

"Yes. Perhaps I'll share another story."

Serving 2

The next day I brought the gin as promised, and eight more cakes. I sat by the bed as before. There was no reservation this time, no halting guilt; he attacked the cakes with gusto, fully content in our conspiracy, encouraged by the sound of his wife sweeping outside. He said, "Tess remind me last night about that poor boy's death. Such an awful thing." And he actually looked remorseful.

"What boy?" I asked.

He blinked. "Your friend, of course. Clare's son."

"It's okay. You can say his name. I'm sure you remember it." He fumbled, his eyes going up in his head as if straining to recollect. "After all, we did work for you in the woodwork shop that spring, in this same yard."

A thought made his mouth tight. He stopped chewing. "Oh yes," he said feebly. "Now that you mention it. But that was so long ago. You have a story for me today?"

"I do. This one is about a carpenter who one spring is charged with the care of two puppies. This man is supposedly god-fearing, but his evil instincts get the better of him and he kills the puppies, drowns them at sea…"

He watched me curiously, weighing each word. I wanted them to pierce his heart. When I finished, his mouth was clamped shut, his eyes, white and bloodless, were drawn up in his head. I thought he was avoiding my stare, but it was something else entirely. He suddenly appeared in distress, taking shallow, rasping breaths and rolling his eyes. He clawed at his throat. "I think the sugar spiking," he rasped. "Too much sweetness in the blood. Can you get me a glass o' prune juice from the fridge." He had consumed at least eight cakes.

I came back with the juice. He drank with noisy, hurried gulps, the glass trembling in his hands, then he fell back limply, his chest rattling with each laboured breath. I wiped the juice dribbling down his chin with my handkerchief. His neck looked thin enough to snap like a twig. *Snap it! Snap it!/ Smother the sonuvabitch with the pillow!/No not yet —*

"Thank you," Brother Mac said, watching me suspiciously. I looked down at him, then pushed my face close to his. His dark hairy nostrils smelled like a rat's nest. I nearly gagged. Understanding passed between us. He held his breath. Not yet, I said with my eyes, not yet, you haven't suffered enough.

I leaned back and said, "You know, when I was a boy no bigger than that table over there, sometimes when Mama sent me to the shop I would pinch the change to buy peanut butter cookies. And whenever she suspected the count was wrong, she'd ask me if I'd spent the money and I'd lie. Then she'd tell me to say 'ah' and she'd check my tongue and smell my breath. Yet no matter how much she beat me for lyin', I kept on doin' it. Why yuh think that is?"

He mashed his mouth inwards, his features collapsing. "The temptation was too great. You just had to have the cookies, regardless of the consequence."

"Consequence… that's a good word… What would you have done in my stead… to avoid the consequence?"

"Me?" He waved me off jovially. "Go on now, heheheh… don't get me started, I would've –" He'd begun brightly then checked himself. "Ah never min' all dat… Past words an' deeds is ol' bone. Let time bury dem an' let no dawg dig dem up. But rest assured, I got away wid more than my fair share of mischief in my day."

He began looking for something in the bedside table drawers, fumbling for the insulin pen. "Here. Can you give me my injection, son. You know, it's partially your fault de sugar spiking eh, nuh. It's the least you can do." I clenched my jaws, but before he could see my reluctance I uncapped the pen and injected him. "Thank you," he smiled, and inspected the cartridge. "There's only a little left… and I won't be able to replace it till next month. These things ain't cheap, you know."

I got up and my knee knocked the insulin pen off the table. "And what about that which can never be replaced?" He furrowed his brows at me as I left, and when he called me to retrieve the pen I ignored him. From the doorway, I watched him crawl out of bed headfirst on his belly.

Serving 3

The next day he wasn't expecting me and was dismayed by the visit, especially when Sister Mac used the opportunity to visit a friend down the street. He looked almost fearful to see her go. But I bribed him with some mangoes I'd picked that morning. At first he stalled, but couldn't hold out. Soon he was stripping away the skin and tearing the flesh between his teeth. When he was done, he became talkative again. "Yesterday, you talkin' 'bout when you was a bwoy? But lemme tell you, when *I* was a bwoy, I could never have a whole mango to myself. I always had to share it with my brother. He ate the belly and I sucked the seed." I closed my eyes. I remembered Tristan's choked pleas in the shed. "I sucked it dry dry," he reminisced, "till it white like salt."

"That's the way to eat mangoes," I agreed, pulling the chair closer and leaning forward, speaking in his ear. "You must grip it in your bare hands, like a small boy's head, and ravage it. You must satisfy your craving till there's nothing left but skin and seed, skin and bone, then you can always have another one, eh."

He stopped eating. There was fear in his eyes.

"I have another story to tell you," I said.

He made as if to rise from the bed, looking around for his crutches. "I need some fresh air," he said. "Excuse me, I think I've heard enough of your stories."

I gently pushed him back on the bed. "No, I don't think you have."

He didn't resist.

"Here," I said, patting his shoulder. "Have another mango." He shrank from my touch.

I cracked my knuckles and leaned back in the chair. "The Indian mongoose, newly introduced to the island to exterminate rats and other vermin destroying the sugar cane crop each year, was walking through a cane piece one day and came across a Jamaican yellow boa…"

At the end, I asked him the same question Papa had once asked me: "Who are you in this story: the mongoose, the snake, or the snake's children? The murderer, the coward, or the hapless victim?"

"I don't know," he said through clenched teeth. "But I get the feeling you're about to tell me." He said this with a tone of defiance. I'd lost the advantage, but I couldn't back down now. I sucked in air hard, balled it deep in my stomach, then let out: "You are the murderous mongoose! You murdered Tristan that afternoon and I watched you do it!"

I was expecting shock, false penitence, rage, anything. But he was calm. "That was a long time ago," he said meekly. "I was a different man. A sinner, as I am now. But I've repented, son."

"Don't call me that! I'm not your son!"

His face went slack and solemn, his hands folded in his lap. In their skeletal state they looked like cruel claws. "It wasn't my intention to open your eyes to that kind of evil in the world. But I'm not sorry that I did. The wrath of God has been unsparing ever since, beating me with many stripes for staining the soul of the innocent." He spoke with the lyrical triteness of a Sunday sermon.

"That's all you have to say after all these years?"

"You're angry. You have every right to be. I deserve your condemnation. I regret what I did to that boy. He's gone – God rest his soul – but I can still beg your forgiveness." I looked at him steadily and trapped under my gaze he lost his composure and beat his fist into the bed. "I'm sorry! I'm sorry, okay! What more you want from me, eh? What you want me to do – cut out me heart and put it on a table for you? Would that make you satisfied?" I went to the kitchen and came back with a knife and put it on the bed's edge and leant forward, my eyes on his face, tapping my foot to the ticking clock above us. *Tick tick tick tick tick.* His loose lips quivered. "Oh God dear Jesus no…" *Tick tick tick tick tick.* He started wringing his hands, his mouth open and collapsed.

I whispered, with my finger to my lips, "Shh! You hear that?"

"What? What is it?"

"Shh! Keep your voice down!" I removed my finger and gave him the goblin grin. "*Tick tick tick…* That's the sound of your heart, beating with that horrible muffled sound… like a clock wrapped up in a bundle of rags. Don't you hear it?"

He felt his bony chest. "Yes! Yes I hear it!"

"Isn't it an awful and disquieting thing, as if it's coming from a tomb?"

"It's absolutely wretched!"

"Don't you want it to stop?"

"Yes! Yes I do!" He grabbed the knife and held it in his trembling grip, then his fingers went rigid and it fell to the floor. He pounded his forehead with his fist. "I'm sorry," he mumbled. "Please! I'm sorry, I'm so sorry…"

I closed my eyes against a surprising warm sting of tears. "You know, I spent a long time contemplating that story, not knowing who I was, thinking I must be the coward, that I had left the Tyger to devour the Lamb that afternoon. But I am not the coward or the victim, and certainly not the murderer. I am the storyteller. I am the eyes that see and the mouth that tells. And I will keep telling this story until the world listens."

"That's your right," he said quietly. "And I'm satisfied the experience has brought you greater self-awareness."

I rose from the chair. "You have my forgiveness. Be at peace."

The words puzzled me even as I said them. But I found myself letting go of my bitterness. I just couldn't carry it anymore.

He turned away from me, burying his face into his hands as if to sob. "Thank you," he murmured, "...thank you."

"I've said all I've come to say."

He stretched his hand out and I pulled back. "Go with God."

"I'm afraid I go alone."

"It doesn't have to be that way," he said, his voice regaining its assurance. "When you find him, you'll truly find yourself."

A final remark rose to my lips, but I held my tongue. After I'd left the room I turned back and crept up to the door to watch him. He was hunched over, hoarding the remaining mangoes behind the headboard.

A few days before my departure, I cried when I heard he had lapsed into a diabetic coma. His suffering had brought no closure, no consolation. I was leaving so much behind: place, youth, but not memory. That cup would never pass.

PART II

THE CITY STIRS – PAPA'S REQUIEM

CHAPTER 1 – MONTEGO BAY PASTORAL

In Jamaica there are three things you don't do on a Sunday: you don't cook rice and peas without coconut milk, you don't beat your children, and you don't – not as a self-respecting, God-fearing woman – go to church without wearing a hat, or at least a decent wig. The first and third rules taken care of, my grandmother was an expert at flouting the second. Took to breaking it with more resourcefulness than congregants breaking bread at Holy Communion. With her right hand she would slap and pinch and pull till your skin was sore and puffy, and with the left hand upraised, as if swearing an oath, she warned you to keep quiet, else your punishment would double. But this was a ruse. Whether you protested or not she kept on hitting you until she felt satisfied.

This morning's punishment was special. I had defied her, had opened my mouth to speak in a strange tongue, had said no when I should have said yes. I felt that righteousness was on my side; it was how I imagined Deacon Sharpe must have felt on that great Christmas morning of the 1831 slave rebellion. But my courage hadn't lasted long, and my palms felt slippery as I imagined the hangman's noose around the Deacon's neck as he stood on the gallows in his Sunday best. Unlike him, I wouldn't have the solace of even a great parting sound bite to seal my place in history.

"Phyllis, why you don't let the bwoy do it half and half. Go to summer school for a month, then go to work with Mackie for a month." This was Papa, sitting across from me at the kitchen table.

"Clarence, don't draw me tongue!" Mama snapped. "This don't concern you."

Papa shrugged and sipped his tea. He didn't have the strength to argue. He was going through another of his spells when he'd wake up in the morning with his insides scrubbed raw, and hard food was off limits. Such moments came after his dream when the gift of prophecy was sealed inside him, barred from ever coming out, his belly a mouth sewn shut with cords of fire.

"An' is not even summer school," I mumbled, spooning my porridge listlessly, my elbow propped defiantly on the table and my palm pressed against my ear, "is a writing workshop... an' it's free."

Mama glared at me. "A writing wha'?" She rolled her eyes in her mocking way. "What a piece o' fanciness. Look here, mister man. The only workshop you goin' is Mackie woodwork shop, bright and early tomorrow morning. Get that in your head! You coulda pout some more..."

1. The Jesus Carpenter and the Jacket Man Crisis

The matter of contention was that I'd already signed up for a three-week writing workshop at the parish library. The library people had come to school in April promoting the event, handing out flimsy, puke-green pencil cases and *Reading Maketh a Full Man* lapel pins.

Now here I was, two months later, gainfully employed and woefully depressed, conditioning my mind to face the rigours of hard labour. My grandmother had got me a job with none other than Herbert Macintyre, aka Brother Mac, aka the Jesus Carpenter, an eloquent preacher and deacon at the Burchell Baptist Church (the church of the great Sam Sharpe) and a carpenter of not inconsiderable repute, though more famous for delivering promises than actual furniture. He had even been charged once with defrauding his renters by tampering with an electricity meter. I had also witnessed his depravity four years before, the incident that had changed my life.

To start with, Brother Mac's Woodwork Shop, as the legend outside the shop declared, wasn't really his. It was one of many rented units at the Bogue Industrial Estate in Montego Bay, just across the street from the sewage plant whose aluminium covers shimmered like a sea of glass in the sun. The estate was owned by Fitz-George Henry, aka the Jacket Man, a former drug lord and gangster of the 1970s political scene who'd been sentenced to twenty-five years in prison, and who, like a good many people with a wall to their backs and time on their hands, had searched for God, found him and got early release.

Henry's history with the Baptist church was short-lived but lively. He became a member soon after leaving prison in 1990, but his forays into public life soon brought him into conflict with the church. The last straw was when he bought a license from the Gaming Commission to build several casinos. The Baptist Council of Churches came down like a scourge on his head. He was disfellowshipped, cast out from the flock, banished to roam the wilderness of the spiritually slothful. Three years later, with the acquisition of the Fletcher's Land property, he had rubbed salt into the church's wound. They had planned to acquire the site for their new western conference centre. Henry was intending to build a permanent home for the world's largest reggae festival: Reggae Jammin' Jamfest Jamboree.

The Church, not wanting to appear bitter, had extended an olive branch. At a parochial prayer breakfast, to which Henry was invited, the Archbishop had tried to broker a peace with their wayward son, wishing him success with his new venture. Henry, in return, had offered to allow the church to play a role in the development of his new property.

This was where Brother Mac came in. The Church commissioned him to build seven hundred foldout chairs for the VIP section of the venue, over a period of three months.

When I started working with him, Brother Mac was already into his second month, having started in May, the chairs due for the end of July. The festival would start in August and run for a week.

Brother Mac had worked for Henry before, so you had to think that Henry, with his knowledge of Brother Mac's highly individual work ethic, must have trusted his reputation to keep Mac in order – particularly the stories of the licensed firearm he allegedly toted below his coat, and the legend that he'd killed his wife and buried her beneath the tiles of his pool at his Plantation Heights mansion, then reported her missing. This had earned him the nickname, Stonewall Henry. You'd hear idling estate workers singing under their breaths:

One two three four Jacketman a come
One two three four, Jacketman a come
Wid de moneybag a knock him belly bam bam bam
Wid de gunstrap a knock him belly bam bam bam…

This was when they saw the blue Mercedes pull up by the gate the last Friday of every fortnight, when Henry personally doled out brown envelopes of cash and checked on the general status of things. Then they'd take flight like zinc sheets in a hurricane across the grounds.

But despite all this notoriety, we were fixing the Jacket Man's business, swindling him. From Day One. What we were doing was this: since completing the first three hundred chairs, we started renting them out to various church groups for weeks at a time. They needed the chairs for their summer tent crusades. We'd rent a hundred or so chairs to a particular church for one or two weeks. And since we had completed Jacket Man's quota a month early, by working sometimes up to nine p.m., we had the full complement of chairs at our disposal. We could rent to three or more clients at a time, depending on demand.

When the chairs came back, all we had to do was a little refurbishing, scraping off globs of candle-fat or gum, then applying a light coat of varnish, depending on the state of disrepair, before sending them out again. For the rest of the day, with no more chairs to be made, we had time to ourselves.

I passed most of the time reading. I'd gone back to the library, following the row with Mama, to borrow a few books on the workshop's reading list. My confidence had sunk when I saw it was the portly, overly dramatic librarian on duty. I'd never had a good relationship with this man, even as a child borrowing books from the Young Readers section. I had selected Naipaul's *A Flag on the Island* and Fitzgerald's *The Great Gatsby,* and brought them to the counter. He scowled at Naipaul's author portrait and leaned towards me confidentially, "*This one*, I have it on good word that his greatest desire is to be buried at Westminster Abbey, hmph!" Then he looked at the Fitzgerald book affectionately and pressed it to his breast, and looked at it again, his face sad, his lips quivering. "What a wasted life," he crooned (and the fraud was actually dabbing tears!). "A genius should never marry. A talented man maybe, but a genius no." Then he stamped my card and held the books out to me, though I had to wrench them from his fat fingers.

Gatsby I'd read before so I skimmed through it and loaned it to Renee (Brother Mac's secretary and mistress) telling her that it wasn't one of those stuffy classics that would leave you comatose before lunch, but the story of a great romance – not unlike the Mills and Boon paperbacks she devoured daily. I took my time enjoying the Naipaul stories.

All was bliss. (And I was making so much money!) My summer couldn't have been going any better.

But with time we got complacent. It was our greed that did for us, because we weren't just renting to tent crusades anymore, but had started taking commercial orders. The money was better, the engagements shorter, and we liked to think there was less risk involved, since most of the orders were one-day gigs, for business conferences, wedding receptions and so on.

So that Tuesday, when the little green van from the Freeport Business Expo returned, just after three in the afternoon, calamity was the last thing on our minds. Brother Mac, Demoy and I had been enjoying a round of dominoes, and we went out to help unload the chairs in good spirits. But there was Jacket Man, wearing blue overalls and work boots like the other workmen, but given away by his dark glasses (which he was never without). With his small frame, he looked like a boy playing dress-up. But there was no child's play in his body language. I recalled the story of his wife rotting away below the tiles. In our haste to fill the order, we had forgotten to vet the clients properly, to check if there were any risks. We were about to pay dearly for that oversight. We had rented the chairs to one of his many subsidiary companies.

He was walking coolly towards us, his jaw muscles twitching. I saw now that the grim-faced workmen weren't really workmen, but his bodyguards. I felt like running, but my legs wouldn't carry me. Demoy, on the other hand, had bolted right past them, before two bulky bodyguards cut off his escape. Brother Mac had spun on his heels and made a dash for the shop. "Renee!" he was shouting. "Renee!"

I found my legs and followed him.

Renee came dashing from the backroom, with a startled and expectant look on her face. With her right hand she was preening her hair, with her left she was clutching *The Great Gatsby* to her bosom.

"Renee!" Brother Mac was on his knees, blowing raggedly through his open mouth, his hand over his heaving chest. In retrospect, I can see how this gesture could have given her the impression of a man in the grip of an epiphany of passion, a man about to confess his undying affection.

Renee started crying.

"Renee."

"Yes, Mackie."

"The book."

"The book?"

"The book. Quick! Burn the book!"

"Huh?"

"Burn the book!"

She was off. In an instant she was back from the storeroom, armed with a lighter that she now held to *Gatsby's* spine, the blue plasticised cover already curling back on itself. I couldn't move. My head was swimming. Everything was happening so fast.

Renee's eyes were bright with excitement. "Mackie, me *doudou*. See me burn it there. For our love, darling. To consummate our love."

For a split second Brother Mac's infirmity vanished and he became sober with rage. "Not that book, you stupid cunt! The receipt book! *Jacketman a come!*"

But before Renee could shake off her paralysis, Jacket Man was standing in the doorway, instructing his cronies to seize the books from the backroom. They pushed past us as *Gatsby* turned to sacrificial ash in Renee's hand. When the flame reached her fingertips she drew a sharp breath and flung it across the room. The Buttonmen (they looked like the characters in the first *Godfather* movie) came back. They had the receipt book, with all the yellow duplicate copies of our illegal transactions still intact. (Why Brother Mac had kept such damning records lying around the shop, I really can't say. Ego? Recklessness? Or just plain insanity?)

The Jacket Man put a hand on Brother Mac's shoulder and sighed wearily, like a father disappointed in his son. Brother Mac, still kneeling, fumbled with the insulin pen he'd taken from his breast pocket to inject himself. The sudden stress was spiking his blood sugar. One of the Buttonmen slapped the pen from his shaking hands.

"Mackie." The Jacket Man's voice was like liquid death. "I think you should come with us."

Brother Mac didn't resist. Rising slowly to his feet, his face as lifeless as a carving, he turned to follow the three men outside, sandwiched between the Buttonmen.

Picking up the insulin pen, Renee ran to them and forced it into Jacket Man's hands, saying, "Please, you have to stick him in the stomach."

When Brother Mac heard this he yelped like a cold puppy.

The blue Benz had arrived outside, as if by magic. By now word had got around and there was a crowd outside, with a kind of subdued sadistic expectancy playing in their eyes, now falling back theatrically to let the men pass. They got in the car, Jacket Man in front with the driver, and Brother Mac in the back, still squashed between two Buttonmen.

Back in the shop Renee was sobbing, her breath catching in her throat when she tried to speak. "What they going to do to him?"

"I don't know."

She was packing up her things feebly, kneeling to retrieve the remains of the book. I reached out and grabbed it from her. She looked at me pitifully. "You must forgive me, I didn't mean to burn your book… Is just that… well… you see what happen. I don't need to explain. I'll pay you back for it. I promise."

I was moved to sympathy. "I know you didn't mean it."

But then her expression changed to curiosity and she said, "But tell me, will Jay and Daisy ever get together? What will happen to Jay, eh?"

I looked at the ruined book, burnt all the way through to Chapter 9, page 198, where Klipspringer was sheepishly asking Nick to send along his tennis shoes. "You killed him…"

She didn't say anything. I took up my things and left. I didn't even change out of my work clothes. Demoy had vanished.

My head was still swimming when I ran out into the street. I thought about stopping at the police station a few blocks up the street, but then couldn't think what I would actually say. Was there even anything to report? I hurried home to tell Papa.

When I got home I saw our bull, Winston Churchill, standing staidly in the yard, managing to look noble, impatient and righteously indignant all at the same time.

2: Anchovy: the Early Years

My grandfather reared animals on property he owned in a place called Goshen, just about three miles from where we lived in Anchovy, next to an abandoned textile factory. On Sunday we had to accompany him there, Tristan and I, to help him to clean them, give them food and drink, and various other things livestock farmers busy themselves with. It was torture. I'd go to bed on Saturday nights with a heavy heart knowing that it was cow bush the next day. It was enough to spoil my whole weekend, just thinking about it. My grandfather knew this and tried to wring as much distress out of me as he could by giving me really hard tasks, like casting and tying up Winston Churchill, or picking ticks off his black skin while he grazed, which the bull hated. Tristan was Papa's hero on Sundays. He could cast the cows like a cowboy and could talk to them in a language they apparently understood; they would nod and moo at him when he spoke softly, or bellow and shift their weight clumsily when he wagged his finger at them and cursed, tying them to a post or getting them to move from A to B. He always played up his skills for Papa's observation, in the same way, I began to realise, that he did while we were in school. In his efforts to win the teachers' good graces, there always seemed a need to play up to their authority, or their suspected homosexuality. I would watch him. Sometimes he would make a show of grabbing a male teacher's cigarette in the dining hall, like a girl flirting with a boy she liked, or offer his services as a food taster to his "lieges" at the head table, and mime sipping their soup, then grab his chest and fall to the floor as if dying of poison, while the masters laughed and clapped. The gay masters on campus knew exactly what he was doing. They would exchange knowing smiles while they smoked their expensive cigarettes and watched him performing for them. Once I overheard Master Livermore inquiring who the "live-wire" was from his familiar, the skirt-chasing Master Beaumont, who was Tristan's academic adviser. Beaumont had replied, "Look at him, Alfred. Can't you tell the mother is beautiful? The boy is her 'dead stamp'! I visited her house last Monday." Livermore, smiling like a judge at a beauty pageant, had tapped off his cigarette ash and studied Tristan holding forth and had said, "Yes… he *is* beautiful." But in playing up his skills for Papa's praise, Tristan would sometimes get it and sometimes wish he hadn't striven for it. Once when Papa had instructed me to pick the ticks off Winston Churchill, I was doing so and cursing him under my breath. Tristan had come over and started exploring Churchill's genitals and scrotum. He looked so earnest I couldn't laugh. I even started taking my exploration more seriously. Papa had walked over to us and frightened us with his outburst. "But bwoy, is what you doing? Who tell you to do dat?"

Tristan looked at him with a wide-eyed stupid look that he knew made him seem vulnerable. "I jus' lookin' after Winston Churchill, sar. I know Chauncey wouldn't do a good job."

We crossed eyes briefly and I made it known to him that I hated him perfectly. He didn't mind.

"Damn fool! I tell yuh to feel up de bull balls eh? Since yuh so eager to clean dem, yuh might as well do a good job. Chauncey move from deh so!"

I moved away quickly and stood by his side, leering at Tristan. His eyes were now the ones that communicated perfect hate.

"Yes, Missa balls-cleaner, make sure you remove every las' tick from offa dat bull yuh hear me?"

"Yes sar." Tristan was morose.

"And don't move till yuh find every las' one. 'Cause if you should ever say you done, an' I fin' one tick pon him, I go tear yuh ass for you. Damn fool."

Tristan stayed there the whole evening, looking for ticks, no doubt thinking he'd found them all, but then having to start all over again, since a new one might have found its way on to the bull while he was busy looking elsewhere. I sat reading an English translation of Leopardi's *Discourse on the Life and Works of Fronto*, while Papa went off somewhere. When he came back and it was time to leave, Tristan was crying, feebly picking at Winston Churchill, who was quite annoyed now. Papa walked over to them and gave Tristan a long, sarcastic look, rubbed his hands over the bull's body, legs and head, then held his left hand up daintily, his index and thumb kissing, with a tick supposedly cradled in between. It was so dark, none of us could tell if there was a tick held there, but who were we to question him. Tristan started bawling when Papa grabbed him by the front of his shirt and started slapping him skilfully all over his body with the blade of his machete, careful not to twist it to cause it to cut him or hit him awkwardly – since he was writhing – or allow the blade to make contact with any of his pressure points. I laughed my head off – at a safe distance. Cruel behaviour like this was what we boys were raised on in Anchovy.

My grandfather had a standard test for manhood. He'd open a coconut with three machete cuts, then order you to do the same. He'd done this to my father and Sheila when they turned thirteen. When it was my turn, I blundered my way through six coconuts before Papa lost his patience and went off to milk the cows. Tristan had been watching. When Papa left he took the nut from my hands and opened it with two slashes! I don't think even Papa could do that. However, instead of thanking him, I sneered and said, "How come a faggot like you can do that and I can't?" Even then, we both knew he was gay. He smiled and his eyes were full of triumph. Sure enough when he returned, Papa knew it wasn't me.

3. Homosexuality in Montego Bay – Worms! Worms!

Crab cakes, crab cakes, baker's man
Show me your guts as fast you can...

The city had its own test for manhood, too. The sign that everyone saw was of a straw-hat wearing *gal*, arms outstretched, laughing on the airport billboard: *WELCOME, LIFE'S A BEACH IN*

MOBAY! On the back of this billboard a graffiti artist had painted: *Social Etiquette: If you see a blind person approaching, step out of his way. If you see a faggot approaching, punch him in the face. Have a nice day* (followed by an orange smiley face). As boys we adopted this attitude uncritically, in the same way we never questioned the savagery and stupidity of the crab cakes game. Harry had concealed a live pea crab in a *joo-joo* berry, and mixed the tainted morsel in a bag of these suck-and-swallow sweets. He shared them with us as we sat on the Sunset Beach wall watching airplanes taxi and take off. Harry had shouted, "We have a winner!" when Sanjay held his stomach and groaned. The rest of us, now alive to the prank, thanked Diego Tobago that we'd been spared, then clapped and sang, "*Crab cakes, crab cakes, baker's man. Show me your guts as fast you can...*" while Sanjay ran retching to the nearest toilet. Papa had fondly told me that as a boy he'd ended up in hospital to have a parasite removed after swallowing a crab cake, yet even in extreme situations like this you were expected to keep a stiff upper lip.

But when I swallowed a crab cake the day Chicken Friday was assaulted, there was no way I could keep my upper lip stiff.

A gay man in Montego Bay, dubbed the gay capital of the country (a label which Montegonians fiercely resisted with knee-jerk homophobia) had to be very resourceful. I saw this from an early age. Chicken Friday was one of the few openly gay men we knew. He walked the streets most mornings with his blind father, taking him to the clinic or the park. Sometimes people called him names, but Chicken Friday cursed them right back. "Battyman!" someone would shout. Chicken Friday would retort, "And proud of it." He had a reputation for being fierce, and on the whole was left alone. Nearly everyone looked kindly on his devotion to his father. It was his saving grace. People saved their venom for those undeserving gays without a blind father. No certificate of merit for them; they got spat upon and occasionally beaten. As boys, we paid Chicken Friday the courtesy of pretending he was like everyone else, turning a blind eye to his nail polish, beads, figure-hugging jeans, his processed hair hanging over his forehead in a lush comb-over, looking like a 60s R&B singer, though sometimes ruffled like a rooster's comb. When he was in a good mood, he would swing his hips and snap his fingers and sing things like: "*A dem have de shape wah give de man headache, Jamaican man dem full up a shape.*"

He was a baker at the delicatessen on St James Street. When he worked at the front, customers would try to engage him. Women would ask him for beauty tips. Male customers, jealous of his popularity with females, would jeer him good-naturedly or shoo him to the back of the shop. Chicken Friday, hands on hips, would tell them, "Y'all don't mess with me. Remember, I handle your food!" To us schoolboys he showed kindness. We weren't supposed to leave school during lunch, and on more than one occasion, when Vice-Principal Brown drove into the deli's parking lot while we sat inside, Chicken Friday signalled to us, giving us time to duck through the side-door and escape. I'd wanted to think it was a mark of people's general fondness for Chicken Friday that the deli was the most popular in town.

But an incident there turned everything upside down.

One afternoon, Mola stood at the head of the line, in front of the cash register, and Chicken Friday checked his tray and said, "Twenty-eight dollars, schoolers."

Mola checked his wallet, hesitated, then turned to Russell Alvaranga. "Russell you have enough small bills? I'll pay you back when we get to school."

Alvaranga said, "How much you have?"

Mola said, "A hundred large."

Alvaranga shot him an annoyed look. "Why do you do that, Sanjay?"

"Do what?"

"Talk like an American – that annoying yankee lingo all those tourists passing through your family's duty-free shop leave behind like worthless souvenirs. Those stupid slangs."

At the counter, Chicken Friday chuckled and said, "Oi! Mr. Alvaranga, leave your friend alone. What if de bwoy want to spice up him speech? Why that mus' bother you? Why you Montegonians so small-minded an' begrudging?"

But Russell wasn't through. "It's not the same, you numb-skull. A hundred dollars isn't 'large' in Jamaica, it's chicken shit. See, that's where you're wrong, Sanjay, you don't measure the two countries on the same scale; it's incongruous."

Chicken Friday cleared his throat dramatically. "*Ahem*, incongruous, eh. I should charge you extra for droppin' dat big word on us." Then he goaded Sanjay. "Indian, you really goin' to make him mash you up like that? You 'fraid to cuss him back!"

Mola said timidly, "So I should say a hundred small, then?"

Russell covered his eyes. "Oh Jesus…"

Chicken Friday cackled and slapped Mola's shoulder. "I would ask him de same t'ing. Anyway, pass it here, Indian, I can change it."

When we sat down to eat, Alvaranga watched me suspiciously. "Knuckle, why you not eating? You fasting?"

I sipped a bottle of coconut juice and said, "I have tapeworms. I passed one in the toilet this morning."

A fat woman beside us said loudly, "Some of us are eating here."

We ducked our heads and giggled.

Harry whispered, "Ooh, that's nasty. I haven't had those since I was eight."

"Good for you," I said, "I'm passing all these suckers on my own, without taking that foul stuff my aunt makes us drink."

Tristan bit into his croissant. "Good luck with that."

Just then four men entered, wearing hardhats and dusty overalls. They weren't Montegonians; we could tell by their accents, and they were asking for "sugar loaves" instead of "sugar buns". They acted with deliberate crudeness, spoke loudly and looked around brashly. When they saw Chicken Friday at the cash register they sniggered and passed remarks that he ignored.

The one who stood at the head of the line shoved the money at Chicken Friday. Chicken Friday glared and handed him his change. The man said, "Don't eyeball me, you fuckin' faggot."

"It takes one to know one…" Chicken Friday said. "Nice earrings by the way," and blew him a kiss.

The man lunged across the counter. Chicken Friday stepped back but then reached forward and pulled the man's earring. He howled, staggered backwards, and jumped about in pain. His friends rushed forward angrily. Screaming customers stampeded from the shop. The manager, a stringy old Chinese Jamaican, quickly bundled Chicken Friday into the backroom and locked the door. By the time we stood on the pavement outside, a squad car had pulled up.

43

We hurried back to school.

The next morning after assembly, Mola showed me the newspaper. "Chicken Friday is finished in this town," he declared.

The front page of the *Sun* carried a picture of Chicken Friday in a brown tank-top below the headline: *"Famous Citizen Held in Assault Case."*

The *Sun* said Chicken Friday was at the Barnet Street jail.

On the day of the bail hearing, people lined the street where the old redbrick courthouse stood. We had skipped classes and gone into town. We stood on the second-floor balcony of the *Homelectrix* furniture store beside the courthouse.

Because the complainant was not Montegonian, many people sided with Chicken Friday, but others, who'd long wanted to vent their disgust over him, finally had occasion.

As blue-striped policemen escorted Chicken Friday across the street, one woman shouted, "Chicken Friday, hold up your head!"

A man shouted, "Lock up that Sodomite and throw 'way de key!"

Chicken Friday looked bedraggled; his perm was dry and matted over his bruised face; there were cuts on his arms; he had the mute, terrified expression of an animal looking at the butcher's knife.

He failed to make bail.

The trial was set for Friday morning, four days away.

Alvaranga said, "We coming here early next time, before the crowd."

On the trial morning, we sat below the courthouse steps on newspaper sheets. We'd been there since seven. When one of us needed to use the courthouse toilet on the ground floor, he left his sheet and knapsack over his spot so it wouldn't be taken, because by 7:30 both sidewalks were packed. The bums who slept outside the courthouse shambled away, muttering curses, with cardboard beds tucked under their arms. A man standing beside me surveyed the crowd and whistled. "Chicken Friday making history, bwoy. This is the trial of the century."

At 9:45 a.m., two blue-stripes opened the station's iron gates and marched out with Chicken Friday, dressed in a pale-blue jumpsuit and handcuffs, but it wasn't his wardrobe that shocked us. His head was shaved to the scalp! He looked as pitiable as a shorn sheep. A woman said ruefully, "All that beautiful hair…" Chicken Friday trudged across the street, his chin buried in his chest. No one said a word. He and his escort were just ascending the courthouse steps when someone pushed through the crowd. Bystanders, alarmed, fell back. When the blue-stripes turned to see what the commotion was, a man uncorked a small brown bottle and threw the contents into Chicken Friday's face.

"Acid!"

People shrieked and took cover.

Screaming, Chicken Friday grabbed his face and went down. The man, whom I recognised as one of the hardhats from that day in the deli, ran through the lane between the courthouse and *Homelectrix*. Police gave chase. Chicken Friday screamed and squirmed on the ground. His cries did not sound human.

"Monkey lotion," an onlooker said. "He's finished."

Monkey lotion was slang for car battery acid, commonly used in assaults.

He continued screaming and clutching his face. People just stood there. Nobody wanted to make a public show of sympathy.

Moments later we heard sirens. Someone had called an ambulance. It was time to leave.

Wriggling through the crowd, we hurried back to school. When we got to the lower gate, Brown was standing there, speaking quietly to guards on duty. He marched us to the principal's office. Other truants, who'd made the journey in different groups, were also rounded up.

They lined us against the wall of Dr. Leaders's lobby. I was too distracted to be scared. My head was full of all I'd witnessed. Brown was shouting and flexing his cane. I could see fear on my friends' faces, but what I saw was the circle of faces standing over the suffering man. My brain refused to accommodate anything else. I felt faint. Dr. Leader asked me a question. I couldn't understand what he said, but mumbled something. "Speak up boy!" he shouted, holding the quivering cane – which was labelled WRATH OF MONTEGO BAY, in green marker ink – above me, poised to strike. When I tried to speak, I had to clamp my mouth shut because a wave of nausea rippled through me. Something wriggled in my underpants. The secretary's voice broke my daze. She was pointing at my shoes and screeching, "But this boy has worms, worms!"

I looked down. I'd passed a worm that slithered down my pants.

They rushed me to the sick bay where the nurse gave me the same bitter medicine, Biltricide, which I was scrupulously avoiding at home.

I was sent home.

When I arrived, Mama and Aunt Girlie were naturally surprised, and stood over me in the den, waiting for an explanation. I spoke to the carpet. "I saw it all, Aunt Girlie... everything! They didn't even try to help him. They didn't even try..."

I kept hearing his screams, kept seeing his blind father knocking about with his cane, shouting in vain, "Errol? Errol!" before collapsing in tears amid the mob on the courthouse steps.

I stayed home two days from school. The assault had made the news, and that night on TV they interviewed a famous gay activist and intellectual and asked him his thoughts on the attack. He took a prepared statement from his green herringbone jacket and read in a slow, careful voice, "We, the prisoners of the gulag, have always considered ourselves soldiers of misfortune, for we fight at the battlefront everyday, whether we want to or not, and we fight not for the mother country, but for survival. It is at the point of death for us, gay citizens, that we acknowledge that the death of a man who comes from nothing, has nothing and will return to nothing is always freedom and never a sad farewell." Then he refolded his paper, replaced it in his jacket, took off his glasses and wiped his eyes. The news reporter tried to engage him but he would say nothing more. The TV and radio stations were abuzz all night with his cryptic comment. I could not say for sure that I knew what he meant, but I felt their import. The first thing I did the next day was look for his quote in the papers and cut it out and put it in my scrapbook and read it over and over again.

By the end of the week, we learned Chicken Friday's fate. The acid had burnt off half his face before paramedics could help him. He lost an eye, and his lips and nose were mangled, but he would live.

The tragedy proved too much for his father. A few days later, he suffered a stroke and died.

That Sunday, Aunt Girlie took me to Pastor for counselling.

We talked in the vestry. Pastor told me the church had started a fund to help with the old man's funeral, since he had no other kin. I asked if they couldn't also start a fund to help with Chicken Friday's hospital bills. He looked at me seriously. "That might send the wrong message of what we're about. See, we cannot appear to... endorse certain lifestyles."

I said, more to myself than him, "Faggots don't count, eh."

Aunt Girlie said, "Watch your language young man," and apologised to Pastor.

Pastor smiled patiently. "Homosexuals do count, Chauncey, as sinners who need saving."

"But not as humans who need help?"

He blinked, then said, "We're not as heartless as you think, boy, just not naive."

The following week, I was sitting in the French study room of the Lower School library, reading my story "Worms! Worms!" to Master Harding, when I said, "I don't think I'll ever go back to the deli."

"In 1978, when I was a teenager, I saw a man slit another man's throat at Jarrett Stadium for looking at him 'funny'." Master Harding drew a finger across his throat. "The hooligans cheered as if a goal had been scored. Things were bad back then. Men like Chicken Friday couldn't walk the streets."

I said nothing.

He squeezed my shoulder. "Don't beat yourself up. It's not like Chicken Friday was on fire and you had a bucket of water."

"But he *was* on fire," I insisted. "We just couldn't see the flames."

"The flame is in your heart, son. Don't let it die. Because that is what will burn away the savagery."

But I continued to play my game of hypocrisy, even after Tristan's death.

4. School – Take Out Your Penis

If there is one thing Chester College excelled at it was making you feel inferior, as if you weren't good enough for the school, as if your place among the nine hundred or so student body was never really secure and could be snatched away at any minute. You never lost that feeling of insecurity, of competition for survival. When we bowed our heads in prayer at Monday morning devotion, Reverend Myers would clutch the library's rails, tilt his head to the sky and beg God for the assurance that even if our brains should became so addled with the wine from the Whore of Babylon's cup that we forgot how to count our fingers and toes, we should never (ever!) forget to count the blessings of being among the chosen few of Montego Bay and St James, whose names were inscribed in the student registry at 15 Orange Street.

This was the burden you were sentenced to walk around with for five years (seven if you made it to Sixth Form), and the cross strapped to your back became heavier with each step to Golgatha.

Even now, when I look back at all the money spent on extra books and lessons while in prep school, competing for one of the few scholarship places each year, at all the years I was kept on a diet of "brain food" (broiled fish, brown rice, avocados, prunes, oatmeal, unsweetened peanut paste, two cod liver oil tablets after each meal), at all the hours spent cramming till my head hurt, I can't help feeling that the payoff has been stingy, the fruits of my labour unsweet.

As a country boy, you had to know your place, no matter how bright you were. The masters conspired with the boys from well-connected families to mock you, so we boys from Anchovy always banded together. Masters took pride in showing off their learning to reinforce your sense of ignorance. I confess I took pleasure in playing them at their game. Once, in lit class, Master Harding caught some boys with a Playboy centrefold hidden in a *National Geographic* magazine with a pack of wolves on the cover. Instead of scolding them he recited, "Would that I saw it eaten by wolves, which would rather keep itself for the worms than for the relief of that poor lady." Nobody had the slightest idea what he was talking about – he liked to awe us with his literary quotes.

One of the perpetrators asked, "Who said that, sir?" Master Harding was about to reply, when I answered with another quote, "I myself, who Don Quixote of La Mancha is." The boys looked from Harding to me and oohed and aahed. He stared me down, as if a joust was about to begin. "Art is merely the refuge…" "W. Somerset Maugham," I cut in before he could finish. He got a bead on me with his eyes, ready to go in for the kill. I could see him searching his head for some obscure googly. He said, "Amen: said my mother, piano."

"Amen: cried my father, fortissime," I answered. "Sterne, *The Life and Opinions of Tristram Shandy*." He turned to the board and began writing furiously, spilling chalk dust all over the floor. Then he said, "I suppose it's rather good, Knuckle, that your contribution today amounts to more than that quaint smell of mosquito coils you rural fellows all seem to have in common." The boys laughed and shaved their fingers at me; he'd won the joust, but he would have his comeuppance.

You see, Harding, who was also the head of the language department – which meant that he got to walk around in a white coat, a vanity he always ditched whenever doctors and dentists came to the school to give the boys checkups – our dear Master Harding had something of a flaw we liked to exploit. In class, whenever he told us to, "Take out your rulers," we'd bug him by replying, "Take out your penis." One day he slipped and said, "Take out your penis," and we responded, straight-faced, "Why, sir, certainly. But did you mean, 'take out your rulers'." Dr. Leader and a phalanx of suits from the Education Board had been observing the class and Harding, already flustered, had licked his lips and responded limply, while gripping the ruler in his trembling hands as if about to snap it in two, "Yes… yes, that's what I meant."

But later we became good friends when he became something of a mentor, even a *brother*. He read my early stuff and gave me advice, even after I'd moved on to the university and kept sending stories to him; he never failed to repost them, covered in his red editorial ink. It was to him alone that I'd ever show the most recent stories.

5. Books – Gacha! Gacha! Gacha!

I was eight when Vic Reid died. I was too young to understand his importance, but I remember that morning, walking to school, I saw Diego Tobago. Whenever you saw him on the streets he always had his hands in his pockets with his eyes searching the sidewalk while mimicking the sound of a telegraph. "*Gacha! Gacha! Gacha!*" Then he'd hold up the imaginary telegram and read it aloud. Many people in Mobay had known Tobago when he was still sane, including the masters at school since he was a past student of Chester. Tobago had gone away to Cornell University and came back to Mobay a broken man. Some said he'd studied too hard at Cornell and had a nervous breakdown. He said to me that morning: "*Gacha! Gacha! Gacha!* VIC REID DIED TODAY. STOP. THE MAN WHO WAS OUR MARK TWAIN. STOP." It wasn't till two years later, when I read *New Day*, that I realised what he'd meant. Reid wrote in dialect, like Twain, and this was a discovery for me. I read his novel over and over again in the glow of the nightstand lamp, and even when the book was closed, my mind was walking through the pages. I knew this passion would rule me for the rest of my life. I read with hunger. I spent whole nights reading, and even in lessons would read books with feverish energy under the lid of my desk, while the teacher spoke. I read in the bus, on the toilet, even walking down the street.

I'd stay up and listen to RJR's *The BBC's Archives: Caribbean Voices*, old grainy recordings from the 1950s, so I could hear Selvon's recitation about brown stumps of teeth, the gentle tide of Lamming's genius breaking over my soul, Mittelholzer's fire consuming him while the world turned its back. When it was time to sleep, I wanted them to be quiet, but even if I plugged my ears, that's what I heard.

Once I heard masters in the coffee lounge disputing the point over Dostoevsky's translated text that says, "Man and wife will grow close in spirit." "Surely he wrote, 'man and wife will grow *closer* in spirit'," put in another master – and they put great store in this trifling point of contention. I stayed there, lapping up every word. Seeing me hanging around, they asked my opinion and I chose my words carefully. "My favourite writer is V.S. Naipaul."

"Why is that, boy?" "Sir, the thing I like most with Naipaul is the paper-dry prose and tart humour, all enough to make you wince, then laugh out loud in the same take, and that unerring ear for rhythm that he has. After you get locked into the beat of the sentences you can actually feel the music playing out in your head, like a symphony." They exchanged sly glances. "Paper dry prose eh…" They prodded further, "And which is your favourite story?" "'The Raffle'. It's about his adventures as a schoolboy in Trinidad. It's the only story in which he refers to himself by name, which gives it an intimacy the others don't have." "What do *you* think of Naipaul, Sir?" The master made a face and drawled, "…There's something to be said about a writer exploring the same theme over and over again, of the dispossessed barefoot colonial facing the psychosis of alienation, till the writing becomes a parody of itself, loses it's bite, like an old toothless lion roaming the wilderness of thematic relics." I wondered when I'd be able to use words like those so confidently and effortlessly.

I was fourteen when Sam Selvon died. Diego Tobago was still on the streets, and he gave me this news too. I went home that afternoon and looked at Selvon's author portrait on the back of *A Brighter Sun*. The photograph suggested something to me – the timelessness of his work, the tradition I was so eager to join. That was a turning point in my life, sitting that afternoon on the bed with his book. I felt the hunger to create a legacy. When you're that young, you think people like Selvon are invincible. Then you realise they're mortal, too. It made me understand I needed to make the most of my talent. I sat down at my desk that same afternoon to write because a telegram was in my head. *Gacha! Gacha! Gacha!*

6. Friends – *This that and they paid Diego Tobago*

All of us, except Russell Alvaranga, were childhood friends who had gone to the same prep school and grown up in the same neighbourhood, though Mola, a sixth-generation Jamaican Hindu, lived in the affluent section of Anchovy. Tristan was the oldest by almost a year, and had got into Chester on an athletics scholarship. He had the physique and good looks to match his personality, and seemed to possess all the energy of life, but little of its happiness. There was a detachment and guardedness about him, as if he would never allow himself to be caught out. Among the four of us, he and I had a special bond. It had been that way ever since I can remember, living just two houses apart on the same street. That bond had been deepened and complicated after the spring of 1989, in a way neither of us could have foreseen.

When Montegonians say, "This that and they paid Diego Tobago," it's a way of skipping over the details of a conversation the speaker deems unimportant – yet at the same time saying you've paid the elided details their just due. For instance on the afternoon Chicken Friday was assaulted, I passed two women catching up:

Lady#1: Girl what happenin' in Mobay these days? I jus' come back from Ochi.

Lady#2: You ain't miss a t'ing, girl. I still cyan full me basket at market and sumaddy finally fricassee Chicken Friday, this that and they paid Diego Tobago.

Nobody knew the origin of the saying, whether Diego Tobago was ever a real person, a figure of local folklore, or whether Montegonians had attached the name to the telegram-spouting lunatic as a kind of running joke. I never paid Diego Tobago as far as Tristan – the beautiful boy I loved and lost – was concerned, and I suppose all that follows is the beginning of paying that debt.

CHAPTER 2 – LADOO'S LEGACY, PLUS THE DELPHONIC SPLIFF

A week before I started high school, the only memorable token of kindness had been from a peanut vendor. It was a Tuesday morning. We'd gone downtown early to buy bolts of khaki and shoes at Aziz's Haberdashery before the morning rush began. Madmen, old prostitutes and drunks were still being shooed from the main street by the municipal sweepers. It was 1991. Jamaica's streets teemed with box-shaped Ladas imported from Russia (Montego Bay back then was known as Ladaville. It had the highest concentration of these cheap cars, most being used as taxis). This particular peanut vendor had noticed us passing and recognised my face from the cover of that morning's *Montego Bay Sun*, as one of the four recipients of the Marcus Garvey Scholarship. As Aunt Girlie and I crossed the cobblestone walkway, he parked his cart and ran over to us. Smiling, he took a sealed tin of Nugget shoe polish and a horsehair brush from the moneybag round his waist and offered it to us, "Nice Miss, for the young Garveyite. I hope he wears black shoes." My aunt had courteously refused, but his mouth was sweet and she had softened, taking the items and thanking him. I overheard Aunt Girlie telling the story that same night with relish to everyone in the kitchen when they thought I was asleep. I had discovered something about my aunt that day that annoyed me: she wilted in the presence of persuasive men.

Two years on, I was returning to the hill for the start of the new school year as a third-form student, standing in the courtyard by the seventh grade block on Monday morning, where Reverend Myers, towering before us on the library's balcony, had just finished imploring the throne of grace for a renewal of our store of gratefulness, and a little extra blessing for Maggi, the Agricultural Science department's resident sow, who was heavily pregnant and close to delivery. The over-dramatic librarian from the parish library then took the podium, after a brief introduction from Ms. Huntley, his counterpart at our school. He was wearing the same tawny suit and blue tie he'd worn that day when I returned one book and reported the tragedy that had befallen the other. I'd paid the recovery charge but he'd been livid that I had destroyed his favourite book. If he'd had his way, he would have taken scissors to my membership card.

He came to school to give self-important speeches on library promotions and the like. We never took them seriously. Sometimes we booed and jeered: "Just give us the flyers and shut your mouth," or shouted, "No more of this man, give us Barabbas!" This morning, he was plugging the upcoming Jamaica Library Services Short Story Competition, a follow-up to the workshop I'd missed. He was whipping himself into oratorical frenzy, waving an imperious finger, "...and we have a policy at the Parish Library: to always have lunch on time! Now you may be wondering what this has to do with –" but he didn't get to finish. We started pelting him with pebbles from the courtyard. He yelped and shielded his body, jumping around as if the pebbles were firecrackers falling at his feet. Dr. Leader ran to his rescue and escorted him off the balcony and down the steps, his eyes still wide with terror.

When Reverend Myers retook the podium, he quickly recognised that we were too keyed up to have even a fragment of attention span left. He frowned, raised the microphone to his lips and droned, "Good morning, boys," and assembly was dismissed.

I was sitting in History class that morning, listening to Master Gordon-Marsh reviewing the finer points of the slash-and-burn method, when a seventh grader came to our classroom door and told Gordon-Marsh that Ms. Huntley wanted to see me.

I was excused from class – the boys *oohing* and making catcalls: "Knuckle's off on his date with the Table Lamp! The lucky good-for-nothing!" Ms. Huntley was sitting at her desk, stamping and arranging books into neat piles by her feet. When I entered, she didn't turn, just said in a spiritless tone, "Thank you, Billy." The boy excused himself, padding off silently.

"You wanted to see me, Miss," I said.

"That's not my name, boy! I'm nobody's Miss, especially not yours."

"Ms. Huntley… I beg your pardon." This woman didn't like me, not since she'd caught me looking up her skirt with a mirror set in the base of a sharpener back in grade eight. Bosomy and thick-waisted, with short, heavy legs like a table lamp, she'd been invigilating a term exam when it happened. She had marched me to Dr. Leader's office for punishment, but I had gotten off easy: a caning and three demerit points, not even a suspension. She'd been adamant that I should be expelled.

I had been mortified by my stupidity – to endanger my academic life in such a way. Now, thanks to my action, Ms. Huntley specialised in long skirts, and whenever I went to the library, I had to negotiate her hostility, having her toss books to me instead of handing them, and having to listen to her curse Dr. Leader under her breath, calling him a 'fat-headed sexist pig'.

"Somebody's waiting to see you," she said gruffly, jutting her chin in the direction of the Reading Room.

It was the dramatic librarian, now looking more composed. He gestured languidly to the chair before him. I set my face; I had made up my mind to be rude to him. "If this is about the book –"

He stopped me with an upraised hand, then patted his face and the back of his neck with his handkerchief, making cooing sounds between his rounded lips. "Oh, the heat in this place. It's like sickness in the bones, man. I hear you're quite the writer, that you regularly contribute stories to the school paper."

I remained quiet. He leaned forward and placed his hands flat on the table. "Well then, I'll come straight to the point. What I had intended to convey this morning – before I was so savagely assaulted – is that there is a preliminary competition to select the best short story from each school. But since most of the staff here have put forward your name, I'm considering choosing you as the automatic candidate. But, mind you, only considering. I thought I should inform you just the same."

"Er… thank you," I said lamely.

He took a notepad and pen from his breast pocket. "Your full name, please."

"Chauncey Knuckle. C-h – "

"I can spell!" He finished writing and replaced pen and pad. "Any questions?"

I shook my head.

"No? You don't want to know if there'll be any prize money, a scholarship?"

"That's fine. Winning is reward enough."

He seemed impressed. "Tell me something, why do you want to be a writer?"

"I already am a writer."

He smiled. "That's good, that's good. You have confidence. You'll need it when you don't have anything else." He rose from his chair and stuck out his hand. "I'll be seeing you soon, Mr. Knuckle... and I don't need to tell you to get started on your piece. No time like the present."

Back at her desk, Ms. Huntley was talking on the phone and rolling her eyes contemptuously as I passed. I smiled and said quietly, "Goodbye, Ms. Cuntley," then stepped out.

As I approached my classroom, I heard Master Gordon-Marsh saying, "Why do I hear talking? Can pens talk? Can paper talk?" Harry, sitting closest to the door, shot me a warning glance. "Pop quiz," he mouthed. I backpedalled and trekked across campus to the idlers' den by the industrial block, to while away the rest of the session.

They always sent us home after lunch on the first day back at school. We would make the most of the half-day off, eager to play the fool before the drudgery of school life began. When we got home that afternoon, we stopped at Harry's house. I wanted him to take my picture for the library's circular as one of the short story competition entrants. I wanted it to look exactly like Sonny Ladoo's on the back of *No Pain Like This Body*, so I'd brought the novel in my knapsack and we stopped at a roadside vendor for a pack of cigarettes. I borrowed Harry's dark blazer and Chester tie and showed him the picture on the novel. "OK, Harry, I want it to look exactly like this."

Harry studied the photograph of the handsome Ladoo holding a cigarette to his lips.. "Gotcha... the cool professor look, eh."

"Exactly like that. With one half of my face in shadow."

Harry fiddled with his father's camera. "Sheesh, Chaunce, don't have a cow, man."

"Don't make me look pretentious!" I lit the cigarette and posed. "I wish I had a moustache like Ladoo's."

"Stop bitching and stay still. You want me to take this or not."

Tristan, sitting on the steps of Harry's garage, looked up at us. "What are you doing? You know they'll never publish your picture smoking a cigarette."

I ignored him and put the cigarette to my lips. "All right, Mr. De Mille, I'm ready for my close-up now."

Harry snapped away.

After, we went up to the flat concrete rooftop with a pair of binoculars, took off our shirts and sat enjoying the breeze. Nobody in the neighbourhood knew we were home and we liked it this way. The housewives had a way of wearing only big T-shirts and underwear in the afternoon heat and coming out to their back steps to talk on portable phones or paint and clip their toenails, while sitting like market women with their legs wide open. We took turns with the binoculars.

Harry, studying the back of the novel, said, "Damn... you know Sonny boy was only 28 when he died? And only published two novels?"

"At least he didn't live long enough to see himself turn into a failure," I said. "He went out on top."

"That's what she said."

Ever since we were in kindergarten we had a habit of turning everything into a competition, and soon were silently competing to see who could smoke the most cigarettes and finish the pack.

Suddenly Harry said in his Alex Trebek voice, "Now let's have a look at our Double Jeopardy categories: What's Up Pussycat?; Beef Curtains and Other Savoury Schoolboy Snacks; Girls I'd Like to Fuck This Year; Before and After."

Tristan chimed in: "And, Who's Eating Gilda's Grapes?"

Gilda was Harry's older sister, the most beautiful of three creamy-skinned girls, the most ravishing in the village, and a straight A student and deputy head girl at St Helena's, the Catholic girl's school across the street from Chester. Harry, the only boy and the baby of the family, the wash-belly, whom his mother doted on, had always been comfortable with his other role as the black sheep. He never wanted to change his pigmentation. His parents had needed to hold the proverbial gun to his head for him to study for his externals, and even so his father, a vice principal at the community college, had to lobby Dr. Leader for a place at Chester because Harry's grades were barely good enough to get in. Now he gave Tristan the stink-eye. "Tristan, I swear, man, say my sister's name again and I'll shove your fucking teeth down your throat. I don't care if she's your ex." Harry had "the kicks" for Gilda. He wasn't ashamed to tell us he'd peeked on her while she undressed. If anyone else had told us something like this we'd have been disgusted, yet with Harry we laughed it off.

To break the tension, I piped up, "I'll take Before and After for $600, Alex."

Harry, still staring daggers at Tris, said, "Oh, Chauncey, you're no fun. OK... Harold Sonny Ladoo's debut novel and the author's oeuvre."

I rang the imaginary buzzer. *"Beep!"*

"Knuckle!"

"What is: There's No Pain Like This Body of Work?"

"Good for $600!"

The sides of Tristan's mouth were dancing, and he said to me nonchalantly, "Chauncey, how do you like your grapes... washed or unwashed?"

Harry sprang up. "OK, I'm fuckin' you up!"

Tristan scampered round the big red metallic water tank, his laughter echoing on the roof. I had the binoculars on a woman across the road, sprawling on her back steps, fanning a coal pot, she closed her thighs quickly and looked up to the roof. I ducked down and giggled, my heart pounding. "Dat pussy has jaws like a bulldog..."

We calmed down and resumed smoking. Tristan stretched out his legs. "This is good, just kicking back like this, mellowing out. We don't do this enough since starting school."

"I concur."

"The city, gentlemen, is what destroys the mellowness of rustic cherubims like ourselves. And I have something to make this moment even mellower." Harry ran down the wrought iron steps and came back moments later with a handful of pungent weed in chunks and *Rizzla* smoking sheets.

Tristan grabbed the weed greedily from his hand. "Sonuvabitch! How did you get your hands on this?" He sniffed it over and over again, smiled broadly and pummelled Harry's shoulder.

"Ask me no questions I tell you no lie."

I'd already had my ruler ready to slice up the chunks, flexing my fingers in delight. I said to the ruler, "OK flimsy six-incher, let's make one thing clear, as a ruler, you're a joke. First of all, you're barely longer than my dick, and let's face it, you're basically only good for two things: gathering eraser bits together and playing coin football. But now you can redeem yourself – "

"Chauncey, shut up and cut the weed," Tristan cut in.

After cutting, we crumbled the tobacco and ganja together and made lizard-tail blunts.

"Pity Sanjay is missing this," I said.

"Fuck Mola, the town rat," said Harry. "He never comes to this part of Anchovy anyways. And why are we always having to go to his house when the holy Hindus never once allow him to come to ours? I'm done going there, even if it hurts his feelings."

"It's not his fault."

"Don't pick up for him, Tristan," said Harry. "Fuck! This *kotch* is good."

We touched foreheads and blew smoke in each other's face. I said, "You remember that time we went to Mola's to play his TurboGrafx-16 and Harry waltzed into their rec-room looking for the TV remote and saw Mola's senile baba sleeping naked in the massage chair?"

Harry smiled at the memory. "She had bush like a ball of snow – *soo* sex-a-a-y! And what if I told you –"

"Please don't," said Tristan.

"What if I told you," Harry insisted, "that I took a mental picture and rubbed one out as soon as I got home."

"You just had to go there."

Harry said eagerly, "But you should try it, Tris, snowball gazing. An' forget all I said, hehe, let's go back to Mola's."

I stood giddily and almost fell and Tristan caught me and said, "Woah, easy there," but he was wobbling too.

I said, "Let's call ourselves The Wobblies. I officially declare this roof Chill Country."

Harry said, "Great! Let's draft a Charter of Rights."

I said: "One: Laziness – not ignorance – is truly bliss. Two: Let the Indians and the Gypsies have their summers, we'll create a season apart to make them weep with envy."

"That's a sweet phrase, Chaunce," Harry said. "A Season Apart. You should make it the title of your first book."

"Three: When enjoying this lassitude, never – ever! – let anyone disrupt it, no matter who or what is knocking at the door. Four: An amendment to Rule#3: unless, of course, it's the weed-man knocking."

"Chill Country needs a motto," said Tristan.

Looking at the back of Ladoo's novel, Harry said, "There is no happiness higher than rest."

Tristan smiled. "There is no happiness higher than rest… I like it."

A story was forming in my head. I already had a working title: *Montego Bay Pastoral – A Close Encounter with the Jacket Man.* I said seriously, "I'll dedicate this story to Ladoo's legacy."

"Amen, brother," Harry said.

"To Ladoo's legacy," Tristan giggled. "Poor bastard died too young."

"And to the Wobblies!"

"To the Wobblies! There is no happiness higher than rest!"

Harry stood and recited from the back of the book:

> *There is no happiness higher than rest*
> *There is no fire like passion;*
> *there is no losing like hatred;*
> *there is no pain like this body;*
> *there is no happiness higher than rest.*

CHAPTER 3 – BURNING OF THE SHELLS

"No fair!" Mola and Alvaranga said. "How could you have formed the Wobblies without us?!"

We were sitting on the bench encircling the almond tree in front of the eighth grade block. Tristan said , "Listen to him… Town rat, you weren't there with us that afternoon, remember. You never smoked, therefore you never wobbled."

Mola smiled. "Oh, I see what this is about – zip code prejudice."

"But," said Tristan, affecting an avuncular tone, "we're not as heartless as you think. We're willing to grant you, and you, and even you, Stennett, immediate charter membership."

"Oh bless your heart, Tris," Mola said, half-bowing.

"Should we teach them the Charter of Rights?"

Harry said, "No induction ceremony is complete without it."

Tristan said, "Oh all right, on your feet."

Mola, Alvaranga and Stennett stood up.

Tristan said, "Repeat after me: There is no happiness higher than rest."

"There is no happiness higher than rest."

"I now pronounce you Wobbly, Wobbly – and wife." He slapped Stennett's stomach so it jiggled.

They sat back down. Alvaranga said, "Y'all won't believe what happened to me this weekend. I took a drive out with my cousin on Saturday morning to buy fresh lobster at Whitehouse, right."

"Right."

"Then we sat and ate peppered conch on the seawall. I met this local girl and chatted her up, got her number and everything, then we said goodbye and I went back to the car. When we pulled out of the parking lot I just happened to see her getting up from the wall to walk down the street. Guess what!"

"What?!"

"She was crooked! She had a curved spine and was leaning down the lane like the letter S, or that gimp vendor, Tippy."

Tristan's mouth fell open. "Mi pussyclaat…"

Mola slipped from the bench to the tree roots, laughing and holding his belly.

Stennett stared hard at Russell. "What did you do?"

Alvaranga said, "Man, it was like a punch in the stomach!"

"I can bet…"

"My blood ran cold. I took the paper with her number and tossed it through the window."

"What a waste," Harry sneered. "You could've given her a pity fuck. A girl's got to have some action you know."

"Damn skippy," said Tristan. "Sex with the letter S; you got to start somewhere in the alphabet."

Mola was still laughing and wiping tears from his eyes, sitting on the ground. "Nah, she's not waiting on your call, Russ, she's back on that wall to bait some other poor bastard."

"You know what she is?" Alvaranga said. "She's a mermaid showing off her bra and sexy midriff, catching the fellows' eyes on the beach."

"The beach…" repeated Harry.

"The beach?" they all said, except Stennett. "Nah! This early? We couldn't. We just couldn't!"

Harry smiled. "Yes we could…"

Stennett took some Blowpop lollipops from his bag and handed them out. Harry struggled to open his and glowered at the sweet. "Da fuck…? Why are these things so always damn hard to open?"

"It's like trying to pull Excalibur from the stone," Tristan said.

"Those people at the packaging plant take their jobs way too seriously," said Sanjay.

"They're sadists!" Harry screamed, clawing at the wrapper. "They're goddamn sadists! Argh!" He flung the sweet to the ground and stomped on it repeatedly. "Argh! Argh! Arghhh!"

We all looked at the crushed sweet, then back at Harry, breathing sharply.

"Now you feel better?" said Tristan.

"Damn right I do!" said Harry.

"No you don't," said Sanjay.

"No I don't," said Harry.

Russell said, "Right now you're saying to yourself, 'You've been an ass, Harry, crushing the poor sweet with all the tyrannical excess of a modern day Caligula.' Now you're dying for the cool minty taste of a Blowpop on your tongue."

He looked at us, savouring our sweets to taunt him. "Fuck it," he said, then quietly, "…Stennett, you wouldn't happen to have –"

"Nope," said Stennett, licking his lolly, then offering it. "You want a bite?"

Alvaranga looked at me. "What's riding you? You've been glum all day."

Mola said, "He told me this morning – is it OK for me to tell them, Chaunce? After all we're your bestest friends an' we care about you – he told me this morning that he's pregnant an' he doesn't know who the father is."

I laughed shallowly and said, "The story I'm writing has stalled. I'm having trouble with the ending."

"Somebody spread out the sympathy blanket," Russell ordered.

Tristan and Mola spread the imaginary blanket on the ground.

"Now go get him a pillow."

"Let's go to the beach," said Stennett.

Tristan gave him a disgusted look. "Fatman, where were you? We just had that conversation two minutes ago. Are you really that slow on the uptake. Is your heart and brain pumping sludge?"

"Sewage," said Russell, pinching his nose. "They're pumping sewage. *Damn* he stinks!"

"Stink *and* slow."

"He's like a zombie snail."

"Except he's alive… Is he alive?" I leaned closer and peered into Stennett's eyes with the Blowpop as a flashlight.

"No, that smell is sewage, his heart is definitely pumping sewage. *Wooh,* Stennett, so early in the day? We definitely have to take you to the beach for a bath."

"Are you a Wobbly or not, fat man?!" Harry barked.

Stennett, as quick as he could manage, shot to his feet. "A Wobbly by name and girth, Sir!"

"And brain mass?"

"And brain mass, sir!"

"Good response, Stennett," Mola said.

"Why you staring like that?" Tristan asked. "I have something on my face?"

"Hehe…"

"What's so funny? Stop staring like that, you fucking faggot. It makes me uncomfortable."

"*Damn*… hehe… you guys… Tristan is so black… Look at him… Tristan is so black that… look at his hands… it's like he's wearing gloves."

"Fuck you, Harry."

"The fucker's handsome though… no homo."

Russell said, "Yea, he's the best looking of the bunch of us."

I said, "That's what the girls always whisper whenever we stand by Carol's Wall trying to look cute."

"When boys are really handsome," Stennett said, "they seem almost too good for the girls because of their superior looks."

Harry turned on him. "The fuck you just say…?"

"Nothing… Was just thinking off the top of my head."

Tristan said, "Still, with the staring… you fucking queer."

Harry teased, "You're the queer, Tris, and I'll look at you as long as I want."

"Take that back Harry."

"What? Are we in prep school?"

"Harry, I said take it back."

"Why? I hurt your feelings?"

"I'm not telling you again."

"Always so calm and cool. Turns up his nose at the best pussy we're all dying to even sniff – like he's playing hard to get. Wha'ppen, Tristan? You think pussy poison?"

I said, "Guys come on… knock it off."

Harry blew him a kiss. "Boo-hoo! Look at you with your shy dick –"

"Take it back! Don't test me."

"Hehe! Oh he's mad now. Standing all up in my face."

"Stop this minute or I'll –"

"Or you'll what? Stop or you'll what? I guess the truth hurts eh. Look, he's going blue in the face. Ahahaha!"

"Fuck you!"

"Guys! Guys!"

"Cut it out! Stop!"

"Tristan, let him go!"

"He can't breathe, Tristan! Let go!"

Russell said, "OK… OK. Both of you take a deep breath… Now, shake hands. I said shake hands! There… that's better. And stop staring each other down like fucking zoo critters! Tristan, shame on you, you know how Harry is. The fucker never knows when to stop joking around."

"Fuck him…"

"Harry…"

"OK, OK. Not another word. Zip. Sorry Tris. You know I love you, brother. No homo. Would fuckin' kill for you. Now come here you big lump. Gimme a hug. It's a shame to see that handsome mug so glum."

Then Mola, the Cool Assessor, planned how best we should leave the compound undetected.

It was the third Tuesday of the new term. We did this from time to time, ditching school.

We left during the second period, taking the shortcut behind Bailey House that came out at the bottom of Orange Street. We weaved through tourists fresh off their buses milling in and out of duty-free shops, or stopping to examine craftwork by local artists selling on the piazza. A tourist sat on a stool near the entrance to a shop, having her blonde hair cane-rowed after the local style, her face tortured, the braids too tight. Harry nudged my arm and pointed at one of the fruit maidens, discreetly scratching her perspiring neck and unwittingly misaligning the shoulder-length wig with her fingers. "I'll give you fifty dollars if you snatch off the wig."

Stennett jostled between us and blurted out, "I'll do it!" Harry ignored him.

The fruit maidens, dressed in red, flowing plaid skirts, white peasant blouses and plaid head-ties, sat along the walkway with baskets of fruit cradled in their laps. Their fruit wasn't for sale – they were waiting to have their pictures taken with visitors for a modest fee. But that's where the modesty stopped. Nearly all these women were on the game. This was their morning trade or "soft work", as they called it. After having their pictures taken, they baited white men into the nearby bars. The fruit baskets and costumes then changed hands and someone else occupied the seat, like a game of musical chairs.

From being small, we knew all about Montegonian marriages, when a tourist pays for the exclusive services of a prostitute, say for a fortnight or even a month. As boys, we'd see these smiling foreigners parading the city with local girls on their arms. These girls weren't shy. They'd roll their eyes and cluck their tongues at disapproving stares and blow kisses to us small boys and pat our heads. They called the men, "Daddy", or "Sam".

But when the tourist season ended and business dried up, so did their merriment. Many moved back to compete in over-crowded brothels, to a life of scrounging and physical abuse. As they got older and were no longer marketable to tourists, this became their permanent trade.

When the six of us got to the steep incline on Kent Ave that led down to the beach, Tristan pushed me down the small hill. I stumbled and fell, but the hillside bush broke my fall. When he followed me down, I grabbed him round his neck, leaned in with my hip against his and threw him, then jumped on top of him, my knees on his chest. He shielded his face with his hands and mewled like a scared puppy, feigning surrender. I laughed and smacked the side of his head, then pulled him to his feet. I realised I had an erection. He saw it, then looked at me suspiciously. "What does that mean? Does it mean you're like me?"

I stumbled for something to say, and finally managed, "Ahm… it's probably just an adrenalin rush."

"Yea…" he said, still watching me, "…that's probably it." He stood there, sucking at the inside of his cheeks and bunching his lips, a sign he was turning something over in his mind.

"What you thinkin' 'bout?" I said.

"Nutten much," he said. "It's just that something sorta strange happen this morning."

"How strange?" Harry asked, coming up behind us. I jumped, wondering how long he'd been standing there.

Tristan said, "I was goin' up the steps of the bus park an' saw a parakeet with its back to me. I crept up real quiet an' grabbed the tail feathers. But the bird didn't move. It didn't even flinch. I was so surprised I let it go. But it didn't fly away. It was only after I hear someone comin' an' turn to look that it fly 'way."

"Did you look in its mouth?" Harry said.

"No. Why?"

"Because he had a message for you, dummy, that's why. When a wild bird doesn't fly away from your approach or flinch at your touch, it's because it has a message for you."

I rolled my eyes. Harry thought himself an expert of the occult.

"Any bird?" Tristan asked.

"Any bird," Harry answered firmly.

"Will it come back?" Tristan looked disappointed. Was he actually taking this seriously?

"The opportunity has flown, my friend. But who knows, if it's important enough maybe it will. Just be more careful next time."

I looked around the beach. Three boats with faded strokes of mismatched paint were strewn along the shoreline, with fishing nets draped over their bows. The nets shone in the sun's glare and a lazy surge of water animated their edges. I walked over to an almond tree and began undressing. Stennett watched me as I did this, biting and releasing his bottom lip till it flushed.

"What happen?" I asked, "Why you staring like that?"

Harry snickered. "Fat faggot, he looks ready to rape you."

"I didn't bring any shorts," Stennett said lamely.

"Swim in your underpants," Mola said.

Stennett removed his glasses and crinkled his nose. "I'm a briefs man," he said.

"So they *do* make them in that size," Harry said, kneeling to undo his laces. "You learn something new every day."

"No worries, man," I said. "Just swim in your brief an' put it to dry a little time before we leave." Harry and Alvaranga glared at me as if I'd just revealed a secret handshake. I knew they disapproved of my being so accommodating to Stennett. A boarder, he'd befriended us at the beginning of the term, after transferring from Munro that summer. Before Munro, he'd been expelled from Knox College in St Ann in his first year. When we asked what had happened, all he would say was he had "met with difficulties" at both schools. We didn't press him. He was still working hard to win our approval and acceptance. We weren't making it easy for him.

After changing out of my clothes, I walked to the old concrete pier at the north end of the beach and watched the hanging beards of green moss float down into the water from truck tires chained to the pier. It was a ritual of mine. It gave you the illusion that as the sea roiled, the platform would move beneath your feet, and your body would do a slow rolling dance – a child's game, but there was something mysterious and captivating about it.

I hopped off the platform and walked back up the shore. The wind had become sharp, what the fishermen called a cutlass wind because it cut the nostrils cleanly like sugarcane steel. The beach curved jaggedly along the contour of the land. The sunlight made the blue-green water sparkle with each ripple, as lucid as glass.

We swam for about an hour. Then Tristan and I stood on the shore, shoulder to sandy shoulder, grinning at each other while rocking back and forth, our hands outstretched, opening and closing our upward-facing palms and chanting in unison: "Bogue Boy, Bogue Boy swim a little closer." Bogue Boy was the name of the one-eyed shark that terrorised Montegonian fishermen and swimmers. On land you were safe from his menace, so children would boldly chant his name. Of course, no one had ever seen Bogue Boy, which was why his myth was so enduring. It was deliciously exciting to stand on the beach and look for the telltale shape of a shark's fin in every swell and flattening of tide, to feel secure in the knowledge you would never see it. *Bogue Boy, Bogue Boy, swim a little closer.*

Later, sitting below the almond trees, we watched the water shoot up the shore and slide back down, leaving the sand covered in clusters of iridescent bubbles. We were the only ones on the beach. Harry got up and walked around; he found a half-finished lighter and began searching the underbrush for hermit crabs. He found one and pinned it to the ground and lit the back of its shell; when the shell got too hot the crab had no choice but to crawl out. It scuttled about frantically, aware of its vulnerability and impending death. Its soft slimy skin, now covered in grit, would soon curl up and dry out, if some other predator didn't attack it first. We joined him, searching for crabs and taking turns with the lighter. It was cruel, but we couldn't resist the compulsion. When that bored us, we swam again, then lay on our backs, spread-eagled on the sand, trying to outstare the sun and shift it from its position in the sky.

Two older Chester boys, sixth formers, had wandered onto the beach and were watching us with condescending smirks, talking loudly. One said, "She blew me you know."

"If a girl blows you and you're reporting, say she 'blowed' you, not 'blew' you." He shook his head in pity at his friend's ignorance. "You show your greenness by saying that."

I felt a sudden ache for the girl.

Russell said, "I want to wet my whistle. I want to speak in the corrupted past tense."

Harry said, "You should've kept the gimp's number; that right there is a sure head."

Stennett was smiling to himself.

Harry looked at him. "What's so funny?"

"My baby sister… she calls her toes, foot fingers, hehe, isn't that cute?"

Harry shook his head. "Oh brother…"

Stennett said, "I read that this beach is a former docking station for banana ships."

No one said anything.

After a while Harry said, "I don't understand why we have to go back to Marzouca Estate for another field trip. We went there in seventh grade."

"Oh, but you're missing the point, Harry," said Alvaranga. "What better way to be educated in the past glory of your forebears, than visiting the fields where they toiled for freedom? And what's more marvellous than Backra's mansion on the hill?"

"To think they still have blacks up there dressing as slaves and role-playing plantation life, giving tours to white people," Tristan said.

"It's past absurd, it's downright criminal," said Alvaranga.

"The food is great, though," said Tristan. "That roast pork with plantains an' rice an' peas is …" He smacked his lips. "Mm, mm… it's to die for."

"Man shall not live by bread alone," Alvaranga said. "We

should boycott the whole thing, take a long overdue moral stance."

"I not taking a failing grade for geography," Mola said. "You might as well repeat the school year."

"Mola, you disappoint me," Harry said. "But then what should we expect from an apathetic Hindu."

Mola knew better than to take Harry seriously. Harry had a likeability than none of us could match. His weakness was his lack of self-restraint. Without being too handsome, his face was fine-featured and feminine, and his big dewy eyes looked sensitive.

Talk of the estate triggered an idea. It was a tradition of ours. We would do a skit about something that was nagging us just to have a laugh about it. The fun was the improvisation, and Harry was quite good at this, something of a wit. I sat up quickly. "OK, casting call! Russell, you will be Mr. Moses, the labour union official come to inspect conditions on the estate. Harry, you will be Edwin Marzouca. Tristan, Stennett, Mola, you're the black workers."

"Why do I have to be Edwin Marzouca?" Harry asked.

"Because you're the brown man," Tristan said, springing up and pulling Harry to his feet.

I watched Tristan's magnificent features under the halo of sunlight. The skin on his face was smooth and tight, flawlessly fitted over his skull. His nose wasn't too small like Stennett's, nor was it big. It was perfect. He had thin black lips that seemed even blacker when he opened his mouth to show strong, even teeth. Their whiteness flashed like fire in the sunlight when he tilted his head back to laugh. There was a toughness about his muscular body that completed the impression of godlikeness, especially when the seawater crashed against his legs planted in the sand. But then I saw his knees, and the scars where he'd knelt on sandpaper that afternoon in Brother Mac's woodwork shop. He was suddenly damaged, pitiable. Whenever I saw those scars it was all I could do not to beg his forgiveness. When I looked up at his face I saw he'd been watching me, and that we were thinking about the same thing; his face darkened; I looked away before he could hold my eyes.

My hands went up to signal. "Action!"

Harry puffed out his chest and folded his hands behind him, walking alongside Russell on their imaginary tour of Marzouca

Estate. "And what of employee benefits, Mr. Marzouca?" asked Russell. "How is the estate meeting the workers' needs?"

Harry said, "We're meeting them just fine. You see that orange grove over there. That's the workers' healthcare plan. They're allowed one orange each day. Plenty vitamin C, and quite tasty, too. You're welcome to try one."

I was already chuckling. But Harry didn't break character, neither did Russell. Consulting his imaginary clipboard, Russell said, "And what about their retirement plan?"

Harry, mimicking Marzouca's aloof uptown drawl to perfection, waved his hand at the sea. "You see that sugar cane field over yonder? Let's just say that after the niggers stop working at the big house, I have a sweet surprise in store for them."

Russell cracked up. I fell backwards in the seaweed vines, sick with laughter. Harry grabbed Tristan around his waist. "Mr. Moses, how about taking this fine negress back to the city with you, courtesy of Marzouca Farms?"

"All right that's enough," Tristan said, breaking free of Harry's embrace, "quit while you're ahead." His mood had shifted ever since he saw me looking at his scarred knees, and now he walked away from us down to the shoreline.

There was a lull in our gaiety. Stennett plopped down beside me on the sand. "Chauncey, how's your story coming?" he said.

"Didn't you hear me? It's not. I was hoping to get away from it by coming here." I watched Tristan looking out to sea, sitting with his arms thrown back. I could only see his face in profile, a face that seldom betrayed any other emotion than abrasive cheerfulness or sudden sullenness and withdrawal. I thought of the features I feared most, the ones I couldn't see – the eyes I sometimes caught watching me when he thought I wasn't looking.

"There's another story I have in mind, though." I spoke loudly so he could hear. "It's about a carpenter who is charged with the care of two puppies. But his evil instincts get the better of him and he kills the pups and drowns them at sea. But since they're innocent souls, their spirits rise from the water and return to haunt him, taking up residence in his testicles, which swell to the size of cantaloupes. He tries to have the swelling operated on. The doctors won't touch it. It's not hernia, they say. It's not anything they've ever seen. Now, whenever this carpenter walks, ghostly yelps can be heard coming from his balls, but only he can hear them."

"Now that's what I need to take with me to Sugar Navel next week, a pair of barkin' balls," Harry said. "That would surely scare up some free pussy."

We laughed. Tristan remained apart, watching the waves rising and crashing. His silence lacerated my shame. Who was I kidding? I was the one who'd been in league with the Jesus Carpenter all summer. I was the dog who deserved to drown two times over. If Tristan realised this was another of my peace offerings, he didn't show it. I wanted him to acknowledge that I'd suffered too. Sometimes I had the impulse to hurt him, so he would stop playing the victim, licking his wounds. Other times, like now, I had the impulse to plead to him.

We saw Dennis the Epileptic approaching us from the south end of the beach, picking boogers and chewing his nails, his eyes glued to the sand, looking for anything valuable left behind by swimmers. He had the habit of sexualising the hymns the nuns taught him. Now, instead of singing, "*I feel like running, skipping… Praise the Lord*," he sang spiritedly, "*I feel like fucking, jizzing… Praise de Lawd.*" Harry put his fingers to his lips and whistled. "Hey! Booger T Washington!"

Dennis looked up, pretending to see us for the first time. Harry beckoned to him. He approached cautiously, wary of our antics, especially Harry's, who was always tormenting him. But when Harry went over to his clothes bundle and took out a shiny five-dollar coin and showed it to Dennis, he quickened his pace, breaking into a little jog up the beach, holding up his filthy sweatpants by the waistline. When he was close enough to stretch a hand out, Harry wagged a finger: "Ah ah, down on your knees." Dennis stopped, cocking his head like a bemused puppy misunderstanding its master's instructions. Harry held the coin above his head. "On your knees, you filthy wretch!" Dennis dropped to his knees. Harry coaxed him forward with the index finger of his free hand, the coin still held aloft. He held out his palm with the coin. When Dennis made a grab for it, Harry pulled his hand back so Dennis clutched air. We watched the performance with amusement. "Not so fast, Dennis," Harry said. "Kiss my feet." Dennis lowered himself slowly, his eyes still on the coin glinting in the sunlight, then shuffled forward quickly to grab Harry around his waist. Harry, taken by surprise, backpedalled and nearly fell and pushed him off. "Damn, Dennis, you stink!" He brought the coin to his lips and spat on it, then threw it over Dennis's head. "Fetch." Before the coin fell Dennis was leaping backward like a cat. He missed, and the coin sank into the underbrush. He darted after it and searched feverishly, and had soon found it, not caring to wipe away the spittle. Harry called to him again, this time holding up a ten-dollar bill. Dennis's eyes shone. Harry said, "Den Den, dance for Daddy." Then he turned to us. "That's what the pervs under the bridge call him, Den Den."

None of us spoke or moved, not even Mola, who considered himself the moral lynchpin of the group. We were too curious to see what would happen.

Dennis had two lives, two faces. Just that morning, we'd seen him by City Centre, standing behind Sonaa Puckoo, a local artist, who'd been sketching the tourist woman we'd seen having her hair braided. While Sonaa Puckoo sketched, Dennis had mimed his strokes, drawing a phantom portrait of his own on an invisible canvas with a fierce look of concentration on his face. Amused tourists had thrown him money. He did creative hustles like this in the daytime; sometimes he washed cars by the courthouse; in the evenings he attended bible classes with the nuns at St. Helena's Church and had supper. But at night it was a different story. He was a different performer. He slept below Carol's Wall Bridge with other bums in an encampment of board and tarpaulin shacks. There, many of the bums provided sexual services. Their clients were mostly upper-crust men, untouchables, in dark suits and darkly tinted cars, who parked by the roadside, then made their way down to the encampment under the anonymity of night. If we were in the city after nightfall, we sometimes harassed them by shining flashlights below the bridge and watching them scatter like roaches. In desperate flight, you could never quite tell the suits and bums apart: they all had wings, feelers, hairy legs and thoraxes. But now Dennis looked hesitant. The look in his eyes had changed. He seemed set to defy Harry, as if he'd recovered a smattering of self-respect. Harry blinked in surprise and anger,

73

the freckles on his high cheekbones glowing pink. "Oh, so you will turn tricks under the bridge, but you too proud to dance for money. Bravo, Dennis." Dennis began getting up. Harry stepped forward and forced him back down with a foot on his shoulder. "Not so fast! Isn't this how the nuns tell you to earn your salvation, on your knees?"

"Harry, that's enough." Tristan's voice was firm. He was standing with his hands at his sides, his fingers curled.

"Wait, I'm not through," Harry said.

"That's enough!" Tristan repeated.

Harry saw that Tristan was serious. We all saw it.

"All right, all right," Harry said, "don't bite my head off." He removed his foot from Dennis's shoulder. "We just having a little fun, right Dennis." He looked at Tristan. "What's it to you anyway?"

Mola said quietly, "Harry, give him the money or let him be."

Dennis watched the exchange keenly. When the prospect of getting the ten dollars seemed lost, he shuffled away from Harry. Harry glared at him. "Dennis, you know what? You're the lowest form of human scum. You're filth, slime. You're fouler than a festering pustule in a dead donkey's decomposing rectum. But praise God! You're a child of the King. His royal blood flows through your veins. Sing with me, Brother Dennis! 'Oh yes, oh yes. I'm a child of the King'."

Dennis began humming the hymn, swaying from side to side with his eyes closed, then broke out in a rich baritone, "Praise Gawd, praise Gawd. I'm a chile of de Ki-i-ing..." Then he opened his eyes wide and startled us with a deep voice. "De King Crow! De King Crow! Ahahaha! Ahahaha!"

The performance was too strange for us to laugh. Tristan hawked and spat, and walked over to his clothes bundle. It was time to leave. The sand was getting hotter underfoot. We dressed in silence. Harry made faces behind Tristan's back. The sun was high overhead now. It might have been noon. A fisherman had come on the beach while we were distracted and was attending to his boat. He studied the sun with his hand over his eyes, then studied the sea; he dragged the fishing net from the bottom of the boat and began stretching it over the sand, sucking the pulp of a lime between his teeth to prevent dizziness as sunlight penetrated his smooth scalp. His concentration made his dark sinewy body a single muscle. He was in his own world. We didn't exist.

The sea was much calmer now, the after-tide creeping weakly up the sand. I watched Dennis standing waist deep in the sea, his hands clasped under his thickly bearded chin; when he was through praying, he dipped himself. "What's he doing?" I said.

"He's baptizing – cleansing himself," Tristan said. "I've seen him do it before. He probably does it every morning."

As we left we heard Dennis sing with his childish lilt. *"Praise Gawd, praise Gawd. I'm a chile of de Ki-i-ing."*

Russell said, "I'm going to put it on a plate for you… Ready?"

"You can't put anything on a plate," I said, "you don't even know what the phrase means…"

"Shut up and listen! She said, Russ, I can't give you my best, I just can't… There's someone else. And then I said – and by this time I had my hand in her bra. Then I said, 'If you can't give me your best, Katelyn, I'll take the scraps. Let him have your best, I'll take your worst'."

"Booyaka!"

Mola beamed, "Man! Finger 'cross the throat, Russ! Put it here!"

"You'll take her worst?" said Harry.

"Yup."

"That was the line that got you in?"

Tristan said, "Hmm, for a man who got his dick wet, you don't seem that happy, Russ."

"Jus' this feeling… I don't know… You lose something after you come inside a girl."

"Interest?" said Harry.

"No, something else… Something almost… cosmic."

"I get the same feeling when I rub one out in the planetarium," said Harry.

"Look at him. Still musing… You'll have plenty to consider next week."

"Sugar Navel! Yay boy."

Sanjay said, "I hear they caught some eighth graders planning a rogue mission last term. The Upper Schoolers blacklisted them."

"Amateurs."

"Stupid little sluts," I said. "Don't they know the Beer Kaiser is the only man that can get you through the door."

"I heard he's the head of New Lots," said Russell.

I said, "I hear if you meet him personally, you have to shake both his hands, as if it were the most normal thing in the world."

Harry laughed, "Ol' Curry Beard, heheh. Funny the way he keeps dying his beard to hide its natural pigmentation."

Russell said, "Guess who I saw Sanjay swapping spit with at the Odeon Friday…"

"If you open your mouth I'll –"

"Liquorice Lori."

Harry choked on his soda. "The boot-black chick from Helena's? Ho-oh! What got into you Sanj? You think if you marry her and change her name the pigmentation will follow? That's not the way it works, son. Nuptials won't change the melanin count." Harry clapped. "But look at you, Mola… goin' against the grain, defying the Hindus."

"And disinheriting himself," said Tristan.

"Look, the Kaiser's over by Agri Sci…" said Russell getting up.

"He loves to hear himself talk doesn't he?"

Harry frowned. "Something about him doesn't add up, something doesn't make sense."

"He's big time, got to give him that," said Sanjay. "He doesn't have to make sense, but everybody wants to be the Kaiser. Look at all those losers over there by the chicken coops, hanging on to his every word, trying to catch his essence."

"Trying to catch the Holy Ghost."

"And we're here talkin' about him when he doesn't even know that any of us exist."

"My god I want to kiss the man!" shouted Harry.

"Let's go and catch the spirit before they suck him dry," I said.

When we met the Beer Kaiser, aka Andrew James Hurlock, by the turtle pond in the old garden, it was actually my first time meeting him. Before that day I had only known he existed through the magnitude of his myth. He appeared to the untrained eye as one of those well-adjusted students who didn't like to limit his educational experience merely to the academic. He would tell you this himself, being a first-rate philosopher who drew crowds to impromptu lectures all over campus. He'd spent the better part of a decade at Chester, pursuing this holistic development and repeating three grades in the process. Now he was an Upper Sixth former, and leader of the New Lots Society, the school's mysterious fraternity. He looked nothing like I'd imagined – short and stocky, with an auburn complexion, fully bearded with puffy cheeks and close-set eyes like a pig's. Some said his name had to do with the fact his mother was German, others that he had a beer habit, but everyone knew never to commit the unpardonable sin of asking its origin. He would swell up like a frog and dismiss you from his presence. This meant banishment from the school community, to be treated like a leper. Some of the boys called him Curry Beard behind his back, because of his reddish-brown facial hair that he dyed black. The dye job was so obvious it looked ridiculous, but it was all a part of his smokescreen, a smokescreen I wouldn't begin to penetrate until the Bailey House Trial.

He was presently apprising us on how to comport ourselves inside the brothel, since this was crucial to how we would be "received by the hostesses". I assumed this meant the prostitutes, though from the reverent way he was talking about them it was hard to tell. The pig-faced hypocrite! I couldn't wait for the stupid speech to be over so I could escape his smug presence.

The other boys were hanging on to his every word. One idiot asked if he could bring his camera, to take pictures for his scrapbook. The Beer Kaiser sighed and said quietly, "Nerd, leave us." The boy walked away shamefaced. After that, there were no more questions. It was time to discuss strategy.

The excursion was two days away. Since there were four ninth grade classes, there would be four groups, each consisting of around thirty students. Our excuse for leaving school en masse had already been taken care of, the plan being more or less the same each year. We were going into the city to raise money for some new project or other on campus. This year it was the renovation of Bailey House. The tricky part was being allowed to leave school without a teacher playing chaperone. But as the de facto Social and Entertainment Coordinator, and a twenty-year-old sixth-form student, the Beer Kaiser was more than qualified for the job. So while two groups would be out roaming the streets, soliciting charity for our worthy cause, two groups would be inside the brothel, and back out again when it was time to change shifts.

On the day of the pilgrimage we gathered in the parking lot at 10:15 a.m.. You could see the eagerness in the limbs around you – fingers drumming pants' seams, feet tapping, teeth chewing nervously into lips. We organised into groups, each person given a soup can with the label removed and a coin slot cut into the top. The Beer Kaiser stood at the head of the lines: the general inspecting his troops before the final push, Moses taking a head count before the Exodus. After roll call, he hung his clipboard around his neck, clasped his hands behind his back, and stood in a wide stance. "Gentlemen, today we will…"

I bowed my head and whispered to Tristan, "I hope he chokes on his slimy tongue."

Tristan chuckled.

"Did you say something, Knuckle?" the Beer Kaiser said.

After recovering from the surprise of him actually knowing my name, I responded in a faltering voice, "N-no, sir. I did not."

"Good, that's what I thought."

The speech finally over, I double-checked my pocket to make sure I had my wallet with the money and condoms. We started filing through the gate, walking two abreast. Russell Alvaranga was ahead of me. I tapped him on the shoulder. "How long you been dreaming of this day?"

"Just last night, then I woke up and had to change my underpants."

We had a good laugh about it, except Mola, who was still acting as if he was being dragged along against his will.

The night after coming home from the brothel, I sat at the study table in my room writing a draft in the back of my notebook. I soon realised I had no emotional connection to what I'd written; something was coming between me and the words on the page. I sat trying to think of what this impediment was. I read:

…the air inside was musty and stifling, with cigarette smoke floating everywhere like poisonous smog. Dull red bulbs gave the ochre-coloured interior a pale, sickly glow that was as unattractive as the sleepy-looking people slouching in threadbare couches in the corners, smoking with pained faces, as if disgusted with themselves for being there. Wishy-

washy girls plodded around the bar with sour expressions. One girl gyrated lazily on a pole at centre stage. She never once looked into the audience, and kept pulling on the loose strap of her thin red bra that sagged with the weight of her slack breasts. I bet she had about a dozen children. They must be whom she was thinking about. My heart raced in my chest; I got up and pushed past an old man who was holding out necklaces of red, yellow and black beads to me: 'Hey Joe, wanna buy a souvenir?' He was so drunk he didn't even recognise that I wasn't a tourist. Then again I could have been. I could have been anybody...

The more I read, the more sterile the words felt, as a form of self-deception. But another story was testing its teeth, its bite becoming sharper the more I reflected on my conversation with Tristan that afternoon at his house. By the time I turned to a clean page and began writing, the feeling was throbbing like a toothache. What a sweet pain it was! At the top of the page, as a working title, I wrote exactly what ran through my mind at that moment: *A release is coming! The stone is being rolled away.*

The next morning, the new draft completed, I told my friends about the Shadowless One.

"It happened during Market Week, just before Christmas. A small-time vendor goes to Cayman for a few days to buy stock for her store and leaves her teenage daughter home alone. A man breaks into the house while the girl is asleep and brutally rapes her. Because it's dark, and because the man is masked, she's unable to describe him to the police. But the only thing she's sure of is he's local, because she knows the voices who are regulars on the football field across from the house where she lives. Needless to say, when her mother hears the news she's devastated, and rushes home immediately. Where her daughter and the police had failed, she would not. She consults an African Revivalist priest and tells him what happened. Lack of positive I.D. and all. 'Not to worry,' says the old man.

"So one Saturday, while the men are playing football, the woman, her daughter, and the priest walk onto the field. The game stops. The holy man claims the culprit is standing right there. And he can prove it. Nervous laughter breaks out. He spreads his mat on the earth, does his incantation, brings his palms together and kisses the ground. The spell is now officially in effect, and will reveal the culprit as clear as day. He's now cursed, the priest says, with a form of living death, and the undead have no shadows. In the morning, everyone on earth has a shadow, except for this man among the group who, through guilt, quickly looks down to find himself shadowless. His friends shrink away from him in horror. The woman screams and charges to tear him to pieces, but the holy man restrains her and tells her it's not necessary. His fate has been sealed. And sure enough it is. He never recovers his shadow. When he puts his hand over his chest he doesn't feel a heartbeat. Food and drink have no taste. He never again takes a shit, never again passes urine, never again sweats or sleeps. He can't even shed tears for his miserable state. His family turns him out, not wanting the curse to spread to them. The community banishes him. When he turns himself in to the police, he's shunned. Now he roams the land after sunset, leaving behind no footprints."

We were sitting on the stairwell of the Art Block on the western side of the school campus. Art class had finished early. We were all silent, until the bell shrilled for the beginning of recess.

"What happens to the girl?" asked Tristan.

"The Shadowless One returns to her dreams every night, and rapes her over and over again." He watched my face as I said this, chewing a straw between his teeth.

"I don't know if it's suitable for the story competition, though," Mola said. "It's too… sinister."

"Forget the competition," I said. "I'm not inspired to write for it."

Russell hmphed, a sound that said: *Aren't we high and mighty this morning*.

I took a deep breath and waited. Alvaranga had a talent for getting on your nerves. He said, "But if you should win, Knuckle, that prize money would go a long way in clearing up a small detail."

"Seriously, Russell? You want to bicker about money right now?"

He hopped off the railing to give passage to some boys running up the steps. "I'm just offering practical advice."

Like hell he was. Truth be told, sometimes none of us liked Russell Alvaranga, nor knew exactly why he'd started hanging out with us, since we'd never been friendly to him at the beginning. But his case was different from Stennett's. He needed no one. The spoiled brat from a family tree laded with money, his father was chair of the School Board, and his dead relatives had helped form the Old Boys Association. He was biding his time – already a prefect – before moving on to becoming head boy or form president. It was enough to make you sick, the way people would line up to kiss his ass, masters and students alike.

I'd bought a used computer from him over the summer – an IBM XT with word-processing software – with the money I'd made, but still owed him six hundred dollars.

"You'll get your money," I said. "Just don't bitch about it."

"Who's bitching?" Alvaranga said. He turned to Stennett, "Fatty, what you think? Am I wrong to ask for what's mine?"

"Not to sound indifferent," Stennett said, "but I'd much rather hear how you guys got on yesterday."

Mola said, "I heard some of the girls whispering that the Kaiser never allows any of them to see him naked."

This was intriguing. "What could he be hiding?" I said.

"Probably some deformity," Alvaranga said.

Mola chuckled. "Maybe he has a third nipple."

Stennett said, "The Kaiser is a bit bottled-up isn't he? I guess it adds to his mystique." I smiled. It was a sign of the traction he was making in our group that Stennett could casually offer observations like this. I was impressed.

Russell nudged Harry. "How did you do?"

Harry made a face. "Man, that black stone burned me up. I had to put my dick under the tap."

We laughed.

"No joke," Harry continued. "The girl came into the bathroom and saw me and made a disgusted face. She thought I was washing her off. But then I explained what happened and she ran for a tube of vaseline and came back and doctored me up real good. So talented these prostitutes."

"Bless her soul," I said.

"No no bless *my* soul," said Harry. "I gave her a generous tip for her trouble, then gave her a taste of her own medicine." He winked at us and it took a while before we caught on.

"Oh no," said Tristan beaming. "You dawg!"

"Woof!" said Harry grinning. "You should have seen her lips; dem shine like she nyam chicken back."

While our laughter echoed, Stennett's jaws had dropped. "That's downright diabolical…"

Harry bowed. "After she finished I felt the black stone wearing off. My balls tingled and shrank till they hurt, man, and my dick went numb. Those sneaky Chinese…"

"Perhaps all that Chinese writing on the box was a warning with instructions," I said.

Russell said, "Careful boys, black stone is a little like Vicks Vaporub. You have to double the dose as your sensitivity declines and all roads lead to impotency."

"The expert here," mocked Harry.

"I've used it a couple times."

Tristan said, "What? Vicks Vaporub on your dick?"

"No no," I said, "he means Vaseline on his lips."

"No no," said Sanjay, "he means Vaseline on his dick."

Russell turned to Tristan. "Tris, I see you and Knuckle bring a nice piece o' skin upstairs yesterday, man." He looked at me accusingly. "Why you never put *that* in your story? So what happened?"

Tristan got up and tucked his art portfolio under his arm. "I don't have no more time to waste. I got to make some sales before class. An' why you askin' me when you have the storyteller sittin' before you?"

All eyes were on me now.

I saw a group of eighth graders downstairs 'bumming' a classmate on his birthday; they had all lined up to give him celebratory kicks. I drew attention to what was going on. The birthday boy was clinging to a concrete pillar by the steps, groaning with each kick, then massaging his buttocks. He clenched his teeth and squeezed his eyes shut. Harry smiled. "You know… I think the little bugger is enjoying himself, he's moaning like he's being ass raped, but those might just be tears of joy." Then he called down, "Be grateful now, dear. You only turn twelve once." We whistled and hooted, "Happy birthday! Keep the kicks coming!" and waved at the boys.

I was praying for the recess bell to shrill to rescue me from having to fabricate a lie.

The day before, when we arrived at Sugar Navel, the first person to greet us was a vendor with a gap-toothed grin, standing outside the entrance. When he saw us coming, he sprang off the wall, launching into his spiel: "See it here, see't here! Everything you need: black stone, peekash, Operation Desert Storm – yes, yes, me have it. What for de schoolers? Me have de medicine to make de cock crow an' make de hen bend low. Lash dem till dem bawl out, bedroom bathroom all 'bout. Yes me have it." We stepped closer to examine the bag he held open. He took out a small bottle of brown liquid. "Ensure yuh cock wid Pull Me Cock, don't make it drop nor flop – Pull Me Cock Roots Tonic – 100% percent natural. Don't gimme nuh coke, don't gimme nuh crack, jus gimme de Pull Me Cock *wap wap wap*! Right round de clock yuh do it nonstop! An' yo, yuh see when yuh drink dis, schoolers – yuh gi' any gal back-shot, body press, wheelbarrow, air-fly, lap-fly, lapskuchie, touch-yuh-womb or kidney or liver or maw! Make she all belch, cough an' sneeze an' please! Ensure yuh cock pon Pull Me Cock!"

Harry had ignored the proffered bottle and selected black stone, a Chinese aphrodisiac that was small, black and hard like granite. "How potent is this?" he asked.

The wordsmith squinted in confusion. "Poison?"

Mola smiled. "He doesn't know what 'potent' means."

"Never mind," said Harry, paying for a piece about the size of a kidney bean wrapped in clear plastic. As soon as we stepped off, other boys flocked to the Pull-Me-Cock peddler and he began a roaring trade.

There was that graffiti again on the curb outside: WHO LEFT THE TYGER TO WATCH OVER THE LAMB? We'd been seeing it all over town recently. We saw Ghost, the Fullerite vendor with almost beet-red skin and a skeletal face. Just a few months later, he was found in a codfish barrel at the mouth of Fuller Canterbury with his throat slit. He used to roam the streets with a pushcart balancing an old fridge filled with coconuts and oranges in an ice bath, shrilling, "Ice cold jelly jelly jelly jelly jelly... cokinaat!" Now he said in his high-pitched, womanish voice,

"CC bwoys, wash off yuh heart wid a jelly before yuh enter de establishment."

"No Ghost," I said, "you should sell us the jellies to wash off our hearts after we leave."

"That won't be long," Ghost quipped. "None a yuh lastin' longer than five minutes when mooma twis' it (he swung his hips to one side) an' squeeze it (he swung his hips to the other side) an' pull de venom outta de one-eye snake like a dancin' mongoose. Dey clamp de cocky suh, dey squeeze de pussy lips suh, an' yuh money done. Next customer! Same treatment!" We laughed and looked at each other and Harry said, "We stand duly warned, Ghost." Ghost said, "I'll be waiting right here," then added, "when yuh go inside ask any o' dem girls if in all dem years of professional service if dem ever fuck a ghost. Dem fuck man, puss an' dawg, even policeman baton, but dem never fuck a ghost!" Then he eyed a group of tourists crossing the street. "Aaarinjj! Wha' happen pretty bunununus white lady? Chat to me nuh! Don't pretend yuh come all dis way to only look at two foot long wooden cocky, see de real ting here co-o-ming!"

A middle-aged man with a broad, handsome face and grey stubble all over his cheeks and chin, pretending he was blind and knocking about with a cane, now dropped his act, approached and said, "Psst! Boys! Come this way. Haitian pussy, cheap cheap. Jus' follow mi down dis lane."

Russell said firmly, "No thanks, I've heard about that refugee pussy."

The man smiled and licked his lips. "What you hear, bwoy?"

"That you can't wash the stink off."

The man lifted his sunglasses to regard Russell, then laughed softly and lowered his glasses. "OK." He stepped closer and took a blue portfolio from his jacket, licked his thumb and showed off the girls like a model agent. One with low cut hair was so beautiful she made me drool. I pointed at her picture the same time Harry and Sanjay did. I said, "How 'bout this one?" The man smiled; he knew he was getting through.

"This one?" he said, though he knew well enough she was the one we pointed at. "This one is young and strong, she jus' come off de boat, landed in Portland las' week. They call her the

Cockchafer." Russell sighed in exasperation and put a hand on Harry's arm but Harry pulled away. "We're wasting time here," Sanjay said. "Give us your card and we'll be in touch some other time."

"An' remember, cheap cheap."

"Money was never an issue," said Russell testily. "Goodbye, slave trader."

"Goodbye, rich prick," said the man, blind and knocking about with his cane again.

Inside, it was too much to take in – the pole dancing on centre stage and lap dancing in the glass-enclosed V.I.P Red Room, where Arab merchants from the city centre sat together in a semicircular couch arrangement, laying down their wallets on the tables to tempt the girls to go down on their knees for greenbacks; or upstairs in the drinking lounge, where Montego Bay's finest – policemen, firemen, Jamaica Tours bus drivers – were drinking and feeling up the "hostesses" before heading back to work after lunch. But we had roughly forty minutes before changing shifts with the next batch of boys.

I watched a girl walk in, wearing a mint-green blouse with low-cut shoulders, black leather mini skirt, stockings and fashionable black boots, the straps of her large handbag slung casually over her shoulder. I watched to see if she'd go and change into the standard uniform of black leather bra, booty shorts, stilettos and glittery body paint, but she did not. She was catching favourable stares from most of the men, but some of the girls were giving her hard looks. She was young, couldn't have been more than sixteen, with a small, smiling, pretty face. She looked self-possessed, not too eager to please. I'd made my choice. Even if she wasn't on duty, I'd find a way to convince her. I waited until she had walked over to the bar, rolling her ass to the music. I took a deep breath and walked over. Soon I was talking her ear off, but without much success. She kept looking in my face with calm, cool intimidation, waiting for my next line, my next failure, wanting me to understand that I was failing, that she was in control. Smiling mockingly, she said, "Trus' me honey, you cyaan afford me. Keep you likkle milk money in you pockit. Plus, me don't work here no more." Her voice betrayed her country background; it explained why she chose to communicate through body language rather than conversation. I persisted, until finally I wore her down and she said, "Buy me a drink."

After buying her two drinks, things became easier. She allowed me to get closer to her, to touch her, but only on her back and arms. Then she saw Tristan walking over and her face lit up. She offered to buy *him* a drink. The three of us talked a while. Without my actually knowing how it happened, we reached an agreement. She took us both by the hand, a bit condescendingly, walking slightly ahead of us, up to the rooms upstairs, promising to give us a schoolboy special – a two for the price of one deal, on account, I knew, of her liking Tristan – and a little "bonus". I darted eager looks at Tristan behind her back, but he seemed bored. Two men passed us, one snarling, "Man, dat pussy was worse than lukewarm beer. I want a refund." His friend responded, "What yuh say? It 'taste' worse than lukewarm beer?'"

In the room, it was a different story. We couldn't get her to shut up. She began telling us her life story: how she grew up in a big family in Cambridge, rural St James, and had left home at fifteen to make her way in the city, with only eight dollars in her purse. She had worked various jobs on the Hip Strip – as a waitress, a masseuse, an exotic dancer, and here at Sugar Navel. Now she worked almost exclusively for a high-end escort agency, with some of the most powerful men in Montego Bay on her client list. They took her for exclusive weekends at their private villas; they took her to brunch at the Yacht Club on Sundays. One of her regulars was an American who worked at the U.S. Consular Agency in Ironshore so she had got her visa "easy, easy," so she could go for shopping sprees to Miami. Sometimes, she said, there wasn't even a sexual relationship; all they wanted was companionship, a refuge from marital monotony. There were also the kinky ones, for whom she had to do unspeakable things, "party favours", she called them. She wasn't naïve. She knew success came with a price. And though she wasn't boasting or complaining, there was vulnerability in her frankness; she seemed desperate to talk to someone, and perhaps thought us suitable since we were outsiders to her world, sheltered boys who had made a temporary incursion. I saw Tristan watching her from where he sat on a chair beside the door, a scowl arching his mouth. He got up to go to the bathroom. When he came back, he had a mischievous twinkle in his eyes. He said, "The bathroom has a queer bit of indignity."

"What's that?"

"It has fresh flowers but no soap."

I laughed, shaking my head.

"Wha' dat?" the girl asked peevishly. "A Chester boys' joke?"

She no doubt felt annoyed by our preppiness. I hastened to smooth things over. "No," I said. "It's just ironic that –"

She jumped down my throat. "I know what irony is!"

Tristan seemed pleased. He watched her in his peculiar way, with an expression between a sneer and a smile playing on his lips.

When she rose with her bag and went into the bathroom, I hastily began undressing but Tristan didn't move. I ignored his reluctance. But when he got up to leave, I grabbed his hand. "Don't fuck this up for me!"

"Why do you need me here?"

"Don't play dumb! You're the one she likes. If you leave now, it spoils everything."

So he stayed, sitting sullenly, with his hands folded over his chest. There was a low table in the centre of the room with a tray of sweets, snacks and condoms, all in colourful wrappers – customer service, and a safeguard. Montegonian prostitutes never allowed customers to use their own condoms. The city had the highest HIV rate in the country and prostitutes feared deliberate sabotage. I took a lollipop and popped it into my mouth, trying to relax, thinking of how beautiful the girl was. I wished I could have had her for myself. I liked her prettiness and frankness. Yes, she was coarse, but not as impersonal and condescending as the older girls downstairs. But who was I kidding. As she went to the bathroom, she made a shovel with her fingers and made crude scooping gestures, back and forth, below her crotch, mimicking the twang of an Asian tourist one might come across in the city with a big smile and an even bigger Nikon camera round his neck, saying, "Me, wash wash, you wait." I didn't find it funny. Yes, who was I kidding.

When she came back, her demeanour had changed. She was now less talkative, unsmiling, but sufficiently casual and open to put us at ease – her professional face. She wasted little time. Sitting on the edge of the bed, she put me to stand between her legs, slid down my underwear and took me into her mouth, all in one fluid motion, slowly raking her fingernails over the pit of my stomach, stretching her hand up to feel my chest, to tweak my nipples. I shuddered with pleasure while gripping her shoulders. When I looked over, Tristan was glaring at her; it was making me uncomfortable. I motioned towards him. She got up and walked over and sat on his lap. She began kissing his neck and chewing his earlobe, but Tristan turned away his face. When she felt the front of his pants, she smiled. "Wha' happen, boss? You shy? Lemme help you wid dat." It might have been the half-mocking way she said it that blasted everything. When she touched him, he recoiled, stiffening with rage. He slapped her hand away, lifted her by the waist and dropped her on the narrow bed. He sat on her belly, just below the ribcage so it was hard for her to breathe, then covered her mouth and pinched her nostrils. Her eyes bulged with shock and she squirmed under his grip, his palm absorbing her screams. When he removed his hands he began hitting her about the face, till her eyes watered and her face turned red. She could only moan, stunned by the assault. All this was having a disturbing effect on me. Part of me wanted to stop him, but the other urge was a swooning arousal. I started touching myself, watching him intently as my own pleasure mounted. It was exhilarating, as if some part of me I never knew existed had been violently awakened. Only when I realised he wasn't letting up, when I saw her arms flailing, slapping weakly against his sides and belly – when he seemed set to throttle her – I jumped up and shoved him off. "Tristan! You go kill her, man!" He steadied himself and stepped off the bed, his chest heaving, beads of sweat wetting his face.

The girl raised herself slowly, still stunned from the blows. She crouched on all fours in the middle of the bed, her tongue and teeth raking over her bleeding lips. She crouched at the foot of the bed, her hand over her ear, checking for blood. Burying her face in the sheets, she kept saying miserably, "Me ears a ring. Me go deaf. Oh gawd me go deaf."

I took two fifty-dollar notes from my wallet and tossed them on the bed. Tristan kept looking at his hands and grimacing. For a moment, I thought he would attack her again. An awful mixed-up feeling of spent rage, shame and confusion was in the room. We avoided each other's eyes. I saw him fingering two white, filigreed cards perched on the end of the shabby dresser. "Look Chauncey," he said giggling, "the whore was going to give us her business card, he-heh." I gave him a scalding look. I felt like I wanted to hit him. The girl had crawled back on the bed. We left the room in silence.

Downstairs, the others were already gathered, fresh from their conquests and beaming with satisfaction. The Beer Kaiser came down the steps moments later, flanked by two girls, and said, "Gentlemen, are we ready to go?"

As we left, a new dancer was taking centre stage, dressed in a shimmering golden bikini with sequin-spangled tail feathers. The announcer lilted: "Now coming to the stage is the Golden Hen, who lays eggs for the gentlemen, or as they're called around these parts, the paying cocks." The men guffawed and beat the tables and crowed like roosters.

When I got home from Sugar Navel, Papa called me around to the backyard. Sheila was packing a crocus bag with yams, cassavas, ackee and breadfruit in the storage shed next to the laundry room. "Take this over to Clare's," Papa said.

"An' tell Tristan to come for dinner," Mama shouted through the kitchen window. "Bwoy children don't belong in the kitchen. It's a shame Clare leave him everyday to cook his own supper. One day, the poor thing goin' to burn that house down." I took the bag and left without bothering to change out of my khakis.

Tristan's house had a galvanised roof that was brown from rust. I walked across the yard, and went up the steps, pushed the door and went inside. The windows in the living room were closed, the curtains drawn; the room had the sweet chemical smell of his mother's cosmetology products. This was where she accommodated neighbourhood women when she wasn't working in the city. She practically lived in the room. Her bed things were still on the couch. I often thought of Tristan and his mother more as roommates than parent and child. He called her Clare, like everyone else. He was sitting on a stool in the kitchen, shelling dry corn on the kitchen counter. I placed the crocus bag on the floor. "Papa sent this for Clare." He said nothing.

It was a sign of wealth among Anchovy residents how many rooms you'd added to your small government-built house. We had added eight. The extended kitchen was the only addition Tristan's family had made, and the inside walls, which had never been painted, were already grey and black from smoke, which made the room darker than the rest of the house. Here was where he spent most of his time.

The corn he was shelling was payment from Papa for working on the farm on weekends. Papa respected his industry and had offered him the salary of a part-time farmhand, but after hearing the amount, Tristan asked if he could have the leftover corn from the animal rations at the end of each week instead. He would use it to make asham. He could make a sizable amount and make decent money selling it at school during recess and lunchtime. I watched him pounding the parched, shelled corn in the wooden mortar, then sifting it and adding sugar. So easily, so skilfully. It was another notch of superiority I had no right begrudging, yet whenever he offered me a portion I would pettily refuse just to spite him, even though I was dying for a taste, because he made it well, like a real country boy.

Watching Tristan gather the leftover corn on the farm one day, Papa had observed that he had his father's resourcefulness, but hopefully none of his guile. After Philpot left the family, Papa became protective towards Tristan and his mother. Mama disliked his attention to Clare, whose beauty attracted men, but she was never cold to Tristan, though she often fussed with Papa when she caught him putting money in envelopes for Sheila to take to Clare. I found Clare's photo in Papa's wallet once, as I was lifting money from it while Aunt Girlie gave him his bath. What might have mollified Mama was the fact that Papa could never consummate his dalliance because of his impotence.

Tristan had his mother's face. It attracted men, too. From a very young age, he was made aware of this. At first, you didn't see the resemblance until he smirked; then they looked exactly alike.

His father, Philpot, was a samfie man, known as the smoke blower. Whenever he opened his mouth it was to blow smoke in your face. By the time it'd cleared he'd gone. That's how he had got Clare, Mama said, since he was twice her age and as ugly as sin. The smoke was just clearing from Clare's eyes. That's what the neighbourhood women shook their heads in pity about. Tristan had never forgiven his father for choosing his business over his family, for leaving them destitute and vulnerable, the house as yet unpaid for. He was ashamed of their poverty among his better-off friends, and was determined to make something of himself.

After shelling the corn, he put it into a pot and placed it on the stove. When he turned the knob there was no gas. He kicked the gas cylinder and sucked his teeth. "Nothing works in this house."

"You comin' for dinner?" He didn't answer, and began searching aimlessly through the cupboards. This was his routine to save face whenever I offered him charity. "What you doing? I said. "Even if you find something, how you goin' to cook it?"

He found a half box of cigarettes and a green glass lighter. "Let's have a smoke."

We sat under the cool shade of their star-apple tree. We smoked easily for a while, crunching dry leaves between our toes, silently competing to see who could make the leaves crackle loudest. Finally, I said, "Why you hit that girl like you did today?"

He looked at me, smiling. "Why you beat your meat like a monkey while I did it? You enjoyed it, no?"

I knew I had been excited by the indirect sexual contact between us, a sexual jealousy and possessiveness I'd experienced towards him before when Gilda, Harry's older sister, had dated him. Once we had double dated and I couldn't bear the sight of Gilda kissing him or smiling at his handsome profile while he stood at the box office getting tickets. When she slipped her hand down his jeans I couldn't breathe. My date noticed my preoccupation but wrongly guessed its cause. She sucked her teeth and went cold the whole night. I was secretly happy when he said to me, "I feel like I carryin' sandbags tied under me armpits." When he finally cut Gilda loose, I could breathe again. My excitement over the violence at Sugar Navel was different and more uncomfortable.

His eyes went dull, his face remote and heavy. He said slowly, "I wanted it so bad, Chaunce, to have sex with her, I wanted to do it so bad… but I couldn't."

"Maybe you wanted it too much."

He looked at me with a bewildered hurt.

"Don't beat yourself up," I said. "It's just not in your nature."

"I'm sorry."

"Sorry for what? You have nothing to apologise to me for."

"I felt like I was letting you down. Then I just lost control."

"Forget it."

He now looked angry, offended, but the anger had no focus, was still groping around for its reason to exist. "I didn't like what she was saying. But then I realised I was being a hypocrite."

I waited for him to continue.

He watched the cigarette burning slowly between his long fingers. "You know what I don't like? I don't like when people leave half-finished cigarettes lying around. Clare does that. Either you smoke it off or you don't smoke it at all. Either you destroy something completely or you leave it alone." The look in his eyes was the one I'd seen four years before inside the shed: him and Brother Mac. He knew what I was thinking about; it pleased him. Something flashed in his eyes. He bowed his head, sucked off the cigarette and stubbed it beneath his heel. "See," he said, "as simple as that."

My mouth felt dry. I knew where this was going and I wasn't ready to go there. I wished I hadn't come. I flicked the cigarette towards a stagnant pool of water below a drainpipe leading off their kitchen. It fell short and landed on a pile of dry leaves.

"Half-finished cigarettes, Chauncey. You want to burn down my house?"

Wisps of smoke rose into the air. A small orange flame sprouted. The dry leaves sparked and cracked. He stood and walked to the pile, watching the fire devour the dead leaves, the smoke swirling about his ankles. He said with his back to me, "You remember when we used to go to cadet camp, an' you showed me that trick of how to avoid gaggin' when brushin' the back of your tongue? You showed me that the trick was focusin' on your reflection in the glass. That way, you feel as if it's not you who doin' the brushin', but your image, an' *you* become the reflection, because you sorta trick your mind." He smiled grimly. "Well, I don't have to pretend any more. I've developed a pretty strong gag reflex. I don't feel a thing when it's happenin.' I don't even flinch when they're touchin' me."

I shot him a startled look. Had I heard him right? "What?" I said. "When *what's* happening? When *who's* touchin' you?" He ignored me, and began digging up dirt with a shovel and throwing it over the fire. His manner suggested that we had said enough. I knew I couldn't sit at the same table with him to eat, to look in his face. He knew it too, and made no attempt to follow me. I got up. My legs felt weak.

"Give Mas Clarence my regards," he said mockingly.

"I'll tell them you found something to eat," I said. I took a ten-dollar note from my wallet and stretched it out to him.

"I don't want your money." The hostility in his eyes was unmasked. As I walked away he called, "I didn't tell you how much I liked your story that day at the beach, the one with the barkin' dogs. But don't you see you have it all wrong. Don't you realise it's him barkin' inside us an' not the other way around? You think him lose a night's sleep over what he did?"

"I'll bring you some kerosene for the small stove then," I said, my voice thick in my throat.

"Don't bother." He went inside, banged the kitchen door shut.

On my way home, I thought about the way he'd spoken, my sudden and strange arousal at the brothel, but most of all, I thought of my weakness. I'd run away that afternoon and I was still running. I couldn't seem to help it.

When I got home, Papa saw the consternation on my face. "Something wrong?" I shook my head. "Where's Tristan?"

"He's asleep," I said, and hurried in before he could pry.

I wanted to talk to someone. Reverend Myers? But how could I reveal such a shameful thing? People's opinion of me had always been important. I wanted them to think well of me. Deep down, I thought people should make concessions on my behalf, should be a little jealous of my gifts; I was marked for achievement and therefore entitled to their respect, even as my own actions filled me with self-contempt.

At times I'd felt I lost out to Tristan for Papa's affection. After we'd both won places at Chester College, were both reported in the *Montego Bay Sun* with a photo of us standing side by side, as we'd done so many times since we were toddlers. Papa practically adopted Tristan. He took us both to see his tailor on Victor Street to take measurements for our graduation suits. At the tailor's I listened to them talking, two old friends catching up, but it was Tristan whom Papa bragged about, his athletic success, his dutifulness to Clare, his proficiency on the farm. My name barely came up. I'd won the Marcus Garvey scholarship, one of the top four places in the island, and though Anchovy folk congratulated me, Tristan's accomplishment had more meaning because of his straitened circumstance. I could've afforded to go to Chester without a scholarship; he couldn't. At the time I was so blinded by resentment I couldn't appreciate this. I couldn't feel happy for him. I tried to undermine him in any way I could, with a sense of entitlement fed by my anger at having been usurped in my grandfather's esteem.

One April weekend, one of the cows wandered off in Goshen. We set up search parties. Sheila searched one area, Papa another and Tristan and I searched together. We spent the whole afternoon looking. Evening came. I cursed Papa's name for every insect bite and scratch I got and threatened to quit. I tried to distract Tristan from his keenness on the search, which made it even more oppressive. "Tris, let's play movie quotes. Name the movie: *When a man with a 45 meets a man with a rifle –*"

"Not now, Chaunce."

"Oh lighten up, the stupid cow is probably dead anyway."

He sighed and looked at me. "Is everything a joke to you?"

"Is everything so fuckin' serious to you?"

"You know, if you put half the effort into your chores as you do in your writing –"

"What? I'd measure up to you? I'd be worthy to lick Papa's boots?"

"I ain't trying to take anything from you, *hombre*. It's all yours; could never be mine."

"But you wish it was, don't you, *hombre*? You think you deserve it. That's why you break your back trying to earn it."

"I only break my back when I have to do my portion, then do yours properly."

"Oh! The Prince of Knuckle Manor speaks: the heir apparent."

"Your mout' is set on a spring like a little bitch. I ain't goin' to toe to toe wid you. Just keep up and don't slow me down."

"Don't call me a bitch, you fuckin' queer!" I sprang at his back but he sidestepped and shoved me by my neck to the ground. I got up and rushed at him and he caught me in a headlock.

"Let me go, Tristan."

"Not until you promise to quit your foolishness."

"Let me go!"

"You promise?"

"Yuh full o' shit like a crab an' I go show yuh who's the bitch."

"I'm lettin' you go now… there."

He walked off rapidly, unsheathing his machete, knowing that I didn't know the wood as well as he did and was likely to get lost. I struggled to keep pace. Angry tears blurred my vision. He was soon out of sight and I stopped hearing his footfalls and the swish of the machete through the bush. Then I heard him scream. I stopped; my heart stopped. "Chauncey!" he called out. My heart hammered relief. "Chauncey!" I ran in the direction of his voice, thinking I would give my life to have his favour back. "Chauncey, help!" I pushed my strength to the limit till I found him. "I found her!" he screamed gleefully. He had fallen down a sinkhole, and there at the bottom with him was the cow. He was laughing, stroking the cow's muddy white head, kissing it's wet pink and black lips. "Easy now, girl… Where does it hurt?" Basking in his discovery, our feud forgotten, he grinned at me. "I thought she broke her leg, but it might not be as bad as all that." He gave me that look of satisfaction that I hated so much. "Bighead, aren't you going to ask if I'm hurt?"

I stared at him without saying anything, malice, I suspect clouding my face. His grin disappeared. I said, "Remember when you threw me off the roof?"

"Throw down the rope, Chaunce." I stood there, looking at him and the grateful cow, so exhausted it could barely lift its head to lick his face. Dusk had fallen. Darkness was also filling up my heart. "Chauncey, throw down the rope!" I felt cold inside, shut off my concern for him. "Chauncey, don't leave me here!" I stepped back and bumped into Sheila. He grabbed the rope from my hand.

"What you doin'?" he barked. "Why don't you throw down the rope to Tristan?"

"I… I was coming to find you," I stammered.

"In this darkness? Without a flashlight?" Sheila grimaced and raised his hand as if to strike me for telling such a pathetic lie. I could almost taste the fresh blood in my mouth. I wanted to be punished. I felt the same self-contempt I'd felt outside Brother Mac's woodwork shed when I walked away pretending I hadn't seen anything. That I couldn't hear Tristan's choking sobs.

It was only on the day of my twelfth birthday that we had actually spoken about what happened in the shed. I was hiding on my garage roof while the neighbourhood boys searched for me to give me my "bumming". I was reading *The Divine Comedy* when Tristan snuck up on me. I jumped to my feet and giggled and said, "OK, just one kick, but you can't tell anyone I'm hiding here." The look on his face was vicious, as if he really wanted to hurt me. He grabbed my shirt and held me over the edge of the roof. "What were you talkin' to Clare 'bout in the kitchen las' night? Did you tell her what he did to me? Did you?"

I grabbed his throat: "Let me go! Lemme go! Mi go kill yuh!" He slapped my face. "You told her didn't you?" I spat in his. "Fuck you! Lemme guh!" So he let me go. As I fell I completed a journey – hell, purgatory and paradise in one: him giving me brutal kicks over and over again.

CHAPTER 5 – MARZIPAN

I was placed second in the short story competition. *The Montego Bay Sun* published the top three stories and mine had the caption: *"It's humour comes, as the best humour does, from an acute observation of human nature."* I should've been happy, but insecurity was setting in. I knew I wanted to be a writer but I knew nothing of the vocation. I read aimlessly. Some of the novels I read seemed to demand a frame of reference that I lacked. The foreign authors especially were frustrating; they seemed too self-involved and sophisticated to mean anything to me. And our Caribbean writers were reduced by school to becoming an academic chore, not something (as we were virtually warned) to take pleasure in. Grades were at stake. So writers remained mysterious people, and I realised this was the case for everyone else too. To tell someone, especially your parents, that you wanted to write for a living, was to have them look at you strangely, especially when they found out you didn't mean for a newspaper. Instead I started telling everyone I wanted to be a lawyer. No questions were asked, no funny looks. Everyone approved.

At the end of the ninth grade, when we had to choose our disciplines before entering fifth form, I chose the humanities stream. My grades, except math, were good enough to get into any stream. I hated school. I hated its restrictions, the sadistic beatings and Chester's suffocating formalities: the blowing of the bugle in the lunch hall before we sat down to eat; the "high-coloured" masters sitting in their stuffy robes, despite the heat, at the head table, sipping their soup and looking down their well-bred noses at the rows of shifting black bodies – boys eating self-consciously – as if the sight of us was putting them off their food; the Friday evening dinners at the boarding house with the masters and their spouses – partners or "friends" from the university. You had to mind your manners as the masters held their breath while you spoke, no doubt fearing embarrassment. You realised that this was another exam: your dinner suit felt like a straitjacket you couldn't wait to get out of; polo under the poplars in the Upper School courtyard every second Tuesday of each month – though none of us, except a handful of masters, were accomplished riders, and everyone hated the clumsy lessons doled out by the "professionals" – out-of-work jockeys from Caymanas Park looking to make a quick buck; the classical music over the P.A. system during lunch and the dining-table pop quiz to name the composer (I always answered Vivaldi) and the demerit earned if you couldn't; the useless minutiae we had to memorise – the dates of European history, microeconomic principles, macroeconomic theorems, the physics equations for experiments we never did; the names and discoveries of dead white men (for whom we had to write biographies in the form of "research papers"); the populations of Hong Kong and New Zealand. Useless minutiae.

I received high grades in everything except math. When I was formally introduced to trigonometry it was a poisonous handshake and my grade never rose above 65%. I hesitated to ask my grandparents for a tutor, wary of increasing my workload and reducing the time I had for reading and writing. I paid for this mistake.

Literature class remained a relief. Besides English A, it was the only course I enjoyed. Few others did. By mid-afternoon the classroom was like a boiler room, even with the seaward windows open, with the temperature in the high thirties. Adolescent boys, restless and drowsy, squabbling and sweaty after lunch, were averse to appreciating the finer points of English grammar or the subtlety of a poem. The travails of Scottish kings, soliloquising princes and misunderstood Igbo warriors seemed impossibly far away as the afternoon wore on. No one could bring themselves to care about the real nature of the relationship between Tom and Huck, or wonder why Gatsby gazed at that green light at the end of the dock across the harbour.

Master Harding, appreciating our malaise, would sometimes abandon the curriculum for the final half hour of a double session and simply read. We would select our favourite stories, play excerpts, novel extracts, and read them aloud in class, different voices taking different characters. It felt a little like playing truant, enjoying writers instead of solemnly studying them. The faint feeling of indulgence, of collusion between master and students, would revitalise weary classes like an afternoon tonic.

Sam Selvon always spoke to us through the boredom and heat – even though Master Harding derisively dismissed him as a "literary lightweight and a master of made-up names". Once we got into the stories from *Ways of Sunlight* or another episode from *The Lonely Londoners*, we perked up and were soon laughing, thrilling at his turns of phrase, anxious to turn the pages, competing to read a character's lines, to dramatise certain sections of stories. We were seeing ourselves in a book for the first time – it didn't matter that they were Trinidadians – the way they spoke, the way they laughed at life, the way they thought, the way they were. Literature was no longer about other people's lives, it was about us.

And there was the afternoon Harding asked me to stand and take a bow, and the class formally congratulated me for placing second in the competition, and getting my first story in the paper. We spent the entire session reading my piece and analysing it. These were the days that survived the gloomy memories, that made me feel I was a part of something that transcended academic tyranny.

A bunch of us went to the Civic Centre one Friday afternoon to collect my prize. We were travelling on the school shuttle bus that carried Chester and St Helena's students for free. The bus was packed with girls and boys heading to a Chester football match at Jarret stadium. We were standing in the aisle. Russell was dating a new girl and she was on the bus, a few rows ahead of us. She stood to wave at us, then sat back down talking with her friends, who were giggling and throwing us furtive glances. Harry was in a nasty mood because his hero Ayrton Senna had died.

I said, "What's her name again, Russ?"

"Brittany."

"Damn," said Harry. "She's a bit on the bony side isn't she? What line did you woo her with: 'I have a bone to pick with you?'"

Russell rolled his eyes. "Sticks and stones, Harry."

"And a bag of bones obviously," Harry retorted.

Stennett said, "I think Master Grady insulted me in chemistry class this morning."

"How so?"

"After I gave a wrong answer, he said, 'Stennett, if you were an element on the periodic table, what would you be?' I couldn't think of anything to say. He said, 'May I offer a suggestion? I think you'd be an inert gas.'"

"Oh yea, he got you," I laughed.

"What kind of name is Fatback Grady, anyhow?" said Mola.

"What do you mean?"

"That's what it says on his door: Fatback Grady, Phd."

"Get out of here!"

"I swear! That's his first name."

"Smells fishy to me," said Harry.

"A name can only look or sound fishy, brain fart," I said. "It can't smell fishy."

The girls standing beside us laughed and Harry gave me a hurt look.

"I'll tell you who smells fishy."

"Open your mouth and I'll bust your lip." I meant it because I knew what he was going to say.

Tristan had football practice with the U-15s that afternoon and hadn't accompanied us.

Stennett stared outside at the street, lost in his thoughts.

"How's dorm life?" I asked.

"Every night, I take dishwashing duty, just to feel the bristles of the scrub pad in my skin, just to feel like I'm alive. I don't belong on the dorm."

"Why don't you move off?" said Mola. "Share a student flat."

"Can't right now. My parents are going through a divorce and the dean told them it's best I stay on the campus so they can keep an eye one me, to offer 'moral support'."

"Sorry to hear that."

"Don't be. I've been wishing for a while now that they *would* split up, instead of staying together and hating me for it. Well… my mother is the one who hates me; that's why she shipped me off to St James the first opportunity she got. She was always the strong one, and she never respected him, my father, but that's his fault. He was always afraid to be himself. I always had to watch out for him. But I'm not going to make the same mistake; he married for convenience instead of love and was too weak to break free."

Harry said, "So the bauxite company is your mom's, right?"

"Yea," said Stennett, "she's the CFO. It's been in her family for generations. My dad was a chemical engineer working at one of the plants when he met her. She's fifteen years my father's senior, and he got in over his head; he never loved her, just knocked her up. And here I am, living proof of a lousy decision."

Mola said, "Life is more complicated than black and white choices."

"Listen to the Hindu," Harry mocked, "waiting to marry his brahman-picked bride with a dangling nose chain."

"Fuck you," said Sanjay.

"Imola," said Harry with a woebegone look, "Imola."

Stennett shrugged and said to Sanjay. "You're telling me. Daddy sleeps around, he takes long trips, he indulges himself, but he comes home to hell. To Mommy he's a company man even when he's home; he's always on the clock, her clock, and always 'on her nerves'. She calls the shots."

Alvaranga said, "Give your old man some credit. He's hung in there quite some time hasn't he?" He nudged Stennett. "And I bet he's going to walk off with some shares of the company, eh."

"He's lucky if he sees a dime," Stennett said, "but I guess you're right. I suppose even in hell you have to find a foothold till you can sprout wings."

"There you go," said Harry. "Those divorce papers are the wings he's been waiting on."

Mola squeezed Stennett's shoulder. "You goin' to be okay, man?"

"I'll be fine."

"Oh no," said Harry, "I sense a group hug coming on."

The bus stopped at the bottom of St Helena's hill, and Russell got off with his girl and waved goodbye. Harry called after them, in a wheedling grandmotherly tone, "Watch out for the bones while eating, dear. Nasty things when they get stuck in your throat." Russell, his arm around Brittany's shoulder, gave him the finger.

The rest of us hopped on the streetcar running through the school zone and stood across from some girls heading to tennis practice. A girl with bushy, natural hair caught in a big ponytail came on at the next stop and they mocked and whispered behind her back. When the streetcar rocked they made as if her hair were spikes sticking in them. "Ouch!" they said and giggled. I glowered at the group but didn't know why I cared. I wished the girl would stand up for herself but knew she wouldn't. She was outnumbered. "Bitches," I said.

After we got off the streetcar I jogged to catch up with her. I said pleasantly, "Hey let me help you with your bag."

"No thank you, I'm fine." Her tone was curt, and she quickened her pace.

"Can I at least walk with you to the tennis courts?"

"Suit yourself."

"My name is Chauncey, by the way."

She smiled wryly and shook her head at my persistence. "Hi Chauncey, my name is Marzipan."

"Marzipan? Like the confection. I like it."

She smiled again and I saw her light brown eyes had lost their guardedness. "Yes, like the confection. Don't let me keep you, Chauncey. Aren't those your friends waiting for you?"

"They're fine." I reached out and gently tugged her racket bag, and she loosened her grip so I could take it. "Listen, let me take you to the ice cream station after practice. It's right down the street."

"I know where it is."

"Well…?"

"Sorry, my father is picking me up."

"How about tomorrow then?

She didn't answer but that was fine. She had a perfect figure in her short white skirt and her breasts bounced when she walked. I wondered if the girls behind us, still whispering and sniggering, disliked her because she had matured ahead of the rest of them.

She stopped and looked at me again. "You can't walk me all the way you know; the coach doesn't like girls showing up for practice with boyfriends."

I grinned. "So I'm your boyfriend now?"

"You know what I mean. Let me have my bag back."

"Not before you give me your number."

The look of irritation crept back into her face and she made a grab for the bag, but I held it back. She frowned and grabbed a second time and I stepped away.

She crossed her arms. "Boy, stop playing." I took half a step towards her. Then, sighing with an exaggerated show of peevishness, she narrowed her eyes and beckoned me with her hooked index finger. I stood before her and she yanked the bag from me, but she also took out her pen, took my hand and scribbled her number on my palm, running her tongue slowly over her top teeth and gazing straight into my eyes. She saw how much this excited me. Without saying goodbye, she left me staring in her wake. I looked at the number in my palm, to check that it was really there. When I rejoined the group I showed them the number and beamed at them.

"Looks like a dummy number to me," said Harry.

"Shut your jealous face."

As we walked to the venue, Mola and I shared headphones listening to a new mixtape. On the Disc-man, Biggie said, "*Break both your legs you move in slow mo', got shine to glow mo', 996 grams you need four mo', four mo'...*" Mola smiled and said, "Man, doesn't Biggie make math sound cool." We agreed Biggie was an absolute genius.

Harry said, "You know I haven't started studying for end-of-terms yet."

I said, "How are you going to study for anything when all you do is spy on Gilda and beat off?"

Harry sighed. "Pray for me, Chauncey."

Stennett put in, "You know there's a kung fu technique where you can literally beat the need for sex out of your testicles."

"No thanks," Mola said. "I want to have kids some day."

Harry was baiting. "Really?"

"Yea," Stennett said. "You want me to show it to you?"

"No thanks, fat man; I'll beat my own nuts."

"No silly," said Stennett, "I mean demonstrate it."

"The Shaolin master has the floor!" I announced.

Right there in Sam Sharpe Square, Stennett delivered a resounding punch to his own crotch and immediately doubled over.

"Idiot," Harry groaned, shaking his head. We had to basket-carry him between the three of us to the Civic Centre.

After leaving the Civic Centre we separated. Harry was meeting his sisters by Baywest mall to go to the community college to see his father; Mola was going to his family's store to help out; Alvaranga and Stennett headed back to school. I went to York's pharmacy to fill Mama's prescription. Heading to the bus stop, I took a shortcut through the lane along Carol's Wall Bridge. I saw Tristan near the bridge, by the vacant lot where tinted cars parked after sunset and dark-suited men solicited street boys and the bums living below the bridge. He didn't see me as I walked past on the opposite side of the street. He stood beside a grey Jeep, a few paces from the sidewalk, still in his red and gold striped football uniform and cleats from practice, speaking with the driver of the vehicle. I took a good look at the man. He might have been an accountant, in his early forties – black-rimmed spectacles, a crisp, white buttoned-down shirt. He was smiling as he spoke to Tristan, with one hand on Tristan's arm leaning on the rolled-down window. I wanted to dismiss it as an innocent exchange, but couldn't.

Saturday afternoon, after finishing my chores, I sat on the verandah, watching Papa massaging his toes and listening to cricket on the radio. My thoughts were somewhere else.

"Chauncey!" Papa's voice broke into my thoughts. I looked up, and realised he'd been calling me for some time. "Where your mind off to, bwoy? What's on your brain that you lost in the middle of the day?"

I shifted in the chair. "You don't want to know."

He narrowed his eyes, his bushy eyebrows meeting above his nose. "You're not yourself these days."

"Who is? I'm fine Papa, just tired."

"You have a story for me?" This was a pastime of ours. I read to him from my work (self-censored) or told him my ideas from time to time, and he provided feedback. When the mood took him he'd share anecdotes, sometimes folktales he'd learned as a child, or stories of the miraculous at the Zion Revivalist church where he'd been a member. Sometimes I got the impression he was making things up just to satisfy my curiosity. This annoyed me. Whenever I pressed him, he'd smile mischievously and ask,

"What's more important, the evidence or the belief? What came first – the belief that something existed or the proof that it did?"

I watched him now, noticing how much weight he'd lost since suffering a stroke two months ago, while out working on the farm. The dull, shrivelled skin of his neck, the deep hollow below his Adam's apple revealed how age had caught up with him. He saw me looking at him. He blew out his bristly cheeks and ran his tongue over his teeth. "OK, I got one for you. The Indian mongoose, newly introduced to the island to exterminate rats and other vermin destroying the sugar cane crop each year, was walking through a cane piece one day and came across a Jamaican yellow boa. So struck was the mongoose by the yellow boa's beauty that it mistook it for a god. When the snake rose majestically off its belly and towered over the mongoose, the mongoose cowered in fear and stepped back. But then it stepped on something. It looked down to see a baby snake beneath its paws, and judging from the resemblance and the alarm in the yellow boa's eyes, the mongoose knew it was the snake's child. Yet even with its child endangered, squirming under the mongoose's grip, the snake doesn't move to help it. It just stands there, frozen in fear. For the yellow boa, renowned for its beauty, is equally renowned for its cowardice. The mongoose smiled. The snake had revealed what it was. It trampled the baby snake, then sprang at the yellow boa and ripped his fuckin' throat out."

At the end of the story, Papa asked: "Who are you in this story: the mongoose, the snake, or the snake's child? The murderer, the coward or the hapless victim?" I searched for an answer but found none I felt comfortable with. Papa told me the answer was for me and me alone, that it was only important I be truthful to myself, so should think carefully. I sat thinking and the effort suddenly felt hazardous.

Papa said, "You hear what happen to Brother Mac?"

"No." I found myself automatically wishing it were bad news.

"The sugar beating him to the punch, bwoy," Papa said. "He lost a toe."

"Just one?"

Papa didn't hear. "That man putting up a brave fight against illness for so long now," he said. "Pity to see it catching up with him."

"Yes," I echoed, "a pity."

Papa reached forward and patted my knee. "Now how 'bout that story?"

"I not in no storytelling mood, Papa," I said. "Maybe some other time."

He shrugged and rolled back his chair. "Suit yourself."

I saw Sheila and Fish Tea cresting the hill at the end of our street. They were striding towards the house with purpose.

Fish Tea, the neighbourhood scrap junkie, was tall and gaunt, with a long face and a scar running from his right ear to the corner of his mouth. The neighbourhood youths called the scar his telephone line because it had the squiggly look of a telephone cord stretching across his face. When they saw him coming they'd shout, "Oy! Fish Tea! Who's on the line, today?" Fish Tea often answered, "Your mother, she askin' what colour panties I like." They'd all laugh – though it had been one of the "boys" who'd inflicted the wound as a punishment for one of Fish Tea's various infractions. He had the jaundice and almost toothlessness that afflicted most cokeheads – a few scattered brown stumps in his mouth. There was a desperate energy about his eyes (Aunt Girlie said they reminded her of a Jack-O-Lantern's), as if he felt death breathing down his neck, and every hustle, every scheme, was a frantic attempt to stay ahead. Talk was he'd once been a gentleman; even now he sported a rumpled grey suit, cracked sunglasses, and a black zipper pouch tucked under his armpit. Sheila had on his work boots and dark blue overalls stained black at the kneecaps with tractor grease. Ever since my grandmother forced Papa to follow the doctor's orders and stay away from the farm for at least a month, Sheila had been in charge. He was disgruntled that he'd had no increase in salary. He and Papa had clashed about this and Sheila had threatened to leave. Now Papa looked them over curiously.

"Sheila, what happen? You forget somet'ing?" He pushed the chair toward the verandah rail and squinted. "Fish Tea, is that you, bwoy?"

"Yes, Missa Knuckle," Fish Tea answered.

"Why you dress-up like you going to court? You in trouble?"

"No, Missa Knuckle. W-we here to m-make a p-p-proposal, sir."

"You stuttering," Papa said. "You only s-s-stutter when you in trouble."

Fish Tea looked upset. He didn't like to be mocked. "As I said, we h-here to –"

"All right," Papa said, waving his hand, "don't eat your tongue. You here to make a proposal; I hope is not to sell me any more of my own pawpaws. I need all the free ones I can get. The crop low this year."

One Sunday morning, Fish Tea had showed up at our gate selling a basket of papayas. "Farm fresh!" he boasted. The only thing was the papayas were still green, stinking of pesticides, and freshly stolen from Papa's farm. Sheila had broken his arm with a cricket bat. He wore the cast for months, long after the fracture must have healed, to solicit money from unsuspecting people, till it started to stink and attract flies.

"Missa Knuckle," Sheila's tone was decisive. "We need to talk to you 'bout some business."

Papa drooped his mouth. "This sounds serious. Come, come, sit down. Chauncey, bring me glasses. They bring papers for the old man to read."

Papa heard them out, saying nothing. And I must say that when Papa started questioning them, they'd done their homework, had all the bases covered, threw all his doubts right back into his face; they'd even brought flow-charts and graphs. I never knew Fish Tea had such a flair for business. They weren't stopping at Anchovy; they were going to adjoining communities, had mapped out routes and formulated schedules, covering a wide cross-section of Montego Bay, countless neighbourhoods that were junk rich, they claimed, untapped markets, waiting to be tapped. They were throwing around terms like "feasibility study" and "profit margin". All Sheila requested was to use Papa's van rent free – instead of taking the raise Papa had finally agreed to give him. He was quick to point out that he would only junk-monger on Sundays, his day off from the farm.

Papa was impressed but wary. Fish Tea was indeed the right man to choose as partner, since he never frowned at hard work and was never squeamish about getting his hands dirty – and nobody knew their way around the neighbourhood and knew the people like he did. But Papa had seen that gleam in Fish Tea's eyes before. We knew about the dangers of his exuberance – his slightly less than ethical business code – like the time he sold dog meat in Anchovy Square, passing it off as oxtail. But I was barely aware of Papa turning around to seek me as an ally to dissuade Sheila. My mind was, again, miles away.

The Cowboy's Lunch – May 1989

We were in prep school, around eight years old at the time, during the *Transformers* phase of our lives when everyone had at least one of these toys. Tristan, ever the scheming capitalist, had come up with a hustle. For the poorer boys at the nearby primary school, who couldn't afford a toy, or hadn't some benevolent relative overseas to send them one, we offered to help them out, for a small fee of course. Harry, Mola, Tristan and I worked tirelessly after school and on weekends at Brother Mac's woodwork shop by his house on Grove Street, two blocks away from Poinciana Drive where we lived, making wooden models of the original toys, based on orders boys had made, requesting whichever Autobot or Decepticon they fancied. Soon, with practice and Brother Mac's tutelage, the models were coming out well, with interchangeable parts and our own creative enhancements. Brother Mac had demanded nothing of us, had only seemed happy we were showing interest in woodwork and told us to come by anytime and stay as long as we liked. He was particularly fond of Tristan, who showed a flair for the craft. The praise and attention he lavished on him made the rest of us jealous; but the way he'd sometimes gently rest his hand on Tristan's neck or the small of his back while he worked, smiling at him as though he were a pleasing pet or plaything, the way he'd give him extra duties to keep him after we'd left, was also making me suspicious. In truth I should've known, the warning was always there. Whenever he saw Tristan, he had a lopsided grin and hummed Michael Jackson's *P.Y.T.* under his breath.

Around six one Friday evening, after everyone had left, I went back to Brother Mac's to buy sawdust for the farm pens. As I stood outside the workshop, I heard noises inside – voices and shuffling movements. I pushed the door open slightly, just a crack. There were ripe, closed-up human smells. My eyes gradually adjusted to the semidarkness; I made out two shifting figures: Tristan and Brother Mac. Tristan was kneeling in the centre of the room, stripped down to his underwear, his knees on two strips of sandpaper and his hands bound behind his back with electrical cord; he was snivelling and trembling, with tears shining on his face. Brother Mac stood before him, breathing hard, his thumb pressed into the hollow of Tristan's collarbone and a fan-belt doubled round the knuckles of his free hand; his pants and underwear were puddled around his feet, and his erection looked threatening, like a punishing tool. He hadn't seen me. Through the hazy half-light that had entered the room through the crack of the door, I could see fresh welts on Tristan's shoulder and back, glistening with bubbles of blood. I looked on for some time but couldn't piece anything together in my mind. It wasn't that I was in shock, I just felt weird, misplaced. It was the look of pleading and helplessness on Tristan's face when he saw me, transformed to fear as he watched me stepping back, that I will never forget. Grunting, Brother Mac clasped Tristan's jaw and forced his mouth open. Tristan moaned and begged him to stop. Brother Mac muttered a curse and said, "You coulda cry till your tears touch the sea." I eased the door shut.

As I ran away, in my head was the phrase – he was going to feed Tristan the cowboy's lunch. This was a slang term originating with the village "boys" for when a girl fellated them. It came from their fallacy that American cowboys sat around all the time chewing long brown stalks of beef jerky. They would whistle to us younger boys, pitching marbles by the side of the football field, and say things like: "Chauncey, tell Girlie to stop by my house tomorrow. I go feed her the cowboy's lunch," and laugh and grab their crotches. So Brother Mac was feeding Tristan his beef jerky. I think I thought of it like that, to blunt the obscenity of the act, to pretend that what was happening at that very moment was not only outside my control, but outside my sphere of reality.

When I rushed through the gate, Papa was examining something in the garden. I stopped abruptly before his crouching figure. He lifted the brim of his hat and said, "What happen? Where's the sawdust I sent you to buy?" I stared at him helplessly. "You get into a fight?" He looked beyond the gate to see if someone was chasing me. I opened my mouth to speak, but no sound came. I was still catching my breath. I clamped my mouth shut with a trembling hand. Tears streamed down my face. Papa jutted forward and gripped my wrist, staring searchingly into my face. "Did something happen? Spit it out, bwoy!" I wanted to weep in the safety of his embrace. I wanted him to tell me it would all be fine, that it had been a nightmare and I was now awake. But instead, I recoiled at his touch. I yanked my hand free and ran up the steps, ran into the bathroom and locked the door, thinking I was about to vomit but then found myself unable to breathe. I knelt on the floor, massaging my throat, trying to force my airway open.

I don't think I passed out for long. When I came to, I tasted bile in my mouth. Someone was beating on the door. I curled up on the floor and wept. I felt wretched, anguished at my cowardice.

I lost a part of myself to Tristan that day. *Shalom*.

We never really talked about it after that, nor did we tell anyone else. Now there was a part of him that was constantly shut off, that I could never reach, never truly understand, that would rupture and explode unexpectedly from time to time.

I never forgave myself for abandoning him.

CHAPTER 6 – MARZIPAN II

I wanted to confront Tristan about what I'd seen by Carol Wall Bridge, but didn't know how. I knew I had first to own up to my real reason for confronting him and I wasn't prepared to do this, because it meant acknowledging my guilt. There was a sentence in *Tristram Shandy* that summed up what I felt. "Silence, and whatever approaches it, weaves dreams of midnight secrecy into the brain…" But my silence went beyond guilt, and I knew this quote also connected to something in my own nature that I was coming alive to, something that wasn't content to stay silent and buried anymore. I remembered what Tristan had said, after we returned home from the brothel, about Brother Mac's influence: *But don't you see you have it all wrong. Don't you realise it's him barkin' inside us an' not the other way around?* Sometimes when I looked in the mirror I fancied I saw strains of this influence, and it sickened and frightened me. I started seeing the corruption in things dear to me. I had a favourite old coffee mug, and one morning, I looked at it closely and saw the centurion in his chariot and the cup's old crack that split his chariot in two. I peered at the grime in the crack, and suddenly a tiny maggot squirmed out of the dark crevice and dropped on the table. I yelped and jumped back. Aunt Girlie gave a start. "Bwoy, what's with you this morning?"

I went outside for a walk. A father was taking his daughter to kindergarten and a tabby streaked across the street. The father and daughter watched the animal. The father said, "Fast isn't it?"

The child looked concerned. "Yes," she said earnestly, "but that's dangerous; it should wait on the stoplight like everyone else."

The man shook his head at his daughter's innocence and said, "This is Montego Bay, sweetheart. Everyone breaks the rules, even the animals." I felt that lawlessness mushrooming inside me, and even as I clung to the notion that there was once order and law within me – that I too had once been guileless – I knew it had been disrupted. I was desperately trying to hide this disruption from everyone, including myself, while Tristan was less hypocritical and willing to own up to his altered state.

Russell Alvaranga's family had a condominium, a beachfront high-rise, right along the Hip Strip on Gloucester Avenue, and he had a set of keys for an apartment which he'd lend us whenever we needed to be alone with girls. I was there with Marzipan one afternoon, just lying in bed and talking. I was silent for a while and she said, "What's with you today? Something's on your mind."

I said, "There's this old lady from the neighbourhood who always crosses the street where there is no traffic signal. She just cross herself and say, "Jesus steer the ship," then she walks across. It's never failed. But she nearly had an accident this morning, and it wasn't her faith that failed her, it was her wooden leg."

Marzipan looked at me curiously. "What do you mean?"

"The leg is old and termite ridden, yet she still went around on it. As she crossed the street, the leg must have collapsed and she fell, and a car came this close to hitting her while she lay there."

"Oh my! Did you see it happen?"

I nodded. "I felt absolutely terrified… but it was an impersonal fear, not really centred on her peril."

"Well," said Marzipan, "she should've been more careful." Then she chuckled dryly. "But it's funny isn't it, her own body conspiring against her."

"But technically it's not *her* body that undermined her, it was a foreign body."

She hummed the *Mission Impossible* theme and whispered dramatically, "The invasion of the foreign agents."

"Stop being silly, I'm trying to have a serious conversation."

"Oh you are… excuse me. Well, if it counts for anything, I think the problem was in her head, her carelessness, walking around on a rotting stump, knowingly putting her life at risk."

"Yeah well… Maybe she just couldn't afford a new one, or maybe she was really just waiting for the day it collapsed."

Now she sat up with a pillow held to her chest: "Are you saying she was suicidal?"

"I'm saying she just carried on with life. Maybe it wasn't faith sustaining her, just the need to go on living till the day of reckoning."

"That's a morbid way to look at things."

"Maybe."

"Chauncey, what are we really talking about here?"

"It's not even about faith is it? No one knows why people do the things that they do – cruel, kind or just plain stupid. Life happens to us, Marzie, whether we want it to or not; we don't get to choose our battles, we just have to deal with the consequences."

She said flatly, "I'm not sure how to respond to that, but thanks for the mini-lecture. Now, can we change the subject?"

"Sure… What do you want to talk about?"

"Hmm… OK, you're the language expert, Chauncey, so let me ask you something. Is French bread long or tall?"

"Huh…?"

"Hehe, I know it sounds silly but I need an answer. Is a baguette long or tall?"

"Marzie, what the…?"

"Jus' hear me out… They mounted this food model of a baguette in our Home Ec room, right. I say it's tall but Sulene keeps insisting it's long."

"It's long."

"Hmph! But it's erect… like a pole."

"Well… think about it from the perspective of how you eat it."

"I'm not convinced. Grammatically, I'm not satisfied."

"Sexually, I'm not satisfied, but you don't hear me compl–"

"Grrr! Do you have to make everything into sex talk?"

"Ahahaha! You should see your face… So cute when you're mad…"

"Let go now! I'm serious…"

"OK, she's serious folks. Well, look at it this way… How do you eat my dick? Is it long or… OW! What did you punch me for? That's it! No more questions about French bread."

"Fine."

"Fine!"

I lay back and folded my arms over my chest, trying to clear my head. Marzipan threw her thigh over my midriff and ran her hand

114

through my hair. "You need a trim. I could do it for you, you know. I cut my little brother's hair all the time."

I didn't answer. Instead I mumbled to myself: "*I miss the way I had him, and the way he had me. And such grief can spoil a person's life, especially when the heart beats inconsolably, far away from... To be constantly reliving unspoken farewells, as if rehearsing for the final big sleep.*"

"What's that?" she said alertly. "Are you working on something new?"

"It's something... I'm not quite sure what it is – perhaps the beginning of a story. But there are words in there that don't mean anything, which I have to pare away before I can get going."

"I think it's a poem. How come you never write *me* a love poem?"

I pushed her off and said teasingly, "That's not entirely my fault is it? Perhaps you're just not muse material."

I could hear the soft click of her tongue as her mouth fell open. "Well I never... You're goin' to pay for that, Chauncey Knuckle!" She lunged at me and threw her arms round my neck and wrapped her legs tightly round my waist and bit my ear.

"Ouch!" I twisted and grabbed her and swung her round to face me. She swivelled out of my grasp, slippery as an eel. She pretended not to see my instant erection.

"I know what inspires you." She flashed her panties. She was wearing her bra and school skirt.

"You slut!" The pain of her bite still smarted and I could hardly contain my excitement.

She hid her face in her hands, then made a show of mock hurt. "The names he calls me. Mi shame tree dead."

I reached forward and pulled her back on the bed, then tried to unzip her skirt. She held my hand fast.

"And here I was thinking that you brought me here for the ocean view..."

"Marzie, stop teasing."

"Na-ah... I want a story first – that's the foreplay I require. Then you can have me any way you want."

"Any way?"

"Any way."

"You promise?"

She crossed herself. "Jesus steer the ship."

I looked at her for a long time, searching for the story in her face till I found it. I lay back down with my hands behind my head. She adjusted her body to lie on my chest. I said, "There's a man who believes his face is so repulsive he's afraid to show it to the world. So he walks around all the time on his face."

"How can a man walk on his face?"

"Let's just say he stoops his back so low the world can never truly see it and he in turn doesn't know where he's going because he can't see ahead of him. But one day, on the advice of Blackheart Sam, he swam to the bottom of a murky pond and made himself a face from moss, dead fronds and frogs. And it was so beautiful in its stark originality that he could finally walk around with his head held high. But this mask, he knows, is only temporary; it will soon fall away and reveal his shame."

"What does this man look like?"

"I'm glad you asked," I said. "I'm dying to show you." Then I covered my face and removed my hands to show her my twisted features, and snarled and wrestled her onto her back.

"Idiot," she giggled, hitting my face with the pillow. "That's the worst story I've ever heard." She clamped her thighs on my hand just below the warmth of her panties. "You not gettin' any of me today if you don't –"

Then my tongue was in her mouth. I dragged her to the edge of the bed, stood between her legs and eased myself inside. Soon she was moaning and twisting and tossing her head. I started thrusting. "Don't stop, don't stop, please, Chauncey baby... don't stop, don't stop, baby, don't stop please... Me a beg you, Chauncey, don't stop Chauncey, me a beg yo-u-u..." I reached down and pinched her nipple, then rested my palm on her upraised knee. Her voice dropped to a whisper and she grabbed her legs and spread them wider so I could get deeper. "Don't stop, don't stop plea-a-se, don't stop – do! – me a beg you." She bit her lip and began to moan, her eyes shut. I grabbed her left breast but instead of fondling it, I tugged at it roughly. She reached to caress my face and whispered, "Chauncey, wha' me go do wid you?... Oh god... pussyclaat Chaunc-e-ey, don't stop don't stop don't stop, fuck out me hole." Then she dropped her head back on the bed as I continued thrusting, dipping so I could get deeper inside. She pulled her knees almost up to her neck so I could go as deep as possible. "Don't stop, don't stop please, oh baby fuck me, fuck me, Chauncey, fuck me, fuck de hell outta me, ooh, aah!" Her head was all the way back on the bed and my fingers inched up to her neck. "Aaah, nooo! God no! Jesus Christ! Chauncey aah… yes, yes, Jesus! Chauncey mash up eh… mash up eh baby, ugh!…ooh god!" Without realising it my hand had moved round her neck with my thumb at the base of her throat. She "flashed" her fingers. *Wooiie* yuh ina me pussy deep… mm… don't tek it out don't tek it out." Then she gritted her teeth and her voice climbed. "Oh god – yuh a fuck me too hard, Chauncey! Aaah noo! Pussyclaat! Ayeyaiyai!" But the feeling that had taken over at the brothel as I watched Tristan assault the prostitute had taken over again and I felt almost angry with her. "Take your time… 'zaas Christ…" Her voice sounded raw and faraway and her body was almost limp and her head fell to one side, the moans leaking out of her like drool and getting dimmer as if she were about to pass out or was just too tired to resist. I felt the cum coming up, swelling my penis, rising to the tip. I thrust harder, my hand firmly round her throat, my excitement peaking. "Noo, noo…nooo! Nooo! Ga-a-wd! Chauncey!" Now her face had a look between fright and pleasurable anguish. I was about to come. "Aaah, ah-ah-ah!" The sounds sputtered from her lips with each violent thrust. "Pussyclaat, yuh a choke me!" But I squeezed harder, pinning her on the bed. Her eyes bulged and her hands flailed round my arm. All I could do was thrust and choke her. I had lost control. "Yuh a choke me…" Her voice was low and matter-of-fact, and sounded almost absurd. I couldn't disengage. "Bumboclaat, Chauncey…!" All I could hear was the sound of my own heavy breathing. I felt removed from the room.

"Yuh go pop off me bloodclaat neck! Chauncey, yuh bloodclaat!" Then she flapped around and beat my chest with her palms but I kept choking her. "Yuh bloodclaat – nooo!" She sprang up like a cat and kicked me in the chest, fearing for her life. I staggered back, the semen dripping from my penis. She leaned against the wall, staring wildly through the hair over her face as if seeing me for the first time. I reached out but she flinched and slid back. "Look yah, man!" Her voice sounded reedy and crushed, my handprints were deep in her neck. "De fuck yuh a try do kill me?" But all I could do was stare at her, my hands hanging loose at my sides like an ape's, my knees weak.

CHAPTER 7 – WARRIOR DANCE

At the beginning of tenth grade, while our schedule was still relaxed, we went again to the beach. We went to the south end, where the sea was rougher, the wind strong and biting. Waves hurtled through blowholes in the sea cave behind us, jetting water and air up through the cliff; the hiss was terrifying. The shore was covered in junk from the carnival parade held that Sunday: cardboard swords, silver sequined masks, used condoms and a pair of emerald green plastic wings (the remnants of a ravished fairy?).

We stripped off and sat on the large pink rocks bordering the beach. Two primary-age schoolboys were flying kites, their blue-checkered school shirts tied around their heads like turbans to shield their eyes from the sun and windblown sand. They tried to angle the kites so their red plastic sails would cover the sun; whenever this happened the successful boy would shout, "Eclipse! Eclipse!" and the other one would smile begrudgingly.

Stennett said, "I heard about your grandfather."

"First Winston Churchill dies, now this," Harry said.

"He's not dead yet," Mola said. "Don't kill off the man with your sympathy."

Papa had been diagnosed with colorectal cancer at the end of that summer, just as we were winding up summer school. My grandfather had never put a lot of stock in modern medicine, and continued drinking and smoking heavily, even after his stroke. The doctors had initially suspected gallstones, after his post-stroke paralysis led to other complications. They said they weren't life-threatening, but needed monitoring from time to time. But the pain persisted and his life became increasingly dominated by hospital visits. These offered no relief, only more screenings which found nothing, only taking more of his money and sending him home. He'd given up on the doctor until he developed persistent diarrhoea, a steady stream of putrid inky sludge. Then came weight loss and vomiting, and when he woke up one morning with his eyes as yellow as corn, we knew it was bad. The doctors said it was inoperable, stage four, terminal. They gave him four months to a year.

One of the kiting truants howled in pain and pulled up a few yards from where we sat, hopping on one leg. His kite zigzagged wildly in the wind, tumbling out of the cloudless blue sky. He had stepped on a sea egg. We knew how painful this was. His friend was decisive; he instructed the injured boy to sit and quickly pulled the spines from his sole, then peed on the wound to close it up.

"Let's just hope for the best," I said. "Papa is a strong man. And with medical technology nowadays, you never know."

"Don't even talk 'bout that," said Tristan. "You remember Noah?"

We all went silent.

Noah was a Rastafarian schoolmate of ours who died of bone cancer towards the end of eighth grade. While he was in hospital, Dr Leader would tell us brightly every morning at prayers that his condition was improving, that he was receiving excellent medical care at the regional hospital's cancer unit – supposedly the best in the Caribbean – until, one morning, Reverend Myers announced that Noah was on his deathbed and we should visit him while there was still time. We prayed for his soul and sang a hymn. All the talk of the wonders of science ceased. He died five days later.

"We should make Noah a Wobbly as a posthumous honour," Harry said. "He's earned it. *Man*, sometimes you could get stoned just standing beside him."

"Noah was a scamp," Alvaranga said. "Leader was a spineless coward to let a lout like that run amok all over campus smoking ganja like him at some blasted Nyabinghi festival, trampling on the good name of a school. If I had my way, he wouldn't have set foot on the property to even cut grass."

"Give it a rest, Russell," I said, narrowing my eyes at him.

"You parents never tell you not to speak ill of the dead?" Mola asked.

"He's been dead long enough," Alvaranga retorted. "Plus we gave him a free casket." The Alvarangas ran the largest funeral parlour business in Montego Bay, had even set up shop in neighbouring islands. Business was good, and getting better as the country's murder rate climbed steadily each year.

The injured boy appeared cured. Both now stood at the top of the sloping shore, rocking back and forth on their pink heels and curled black toes, their hands outstretched in the beckoning call we knew by heart, chanting in unison: "Bogue Boy, Bogue Boy swim a little closer."

"The black hands of fate…" I muttered. "They're summoning someone's death."

Harry squinted at me. "But whose?"

"Papa's."

"Or maybe one of us here," said Alvaranga.

"Include me out," said Stennett, "I'm not from MoBay. Bogue Boy doesn't know my scent." Then, still watching the chanting truants, he said, "Those two little shit heads remind me of you and Tristan that first day we went to the beach, chanting side by side." Neither Tristan or I responded. There was tension between us ever since I'd had a meltdown days before during math class – a summer school requirement so I could enter 10-1, the class of my choice.

Tristan was the math whiz since prep school; he could idle in class and not worry about his grades. He often disrupted my concentration – usually by sneaking me a doodle he'd been working on – and I indulged him. Master Laird would warn, "Knuckle, don't let Petgrave waste your time." It was never: "Petgrave, don't let Knuckle waste your time." Sometimes I'd go over to his house for tutoring, but I couldn't stand the way his lips twitched with impatience when he watched me bumbling with problems he gave me to complete. Sometimes he'd snatch the pencil from me: "This is the last time I showin' you this." I had to endure the affront just to see the problem finished. But when he chided, "Marcus Garvey scholar, what you mean you don't understand? How many different ways can I explain the same thing eh? What else you want me to do?" then I couldn't stand this insult. I would leave in a mood, laboriously going over the problem at home and fighting the urge to call him when I felt I had a breakthrough. He sometimes sat at the back of my summer class, marking papers for Master Laird who was also his U-15 coach, and for whom he had a paying job as an assistant, deputising whenever Laird was away on sports-related matters.

Stennett picked up some pebbles and pelted them at the chanting boys.

"Leave them be; they're prayin' to the god of the sea," Tristan said. He got up and walked out to the jagged rocks that tapered out to the sea. When he reached the end, he stretched his body and jiggled his legs, doing a silly little dance he called an octopus tango. "Watch this," he said, grinning back at us, then somersaulted and split the water's surface with a sharp splash. The water rose and fell and frothed over where he entered, then was still.

"Show off," Alvaranga said.

Then we saw Dennis.

He was walking down the shore with a shaggy brown mutt padding beside him. The dog was scavenging the trash-strewn beach, nose down, with saliva stretching from its big pink tongue. Whenever it found something curious, it gripped it between its teeth and brought it to its master. Dennis would inspect it; if he considered it valuable, he dropped it into the plastic bag slung over his wrist, if not he threw it back on the sand. They stopped a few metres from us and sat down, taking a break. Dennis took a half-finished spliff from behind his ear and lit it. He smoked with his head down between his legs. The dog mimicked him, dropping its head onto its paws. Dennis laughed. "Come, Trouble," he said, "come, bwoy." The dog rose off its haunches and went to him. Dennis cupped its face and blew smoke into its nostrils. The dog winced, tossing its head and pawing the sand; it sank to its belly and covered its head with its paws and mewled. Dennis laughed till he was seized with coughing; his whole body shook. He looked unwell. His eyes were red and inflamed and his face puffy and beaten-up. He must have had a rough night on the streets.

"What's he doing?" Stennett said angrily. "That's animal abuse! Fucking cretin."

Dennis glowered at us. We knew from his body language, from the set of his face, that this wasn't a day to mess with him. This was the hardened manner he reserved for the streets, that he never usually brought to the beach. He lay back with his eyes closed, the spliff drooping from his lip.

"Mas' Clarence must be so depressed," Harry said. "I know I would be."

"Don't feel too sorry for him," I said. "Last week he was happier than a pig in shit. He made a killing off a champion racehorse. He's been on a hot streak for two weeks now. Except the horse an' all the money he's making are figments of his imagination."

"Oh dear," Stennett said.

"His behaviour is getting stranger each day. The doctor said his mild cognitive impairment from the stroke might be progressing to dementia."

"It's such a pity his mind is going," Stennett said. "Because the mind is the man. That's what my grandfather always says."

"Forget the damn doctors; let the man have his fun," said Mola. "Life is short an' cruel. He knows that better than most people."

"If he ever comes back to his senses, tell him to bet on Blackadder," Harry said.

"You mean Gassan Aziz's horse?" Alvaranga said, finally piqued by the conversation.

Harry nodded. "Last night I dream I was in a vegetable patch, picking purple tomatoes, an' when I look down I was kneelin' in a cow patty. Shit an' tomatoes mean money. I wonder if I should put down some money on him later today."

"Them Arabs know how to breed a good racehorse, bwoy," Alvaranga said. "If it's one thing they know."

"They know how to t'ief people business too," Mola said. The Molas had made a small fortune from the duty-free business at the City Centre, where they still had a shop. Before the Great Arab Takeover in 1989, when the Muslims bought them out, they had practically owned the industry, along with the three other prominent Hindu families. Mola made it no secret that his ambition was to restore his family's reputation in Montego Bay. It was all he spoke about. He would pick at the blackheads on his oily, spotted cheeks and enumerate the grievances he had against the Muslim families, and as his ire increased, he'd squeeze the pimples harder, popping the zits as if they were the persons with whom he had his vendetta.

"The Hindus were doing nothing for this country," Alvaranga said, "apart from sending money back to India and burning bad oil for other people in business. No offence, Sanjay. Who you think started that rumour 'bout Daddy smuggling coke in caskets from Colombia, just so they wouldn't elect him president of the Chamber of Commerce? The Indians! Without the Arabs, Mobay's economy would've folded long ago. They build the horse-racing business from scratch, the cinemas too, and open supers and dry-goods depots. Put people to work. Now they're lobbying for that casino license. When that happens, Mobay will open up, might even become the number one tourist destination in the world."

"I thought it was the Jacket Man doing the casino thing," I said.

"Fitz Henry is only a front man," Alvaranga said. "The black face. Running the whorehouse means he has a full plate. Daddy says nowadays they're calling him the Tylenol Tycoon because the brothel business gives him a constant headache."

"The Arabs are no better than the Hindus," Harry said. "All they do is shuffle black people around like a card deck, put them in warehouses to lift boxes, or on racehorses with fuckin' numbers on their backs an' whips in their hands."

"Harry, spare us your infantile lecture on the state of humanity. You're born into this world like every other man; you can beat it like every other man. Nobody tying your hands behind your back."

"I've never seen Gassan Aziz," Stennett said. "What him look like?"

"What you think him look like?" Harry said. "Him look like a fuckin' Arab. Always sittin' in his high chair in Jumbo Mart, eatin' horse testicles an' cabbage for lunch. Watchin' the store like a hawk. Makin' sure nobody stealin' anything, with his shit-gut hangin' over his belt like him nine months pregnant."

"Gassan Aziz is nothing but a bearded cunt," Mola said, making a face and squeezing a pimple. "A bearded, pissing cunt."

"You can't fuck him though," Alvaranga said.

Mola replied with scorn, "Russell, how do you measure your ego? By metric or imperial system?"

"By volume, $V=\eth r2h$. Cubic centimeter or feet is fine."

A fish jumped up from the sea just as Russell finished speaking. It meant he'd have a long life. Of all the people, I thought.

Stennett said, "Sanjay, why Hindus don't wear beards?"

Mola shrugged. "They just don't."

Stennett stared into Mola's pudgy, pimpled face a bit too long and it made Mola uncomfortable. "I think they should," Stennett said. "I think it would be a nice look for you, as long it doesn't hide that dimpled chin." Harry and I exchanged glances. Stennett cleared his throat, "No homo, of course."

This was the disclaimer we used to make sure our statements couldn't be misconstrued as homosexual in any way. At Chester, it was used as a matter of course. It was in our way of resisting the label of "a bunch of faggots on the hill", levelled at us by sneering boys and grown men who'd failed Chester's entrance exams and supposedly missed out on a meal ticket to a good life.

An Old Joe screamed, startling us. It kept up its cawing, deep and insistent from its throat pouch. We looked up to see it descending steeply, dive-bombing for fish.

A worried look clouded Harry's face. He looked at the tumbling sea, then around as if he'd lost something. "Where's Tristan?" he said. Then it struck us; Tristan hadn't surfaced since he dove off the rocks. "Look!" Harry shouted, pointing to ribbons of blood untangling on the water's surface. Then what followed took our breaths. A big wave jumped and plunged, flinging Tristan's body clear of the water; when he landed, he skipped on the skin of the surf like an empty barrel, then went under, moving away from us, out to the ocean. We were quick, but Dennis was lightning.

The further I swam, the more the waves pushed me back. I dove below them, but the deeper I went, the more the current rolled my body, forcing my legs apart. I kicked from my hips and speared my hands before me to counter its force, then brought my arms to my sides to propel my body downwards. I closed my eyes to stop the sting of salt. My leg muscles cramped up. For a moment, in the grip of shock, I kicked towards the sunlight of the sea's surface, my chest feeling close to exploding. I surfaced, drawing deep breaths to fill my lungs. When I reached the shore, Dennis was pumping Tristan's chest and the dog was yapping and skipping at his side. Tristan was coughing and gasping, clawing his way back to life. My relief made me dizzy.

Sanjay had called the paramedics from a telephone booth on the street. They strapped Tristan to a gurney and we boarded the back of the ambulance. On our way to the hospital, the medics bandaged the cuts on his forehead and shoulder. He had misjudged the depth of the water and concussed himself on the stony coral of the fringing reef surrounding the islet. Dennis had saved his life.

"Where the fuck did Dennis learn CPR?" Harry whispered.

"From us, we teach first aid classes at St Helena's church." It was the heavyset medic who had fitted Tristan with an oxygen mask to stabilise his breathing. She'd been giving us cold suspicious looks. "And shouldn't you boys be in school?"

"We were doing marine research… for our school-based assessments," Harry said.

The woman snorted.

Russell pointed to Tristan. "Shouldn't you swab his mouth for germs or something? After all, Dennis *is* a bum."

The woman scowled at him. "So him save your friend's life but you still scorn him, eh. Scornful dog always nyam dutty pudding."

"So you're calling me a dog?" Russell shot back; then said under his breath, "Jumped-up peasant."

The woman caught the remark. "Who the cap fit let them wear it. Dennis was where he's supposed to be. Which is a lot more than I can say for you."

"Norah!" her partner said warningly.

"No Alvin, they damn rude! They think because they born with their bread butter two sides they can speak to people as they have a mind!"

Mola pinched Russell's arm. Thankfully he said nothing more.

I watched Tristan strapped to the gurney, his breath clouding the oxygen mask. I thought of how there was always something predatory happening on the beach. A moment before, we had watched crabs nibbling on the tentacles of stranded jellyfish. Seabirds, grey all over with dirty white bellies, had landed to peck at the jellyfish's inner tissue, carefully avoiding the poisonous tentacles that were still alive. Now the reef had drawn Tristan's blood, I felt as if the beach, whose power we had mocked with childish make-believe, had become sinister and cast us out.

At the hospital, they admitted Tristan to the casualty ward.

As we waited, my mind went back three days before and the incident that had made the tension with Tristan. Master Laird, as well as math, was also our form's P.E. instructor, a former Chesterite and a professional footballer whose career had been cut short by knee injuries while still only in his mid-twenties. He had something of a chip on his shoulder, and weakness for catchphrases we found desperately corny: "That's like trying to play ping pong with an egg," which meant that whatever genius method you'd concocted to tackle one of his problems was doomed to failure. He always entered the summer class as if sickened by the sight of us, saying, "All those who didn't do the homework, you know the drill, get out." A quarter of the class would walk out, some having deliberately not done the assignment so they could have the session off. Then he might say, "That included page 17 too." Another five or so boys would get up and leave. On the day in question he looked at the fat boy, Smitty, sweating, his shirt wet after lunch. "Smith, you look frowsy. Get out." Then he droned, "Open your books to section seven; today we're doing quadratic equations." The groans went up. "Oh my," I said, "Smitty's sweat glands did him a favour." Sporadic laughter broke out. Laird hissed, "On your feet, Knuckle." I stood and stared him down. "Are you eyeballing me, boy? You flit around on the football pitch like a girl, but in here you're all man, eh, with that smart mouth of yours."

"No more of a man than you are, sir." I saw immediately that I'd touched a nerve. He had a gimpy left leg and my eyes had flitted to it while I spoke.

"What did you say?" he snarled. I cowered, alarmed at the degree of my fear. "I asked you a question, boy!" But my mouth wouldn't open. "That's it!" he yelled. "Pack your things and report outside immediately!" Then he grabbed his cane off the desk and stormed out, waiting for me to come outside, as if to a duel. I sat down and started packing my things. "Oh Knuckle, you're in trouble now," a red-skinned boy named Richie said. "You hurt Ping Pong's feelings." Tears sprang to my eyes; I ducked my head and wiped my face with my shirt. "What's he doing, crying?" "Poor Knuckle, he's only a wilting daisy after all." Tristan had been in the back of the class, marking papers. I could hear him tapping his feet behind me in annoyance, embarrassed by my weakness. Laird pushed his head through the doorway. "I'm waiting, Knuckle!" But I couldn't move. The boys started

127

sniggering. Tristan walked briskly to my desk and whispered, "Chauncey, what are you doing? Get up!" I couldn't look at him. Instead I opened my notebook and began writing at a frenetic pace: *It's a curious thing, whenever I feel pangs of fear it's like there are lightning bolts going off inside my body. There is no fire like passion, and whenever I feel the urge to write it's like there are lightning bolts inside my head. There is no pain like this body, neither is there any joy like it, and the joy of my talent is like the joy of the discovery of masturbation!* "The fuck is he doing?" someone said. "Maybe he's writing his eulogy." Tristan grabbed the pen and I cried out, "Give it back! I'm not through!" "Yes you are!" he said. "Stop being such a pussy! That's what Laird wants, don't you see? – to get the best of you." I got up and turned on him: "You? Calling me a pussy? That's rich! Who's the one whoring at Carol's Wall?" The boys laughed and beat their desks. Laird, hearing the outburst, put a foot in the doorway and shouted, "That's it, Knuckle! Come out here now, boy! You won't like it if I have to come and get you!" "Yes, Knuckle!" the boys chorused, "Go out there and get in the spirit; take The Holy Ghost like a champ!" "Look at his face; he still wants his pen back, his fingers are itching to write, he needs his fix." I walked outside, trying to commit the rest of the words to memory because I was sure this piece of writing would be rich and good. *Please please don't let me forget any of it before I can it write it down… please. That would be the worse punishment.*

Laird's cane was labelled The Holy Ghost Power. He flexed it and as the first blow almost ripped the back of my shirt, a perverse inspiration struck me, as if the pain had gifted me a weapon. I started singing: *"The Holy Ghost Power is moving just like a magnet."* Laird's eyes started from his head. "Are you mocking me, boy?" The cane came down swiftly this time across my arm. I clapped my hands and shimmied. *"The Holy Ghost Power is moving just like a magnet!"* The boys shrieked with laughter and fell out of their chairs. I began doing a warrior dance. *"Moving here!"* My clapping matched the pounding of my heart. *"Moving there!"* Laird's eyes flashed. "You think you're a man, boy?" He was so livid he could barely speak. "Because you have a condom in your wallet and your little girlfriend 'cross the street, you think you know what life is?" Spittle flew from his lips. Boys were coming out of adjacent

128

classrooms to watch. Now I felt empowered by his apoplexy, keen to land some blows of my own. "*Just like the day of Pentecost!* And you, sir? Are you a man?" "Shut your mouth, you little shit!" Soon, it was as if he was having a coronary, as he muttered what sounded like gibberish. He struck again with the cane, with all his might behind the blow, but lost his balance. I snatched the cane as he tottered and fell and stood over him, The Holy Ghost Power held aloft. "Yay!" went up the cheers. "Knuckle with the KO!" I felt like Muhammad Ali. "You're nothing but a washed-up cripple!" I taunted, glowering at him. Boys chanted, "Finish him! Finish him!" – accompanied by banging desks, doors and chairs. Then Tristan came up behind me, grabbed my hand and wrestled me back into the classroom, saving me from myself and from sure expulsion. But I couldn't be grateful, not in that moment when adrenalin surged in my veins.

I came back to the present when I realised a nurse was asking us some questions and Russell was managing to talk her out of calling our parents. Tristan had already evidently provided them with contact information. Then the Smiling Accountant showed up to visit him, the man in the grey Jeep whom I'd seen with Tristan by Carol's Wall Bridge. I watched as this man wrote a cheque at the receptionist's area. As he walked by us, I thought a look passed between him and Stennett.

When we knocked and entered the ward, Tristan was sitting up in bed, testing the bandages across his forehead, shoulder and chest. Harry gawped. "Bloodclaat, Tris, you're halfway to bein' a mummy!"

"Does it hurt?" Mola said. Tristan didn't answer. He got up gingerly and started dressing. He looked tired, but his eyes had the clarity of someone whose mood had been brightened.

"Who's that man just now?" Stennett asked.

Tristan looked surprised. "My uncle. What's it to you?" His voice was shaky, and he avoided our eyes.

"Really?" Stennett sounded sly. "You're very lucky to have so generous and caring an uncle. Some boys would be… jealous."

Tristan sucked his teeth. Retrieving the prescription from the bedside table, he scrutinised it before stuffing it into his knapsack and hurriedly walked out ahead of us. We rode the elevator to the first floor and he stopped at the pharmacy.

Eager to cast off this ill-fated day, we said our goodbyes and separated. The grey Jeep was waiting in the parking lot. There along the wall was the graffiti: WHO LEFT THE TYGER TO WATCH OVER THE LAMB? A year on and we still didn't know who was writing it. But the artist would soon have the city eating out of his hands.

Later that afternoon when he came over to my house, Tristan's mood was lively and affected. I wasn't surprised. It was what I was expecting. He flopped down on the bed beside me and slapped my thigh. "Lazy bones! I'm the one who should be in bed remember. What happen? You hurt yourself jerkin' off?"

I'd been reading *A Cow Called Boy* fitfully before he came in, but I pretended to be engrossed. "Why you never offer us a ride home with your uncle? What happen, you 'fraid we'd embarrass you?"

He rested the heel of his hand on his forehead. "Look like I go have to start wearin' a helmet to the beach, bwoy."

I put the novel down. "What you think you doing? What you think goin' to happen to you?"

He stared at the ceiling, his hands folded under his head.

I eased up on my elbow to look in his face. "Just remember, whatever it is you're involved in is your decision; no one forced you. You're going down this road yourself. My advice is turn back before it's too late."

"Your advice, eh," he said. "An' what if I don't feel like takin' it?"

"Stop thinking 'bout yourself alone! How you think Clare goin' to feel when she find out 'bout this? An' don't think she not goin' to find out."

"Find out 'bout what?"

"Stop playing the fool."

"So you give your advice so you can wash your hands clean of me, eh, so you can feel satisfied you did your moral duty."

"Don't flatter yourself. I'm not lookin' to you for a clear conscience. That's not yours to give."

He was quiet, moving his tongue over his lower lip, then said, "You ever wonder what happened that day after you left?" His lip was puffy and discoloured. His face was blank; he seemed to be focusing on a point in the ceiling. When he blinked, the tears ran

130

from the sides of his eyes. I'd never seen him cry since that day in the shed, but it made me angry instead of pitying.

I sat up. "What does it matter now? Stop bein' a fuckin' victim!"

"That's exactly what I'm doing. Now I get paid for my humiliation. And most times, Chauncey, I enjoy the sex!"

"Please leave," I said, sitting with my back to him. He got up angrily and walked out of the room. When he opened the door, Papa, who was in the hallway, questioned him about his injury. Tristan lied smoothly. When he left, Papa wheeled himself into the room.

"What's happenin' between you two?"

"Nothing. An' you shouldn't eavesdrop."

"Everybody passin' them place with me these days," Papa said. "But man nuh dead don't call him duppy."

I flung my slipper against the wall and sank back on the bed, then took a deep breath. "I had a long day, Papa, I need some sleep."

But Papa wasn't giving up. "From ever since, you an' that bwoy have been closer than batty sittin' on bench. So why this tension, why this sudden pullin' apart?"

So I told a half-truth, of how we'd ditched school and gone to the beach, and Tristan had concussed himself on the reef and would surely have died if it hadn't been for Dennis, and that we were at odds over whether to tell the truth.

Papa's stare sharpened my shame for insulting his concern. "When did you feel that you can't talk to me anymore, Chauncey?" His voice was sad. But how could I tell him Tristan was fighting against the world? How could I tell him I didn't know what was happening inside me? I still wanted to think, diminished as he was, that Papa could find the strength to save us. But that was wishful thinking. This was a battle we had to fight for ourselves.

He left the room in silence and it hurt. I wanted to cry but the tears wouldn't come. How could I have known that this was the last conversation I'd have with my grandfather?

I soon fell asleep.

A sharp wail woke me. I jumped up and ran to the window. When I pulled the curtain, I saw lights jumping on in yards along the street, bulb after bulb. I switched on the light and checked my watch – half past six. Mama hadn't bothered waking me up for dinner. A car alarm shrieked. Dogs answered. The wailing pierced the air again and it came from Tristan's house – Clare! I hurried out to the yard, barefoot. People outside our gate were engaged in hushed and urgent chatter. When I reached Tristan's gate, Sheila and another man were carrying him out of the house. Under the verandah's light, I saw that his face and neck were swollen and discoloured, as his lip had been before. He was limp, his breathing laboured, his eyes going back in his head. Clare was beside them, crying and wringing her hands, her eyes wild with fright, still dressed in her work clothes. Papa was explaining to her that Tristan was possibly having a reaction to coral reef poison that had got in his blood, but she was too panic-stricken to process what he said. A woman said, "Clare, him goin' to be all right." But Clare neither heard nor saw. She boarded the backseat of the van, sitting beside Tristan who was wrapped in a blanket, and Sheila sped off.

An hour later, Sheila phoned from the hospital to say Tristan had been treated for anaphylactic shock because he hadn't taken his medicine. Mama, finally hearing the truth, scolded me. But I was beyond her reproach. I was feeling the full weight of my guilt. The walls were closing in. Something had to give. I'd had enough.

I went to my grandfather's room later that night. All the commotion that evening had strained him. His blood pressure had spiked and he had suffered dizzy spells. Aunt Girlie put him in the backroom to sleep so she could monitor him through the night. I knelt by the bed, listening to his breath softly escaping his half-opened mouth. The top half of his face was taut from the stress of the day, the wrinkled skin of his brow careworn and constricted. I thought he was trying to say something. I could see his eyes moving below closed eyelids. I put my ear close to his mouth but no sound came. I thought he was in the spirit, and I found myself hungering for the nourishment of his strange poetry. When his mouth relaxed, he slept soundly. I opened my mouth to tell him everything, but I couldn't find the courage. I left his bedside confounded with misery.

I woke with a start when Girlie's voice called from the backroom where Papa was. This time, Sheila was carrying Papa. Saliva was slavering down his chin; his eyes looked glazed and unseeing, his body limp. He had suffered another stroke. Filth slithered through his pant leg and a ripe smell of shit filled the room. I rushed forward to help.

Mama sat in a daze at the kitchen table. "What a night," she said quietly, "but trouble always comes in twos." She held a loose tooth in her mouth, rocking it back and forth with her fingers. "When this comes out, you'll be a free man, Clarence. God-speed."

Papa went into a coma that night at the hospital. I think we all knew he would never come back home.

CHAPTER 8 – THE FULLERITES! THE FULLERITES ARE COMING.

Some weeks after Papa was hospitalised, we were in the changing room of the gymnasium when Alvaranga said, "Geoffrey Dyer came to my house last night for dinner."

"You lie," I said.

Alvaranga crossed himself. "Honest to God."

"I thought he was still in Miami."

"I thought he was dead," Mola said.

"Well, he's back from the dead," said Alvaranga.

"What did he and your father talk about?" I said.

"Politics. What else? Trade unionists glad-handing by the Freezone, praedial larceny in St James; this and that."

Geoffrey Dyer was the wealthiest restaurateur in Montego Bay. He had started out on Peckham Avenue back in the seventies, gradually spreading over the city. By the mid 80s, anyone who was anyone was dining at one of the many Seagull restaurants across the city, and they weren't cheap. A meal could run you well over a thousand dollars. The secret of his success was his faith. Dyer was a Jehovah's Witness, and while the Baptists had considerable clout, the Witnesses were the wealthiest holy people: virtually all the hoteliers in St James were Jehovah's Witnesses, and they'd supported him from the start, with corporate endorsements and land grants. With prosperity came an itch for power that needed scratching. Dyer had announced that he was running for office, on an anti-crime platform because Montego Bay was well on its way to overtaking Kingston as the murder capital of Jamaica. But then he boasted that he had sensitive information that linked local politicians to the gangs in town, mainly the Fire-Clappers Crew, run by the Jacket Man. These politicians, he claimed, were using the gangs to intimidate political opponents and were conning the poor with promises of land redistribution schemes in return for votes. Dyer's image had been splashed all over town as the David fighting the Goliath of institutionalised corruption. Then came the backlash.

It began with the usual death threats. Dyer didn't back down. Then about three weeks before polling day, a mysterious gas leak at his main restaurant caused an explosion that killed two workers and practically left him without a face. He had to be flown to Miami for plastic surgery. Saved within an inch of his life.

"You'd think he'd have learnt his lesson," I said.

"Or at least taken a longer vacation," said Harry, walking out of a shower stall and towelling his hair.

"He's been licking his wounds," said Alvaranga, "strategising his revenge, like Napoleon scheming on Elba."

"Ol' shotgun nostrils," Tristan chuckled, kicking off his cleats. "*Man*, Dyer has a fat nose." Tristan had recovered well, and the tension between us had mostly gone.

"You mean *had* a fat nose," Alvaranga said. "After all the plastic surgery, he's practically unrecognisable. All hell soon break loose in this place. You watch and see. People are already behaving like animals. You hear about the Clarks robberies?"

A local deejay had made an ode to Clarks, a popular British footwear brand. Soon practically everyone was wearing them. Shops couldn't keep the shoes on shelves and they took advantage of the hike in demand to spike prices. Some fashionistas with meagre spending power started harassing vendors, snatching the shoes off canvases in shopping arcades or even off people's feet. A shopkeeper ambushed a thief in his store one night and shot him dead, then dragged his corpse to the police station.

"I pay good money for these," Tristan said, taking a toothbrush from his locker to groom his tan Clarks Wallabees, the schoolboy's trend. He seemed to be spending extravagantly these days, his wardrobe getting trendier.

"I hope you're prepared to guard them with your life," Mola said. "Fuller man not making fun to ambush boys at the corner of Hillel Rd – you didn't hear? – an' if you wearing Clarks, all they do is lift up their shirt an' show you their ice pick."

"Don't worry 'bout me," Tristan said, "worry 'bout yourself."

Fuller Canterbury actually adjoined Chester. We shared a strange relationship. During the football season, we were like family; they were our most avid fans, would treat Chester boys like royalty, warmly greeting you on the street. But when football season ended, so did their friendliness. Their eyes grew dull and lifeless in their faces, like cold little marbles. They would ambush you en route to school, robbing you of money, watches, pens, compasses, anything they fancied or thought could be of practical use. If you resisted, the marbles came alive, glinting with the threat of violence.

But lately, their attitude had become unseasonable. Recent events on campus had left us shell-shocked. The sharks were no longer content to stay at sea. They wanted to move among us on land. An invasion had begun.

First there was a robbery. Tristan, Mola and I, and an older boy named Fenton, had been playing coin football after school, under the ackee tree outside the Pantry where the athletes took their meals, when three Fuller thugs surprised us. They snuck up from the direction of Bailey House and kicked over the board, holding knives to our chests. Mola had appeared too shocked to run, but he'd realised the thugs were now eying his Patek Philippe – fresh from his family's store as a birthday gift – and if he'd tried to escape they would've very likely done us harm. They took our watches and wallets and made us empty our knapsacks on the ground, then rifled through the contents. Tristan refused to take off his knapsack. One of the thugs, a vicious boy named Pap Smear, cut the straps of the bag so it fell off Tristan's shoulders. Tristan lunged at him but Fenton held him back. Tristan ranted at Pap Smear: "I go walk on your fuckin' head when I see you! Just wait!"

Pap Smear, who looked no older than twelve, laughed harshly in Tristan's face; the crinkly scar along his neck, where battery acid had eaten away the skin, squirmed like a flesh-eating worm. "Schoolers, if your life itchin' you, don't let me knife scratch it," he said. "How you go threaten Pap Smear, you mad?" His posse smiled admiringly. Pap Smear might have been a poet.

After they left, Fenton promised to get our stuff back. "I know some people," he assured us. But Tristan said he didn't need his help. He would get it back himself.

Two days later, as we walked on Orange Street after school, Tristan stopped us outside a laundromat and went upstairs to an office with darkly-tinted windows. He emerged minutes later with Spider – the reputed deputy of the Fire-Clappers Crew. We were shocked senseless. Tristan was talking with him as if in the company of a familiar. He and Spider went into the laundromat and Tristan walked back to us with a plastic bag in his hand. Inside were our watches and wallets, all the money intact. We felt foolish and a little begrudging when we thanked him. He rubbed it in our faces by not responding. He knew we were dying to ask how he'd managed it. We had all sensed some change in him. This had confirmed it. He had another existence, another life outside our circle. We resented his patronage, his presumptuous maturity. It made us feel like protected children.

The second incident occurred a few days later at a football match between Munroe and Chester, at the school's pavilion. The Pav had as usual been overflowing with people for this derby match. The ticketing system at the gate had broken down because Fuller hooligans had cut a hole in the fence. When campus security tried to save face by requesting to see ticket stubs, they were browbeaten and harassed. The drama took place during the second half. Tristan, Marzipan and I were sitting near the mid-row on the second floor, shelling roasted peanuts into our mouths. Tristan had made the senior team but wasn't on the roster that day because of an ankle injury. Below, I saw Spider pushing his way through the crowd; he was wearing dark glasses, a white fish-net merino (through which you could see his crew's web tattoo below his armpit), baggy blue jeans and a blue bandana tied over his head. When I realised he was heading towards Grantley – a rival from a smaller gang – I knew something was up. I swallowed my spit and tugged Tristan's shirt. Spider stopped an arm's length behind Grantley, tapped him on the shoulder, then stepped back. When Grantley turned, two of Spider's cronies pounced and held him fast. Grantley cursed and struggled. Spider said, "Put out the arm you don't like." Grantley's mouth hung open in confusion, and even as he struggled to break free, Spider dipped under his shirt and pulled out a Cuban, a small cutlass with an elegantly curved blade. People screamed and scampered away, but many stayed to see what would happen. Spider held the machete above his head and repeated, "Put out the arm you don't like." Grantley no longer struggled, but gave Spider a fierce look, as if he understood and accepted that this was part of the "game", that he'd been caught out and was willing to pay the price for his carelessness. I think a moment of mutual understanding passed between them, one could even say respect. A woman pleaded, "Spider have mercy." Grantley grimaced and jutted out his left arm at an awkward angle from his body, as if he already considered it a loss. Spider said, "Don't flinch. Me don't want your blood to catch me." But it was because Grantley flinched, after Spider brought his arm down in one smooth arc, all his weight behind the blow, that the machete didn't cleave all the way through. Grantley grunted and bared his teeth on impact. Blood splashed and squirted. People squealed. Some fainted. Grantley looked from his dangling arm to Spider, then turned to run. He lost his balance and fell amidst the stampede. We lost sight of him. Six people were injured in the melee. The police came, but of course nobody saw or knew anything.

These recent incidents reignited the debate about the construction of a high security wall around the school. But this wasn't as easy as it sounded. Chester College sat on a huge property, and the layout of the land was such that it was hard to demarcate the exact borders of the property, so the school had to settle for sharing ambiguous territory lines with three adjacent communities. Building a wall was impractical and costly, some argued, and hadn't been needed for a hundred years. Now, though, others claimed, the spate of security breaches not only put boys in physical danger, but also made them morally and psychologically vulnerable. Criminals now viewed the school grounds as open territory and were exploiting students for various illegalities: as shills for card games, peddlers of counterfeit foreign currency, even as mules to transport hard drugs abroad.

Dr. Leader had come under pressure. The upper-crust were at his throat, laying the blame for their children's corruption squarely at his feet. They would stop at nothing till either the construction of the wall or his resignation was achieved. On campus, Alvaranga, never a fan of the principal, was leading a quiet campaign.

"Look at Richie," Alvaranga said. "In jail! They catch him at Heathrow with his ass corked with cocaine."

"All those trips…" said Stennett, sprawled out beside Tristan.

"While Leader sitting on his ass," Alvaranga continued, "polishing trophies and printing bingo sheets for barbecues."

"Richie knew damn well what he was doing," I said. "You acting like Dr. Leader tell anybody to swallow drugs."

Alvaranga shook his head. "You're missing the point, Knuckle."

Just then Saul Christie walked in with a mesh bag of soccer balls, smiling that peculiar smile of his with big bright red gums. "What point?" he asked.

"Nothing," Alvaranga said. "Nobody's talking to you, Christie." Christie was our Cultural Affairs Club president; he could be a bit unctuous at times, but mostly had an easy, friendly way with everyone. Russell hated Christie's popularity. He saw it as a threat to his political ambitions.

Christie turned to Tristan, "That was a beautiful play you made today, Tris, when you let the ball run through your legs and turned. How did you know it would beat me?"

Tristan smirked. "Because you were expecting me to control the ball, so you planted your feet to make the tackle, but when I ran with the direction of the ball instead, I caught you flat-footed."

Christie tapped the side of his head. "Gotcha. Don't expect it to work again."

"A good artist never repeats himself," Tristan said. "Consider yourself lucky."

Stennett was rubbing his foot and wincing. He had landed awkwardly while keeping goal and Tristan had helped him off the pitch. Now seeking to exploit his mishap further, he asked Tristan for a foot massage. Tristan leaned over and began massaging Stennett's foot.

There was something at play between them. Ever since seeing the Smiling Accountant that day at the hospital, Stennett had been cozying up to Tristan, and Tristan had been unusually friendly to him. I even wondered if Tristan thought that Stennett might use the identity of his mysterious benefactor to blackmail him. Watching them, Harry and I leered at each other. If what we'd suspected of Stennett, that he was closeted, and clinging to us for protection, then it was only a matter of time before he slipped up and revealed his true colours. The watching, which

139

Harry and I liked to think of as a scientific study, felt almost as satisfying as the eventual outing. But as it turned out, Stennett had the last laugh. Now, though, Harry's and my leer unsettled him.

Christie rocked back on his heels and spread his big arms. We knew this posture. He was always plugging something. We braced for his pitch. "Guys, listen up. I'm inviting you to the Heroes' Day festivities this Friday night at the Doctor's Cave Beach. The theme is: Liberation Today. Freedom Tomorrow. A Look Back!" He brought his hands together and flashed his teeth like a televangelist. "We're going to have a big campfire, and have real Maroons from Accompong come and tell us stories about the bravery of our ancestors. Afterwards, there'll be a social with the St Helena's girls from the Key Club." We looked at each other and said nothing. Christie turned to Harry and me. "Knuckle, you could bring Marzipan. We're in the same junior tennis club, you know. Sometimes she's my mixed doubles partner. Harry, you could bring Cynthia, that little short-hair chick from St Helena's. You guys still going together, right?"

"Yeah, but barely. It's frustrating. Her personality is *so* flat. Being with her is like eating a stale ice cream cone. All you want is the filling, not the soggy taste of the cone in your mouth."

"No crunch, eh."

"No crunch," Harry said.

"Crunch is important," Christie said.

"Crunch is very important," Harry said. "But her snatch is so tight and sugary it's hard to cut her loose." Harry narrowed his eyes at Stennett. "Look at Fats, he's lost. He doesn't have a clue what we're talking 'bout. Stennett, what's a snatch?"

"A vulgar name for a cunt."

Christie laughed and thwacked the locker. "*Hahaha!* Good one, Stennett. Harry, you've met your match."

"It would seem so," Harry said.

Stennett glared right back at him.

Christie wiped his eyes. "A vulgar name for a cunt… my word."

I said, "Speaking of which, I had another run-in with Ms. Huntley this morning."

"Your old flame, the Table Lamp" said Saul, raising his eyebrows repeatedly. "You do bring out the best in her, Knuckle.

What is she calling our dear Dr. Leader these days for letting you off with a tap on the wrist?"

"A classless pig," I said.

Christie sniggered. "Not very astute, is it? All pigs are classless; that's far from an insult. That's like me calling you an ignorant ape, which you are. What does that girl Marzipan see in you?"

Just then Thura Sotwae walked in, prepared to ignore everybody. Harry said in an undertone, "Speak of the foppish devil." Then: "Thura, we were just sayin' how much we like that new billboard in Sam Sharpe Square of you promoting Student Month and masturbating a giant green pencil."

Thura's jaws dropped. "Is that what it looks like, Harry?"

"Yezzir. And your big satisfied grin brings off the effect beautifully."

Thura bolted from the room shouting, "Oh-my-gawd! Vice Principal Brown! A word! The billboard! It has to come down this very day!"

Tristan said, "I think his majesty was upset."

Christie said, "Something weird happened this week. I did the wash for my mom and while I was removing the clothes from the machine, I found this bloated white thingy that looked like a fat dead plastic slug covered with lint, it weirded me out, like... like dragging up some weird junk when fishing at Freeport."

"That's her pantyliner, *buhbuh*," Tristan said. "Don't you know *anything*? She forgot to peel it off before throwing her underwear in the wash. Clare does it all the time – forgetful as a fish."

Christie hugged himself. "Jesus Christ... so you're telling me that... Oh no... mommy..." He stretched out on the bench with open lips and vacant eyes, doing a Brando impression from the closing scene of *Apocalypse Now*: "The horror, the horror."

"Get up, you drama queen," said Tristan, slapping Christie's leg. Stennett pulled him up by his arm. "You'll live."

Christie jumped up, tall and bluff and hearty again.

Alvaranga had been seething ever since Christie's intrusion into our conversation, and he couldn't hold back any longer. "Christie, where do you get off? I'm sick of you coming in here all the time promoting your little bogus soirees. You're not even Jamaican!" He looked to us for support. "His father is that

Bahamian lackey who works for Tony Minott by the Port Authorities. What's the matter, Christie? Were you so desperate to prove you're one of us that you bought all the School Council votes just to become president?"

"I have nothing to prove," Christie said. "I'm proud of my Bahamian heritage, and my Jamaican. One of the reasons Mommy decided to move back here was to trace our roots. They go all the way back to the first settlement of Coromantee Africans on this island."

Alvaranga made a silly face. "*One of the reasons Mommy decided to move back here…* You small-islanders are always trying to hijack our fame."

Christie was unperturbed. "I'll have you know that Sidney Poitier is a proud Bahamian, so we don't have to *hijack* anybody's fame."

"Hah! Don't make me laugh," Alvaranga said. "Sidney Poitier wouldn't be caught with a Bahamian accent in his mouth."

"No more than Harry Belafonte would be caught dead with a Jamaican accent in his!" Christie shot back.

We all aimed finger guns at Russell and chorused, "*Booyaka! Booyaka! afta Shabba Rankin!*" celebrating Christie's riposte. These were the moments we lived for.

Just then Mr. Bremmer, our tennis coach, came bursting into the room. There was a phone call for me by the office and it was urgent. His face said more than his words.

Panic prickled my skin. When we got to the steps outside the administrative building, Mr. Bremmer pointed to the bursar's door on the ground floor, squeezed my shoulder, then left. I knocked twice. My knees felt weak. The old grounds-keeper who always took his lunch on a chair inside the passageway opened the door. I walked along the passageway and took the phone. I knew it was Mama on the line.

"Chauncey? You had lunch already?"

"Yes ma'am."

She paused, and it felt like I'd fallen through the floor. I waited for her to speak. When she did, her voice was soothing, like when she'd smile at me as a child. "Come home, baby. Come home."

I put the receiver down and walked out of the room. My friends were waiting. Mola had my bag packed and ready, in case

I needed to go home. Good old dependable, Sanjay. The Cool Assessor. His family's future couldn't be in safer hands. They realised I didn't want to talk. But I would burn that image into my brain, of all of us standing there that day. It was what I would recall years later.

Elegy I: A New House

I felt as if I'd grown older, as if I'd transformed somehow, like an animal shedding skin; but was not yet comfortable in this new skin. I felt like a stranger in my own body, like a new tenant inside an unfamiliar house. But I knew I would have to occupy this strange house, would have to fill out its strange spaces. I had no choice.

My grandfather was a very wise man. Some of his counsels would come back to me as an adult with meanings I couldn't grasp when they were first given, like eyes gradually adjusting to the conceit of an optical illusion.

When I was a boy, I had a great fear of dogs. Papa noticed this one day while we were going down the street. The neighbour's dog barked at us and I jumped. Papa stopped and said, "Bwoy, don't fear dog. When you see dog, you must walk with dignity, then they will leave you alone."

I decided to try his advice. The next time the dog barked at me, I walked with dignity, my shoulders square, my head held high. The dog stopped barking, cocked his head and watched me quietly, then decided to show me what real dignity was: he squared *his* shoulders, held his head high, and trotted back to his kennel to take dainty nibbles of his food, completely ignoring me. Whenever I walked past him after that, I maintained my poise and he never once barked. Later in my life, I'd be brave without feeling courage, just as I'd been that first day.

When I lost my grandfather that autumn, I lost more than a mentor. I lost the soil that anchored my roots. I lost my compass. I lost my way in the world.

After Papa's death, Aunt Girlie went into a severe state of shock, locking herself in the old stone kitchen in the backyard or sitting in the living room all day, kneading the space between her breasts and watching invisible patterns on the floor.

When my mother died mysteriously in 1983, after an "accidental overdose" of painkillers to cure recurrent bouts of sore throat pain, my father, not interested in raising a child, had dumped me on his parents and fled to America to take up employment on a cruise ship. It was Girlie who raised me, since Mama was busy attending to Papa and keeping house. I developed a deep fondness for my aunt, to the point of possessiveness, but my feelings were more protective than selfish. Even as a boy, I could see that she, by nature a timid person, was in trouble.

We went jogging on the weekends and our way back we sometimes stopped at a neighbourhood bakery to buy the sugar buns we both liked. Once, when they weren't ready, Aunt Girlie had lingered and the fat, warty-faced woman, Millie, who ran the bakery, trundled up to us and rasped, "Sugar buns eh! They not quite ready." We turned to leave but she grabbed Girlie's arm and insisted, "Wait here, Girlie," then hobbled to the back. When she came back she said, "They said they'll be ready by ten o' clock." She showed us her ten fat fingers. "Let me write down your order." "No, it's quite fine, Millie," Aunt Girlie said. "Don't put yourself through the trouble. We just had a craving for them now." "No trouble dearie, by ten they'll be ready. Even sooner. Fresh an' warm, wid de sugar meltin.' Jus' send de bwoy back to get them. How's Phyllis by de way?" "Please it's really –". "No trouble at all, darling. You like to buy anyt'ing else in de meantime? Take a look at those grater cakes."

I had to shout at the woman, "She said it's fine. We wanted them now and we don't want to make an order or to buy anything else." Then I dragged Girlie out of the shop, ignoring Millie's dirty looks.

If, for instance, we stood at a checkout line and the cashier had an impatient look, Aunt Girlie would be too scared to check her change, even if she suspected it was wrong. If she counted it in the car and confirmed her suspicions, she never went back for her money, no matter the amount. She accepted it as a loss. She took this attitude with many aspects of her life: never resitting the CPA exam and settling for a dull bursar's job at a secondary school; in her failed relationships; her settling for a man who spoke big but made more noise than he made sense.

This was Reds, a tall brawny mulatto, big-boned and aggressive, the owner of the supermarket in Anchovy Square. He stayed at the house from time to time, and seemed to wield some kind of magical power over my grandparents, especially Mama. They let him do whatever he wished in our house, eating our food and scuffing up our furniture and rugs with his boots. It was only later that I found out what this power was: Aunt Girlie was barren. This shamed my family. They seemed grateful to Reds for his kindness in staying with her, desperately waiting for him to propose marriage, reminding him of her education and good looks.

The only one who didn't fall under Reds' spell was Sheila. The two men hated each other perfectly – it was beautiful in a way. They never talked, only scowled when they passed each other, were never in the same room at the same time, never on the same side of an argument.

I caught Aunt Girlie looking at my notebook once. As she replaced it on my bedside table and continued cleaning, I said, "If you read that book, you'd kill me." She turned and smiled, her legs wide apart in her thin chemise, the sunlight streaming through it, showing her body and the simple lines of her underwear. She hated wearing bras. She walked over and kissed my forehead. "Boy, your gift makes you so dramatic at times."

I added, "And if Reds ever raises his hand to you again, I'll kill him. He doesn't deserve you, Aunt Girlie, even Miss Beryl an' Clare dem sayin' de same t'ing. An' they know he hit you. Why you take up wid a brute like that?" She slapped my face. "Don't pass your place! Me an' you ain't size. You're still a child – an' watch how yuh style big people. Reds and my business is none of your concern."

I said stupidly, "I'm not a child! I've done things. I'm experienced." She stepped back to take me in, looking me up and down. "*Ho-hoh*. Yes, I hear you tellin' Sheila all about your 'experience', your disgustin' little sex talk." I remembered what I had told Sheila and blushed with shame. "Go ahead, repeat what you said. Go ahead! Wha' happen? You forget?" She slapped my face again. "Say it. You had plenty mout' when you was talkin' to Sheila. She had a pussy like a crab's apron, eh." She slapped my face again. "EH! What gives *you* the right to judge Reds? I'll deal with Reds on my own terms, don't worry yourself. I know everybody in Anchovy talkin' how Girlie is a pushover, but Girlie ain't no fool. An' don't you dare feel sorry for me!" She smiled. "A woman is a born actor, but where are the accolades? Where's the recognition? A man only learns the profession, but a girl-chile instinctively masters the pretence of ignorin' a boy's brute strength that can crush her any time. An' when they older, no matter how much he sayin', 'Baby baby, I love you,' she never forgets what he can do. No blow ever takes her by surprise. All dat talk from dem other women – you don't pay dat no mind – they know well enough what I goin' through because they live it, an' even if they don't, they ready for it if it ever happens. You jus' remember whenever you t'ink to lay hands on somebody, don't forget to praise her first."

At the farm one morning, as Sheila sprayed fertilizer on the cassava leaves, we talked about Girlie.

"Hard t'ing, Chauncey," he said. "Girlie heart full with grief. It's like bad gas trapped in the stomach."

"I wish I could rub her heart so she could burp."

"I know, son," he said, grabbing my neck and pulling me in an embrace.

He had a strong resemblance to Papa, the same height, the same coffee-brown complexion, the same oval-shaped, owlish face and arched nose, the same grin that made the flesh taut at the right corners of their mouths and wrinkled at the left. This had settled Anchovy's longstanding question about Sheila's paternity, though Papa had never acknowledged him as his child. Papa had taken him from his mother, Papa's former mistress, to work on the farm since he was fifteen and he'd been living with us ever since.

He peered at me closely, "Something else eatin' you, man. I know that look."

I sat against a freshly decapitated stump and broke a twig and knocked it against my teeth. "Sheila, I having problems with my girl like you wouldn't know, bwoy."

"Wha' happen now?"

"Is like whenever *that* time comes, since lately, I jus' cyan get it up."

"Don't worry, man, happens to the best of us. Jus' drink some egg whites before bed, get plenty rest an' don't touch your ol' lady for a month."

"It sound like you preparin' me for a marathon."

He tightened his mouth as if stung by a painful memory, then said, "A woman really sucks the fun outta your life doesn't she?"

"But you need them."

He puckered his brows. "No Chauncey, the *body* needs them, much in the same way it needs a cold beer. The mind doesn't need them, much in the same way it doesn't need a migraine."

I laughed. "Sheila, how come I never see you bring home any o' the women you flirt with in the street? What happen, you 'fraid they won't leave?"

Then he spoke in the tone he used when he was giving me and Tristan instructions about some task he wasn't keen on doing over himself because of our ineptitude. "Listen to me, bwoy. Every man hates a woman, because a woman reminds him of his weakness, and because he can't deny this sexual weakness, him lose him freedom and end up hatin' her his whole life – worse if him married – but you see, him really hate himself. You don't understand now because you young. Gwaan, enjoy your schoolgirl – but when you get older, when the urge sets in and you surrender your freedom, you'll hate them as much as you enjoy them."

I grinned. "No it ain't that. You don't believe all that rot. You just too mean to spend your money on a woman. That's what Papa said."

Sheila laughed hoarsely. "I ain't goin' say a bad word 'gainst him."

"How was my father with women, before he got married?"

He grinned. "Your father? Your father was a special case. He hated women extremely, which is to say he had a new one almost every month."

I obliged him with a short burst of laughter, and could have even enjoyed his joke had I not resented my father so much.

"You eager to see your daddy?"

I hadn't thought about this. I knew my father was coming for the funeral but hadn't considered what our encounter would be like after eight years.

The last time I'd seen him, he'd shown up unexpectedly at my prep school, back in grade three. I remember feeling so proud that day. While the children watched us from classroom windows, we crossed the courtyard together, my fingers locked in his, high stepping like a clown on a trampoline: my father fresh from America, reeking of prosperity and fresh-smelling cologne. When I rode off in his spanking new rented car, the fantasy was complete. But then my mood plummeted. I was in the company of a stranger; we had nothing to talk about. I was eager only to get home and see what he'd brought.

But then he hadn't come for my graduation and had sounded annoyed when I called to ask why. Even Mama had snapped at me when I complained. That's when I realised my mistake: I had demanded too much of him.

When he showed up, four days before the Nine Night, he looked the same, only a little heavier around the shoulders. His complexion was a shade darker than Papa's, brown going black, more coffee grit than coffee. His wide-set mouth and high forehead were the only features we shared. I noted that he was compensating for his receding hairline with a thick and neatly clipped beard. His old neighbourhood friends commented on how fresh-faced he looked, how much "foreign life" agreed with him. My father could talk to people as if he'd just slipped out of a room – perhaps had gone to the bathroom – and was returning to rejoin an ongoing conversation. People responded in kind. He was easy and familiar with everyone, except me. After small talk on the verandah, we fell into silence. He fidgeted in his chair, frowning and studying the backs of his hands, just as Papa would have done.

"Chauncey," he finally said, "when the time comes, you know the restaurant is yours, right?"

"When what time comes?"

"I mean... when you finish your studies. Not that I'm telling you what to do with your life... Look, all I'm saying is... it's there. It's yours. No one can take it from you." I said nothing. "You can cook, bwoy?" I shook my head. "Well, I always say, if you can't cook the food, make sure you can cook the books, heheh."

When Mama walked past he called out, "Mama, why you don't teach the bwoy to cook?" I mumbled an excuse and left him to rifle through the old records he was planning to play at the wake. Before he had got the waitering job on the cruise ship, he'd been a sound system operator; it was the sound system that he'd sold to buy his ticket to the US. Now he ran an ethnic restaurant in the Bronx. He'd never remarried nor had any other children we knew of. Aunt Girlie said my parents had been soul mates. My mother had been a young librarian at Girlie's high school and they'd been best friends. It was through her that my parents met.

My mother died when I was three, so I have no memories of my own. The pictures I kept of her stirred no emotion, not even sadness. What meant more was hearing that she had been an aspiring writer, had finished three chapters of a novel, but the demands of family life and her job meant she never found time to see it through. When I thought about that it frightened me and I vowed never to let anything get in the way of my creative ambition. I kept in my wallet a poem she'd scribbled on her maternity clinic card.

TO C.F. Knuckle

The soldier came back from war
and went to the lively restaurant
but was inhibited by all
the high-flown manners
of the customers.
"Me a man who fought and died
for my country, and I come
back to this – civilised chains."
When they asked him
for his order they realised
they were looking at a skeleton
weighed down by
well-meaning medals.

Was that why you left me? Had you been weighed down by a well-meaning life? Had you been in love with death more than your own child?

I thought of how close Sheila and my father had been, the time they'd spent in goodnatured conversation. Now Sheila kept smiling at him, playfully pummelling his shoulder. "Son Son," he kept saying. My father, Son Son, was enjoying his brother's adulation.

I walked about the yard sampling the neighbours' food. Since it was a wake I was allowed a drink, so I took advantage of this and drank all the rum punch I could. As I watched bottles of beer sweating in a silver ice-bath on the steps, a sentence flashed through my head: *I still haven't acquired a taste for beer and a hatred for women.* I thought it a fine sentence, so went to my room to write it down. My cousin, five-year-old Terry, stood silently by my door, the toe of one foot scratching the ankle of the other.

"Chauncey what are you doing?"

"Nothing… just jotting something down." I was fond of this boy, seeing something of my inquisitiveness in him. His family had come over from Manchester and been staying with us for two days already. The night previous, while bathing with him and his younger brother, he said, "Were your balls ever smooth like mine?" I laughed and wiped shampoo in his face.

I went back outside and horsed around with the children, Terry following me. I dodged behind the garage wall and watched him whirling about, wondering where I'd gone, before I jumped out and startled him, grabbing and tickling him to tears. He laughed so hard guests started watching. I made a scissors with my fingers, feinted at his crotch and whispered, "I'm goin' to cut off your little prick, Terry. Then what will you do?"

He screwed up his eyes, then squatted and smirked. "Then I'd have to stoop like this and pee from my bum like Mommy does."

Some of the guests smothered their laughter.

Our neighbour, Miss Beryl, called out, "Chauncey, leave that poor chile alone! Makin' him sin himself!"

I squeezed Terry's cheek. "Yes Miss Beryl…"

At that moment, Uncle Boysie, Papa's younger brother, who worked as a performer with the Montego Bay Theatre Company, arrived with his troupe to help with the organisation. Fish Tea was already there, with permission to sell food at the event. On the first night, he'd rolled his jerk pan and soup cart down into the yard and set up shop under a blue tarpaulin tent by the gate.

The darkness that descended that first evening felt solid and close. We held hands, our heads bowed. Uncle Boysie lifted his face and smiled. "Yes, Clarence, dance with us in your new shoes one last time." We lit red candles and set them in empty beer bottles at the head and foot of the empty casket in the yard. Penny Dreadful beheaded the screaming white cock – symbol of Papa's spirit – and trailed the warm blood spurting from the neck around the casket, plucked the feathers and scattered them at the gate, so Papa's soul would leave us in peace and not torment the yard.

Then the festivities began.

Later that night, while people were busy eating and drinking, mourning and gossiping, Mama said solemnly, "Boysie, you one brother dead. Is only fair *you* give the speech to remember him by."

The mood was tense until Reds shouted, "Speech!" and everybody joined him: "Speech! Speech!"

Uncle Boysie stood, rubbing his belly and belching Red Stripe. He started slowly, speaking in his throat, like Pastor invoking the Lord's blessing on the day's tithes and offerings: "Two pot o' rice, and one black ram. De night before Nine Night de goat did a walk. But on Nine Night de goat throat cut off."

Penny Dreadful rubbed his chin and looked thoughtful. "Look at that… look at that."

Uncle Boysie continued: "We kill him, put him ina pot, with banana boil soft. And people come tonight and everybody eat it off."

People stood and stamped their feet. "Yes! Amen, Boysie! Preach it, me bredda!"

Mama stopped him. "Boysie! You suppose to say something 'bout your dead brother, not about your belly!"

"Damn idiot!" Aunt Girlie said.

Uncle Boysie looked confused and the people guilty that they'd been happy. Uncle Boysie sat down quietly.

It pained me to see him insulted like this. It was what Papa would have wanted, not Penny Dreadful, the village busybody, his face sour and spongy from drink, standing wobbly as he read from the Bible, his loose lips throwing spittle at the coffin.

I thought of how my grandfather's final days had been ruled by fear, fear that his life had become meaningless because of his paralysis, paranoid because of his cognitive impairment. My investigation into his past had left many questions unanswered and I knew I'd never know the whole story. He was far from a perfect man. His treatment of Sheila had especially bothered me, the way he had denied him the love of a father; it had deepened my resentment towards my own father. But it was not a time to bewail his shortcomings but to honour his courage.

As I sat among the now downcast mourners, I wanted to shout. I would not be cowed as Uncle Boysie had been silenced. I wanted to be as strong as the stone elephant Papa once spoke of.

During one of those rare spells of respite from his abdominal pains, Papa's appetite had returned. He made the most of it, had stacks of boiled yams and fried plantains and dumplings piled high on his plate, with callaloo and brown-stewed kidney, and washed it down with steaming mugs of chocolate, the cocoa freshly grated that morning. Mama, delirious with joy over this small miracle, had to tell him to go easy, lest his stomach react to the over-pampering from too rich a diet. He had smiled and said: "Phyllis girl, don't worry, on days like this I have the constitution of a stone elephant. If maggots grow teeth they couldn't destroy this body."

The remark pained Mama. It must have reminded her of his mortality. But for me, it was reassuring. I'd discovered that the stone elephant symbolised unconquerable inner strength for African Revivalists, and this was Papa's way of saying his faith was his last refuge, even as his body was failing him.

We buried him four days later on a remote plot on the farm, after the funeral service at Burchell Baptist chapel. Fish Tea dug the grave and Sheila cast the concrete for the burial vault. While he worked, Fish Tea said over and over again that he was doing this as a favour to the family, since Papa had been like a father to him, that he wanted no reward. When Mama finally succumbed to his pressure and paid him, he said, "Thank you Miss P. You shouldn't have," then counted the bills quickly and stuffed them in his pocket.

Mama cried only when the body was being lowered. No bawling, just quiet contemplative tears. Aunt Girlie stood beside her, dry-eyed and rigid, her handkerchief over her mouth. Sheila was the only man who cried, the son, the villagers' joke, who got to carry Papa on his back but never got to carry his name. *Shalom.*

CHAPTER 9 – THE CITY AWAKES!

From the Notebooks: Red Room

I stood with my back to the circular counter and stools in the middle of the Red Room, half-watching the performance on stage. A female magician with a heart-shaped face, in a black bunny's uniform, black fishnet stockings and top hat, had just blown up a balloon to about two feet long, then began stuffing it down her throat while the audience oohed and aahed. She periodically stopped her performance to rub her chest as if experiencing heartburn. Soon, the whole thing had disappeared. She opened her mouth for the audience's inspection, smacked her lips and smiled. The men roared and clapped. The MC walked on and hugged her: "Suzie, where the hell is that balloon?" She tittered and shook her fluffy white tail, then said coyly, "Not telling." The MC gave her a look of mock exasperation and slapped her rump; she jumped and said, "Ouch!" Someone passed up a glass of beer; it was handed to Suzie who downed it in four quaffs, then burped and held up her glass. Worshipful silence ensued. Then the men went insane. "Suzie, let me lick the foam from your lovely lips!" "Moustache! Suzie has a moustache!" "Suzie, I'm not worthy to the lick the foam! Let me lick the spittle from the glass! Oh Suzie girl!" They threw money at her, big bills, including greenbacks. A man in a pinstripe suit parted the crowd, took a wad of handbills from his interior pocket, bearing Suzie's image as a 1930s cabaret girl, her short hair in finger waves and a serious expression on her face, then threw them in the air, shouting like a carnival barker, "Her pussy game is cold cold cold! She's a genius genius genius!" Suzie kicked up her heel, tugged her top hat and did her famous impression, "Vance, Kitty Vance – that's my society moniker. But the mob all calls me Swingin' Door Suzie… Get me out of this cooler and I'll unbutton my puss and shoot the works." Then she flattened the front row with her machine gun and blew smoke from her fingertips. "Suzie give us a kiss!" She put her hands under her chin, made a pained expression, then pushed out her rosy bottom lip and pouted. "No, it will smudge my lipstick." "Suzie, not you too! That's what

153

my wife says when I ask her for a kiss when she's leaving the house!"
"Suzie, Suzie, not even a chups?" She blew a kiss over their heads that they
grabbed at and scuffled. Suzie looked appalled and said in her ditzy voice,
"Oh no, now what will happen when I start my bubble-blowing trick?"
"Bubbles, Suzie?" She put a finger to her lips and winked at the questioner.
He jumped up and pedalled an imaginary bicycle with rapid high-kneed
steps as if the floor were on fire. "Wooh!" The MC called for quiet. "Paying
cocks! Paying cocks! Pussy has laws. Stop this cockfight now! Suzie is
ashamed of you and has told me she is ready to leave!" They stopped
immediately and looked at her with hat-in-hand contrition." Suzie patted
a few heads at the front. "Now that's better, boys. No rough stuff now."
"OK Suzie!" "There's plenty of me – oops! teehee – I mean there's plenty
more of my kisses to go around for everyone." "Share the love, Suzie!" She
had them eating out of her hands. She took off her hat and pulled out a
Twinkie and said, "Now for my next trick – I need a volunteer." But before
she could continue, the MC hugged her waist and said, "Paying cocks, if
she could do that to a glass o' beer, never mind a three foot balloon, imagine
how quickly she could make…" They jutted forward, ready to devour the
rest of the sentence as soon as it left his lips. "…this Twinkie disappear."
A man at the front clambered on the stage and grabbed her and said, "Yuh
red up yuh lip dem an' not even a bloodclaat kiss me cyan get!" Then he
tried to kiss her. She screamed and crushed the Twinkie in his face and the
bouncers moved into action, dragging the man away. He was licking the
Twinkie cream off his face and laughing like a loon. The audience cheered.
The MC whisked Suzie backstage.

"Encore! Encore!"

One of the girls walked up to me, holding a glass of green apple
vodka. She peered into my face, waiting for me to say something. I
ignored her and sipped my drink. She fidgeted with the strap of her
dress, stepped closer and said, "Can you help me with this? Lemme hold
your drink." I put my glass down and reached behind her neck to get at
the strap. The whole thing came off in my hand and she was standing
before me topless. Giggles and applause came from behind me. I sighed
and cut my eyes at her, feeling I'd been made a fool of. "Why me?" I said.
"Don't you remember me?" "Should I?" "I'm the girl who posed for
your art class a few months ago." Now I remembered, but something
was different. It was a small, neat pair of purple paws tattooed on the
inside of each breast. She saw me studying the tattoos and tossed her long

black wig back so I could get a better look. "You like them?" "They're lovely, but you know you can never pose as a model for the school anymore, right?" She pouted at me: "How sweet..." Then she wagged her finger. "Careful now, a girl might get the wrong idea and start thinking you care about her." Her face was tempting and girlish, then her expression hardened. "I'm done with that – I hated it. Anyway, at least by getting these I was forced to make a decision, that here is where I belong." I finished my drink and she proffered her glass. "Oh! I almost forgot, this is for you, courtesy of the Beer Kaiser." I knew it! I thought it was him I'd seen in the VIP lounge before, but hadn't wanted to stare. Now I turned and looked. He was seated in a group of sixth formers, university-aged youth and middle-aged men in suits, presumably all New Lots, with the Jacket Man in the centre, wearing a red velvet smoking jacket and smoking a cigar. I put the glass down and mouthed, "No thank you," and had a good mind to send the girl back too. A thought snapped in my head. "Was he the one who hired you for the school?" She nodded. When she tugged the front of my shirt I followed her, still watching the Kaiser's smirking face under the heavy red light.

Upstairs she gave me a red satin blindfold and pushed me onto the bed. "I have a surprise for you."

I put it on.

"I know you're peeking through that!"

"Me nah look, man."

"You're looking! I can tell that you're looking!"

"Me not lookin'... seet deh." I turned my face to the ceiling. I couldn't stop giggling. I could tell by the closeness of her perfume and the wavering changes of light that she was moving her hand before my face.

"Leave your head just like that," she said. Then, "Take it off, Amerie... an' hold this."

I realised someone else was in the room.

She mumbled to this person. "No, Amerie, leave the lights on... an' come away from there nuh, girl!"

I couldn't resist anymore. I pulled off the blindfold and blinked. I was seeing double. She stood there with her identical twin, identically dressed in black leggings and long heavy wig and thick black lipstick. "You have enough money?" I nodded eagerly. I took out my wallet and laid it on the glass table with the tray of complimentary sweets, condoms and bottles of rum cream liqueur. I was a Montego Bay man – ready

155

to devour a whore. The sister had a tattoo, too, a lion-claw scratch, three long jagged red marks below her left rib cage, a cover-up, I saw immediately, she'd gotten to disguise nasty-looking knife gashes that reddened and disfigured a good portion of skin all the way up to her armpit. I got off the bed and sat on the chaise lounge on the opposite side of the room and told them that for now I wanted to watch. They stripped down and started kissing, caressing. The mutilated twin kept glancing at me, asking if I wasn't going to join them. I just sat staring. After a while she stopped and climbed off the bed. "Amerie," her twin said. "What you fussin' for? He say he'll join us when him ready." But she was beckoning me to join them over her twin's shoulder. The mutilated twin advanced. I waited for her to make her move, glaring right back in her face. "You're damaged goods," I said, "without your sister you'd be on the streets. Now get your bony ass back on that bed, beat-up patty-body bitch." Her eyes widened, her lips came apart. "De fuck you say, bwoy?" She looked around, as if for a weapon, then tramped round the room naked, knocking stuff off the dresser and glass table, punching the walls. "Is me you want to punch but you wouldn't dare," I said. I whistled the way Sheila taught us to drive the animals and stamped my foot and shooed her. "Fweet! Fweet! Get yuh ass back on the bed, mad gyal!" She flailed her arms and rushed forward: "You feel I 'fraid to fuck you up? Try me! You think you can come in here and run off you mout' as yuh have a mind an' get 'way?" She jutted her pelvis at me and slapped her vulva. "A nuff man still a shawk dung me good-up body! You is a battyman – I know it! I mark you the first time you walk in. Last week, I threaten to out one o' dem so the men downstairs would buss him up, an' he had to pay me double! I go guh downstairs an' tell everybody seh yuh hood cyan stan' up, battybwoy! I go mek de Fuller man dem fuck yuh up! Then you will see who is damaged goods!" She made a march to the door. "Amerie!" the sister cried, jumping before her and blocking her exit. "Yuh crazy, girl? He's New Lots!" I didn't know if she believed this or just said it to dissuade her twin. Amerie went to the television, picked up the remote. I ducked and it zinged past my head. My fingers curled round the ashtray, waiting for her next move so I could crack her head open. But she stopped right in front of me and a playful smile slowly curled her lips. "Sis," she said, "you think we scare him enough? Come see how him face tough. Look how him blowin' sharp, ready to thump me down." The sister walked over and

156

hugged her from behind and nibbled her ear. Their laughter resounded in the room. I looked down and saw the wet spot on my jeans and my erection throbbed, like pain kicking in without morphine.

I had been reading this story when Marzipan arrived at the door. I put the notebook away. There she stood, her hair and blouse wet. I said, "You'd rather use a small cute umbrella and get wet than use a big one and stay dry, eh." She smiled and said, "I'll use a big umbrella when you buy it." She shoved past me and started taking off the wet blouse. "A girl has to stay stylish, you know." I pulled her to me and kissed her deeply. She pulled away. "My birthday is coming up." "Oh yeah, that's right. I'll get you the umbrella then." She slapped my chest and pushed me back. "If you buy me a lousy umbrella for my birthday, I'll kill you!" I laughed and snapped the wet blouse at her. She jumped back and said, "Chauncey, how yuh play so much man!" I made another grab for her, now that the skirt was off. I held her against me but she turned her face away from another kiss and pulled my hand out of her panties. "Slow down, rudebwoy, we have all day. I need a shower."

I sat on the bed and held my fingers to my nose, savouring her scent. Then I went to my bag and took out a public notebook and began rereading another piece of writing:

We raced to the scene of the assault. We had to hurry – the police would arrive soon and the area would be off-limits. The crime scene was by the Lower School, four blocks away from our classroom. The June plum trees lining the walkway were shedding their overripe fruit, and scampering feet had pounded their soft flesh into the pavement, releasing an acrid smell. Boys milled outside the roofless building, jostling to scramble through the doors or window frames still lined with bits of broken glass. When we got inside, we saw a trail of drying blood on the floor. It had collected beneath the double entrance doors and dyed the pink sandstone tiles rust red; there were bloody handprints over the doors too, as if the boys had struggled to get out. One boy said he'd heard Blacka Pearl had carved his emblem into the boys' flesh, a wound below their right eyes that when it healed and scarred over would resemble a coarse teardrop. "A mark of Zorro kind of thing," another boy said, "but without the craftsmanship." We laughed uneasily. Another smart mouth said, "We need a towel-boy to come and wipe up this wet spot before someone slips and really gets hurt." "Wet spot," I thought, glancing guiltily at Officer Crabbush, then at my crotch. My mind was playing games again. When I looked back at Crabbush, her speech bubble said, "You've been a naughty boy, haven't you?"

Painted on one section of the wall was a life-size image, beautifully rendered in bright colours, very professionally done, most likely by one of the art students, and lifted from one of the American pornographic comics the boys passed around behind the gymnasium. It depicted a voluptuous blonde policewoman, with her blue uniform skirt and red panties torn to shreds to show her buttocks and sandy-brown pubic hair. Her blouse, decorated with a silver badge, was ripped down the front, her white brassiere ripped open to reveal perky breasts. Her hair was dishevelled and her face battered and distressed. She was standing in a telephone booth, her baton in one hand, holding the telephone receiver to her lips. She was saying: "Yes, this is Officer Crabbush. I'd like to report a rape." We'd laughed at it many times before, though this morning that was harder. "At least she stays a while longer," Harry said. "It's a crime scene. They can't touch anything." The thought of her being painted over or destroyed suddenly felt too oppressive to consider.

At a special assembly that morning, Dr. Leader was on the warpath. Even Reverend Myers seemed to flinch as he handed him the mic after the scriptural reading. It was still chilly, but dark patches of sweat marked Dr. Leader's bush jacket, as if his rage had made him feverish. We used to think he resembled Vladimir Lenin: the moustache, the beard, the furrowed eyebrows over small intelligent eyes, though when we called him, Great Leader, we did so with an ironic smile. This morning, though, no boy dared smile. Now he tapped the mic and spoke in a voice that was thick with a kind of dread. "I told the janitors that even after the police are through with their investigation, not to wash away the blood from that building, because I want it to serve as a reminder of the role all of you play in this, that you are equally responsible for those boys' predicament, as if you had laid hands on them yourselves." He paused, waiting for the words to sink in, looking over the mass of motionless bodies from his position two floors up. We kept our heads low and looked contrite while slipping each other wicked grins. "I want each and every one of you here to ask yourself the question: 'Am I my brother's keeper?' Can any boy here answer that question with a straight face ("No – not a straight face," a grinning boy whispered) and a clear conscience this morning? When one amongst you – some nasty scoundrel who might even be standing here! – one whom I've learned you all call Blacka Diamond or some such nonsense, has beaten two of your fellow Chesterites to within inches of their lives. Yet you shield him! Imagine, none of you here has the courage, the compassion, to stand up and be counted. The report from the hospital yesterday is that one of the victims has permanent damage in his eardrum. Half deaf! Before he's even old enough to begin enjoying his life." He paused again, twitching his cane behind him and studying his pointy black shoes, searching for his next words. "If this is all you've learned in your days here, if this is the sum total of your education, then you have wasted your time and the institution's resources. Education should teach you to be humane, to be citizens of the world, not self-serving cowards."

Someone shouted, "Ask Officer Crabbush. She saw everything."

We laughed, but Leader pounced on the remark so quickly, and with a voice so menacing, it frightened us back into silence. "Who said that?" The quality of his anger, now amplified over the loudspeaker, not only intimidated us but made us remember ourselves, that we were boys standing before adults. All the play fell out of us. When he said, "If you let me leave this landing to come down there, God help you," we responded to his authority. A circle quickly opened around the guilty party, leaving him dead in the centre like a target. It was Tristan.

Dr. Leader met his eyes. "What are you waiting for – a horse and carriage? Start walking!" Tristan moved forward without hesitation, a fierce determination on his face. The cane behind Dr. Leader's back twitched rapidly like an agitated tail. The other teachers on the landing – Reverend Myers, Mr. Brown, our vice principal, and Ms. Huntley, the librarian – all assumed the grim expression the occasion required.

When Tristan mounted the platform and stood a few paces from Dr. Leader, something sensational happened. We heard a sharp whistle behind us and there at the edge of the assembly, along the gravelled path fringing the asphalted walkway, stood Blacka Pearl! The boys moved back in a wave; the look on his face was murderous. He was wearing a long stonewashed trench coat, barely recognisable as a Chesterite – he was all Fullerite! Teachers and students alike started murmuring excitedly. VP Brown darted into the library and tripped the emergency

159

alarm. Ms. Huntley whispered to Dr. Leader who Blacka was. Blacka took off the blue bandana round his head and tied it round his neck, the gesture meaningless and menacing at the same time.

"Leopold Wylie," Leader said over the mic, "what do you have to say for yourself, boy? And don't you dare move! You're surrounded. The Area One officers are everywhere. You're trapped."

RUUURRRP! went the alarm. Blacka threw off his trench coat, under which he wore his school uniform, lifted his arms slowly and made the Fire-Clappers gesture, two Os with his index fingers and thumbs. His shirt armpits were cut out, and we saw the spiderweb tattoos! Tristan, standing on the platform, lifted one arm, and returned the salute, and the assembly, in a sudden access of collective mischief, all raised their hands in the same gesture and shouted, "Fire-Clappers! Pow! Pow!"

Someone called, "Blacka, look dem comin'!" We saw two sets of five police officers running towards us from the direction of the slope behind the seventh grade block and the canteen. Right on Blacka's flanks, security guards were closing in with batons drawn. But Blacka, wily as Zorro, dived into the student body, boys started taking off in every direction across the quad, and Blacka, a Chesterite again, disappeared.

I took out another notebook and looked over a story – for which I'd used Fish Tea as a model – that Master Harding had just handed back to me that day. His red ink commentary at the bottom said, *"The sections dealing with village life tend towards broad satire and the characterisation tends to a mostly comic/sometimes sentimental tragic broadness that is less satisfying. Indeed, some of the characters tend towards the stock/stereotypical figures of rural satire, such as Gully Bishop. Yes, no doubt bestiality exists in such places, but Gully Bishop becomes quite a representative figure."* I thought the criticism was harsh (after all Fish Tea *did* fuck someone's donkey) and I didn't want to give up on the piece, so I wrote below Harding's notes: *Tone of revised story should be careful, studied, sober without being funny, should exude humour, like Akutagawa's 'The Nose'…*

Marzipan came out of the bathroom in her underwear and her head wrapped in a towel, drying her upper body and chuckling to herself. "My baby brother is so clever. Whenever he knows he's being prepared for bed he starts acting difficult. Cheeky little bugger. But Daddy him – ugh! – such a klutz at times, I swear we have to watch him with Jason. Last night Mommy caught him washing the baby with the sponge we use to scrub the bathroom tiles. Can you imagine?" She continued vigorously drying under her breasts and armpits. "The toilet paper here is so soft, by the way, would be perfect for Jay's little bum." She sniffed the towel and dropped it in the hamper behind her, unwound her head-wrap and began drying her hair, leaning her head to pass the towel firmly through its length and ends. Whenever she stretched her arms up to wrap her hair in a towel it all came together – the flatness of her stomach, the bulge of her hips, her mound – that anthill whose warm dark hole I always wanted to crawl into. Once, as she watched me staring below her bellybutton, she said, "You like it?" I gave her an incredulous look. "Like it? *That's* a silly question!" "I'm talking about my nail polish, you horny goat." "Oh." "Those cursed nuns are too chaste for my taste. They even have a litmus test for clear nail polish. I had to apply this after school, just before I came here." I watched her now, wondering if the words in my head could ever match what I was looking at, her unhurried movements, her subtly changing expressions: they contained an elusive grace you could only catch when she was wrapped up in herself, unaware of observation, a quality that was ruined whenever her body was taken over by its coarse passion for lovemaking. "My father, I swear, the man has too much pride, I don't know what he's going to do with it, he gets all cross when all you're trying to do is teach him how to take care of his own child. Chauncey, are you listening?"

"Yea… you should tell him to swallow it."

She looked at me. "Swallow what?"

"The pride, that's what he should do with it."

She sucked her teeth. "You're another one with those shallow comments."

"Why do people always say that? I'm serious, Marzie."

"OK Chauncey… if you say so."

I wanted to continue watching her but the notebook was calling me. I snuck it open; she caught the movement in her peripheral vision and gave me a reproving look. I closed the book. She walked over and tossed the notebook onto my knapsack on the floor, then sat with her back to me, drying her hair. "My older brother got baptised at the university last week, you know."

"Really? What faith?"

"Adventist."

"So what does that mean now?"

"It means he no longer eats pork and pussy."

I broke into a short laugh. "Now that's a special item of news." She glanced around and seemed pleased to have amused me, but kept on working the towel. I hated when she did this – towelling her hair for an excruciatingly long time because she knew I was aching for her and she wanted to lengthen my torture. I glanced at the notebook on the floor, but then she might punish me and turn it into a fuck-free visit.

"I heard what happened at CC," she said. "Who's this Blacka Pearl?"

"His name is Leopold Wylie, an eleventh grader and Fuller native who's been running a gambling den by Bailey House. He started out as a junior partner alongside the Beer Kaiser. But when the Kaiser graduated he took over the reins of operation."

"Oh really."

"Business was so good that boys began racking up horrendous debts – we're talking huge sums of money here, well into the thousands – and when they were late clearing their debts, Blacka had his fellow Fullerites pay them visits on campus to coerce them."

"Was that what happened to those two boys?"

"Pretty much. They tied them up in an abandoned chemistry lab, and stripped and beat them. A janitor found them in the evening."

"How did Tristan get involved with them, the Fire-Clappers?"

"I'm not convinced he's involved; he just seized the moment and returned Blacka's gesture, knowing that would raise his stock among the boys. But if he *is* involved, it's likely through Colours, one of the crew's leaders and a Chester old boy. He has a rather interesting recruitment drive on campus. He has his cronies disguise themselves in school uniform, carrying backpacks and school I.Ds and using their knowledge of the school grounds to evade campus security and approach boys all over campus, giving away baseball caps and Swatch timepieces."

"How long has Tristan been suspended for?"

"Three days."

"Chauncey, have you spoken to him? About the danger he's getting into? He's playing with fire you know – no joke."

I groaned and covered my face and slunk down in the bed. "Marzie, haven't you heard a word I said? It's probably just a hoax; he just took advantage of the situation. Tristan is very astute, you know, he's determined to get ahead in life."

"Hoax or not it's a dangerous situation. It's not funny, and it's your responsibility to remind him of that. You're the only one who can reach him. Sometimes when I watch you two I'm baffled. I swear, even when he's not around, you're emotionally unavailable to me. I'm still competing, fighting for a seat on the bus." She pushed my shoulder. "So get over yourself and talk to him seriously."

"Awrite, awrite." My impatience climbed and I reached over and turned on the bedside lamp and took up the notebook. She glanced around but continued towelling her hair. "Why don't you just bring a hair dryer?"

"Excuse you?"

I regretted my tone immediately. I reached out to touch her back but she pulled away. Now I was desperate to make amends. When she turned round again she was snickering, with her hand over her mouth, a mocking gleam in her eyes.

"What's so funny?"

"When you want pussy your begging face is so long, like a donkey's."

I didn't like the way she was laughing at me. Once when we were at the movies, the heroine told her father she planned on being a model and her father had replied with scorn, *'So you're going to make a living off your vapid looks and waste your brain.'* She had whispered to me, "It's a good thing you can live off your beautiful mind, Chauncey, and spare your poor looks the strain." The remark had hurt. Sometimes her jokes were even crueller – like boys ribbing boys. I knew she hadn't dated me for my physical attractiveness. Once when we argued, she had said hotly, "You know, just this week Theresa told me you're ugly!" I'd told her that if we broke up, I could get Theresa to fuck me. Marzie went silent, perhaps unsure that I couldn't fulfil this threat.

"I've written your poem, you know," I said.

"Really?" She dropped the towel and turned to face me, her face flush with excitement. "Let's hear it."

I sat up, cleared my throat, and recited:

> "I loved you, so I drew these tides of
> men into my hands and wrote
>   my will across the sky in stars
>   to earn you freedom, the seven-
>   pillared worthy house, that your
>   eyes might be shining for me
>   when we came."

She screwed up her lips and plunged her fist into the bed. "You think I'm a fool? Those aren't your words! Seven pillared worthy house mi foot!"

I laughed and pulled her to me.

"Lemme guh! I should punish you for lying."

"But you won't…" When her nipples touched my chest I remembered the brothel twins entangling me like snakes, their wet licks probing my crotch, their pubic hair stubble pricking my skin, their slipperiness in my mouth. Marzipan sat on top of me and it felt like the weight of guilt. I studied her breasts.

"What you staring suh for?"

"You have east-west breasts, your nipples face outwards."

She cocked her head, looking at me slyly. "You're an expert aren't you?" Slowly she began circulating her buttocks over my crotch. When no erection came, I eased her off.

"What's wrong?"

"Nothing…" But she had realised and pretended she hadn't. She started kissing my neck a bit too eagerly, then my nipples. All I could feel was annoyance with myself.

"Stop Marzie."

She moved her tongue below my navel. I grabbed her head. "Stop!" I breathed slowly to relieve my frustration, her head was on my stomach as she stared across the room. I said, "How about a little role play. You can be a lady cop and –"

"No Chauncey," she said, "no more of those games. You can't control yourself when you get excited; something happens to you."

"Fuck it then…" I pushed her aside and got up. I turned the TV on and off, on and off. My heart raced. This was the fifth time it had happened. I said the only thing I truly felt. "I'm going to lose you aren't I?" I was relieved when it appeared she hadn't heard. She went to the mini fridge and came back with a bottle of Schweppes and a packet of Cheesewitz and put her head in my lap. She skipped through the TV channels while trying to put a chip in my mouth.

"Bwoy, fix yuh face; there're other things we can do besides having sex."

"Like what?" I said crossly.

"How about a board game? Where's that scrabble set?"

"You couldn't beat me if I played with half a brain."

She groaned and said casually, "You're in a rich vein of form quite of a sudden. You did the same thing last Saturday at the skating rink with Debbie and Sulene."

I said, "If you ever raise your voice at me again, just to show off to your friends that you have me under control, yuh nah guh like it." I wanted to start something with her but she didn't take the bait. I felt reproached and stayed gloomy while she watched TV and ignored my sullenness. I went to the bathroom and tried jerking off; it didn't work. When I came out she was dressed and set to leave. She said, "How come I didn't hear you flush?" She kissed my cheek. "Walk me to the lobby."

I said instead, "Marzie, pull down your panties." Her mouth dropped open. "Excuse you? I'm going to pretend I didn't hear that." I grabbed her hand as she walked by. "Marzie, please, just let me look at it, I know I can get it up."

"Let go, Chauncey! You're hurting me!" I snatched the bag from her and locked the door and walked back to the bed. She looked shocked, insulted, but I was over the edge. I couldn't help myself. She made a dash for the telephone but I yanked out the line. She stood before me, biting her lip, crying. She kept rubbing her arms and shaking her head. "This isn't you, Chauncey, this isn't you." I wanted to say I was sorry, but my stubbornness had removed me from her distress. She held out her hand. "Give me the key."

I shook my head.

"Chauncey, give it to me!"

"Shut up before I lock you in that closet!"

She looked around frantically, then said, "You need to see someone about this. You need help."

But I kept saying, "Please Marzie, just let me look at it; I'm sure I can get it up." When I approached her she screamed, ducked by me and made for the door, yanked at the lock, calling for help. I had the perverse instinct to scare her more. "Now you see me. This is what a man truly looks like when he stands upright and doesn't walk on his face anymore, when the moss and fronds and frogs are removed." She screamed. I lifted her skirt and pulled her panties down to her knees. Her knees wobbled and she held on to me, snivelling, her face wet with tears. She hugged me but I broke her grip and pushed her back. She dropped to the floor and clutched her knees. "Please Chauncey, this isn't you – this isn't you."

"But this *is* me," I insisted. "Don't you see? Look at my face!"

"No," she said, "you're wrong!"

I sneered: "You love me don't you, Marzie? But can't you see I'm unworthy of your love?" I reached forward and she said feebly, as if exhausted, "No, Chauncey, no." I yanked her to her feet. "Ah fuck it… pull your knickers up."

I unlocked the door and turned away as she hurried out, leaving her bag. I went back to the bed. I also realised that the poem had come to mind because I had Tristan in my thoughts and it was meant for him, and that he would die and I would be powerless to stop it. Another stanza of the poem, bitter like vomit, spilled from my lips:

> Love, the way weary to your body
> our brief wage ours for the moment
> before earth's soft hand explored
> your shape, and the blind
> worms grew fat upon
> your substance.

CHAPTER 10 – A PEEP THROUGH
THE CURTAIN. FRESH AIR AT LAST!

There's not much to tell about Jesus Saves, except that he was either a flawed genius or reasonably insane. Perhaps a bit of both. It depended who you asked. But whichever side of the fence you were on, it had to be admitted that he was a remarkable man.

He claimed a dubious relationship to T.P. Lecky, the great Jamaican scientist who created three new breeds of cattle during the 1950s and was awarded the OBE in 1959. He claimed his father was a famous chocolatier from St Mary who'd pioneered coffee-flavoured chocolate and had made a fortune, but then disinherited him because he'd refused to take up the family business and instead gone on a pilgrimage to study Taoism. But it wasn't so much his noble associations that attracted us to Jesus Saves, more his liberality in bestowing thought-provoking advice in the form of random maxims: "It's good to have a clear conscience, but it's better to have clear nostrils," or: "Never trust a man who doesn't like ice-cream," and my favourite: "Only bamboo makes the panda ticklish."

If you asked him what he did for a living, nine out of ten times he'd tell you he was a "curator of culture", that he'd been a Garveyite long before Marcus Garvey became a national hero; that he was a Jamaicanologist, something like an Egyptologist but without the archeological mess. Mostly, though, he was just a graffiti artist. When he wasn't pursuing these disciplines, practising the lost art of pamphleteering, or writing to the government for research grants, he made his bread running small hustles around the Bay. You never knew what to expect from his pamphlets, what hot-button issue was firing his brain.

When we caught up with him in front of the newly refurbished Civic Centre in Sam Sharpe Square, at the Sure Brite Jamboree, he was in typical form. He was dressed in his customary yellow

T-shirt (the words *Jesus Saves* stencilled across the front in black, exclamatory letters), dark shades, a wooden necklace with multicoloured beads and feathers, gold finger rings, his Mohawk and goatee freshly cut, and his gold tooth glinting cynically in his mouth like stolen treasure.

Harry was the first to see him. "Guys, there's Jesus Saves! We should say hi."

When he saw us coming, he folded his newspaper and opened his arms as if to greet us in an embrace. "Ah, the noble men of the hill," he said. "What brings you to the square this afternoon, besides the obvious?"

"Chauncey's here on assignment," Harry said, beaming at Jesus Saves. "He's the big man at the *Trumpet* now."

We were in grade eleven, our final academic year of school, and as subeditor of the school newspaper *The Hilltop Trumpet*, I was responsible for canvassing local events like this one for the "Community Corner" page.

"Is that so? How the writing coming on, Young Garvey?" This was his nickname for me, a reference to my academic scholarship.

"Not bad, you know," I said, trying to sound indifferent. "I'm concentrating on journalism now, sort of branching out."

"As well as you should," Jesus Saves said, closing his eyes serenely and nodding his head. "The city needs all the journalistic muscle it can manage, mired as it is in mess. Have you seen the paper this morning?" He opened the *Sun* to a headline: *Montego Bay's Favourite Son Feared Among Missing.*

The article was about how, during the night, some thirty-odd mentally ill and homeless persons had been kidnapped from Montego Bay and transported to St. Elizabeth in two St. James Parish Council trucks and dumped at the edge of a mud lake, ostensibly in a clean-up campaign ahead of the Governor General's Parade in November. Some of the abductees had hiked the forty-two miles back to the city to tell a harrowing tale of being pepper-sprayed and roped together like animals. But many were still missing, and the mud lake was being drained in case any of them had fallen in and drowned. The scandal was shaking the city. Montego Bay's mayor had distanced himself from the incident, disavowing any knowledge of its operation, but the people's indignation had grown tails, claws and sharp teeth overnight. They weren't fools, so when the parish council tossed them the truck drivers to quell their bloodlust, they only pawed at them like disgruntled beasts and tossed them back. Their appetites were much larger.

Now their pursuit of justice had a face. It was Dennis's. He was the "favourite son" the article spoke of, who'd also been disappeared, along with his Carol's Wall Bridge coterie. The picture in the paper was of Dennis before he was bearded, before his large brown eyes were bleared with cynicism and his smile still had the benefit of teeth. It showed a clean-shaven, toothsome young man, bright-eyed and hopeful – a driver's license photo perhaps. The article quoted tour bus drivers whose vehicles Dennis had washed, tourists whom he'd entertained, and other citizens giving anecdotes and glowing reviews of his life. The nuns at St Helena's were said to be praying daily for his safe return. The whole thing had the underlying grimness of an obituary. I read it with a lump in my throat. Now Jesus Saves was joining the fight on Dennis's and the other victims' behalf.

Mola said jokingly to Tristan, "Imagine, Tris, you never got to tell Dennis thanks for saving your life."

Tristan looked at Mola as if he'd told him to swallow a stone. "You ever tell me thanks for gettin' your watch and wallet back that day you froze like a coward?" We understood what was happening: he held himself apart, to remind us we were still indebted to him. I thought, too, that the stress of the life he led away from our eyes was seeping more and more into his personality. It was becoming more difficult for him to keep the two worlds separate.

Jesus Saves closed the newspaper and grimaced. "These politicians, they're like those rascals at the market who smile in your face and pick your best fruit from the stall, asking for a taste. But instead of buying, they eat the whole thing and spit the seeds back in your face and move to another stall. We're always giving; they're always taking. It has to stop."

This was what we liked about Jesus Saves: his histrionic sense of morality.

That month, there was a big raffle taking place in Cornwall

County, sponsored by Sure Brite, a popular detergent brand. Contestants had to fill in the missing letters to the slogan: Fo_The S_rest Whit_, To_ake Your C_othes Spotle_s B_ite, and mail their entries to the address provided. The grand draw was today in the Square.

There was a huge crowd. A large stage had been erected on the white brick piazza of the Civic Centre. Sound system operators and cameramen were busy setting up their equipment onstage. There were police stationed close by.

There were performances to get the crowd warmed up. First was a two-man comedy act – a short fat man dressed in a tight three-piece suit and pointy shoes, and a tall thin man dressed as a policeman with a rubber baton and a whistle. The fake policeman kept interrogating the fat man, knocking him over the head with the baton; the fat man would pretend to cry. It was quite funny, but real policemen never laughed. Following them was a midget riding a unicycle and a man swallowing fire. The crowd quickly grew impatient.

When it was time for the raffle draw, Howard Gallimore, the mayor, came on stage with a representative from Sure Brite, a grey-suited nervous little man with a small head and rabbit teeth. They were flanked by two scantily-clad girls.

A surprise followed.

There was a boom from the speakers, a whine from the microphone. Then to the theme from *Hotline*, a big-bellied brown man in an appalling purple suit and sunglasses pranced onto the stage. He spread his arms and smiled a big smile at the crowd. The crowd went wild. Jesus Saves's face went slack.

It was Ronny McKnight, the *Hotline* host. He wasn't the slated MC; it was supposed to have been DJ Bones, a popular disc jockey on *Hot 102*, but if the crowd minded they didn't show it. Ronny McKnight cupped his palms round his mouth and shouted: "For the surest white!" Then tugged his earlobe and leaned forward.

The crowd shouted back: "To make your clothes spotless bright!"

He did a little gyration. The crowd went wild. Then he commandeered one of the scantily-clad girls and soon they were on the floor, practically humping. "*Sim Simma! Who got de keys to my bimma!*" The speakers blared Beenie Man's prerelease. The crowd noise started hurting my ears. The police started blowing their whistles, the sergeant gave a hand signal, and they started wading through the crowd, singling out ringleaders. A heavyset man objected to being collared by a policewoman. The policewoman slapped him. Skirmishes broke out, alarms on police cars started going, as loud as the speakers blaring *Who am I-I? De girls dem sugar!* Riot police in helmets, armed with nightsticks and shields, appeared from nowhere and started beating people. Bottles, stones and chairs were being thrown. The stage crew bolted. The raffle was over. When I looked around, Jesus Saves had vanished.

The next morning, when I woke up, I turned on the radio just in time for DJ Bones's canned intro: a mash-up of an outraged Sarah Jessica Parker confronting the closeted Depp in *Ed Wood/ Dick Tracy* speaking into his two-way wrist radio, then cutting down the City's scum with his Tommy Gun/and a chipmunk soul sample of a Rupert Holmes song. *What kind of sick mind operates like that?/I'm on my way…it's Tracy!…rat-tat-tat-tat-tat-tat-tat!/bullet hole that entered near the top of your vest! Brass knuckles won't help you when your hands ain't clean. And you ain't dressed for this affair…h-h-h-homicide/ DJ BONES!! Raise the dead on those turntables (boy)!* This was followed by a record rewind sound effect.

It was Ronny McKnight again, filling in for DJ Bones, and apparently in good spirits, despite the mortifications of the day before. "This is Ronny McKnight, the Poor People's Guv'nor! Sitting in for the convalescing DJ Bones who will be back next week. Putting a smile on your face. Hah! Paul, before we begin, let me remind the folks in *Radioland* that in a recent survey conducted by the Consumer Affairs Bureau, NCB's Keycard was declared the number one credit card in Jamaica. Why bother with cash? Use Keycard instead. It's today's way of getting ahead. The time by NCB's Keycard i-i-s… ten o'clock! Time for the *Saturday Morning Mix* where *you* call the shots and *we* play the hits! Paul, the phone lines are hot, man. Let's take our first call. Caller, go-o-o-d morning!"

After a short silence the caller said, "Ronny."

It was Jesus Saves. Ronny McKnight yipped like a happy puppy. "Jesus Saves! Is that you, ma brotha?"

But there was only a slow audible breathing on the other end of the line. I turned up the radio.

Jesus Saves finally said, "Ronny, how could you?"

He sounded hurt, heartbroken.

Ronny McKnight said, puzzled, "Ma brotha?"

"There were children there, Ronny, innocent babes who now have the disgusting image of your sweaty jiggling flesh burned into their brains, corrupting them for life."

"I b-beg your pardon."

"Pardon? You're begging me pardon? You scamp! You... media whore! Pardon? I have none to give whatsoever!"

Ronny McKnight gasped, as if he'd taken a knife to the kidney. "Jesus, what's the meaning of this?"

"You're an oaf, Ronny McKnight. And I *loathe* you!"

Ronny McKnight huffed, "Well I never!"

Jesus Saves went on to call him nastier names, speaking faster and faster, slipping in and out of Standard English and patwa. In the end, Ronny McKnight had to disconnect the line. It had happened so fast; the assault so sudden. The station went to break. When they came back, Paul, the studio engineer, said that *Saturday Morning Mix* was cancelled for the rest of the day. Ronny McKnight was "indisposed".

Jesus Saves, though, appeared on another radio station, *Radio 3*, on a magazine programme called *Sunday Scope*. He'd refined his rage into an impressive sermon that ended with a bleak warning: "Someone has to do something about the decadence corroding the pillars of this city, before the coliseum crashes on our heads like drunken Philistines. It's time for King Shango to come out of the shadows."

The moderator stuttered. "W-who – who?"

Jesus Saves was indignant. "Who who...? What are you? Man or owl?"

"B-but I'm afraid I don't understand."

"All will soon be revealed. Look to the east for the coming of a black king!"

It was while we were congregated at the school gate during recess, handing out lapel pins with Russell's image and his manifesto for the upcoming student presidential elections, that we heard a carnival-like commotion, the shrill sounds of pan covers clanging and whistles being blown.

We craned our necks in the direction of the noise and saw a

Rastaman high-stepping down the street, tall and reed-thin, in dark corduroy trousers and a grubby vest, sweating profusely from his armpits, with his thick locks bunched under a bright green tam that stood upright on his head, bobbing like a watermelon with his jerky movements. He was waving an Ethiopian flag and shouting, "Look to the East for the coming of the black king! Behold! Christ in his kingly char-a-cter!"

We looked.

A crowd was coming down the sidewalk behind him, the noise increasing with their advance. They waved branches, palm fronds and sticks. As they passed the gate, dancing and singing, we saw Jesus Saves in their midst, wearing a long flowing white gown and carrying a big wooden cross on his back. He stumbled under its weight and staggered into the street. A taxi swerved to avoid him. The driver pushed his head out the window and shook his fist.

"Take your ass out the street you fuckin' lunatic!"

Jesus Saves said, "Father forgive him. He knows not what he says." The Rastaman rushed forward to wipe his brow with a rag and give him a drink of water.

It took us only a few seconds to decide what to do when they passed the gate. We hurried to catch up.

They stopped just outside the Cage in Sam Sharpe Square, by the wrought-iron gate that covered the dark, cavernous entryway that resembled a yawning mouth. We knew of its use as a temporary prison for drunken seamen, vagrants, and slaves found wandering the town, but mostly to house newly arrived Africans until they were sold at the auction block a few yards across the street. Of all the monuments, this retained its mystery; the air inside was always heavy and dank. Beggars who slept outside said they heard moaning and chains rattling at night. A few paces in front of the Cage, Deacon Sharpe and Paul Bogle, one clutching a bible, the other pumping his fist, were perpetually preaching to three seated slaves and a shifting congregation of loose-bowelled birds.

People on their way to work stopped to take in the spectacle. Two men erected the cross and tied Jesus Saves to it. Above his head, on a rough piece of cardboard, was written: *Who left the Tyger to watch over the Lamb?*

"Aha!" someone yelled. "So it was you all along! Jesus you

crafty cow!" None of Jesus Saves's handlers gave any explanation of what this meant, and Jesus Saves was saying very little. He just hung there, moaning and complaining how hot the sun was. People had their opinions. Some said it referred to the scandal surrounding the Parish Council, that Jesus Saves represented the small man standing up to the brutality of big government. For others, hijinks like this were ordinary.

A woman raised her hand to her mouth. "Oh God, the poor man look like him having a heat stroke."

A traffic policeman on his motorcycle stopped, pushed back his helmet visor and spat through his top teeth. "Enough of this damn foolishness. Cut him down!"

One of the handlers, a well-known legal-aid attorney and public advocate named Cicely Hewitt, wearing tightly drawn Sisterlocks and a beige pants suit, stepped forward and shouted at the officer, "Touch him and I'll sue you! He's a performance artist and this is a performance piece!"

The policeman grimaced. "Is a funny thing... I feel like beating somebody like a snake."

Reporters from the *Sun* and *News* 7 arrived. They approached us, recognising us as students. Russell stepped forward. He told them we were there, too, in the "spirit of protest", that we were facing a matter of injustice, and that he was a candidate in the upcoming school elections. The reporter asked him to elaborate, and there, on live television, Russell delivered his first political address. He spoke of the problem of recent security breaches, and that he advocated the construction of a solid security perimeter. The reporters were intrigued. That same morning they went to the school and Dr. Leader, wary of further negative press, refused to comment. The school board caught wind of what was happening. The pressure mounted on Leader's head.

At the elections for Student President, Alvaranga won in a landslide.

At devotions, after Reverend Myers had Alvaranga swear an oath on the bible to uphold the ethos and statutes of Chester College, so help him God, he turned to Dr. Leader for the ceremonial pinning of the lapel. Dr. Leader, recognition slowly dawning in his eyes, groaned: "*Yo-o-o-u!* The mouthpiece who's been campaigning against me and jabbering to the press."

Alvaranga smiled broadly and stuck out his hand for a handshake. Dr. Leader snatched up his cane and walked away quickly, his tail dancing angrily behind him.

When Alvaranga came down to the courtyard, we threw him on our shoulders and sang the school song all the way back to the Upper School. Harry led the procession, dancing and waving the school flag and shouting, "Look to the East for the coming of the black king! Behold! Christ in his kingly character!"

It would be our group's last triumph, our last moment of unsullied happiness. After that, things started going downhill.

CHAPTER 11 – BOGUE BOY

I said, "You remember that scene in the *Thriller* video when MJ lowers himself over the girl in his zombie makeup and she screams and screams?"

"Yeah," said Harry.

"Well that's how she screamed when I bent over her."

"That's cool – fucked up, don't get me wrong – but *so* cool! And to think, you didn't even need zombie makeup! Have you spoken to her since?"

"Yeah, but she's giving me the runaround. We should take time off, I should start looking after myself, this that and they paid Diego Tobago."

"The runaround? Fuck that. She should give you the 'run away' and leave your ass before you break hers in half." He sighed. "You're such a waste-man, Chauncey. She was such a fine stookie."

I could only look at him and chew my nails. "Yeah but do you get what I'm saying?"

We were between sessions and sitting outside on the Lower Sixth study room's slope. He shrugged and threw some banana chips into his mouth. "Yeah, I get it. You're the Hulk."

"Everything's a fucking joke to you, see."

"No, no, but seriously though, don't *you* see? Think about it, Chaunce, that's exactly what happens to Banner when he's truly amped up; the beast will out, no matter how much he keeps denying himself. It's simple and beautiful, the fact that Marvel never clutters matters by adding an arch-enemy to the formula; that would be overkill. The duality of natures trumps everything."

"*The Glass Menagerie,*" I said. "Appearance versus reality."

"Can we get back to what I was saying?"

"Fuck that. What about The Leader? What about The Abomination? Maybe the Hulk's arch-enemy is clothing."

"OK. Who's making jokes now?"

"I'm sorry... Don't go all moody on me now, I really feel like talking."

"Perhaps you should talk to someone about this, you know... like a professional."

"That's what she said."

Harry giggled and stuck out his hand. "You said, 'That's what she said.' Now pay up."

I handed over five dollars.

He pocketed the money and offered me some banana chips. "How about Master Harding?"

"What...? Why would I tell *him*? He's only my academic adviser."

"Your his protege, aren't you? He sees great things in you."

I waved off the idea.

"But seriously though, that's your alter ego; you can't deny it. Not after what you've told me." He narrowed his eyes and moved his face so close to mine I pulled back. He looked into my eyes, breaking the chips slowly between his front teeth. "But let me ask you something – who gave you that gamma exposure?"

"I'll tell you one day, but not today."

"Suit yourself." He pulled back and leaned against the wall. "There's a new woodcutting machine in the woodwork shop."

I wondered if this was truly a coincidence, or what they called a "sign", that he should mention a woodwork shop just then. I tried to put the thought out of my head. "Ah, don't tell me – complicated, eh?"

"I almost cut my thumb off. It's like that time our civics class went to the Japanese embassy and the toilet there had more buttons than the Batmobile. I couldn't find the flush button. It was all in Japanese!" He laughed and ducked his head.

I threw a chip at his face. "No! You filthy beast!"

"What was I supposed to do? Call someone in to flush it for me?"

"Why are you doing woodwork again?"

"Because I'm failing everything else."

"That's why your father was here yesterday?"

"Yeah, they gave me an ultimatum: shape up or ship out."

"Ugh... that's the school's motto these days, so much pressure since we've entered fifth form. I can bet your father really laid into you."

"Yeah…" He opened the top button of his shirt and showed me a welt on his shoulder.

"What was it this time?"

"An old fan belt from the car." This was the way of Anchovy men, which even educated ones like Harry's father, a vice principal, couldn't escape. They would boast about "branding" their sons, like so much cattle. More than once, Papa had slapped me so hard with his machete, as punishment for some mischief, that it left HECHO EN MEXICO imprinted on my arm, and told Sheila he was free to do the same. Once, when we were seven, Harry ran into Tristan's yard bawling while we were playing marbles and showed us an impressive welt, MADE IN CHINA, freshly impressed into his skin from his father's metal T-square, back when he was still working as an engineer. As much as we felt sorry for him, Tristan had joked, "For all I know that's probably a counterfeit blow," and we fell over in the yard laughing, including Harry. The first time Master Harding visited my house and told Papa my grades were slipping and suggested to Papa that it might be a cry for help, Papa had responded sardonically: "I didn't hear that cry. Perhaps I should lay that cow whip cross him back so I can hear it loud and clear." Master Harding had said with alarm, "No, Mr. Knuckle, I wouldn't advise that." Papa had said, "With all due respect, Mr. Harding, this isn't a cabinet briefing. I don't need *that* kinda advise from you. I know how to raise Chauncey."

Now Harry said, "But I swear, if the ol' queen lays so much as a finger on me again, I goin' to let the puss outta the bag and shame him." The puss-in-the-bag was that Harry's father liked to dress up in women's clothes when no one was around. We surprised him one weekday. He was on a sabbatical and we (Harry, Tristan and I) had come home and slipped through the garage, then tiptoed down the hallway, hoping to surprise the girls – who usually came home earlier than us – so they would scream and chase us. There he was in Gilda's bedroom, trying on fruit earrings and wearing her makeup and a white one-piece with a mishmash of cow cartoons. He saw us in the mirror and spun around. There was breathless silence on both sides. He giggled uneasily and started making feeble puns, pointing at the graphic designs all over the cotton dress. "Look boys, a cowrus line. And here, see – in one ear out the udder, hehe."

I had looked at the floor. Beside me dark wet spots started dappling the carpet; I looked to Tristan, then at the tears dripping down Harry's face. He clenched his fists, drew a sharp breath and held it as if he smelled something repugnant, then exclaimed, "Not a bumbo bloodclaat!" and ran from the room. Later he said to me, "Remember that time we snuck into the ninth grade bathroom at St Helena's and saw that receptacle overflowing with used sanitary napkins, and though the stench was so awful it turned your stomach, it was the *sight* that pushed you back? That's how I feel when I see him, as if I trespass an' see somet'ing overwhelming to the senses."

Remembering this took me back to the time I waited for Master Harding to visit our house, about wanting to write about things, but being held back by fear of what others, my family, my friends, would think.

"Shelf bread" came in my head as I waited for Master Harding, watching Aunt Girlie busy preparing for our special guest. For a moment I despised her beauty and refinement. Before I had knowledge of what they were, she would send me to the shop to buy sanitary pads, and even though the shopkeeper took care to wrap them in newspaper or brown paper, people in the shop would give me looks, and if one of "the boys" was in the shop, he would grab his belly and run outside as if he needed the toilet, and tell his friends, "Spoogie! You woulda never guess wah Girlie have de poor bwoy a do – a buy shelf bread!" And they would point and laugh so hard they almost fell from the wall. I couldn't understand the humour, but I felt hurt and angry, and walked home with tears prickling my eyes. When I handed the bag and change to Mama, she held my chin and lifted my face. "Wha' happen? Why yuh cryin'?" I shook my head vigorously, out of an instinct to protect Girlie. "Somebody hit yuh? Open yuh blasted mout' an' chat!" "Spoogie an' dem…" I began. "Spoogie do what? Dat chigoes-foot wretch, him drop lizard down yuh shirt back again?" "Spoogie an' dem laugh after me when mi buy Stayfree!"

Mama clasped her collar as if in shock. "Godself! Girlie! Girlie, come here!" Aunt Girlie, still in her early twenties, and always smelling of nail polish, walked in with a Danielle Steel novel. "Yes Mama?" "Don't send Chauncey back to the shop to buy your products, yuh hear me?"

Girlie flashed me a look of betrayal and I dropped my eyes to the floor. I was supposed to have brought the bag to her first. I had objected before I went. "But Auntie, Marvin an' dem –." "Fuck de riffraff! Wha' reason yuh have concernin' yuhself wit dem? If dey don't have sense enough to be ashamed for laughin', dey names not even worth mentioning. Yuh 'fraid a people? Dem can eat yuh?" She had ordered me to go in secret and when I threatened to tell, she blackmailed me with hurt looks. But she was full of goodness, like a good cake, and every man in Anchovy wanted to eat her. When I got older and after the practice had stopped, I was still not sure how I felt. I'd wanted to write about these episodes and feelings back then, but was afraid because Girlie liked to read my writing, and I couldn't bear to have her read anything that did not have her approval, so I put it off, though impulse told me to write it when the experience was fresh. I'd thought back then that I wanted to write about homosexuality in my hometown, about Chicken Friday and about all I'd seen but wasn't brave enough to write, and even after I had written *Worms! Worms!* after witnessing Chicken Friday's assault, when the experience was fresh, I had only shown it to Master Harding and not my family – and certainly not to my friends. This too felt like hypocrisy, self-denial. I'd realised then that Bogue Boy hadn't yet bitten out my liver, and I wasn't a brave enough fisherman. Of course, I'd also wanted to write about what happened to Tristan in the shed and more about what was happening to me long before I actually felt able to do it.

So Master Harding was important to me, but even to him I hadn't shown everything. The masters had to visit homes once every school year, during the second term, to give an oral report on our progress. That day students stayed home and the teachers finished their work before one o'clock, then got their roadmaps ready and set out to find the homes of their charges.

I listened to Mama and Aunt Girlie, drinking cerasee tea in the kitchen, gossiping about the master's last visit.

180

In the dining room, I opened a notebook. Aunt Girlie looked up from the brim of the cup. "Chauncey, put away that book an' guh wash your hands; it's minutes to noon." Mama came into the dining room and began setting down steaming dishes on the freshly laundered white tablecloth.

"But this is a feast! When was the last time we ate like this?" I said. "Master Harding should visit more often."

"You don't mind all that," she said. "I have a bone to pick with you, an' we goin' to trash it out before he gets here."

My heart leapt. What had I done? I laughed nervously and said, "You know the last time he was here, he couldn't keep his eyes off Aunt Girlie. Is true. God see an' know."

"Keep God's name out of your vile little mouth!" I knew I was in trouble. Aunt Girlie's face shone at my comment and Mama pretended not to see, setting down the large pyrex dish with jerk shrimp and pineapple salad and another with steamed snappers, while Aunt Girlie placed the small bowls of okra rings in okra slime, and black pepper, each on a table mat. She opened another pyrex dish of rice and gungo peas. Its fragrance rose and sharpened my appetite. Mama didn't set Master Harding's place at the head of the table, which she normally would have done since Papa was no longer there. This was a calculated slight. She was still upset that the last time she visited the school in December to collect my end-of-term report, Harding had said I might need to repeat fifth form, since he thought I wouldn't be ready for the math externals come May. She was going to take him up on this. In the same spirit of simmering anger, she spoke to Aunt Girlie as if I wasn't there.

"That man from Montego Bay?" She knew well enough that he wasn't.

"No ma'am."

Mama spoke on as if she hadn't heard Girlie's response. "He knows he should dip the fish in the slime and not throw it over the meat?" Mama was the genuine article, a Montegonian born and bred, having grown up in Hopewell, the beachfront community beside Barnett Estate. It was at there that she met Papa when she was a young typist and he a young overseer.

"Why is it such a rude thing to throw okra slime over fish in the company of women?" I asked in genuine innocence.

Aunt Girlie said teasingly, "Mama, I think Chauncey is asking for some of your wisdom." Mama feigned deafness and busied herself with the jug of June-plum juice and ginger. Was this something you learned among playground peers, behind buildings and in communal showers? I was determined to know. "Is there a sexual connotation to it?" Mama nearly dropped the jug; Aunt Girlie gave a burst of laughter, then knocked her chest and tried to mask it as a cough. "But you see me dyin' trial," Mama said to the ceiling.

"Chauncey, keep your words to three syllables," Aunt Girlie said, but she was having fun and added after a short tense silence, "To slurp the slime is even worse. A proper Montegonian woman will excuse herself from the table. Isn't that right, Mama?"

Mama said, "Girlie, keep me out of you an' Chauncey argument. It's too grown-up for my ears – not dinner table conversation."

"I think it's exactly that," I countered. "All this secrecy and discretion over slime on a fish seems absurd."

"But doesn't the imagery rather rouse the appetite?" Aunt Girlie had a mischievous twinkle in her eyes. It was the same when she had caught me masturbating on the bathtub ledge while I ran the shower. In my haste I had forgotten to lock the door. She had said, smiling, "Who should pay for all that water you're wasting?" "I—I-h-h…" I stammered, then semen spurted lazily over my knuckles, like a runner limping over the finish line.

Mama said to Girlie, "I hear las' year that when that nice handsome man Master Beaumont visit Clare, you woulda never guess wha' de low-minded gal do. She steam black snapper and okras as if dem courtin', and made sure she garnish each fish with a single okra ring before him have a chance to sit down, so he wouldn't miss the hint." Mama chuckled dryly and imitated a cultured man's voice. "And when de man say, 'I'm sorry Mrs Petgrave, I'm afraid I'm allergic to okra.' You know wha' she do?"

"What she do?" Aunt Girlie asked.

Mama lengthened the suspense. Sheila had come down to collect his lunch, and she shouted, "Don't take off those stinkin' boots inside here! Guest comin!" Sheila growled like a dog.

I said to Girlie, "Black snapper? So wha' dis here we havin'?"

182

"Mangrove snapper," she said curtly. "Now keep your ass quiet so Mama can finish the story." When she came back, Mama continued. "Clare so angry she said, 'Well *excuse me* sir,' and grab up de plate and ready to dump the fish down the sink. 'No no!' the man say, 'I'm not averse to havin' the fish.' Hear de low-class gal: 'Listen, don't play games wid me! What happen? You allergic to marriage too? The only way you eatin' *my* fish is if yuh swallow de okra slime! Get that in your head!' The man so frighten him lose him appetite." They laughed together, Mama with her carefully parcelled sneezing sounds, as if she didn't want the laughter to break her in two, and Aunt Girlie with her goofy long, clear, loud cackle. I had heard this story from Tristan: how his mother had practically foisted a proposal on Beaumont – who had flirted with her in the past – and he had lost his bottle. I was amazed though that Mama should have known it; her craftiness made you feel no secret was safe.

Then Aunt Girlie said, "But, Mama, I want to know why *you* always insist on steaming snapper whenever Harding coming."

I covered my mouth and said, "Ahem."

Mama glowered. "Something in your throat all of a sudden?"

Aunt Girlie and I smiled at each other. I said, "I wonder if we will have black snapper next year." Mama grabbed a coaster off the table and took aim. I held Aunt Girlie's hips and buried my face in her soft buttocks, hiding behind her ample skirt.

"Lawks, Mama, is likkle joke Chauncey runnin'. Why you carryin' on so?"

The radio announced noon.

"He runnin' a little too fast nowadays, but watch out for me an' him."

Now I had to know what my offence was. Aunt Girlie sucked her teeth and snapped, "Chauncey don't you see me holdin' this baking tin?" I was still watching Mama from behind the protection of her skirt.

"Girlie skirt ain't wide enough to hide you when I ready…"

There was a sudden roar of, "*Goal!*" from spectators at a football game at Far Common. Mama said in an undertone, "Ugh… all dem stinkin' mouths open one time."

Aunt Girlie said with sudden alarm, "Mama, he doesn't like

raisins in his pudding! The last time he was here I saw him make a slight face."

Mama said calmly, "Girlie, never spoil a man. How it go look if I change my pudding to please him? This isn't his mother's house; he has to learn to adjust to what another woman cooks." Then her tone changed and she turned on me. "Now what I want to know is – " This was it, she was finally ready to upbraid me. "What business you have – "

Then we heard a car's engine purring outside the gate and Mama and I rushed to the living room window. Despite Mama's promise to be hard with Master Harding, she was suddenly beside herself with excitement. "Girlie, he has a new car, blue sedan, with a lion on the front; he got rid of the two-door fanciness." Aunt Girlie was still fussing over the table, though everything had been prepared. When she finally appeared, Mama said, "Girlie, put up your hair, chile!" She quickly did as bid. Mama shoved me and said, "Go an' open the gate! Move like yuh have life!"

He drove in and parked and stepped out smiling. The day was hot and he was wearing short sleeves that showed off his muscular upper body. Behind me, Mama muttered, "Oh Jesus Christ, Chauncey, where's your shoes?" But it was too late. We shook hands, me feeling embarrassed when he looked at my bare feet. When he saw the stoniness on my grandmother's face, he shifted his gaze to the more pleasing mien of my aunt.

"Ladies, good day." Mama closed her eyes and nodded like a sleepy snake.

I was smiling. I knew I was about to enjoy what would follow.

Inside, he spoke slowly and with great care in response to my grandmother's stiffness. I wanted to laugh, but then thought of the conversation's destination: discussion of my poor grades and prospects. Yet as I watched Harding shifting in his seat, I couldn't help feeling I had him at a disadvantage.

We said grace and started eating.

"I don't think I ask you before where you from originally, sir?"

"Manchester, Mrs Knuckle, and what excellent fish this is."

"My daughter made it."

Each time he spoke his smile broadened. I felt the food would fall out of his mouth. "Kudos to the chef!" Aunt Girlie received the gesture with a demure nod and he looked in her face a little too long before her expression told him to put his eyes back on his plate. Some of the masters were notorious womanisers, and the way they spoke about women, including their female colleagues, in our company, would make even us pale. It seemed they relished shocking us with it from time to time. I heard Beardsley, the top high-school math student in the island, a little god on campus, telling Master Laird of the joy of unlocking a math problem that won the school top honours in a regional competition. "You know when you enter your girl and she's initially dry, then you break through to her wetness and it's hallelujah?" Laird laughed wheezingly like a cat and answered, "Hallelujah."

Aunt Girlie said, "Did you mention last time that you have an apartment by the teachers' cottages, Mr. Harding?"

"Did I?" Harding paused to swallow. "I might have, but I moved off campus last year."

"Oh you did?"

"I used to feel school life was all there was. I came to Montego Bay when I began boarding at Chester as a student and I still can't claim to have any relationship with my adopted hometown; a symbiosis with Chester College, yes, but beyond that, I'm still a stranger to your shores."

Mama lost some of her sternness. "Well there's plenty time. You're a young man an' seet deh, you're already explorin', but be careful of the sharks; they can smell fresh blood, and not a bone in them body ready to settle down."

Harding dabbed his lips. "I don't know if I'm the settling type."

Some of Mama's sternness came back. "I always say a man needs a helpmeet. A man works better when he's married. But the thought never enters his head when he's single."

"How could it?" said Aunt Girlie, forking her salad and watching Harding's simpering face.

"Isn't that a shame?" said Harding. "This fish is really excellent by the way."

Aunt Girlie said, "Sheila caught them himself; he goes swimming and fishing with the boys every Saturday."

"How is dear Sheila?" He addressed me for the first time. "Oh yes, that's right; Petgrave lives next door, eh."

185

Mama said, "Perhaps we should invite you for a swim? Sometimes the whole family goes in the van and has brunch at the beach."

He smiled warmly and made patterns with the food on the bottom of the plate. "You Montegonians. I'm from Middlesex, the landlocked region. I never swim, I hate the boundless look of the sea – sorry to be so blunt."

Aunt Girlie said, "No apologies necessary."

Mama was at a loss. "What kind of man never swims or even pretends to?"

The table went silent, then Harding said, "The truth is never plain and simple, but complex." He looked at me to see if I could identify this quote, but I was stumped.

"Well, excuse our ignorance," Mama said coldly.

Then Harding threw the slime over the remainder of his fish and Mama nearly choked.

"Oh I'm sorry! I forgot! I was to dip wasn't I?"

Mama looked as if she'd inhaled smoke and needed oxygen.

Harding blabbered on, "I forgot that you Montegonians –"

"You Montegonians?" Aunt Girlie sounded slightly irked. Harding realised he'd said this twice, and that he'd possibly lost an ally. "I'm sorry, let me rephrase."

Mama pre-empted him. "The first puss out the bag is the bride."

Harding swallowed his comment, looking at the slime-covered fish as if it was roadkill.

"It's OK," said Aunt Girlie, enjoying his perplexity, "it's quite fine to eat it."

He peeked at Mama's face. "Are you sure? I'd rather my mouth get me into further trouble than my manners. I couldn't bear to insult your hospitality any more than I already have, Mrs. Knuckle."

But Mama had run out of sympathy and small talk. "I don't understand why all the teachers say what they say about Chauncey. He isn't as bad as all that. And that Master Laird is a brute! You should see the pile o' sums the poor bwoy has to finish everyday to 'catch up' with the first stream class. That first stream class must be a damn freight train without brakes."

"But the master wouldn't tell a lie, Mrs Knuckle," said Harding, glad for the diversion. "Or be intentionally cruel. If he assigns that volume of work, it's for the boy's own good."

I ate my pudding quickly and looked from face to face.

Mama said, "I don't know 'bout intentions – I not judging anybody – but that is downright cruel. You don't think other areas of his study wouldn't suffer if things not balanced? You think about that?"

I was wondering how many slices of pudding I could put away. "A man on death row might as well eat," was Harry's famous quip whenever the masters visited his house and his parents had their heads in their hands, listening to his woeful report, while Harry feasted. Aunt Girlie got up and put a slice of pudding on Harding's side plate and cleared his dishes. He hesitated, then used the opportunity to inspect her bosom. Again her eyes caught his, compressed lips showing her disapproval. My mind drifted. When I came back, Harding was raising the idea of a repetition of fifth form. Mama erupted. "He doesn't need all that!" She slapped the table. Harding sighed and knitted his fingers. "It would be a damn embarrassment!" She whispered these words as if she felt people were listening. This was a truth I'd never considered. It *would* be an embarrassment. "He's a Marcus Garvey scholar! How could I ever hold up my head in Anchovy if things come to that?"

"A Marcus Garvey scholar who's failing trigonometry and pre-calculus, who won't matriculate to sixth form because he's stuck in the lowest math stream."

Mama couldn't comprehend this. My scholarship had proven my invincibility. I would be all right.

"Perhaps it's something we should consider, ma'am," said Girlie.

"Girlie, shut your mouth! You little bird-face bitch! Don't fly past your roost with me in front o' stranger. Don't do it! Don't let me have to act low and shame you!"

Aunt Girlie's face reddened; she sucked in her breath and dropped her eyes.

The atmosphere in the dining room felt denser by the minute. I looked over at Harding. He was as calm as a lake! He was probably used to these entanglements on home visits. It wasn't lost on me that this was all on my account. I wanted to say sorry to my family for all the trouble I was causing, but I didn't know how.

Harding finished his cake, wiped his lips and eased back his chair. "If it's any consolation, Mrs Knuckle, I was failing math just as badly as Chauncey, even with a tutor, and had to repeat fifth form." He winked at me and stood up. "You promised me a tour of the farm last time I was here. Excuse us, ladies, the boys need to idle a bit." I sprang up and fairly ran out. He slapped the back of my head in the living room. "Look at all the fuss you just caused." Outside he said, "I heard someone got their learner's license," and tossed me the keys.

When we got to the farm, Sheila and the workers were mulching callaloo beds, scrubbing freshly dug carrots in buckets of water, putting fresh sawdust in pens and blue-bagging banana bunches on trees. They greeted Harding with a mixture of shyness, curiosity and hospitality, all clamouring to "cut him a jelly". I waved them off and they returned to work. An idea occurred to me. I had a mind to test the master and I had him right where I wanted him, in *my* classroom, where I could shed the encumbrances of Standard English and shoes. But first I needed him relaxed. Sheila showed him the pride of the farm, Capricorn, a goat they'd been grooming from birth for entry in the Denbigh Agri Show. "He's a Nubian, isn't he?" said Harding, trying to impress Sheila. This buck was nothing short of stunning – long flowing white mane, all the way down to his hooves; a strong, angular face; a beard like a wizard's; piercing hazel eyes, and arched horns cut deliberately low to give better definition to his main facial feature: his Roman nose. We quickly realised we weren't the only ones smitten by his beauty; he was narcissistic to the point of arrogance. I told Harding, "He never socialises with the rest of the herd, not even his immediate family; never eats grass unless Sheila cuts it in his presence; never drinks water from the trough, nor even tap water; we have to fetch it from the spring that runs behind the property, and it has to be at room temperature, else he only sniffs the pan and kicks it over." Harding laughed and clapped. I said, "He hardly ever bleats, as if he considers it too crude a noise; the only time he does bleat is when he's constipated – then we have to massage his anus so he can pass his stool." Now Harding couldn't stop laughing. "I think you're being a devil, Knuckle, and telling lies on this poor goat."

I smiled, "Perhaps…" I recalled how frosty our relationship had been at first when he would rib me with "country boy" jokes for the benefit of the class. Then I sprang my surprise. I went to the storeroom and came back with a machete and coconut and handed them to him and whistled to the workers. He was as surprised as a child pushed in the middle of a *Dandy Shandy* ring. I announced, "Let's see how many strikes the master needs to open a coconut." The workers' eyes glittered. Like my grandfather, they lived and died by this ironbound rule of masculinity, and now they were watchful and even aggressive in their silence, sniffing out his fear. Harding gave me the slightest sneer of annoyance. I leered right back. There was nothing to be done; he had to follow through. He raised the machete, beads of sweat on his forehead, paused, his jaw muscles twitching, his knuckles white, and brought his arm down as if it didn't belong to him, as if it didn't know its purpose without a cane or stick of chalk in its grip. Sheila had to grab his wrist before he chopped off his thumb at the top of the coconut. The workers grunted in disgust and shook their heads, sniggers all around. Harding tittered nervously, "Thanks, Sheila ol' boy. I suspect you rather saved me a digit there." Sheila said something, but chewed up his words to indistinctness while relieving him of cutlass and coconut. I laughed so hard the workers shot me stern looks, ashamed of my crassness. I said to Harding, "I don't suppose you've been practising on that new woodcutter at the industrial block?" He squinted the sweat out of his eyes. 'OK, you've embarrassed me enough… let's go."

Back at the house, we went into my room and I sat at my desk, trying to find a story from a rash of papers to show him. He sat on the stool sipping refrigerated coconut water the women had offered after hearing what happened. They had cried shame on me, but pointed their mouths mockingly to his back.

"What does it feel like Chauncey, when you're writing?"

"Sometimes, when the writing is good, really good, when the pen sails over the paper with a speed that I find amazing, I stand up and walk around the room and smile. Sometimes, I feel as if I have no parents, just the life that flows from my pen. But there's a downside. You know how they say if Bogue Boy encounters a fisherman, he bites out his liver and not only makes him immortal, but the bravest fisherman in the world? I still haven't met him; my cowardice is still intact."

He beamed. "Let me see your latest piece." I found the story I was looking for. "It isn't finished, though," I warned. I offered the sheets but instead of reading, he said, "Give me a gist." I thought again and said, "It's about a man who is corrupted and sees corruption everywhere he goes. He goes to the restaurant and when his meal arrives he stares at the plate and there's a maggot crawling at the edge of the beef. A maggot is in his brain too, insisting on things… For instance, if he licks a certain flavour of ice cream, the one he had enjoyed the same afternoon he witnessed a certain incident, he might recite to himself, '…and as he thought of these things, Chichikov rolled about the floor, and felt the cankerous worm of remorse seize upon and gnaw at his heart, and bite its way even further and further into that heart so defenceless against its ravages, until he made up his mind that, should he have to suffer another twenty-four hours of this misery, there would no longer be a Chichikov in the world.' Passages like this stick with this man; sometimes he feels as if he's all maggots – he wipes his nose and a maggot falls into his palm; sometimes when his aunt enters his room it's crawling with maggots and she scolds, 'Look at the mess you've made! Pull yourself together! I don't have time for this! Clean this room up!' "

Harding crossed his legs and grinned. "You've got something on your chin."

My hand went up to my face: "Here?"

"No it's wriggled away to your mouth. Here let me get it for you." He smiled at me the way adults do when adolescents take themselves too seriously.

"Suffice it to say," I finished, "this man is hobbling around like a wounded deer on a rotting leg that had been caught in a trapper's snare, though he has managed to escape. He is pretending to be whole, but his heart is all this time heavy with the worry his secret will be revealed."

He handed back the papers. "What I'd like to know is how this man got corrupted in the first place."

"*That* you don't want to know."

"No, I think I do if I am to understand this character and the story better. I'm sure he's not as awful and one-dimensional as you make him out to be. Why aren't you more sympathetic to your characters? You need to learn to write with more compassion so your writing can have broader emotional truth."

"I think I know exactly what you mean."

"Well?"

"Well what?"

"Could you fix that? Could you write something that has that truth, that shows some understanding of the character?"

"I don't know. But maybe these might explain better. Then I offered him the notebook with the stories I showed no one else.

I don't know which stories he read, but when he finished he looked in my face as if he was looking for signs of corruption.

"And what does *this* feel like, when you lose control?"

"It feels like… it feels like one of those cartoons or silent comedies when a car is going full tilt and the driver tries to stop it but the steering wheel comes off in his hands and a crash is imminent." Then I spread my arms and shouted in grim comicality, "*I am undone!*"

He didn't laugh.

"Come now, Master Harding, don't look so dour. At least say *something*. You're making me do all the talking and I might end up saying the wrong thing."

He took out his wallet and handed me a card. "This is Thura Sotwae's father. We were bunkmates back at Chester; he's a urologist, he'll be able to help you with the erectile dysfunction, and can also recommend a therapist if you'd like, but only if you feel comfortable enough to share the *other* details."

I took the card.

"I can make the appointment if you wish." I didn't answer. "Have you shared any of this with anyone else, Chauncey, your family perhaps?" I glanced at my wall clock and he took the hint. I really didn't know what else to say. My family saw him out.

The afternoon I walked to Dr. Sotwae's on Market Street, I wondered how much I would be able to say of what really ailed me. "What's the use?" I muttered to myself. "I am undone. Body rot, body rot." I was imagining myself in the Vienna street scene from *The Third Man* when Harry Lime's giant shadow stalked the length of the building and was more disturbing than the grotesque statue on the dark street corner. "I am the terror of this town!" I shouted up the stairwell.

After a general examination, Dr. Sotwae said in his loud jovial way that I was as healthy as a horse and only had performance anxiety. He kept smiling, boasting of how his son led the upper school in grades and was on the quiz team. He said he remembered my face from the *Sun*. This was no doubt his way of saying that Thura had finally surpassed me. Thura Sotwae was my academic rival even before we met at Chester. He, too, had won a scholarship from a prep school, but with lower marks and from the first day of high school he had me in his sights. Thura was bright but his weakness was his genuine love for learning. This made him vulnerable to studying inefficiently. He was more knowledgeable than I, yet in most exams I beat him because I was a professional studier. His class work was all round more solid, yet I topped him in final exams for grade nine. Once, we got into a fight over a math problem which I knew I had solved. Thura had sneered at my "inelegant methodology", but when we finally took the answer sheet back to Laird's office, he said my answer was correct. Sotwae, the Malaysian genius, went red in the face and I had laughed. He had a very delicate and studied manner, but the day I trumped him on that math problem he lost all that beautiful composure. He flung the paper at me yelling, "You're only book bright, Knuckle! You're only book bright!" Even Laird had to laugh, enjoying his meltdown. I was remembering this when his father said, "Chauncey, are you sure there isn't anything else you want to discuss?" I hadn't told him I had a compulsion to hurt those I slept with, and I wondered if Harding had told him *something*. He finished off by telling me, "Lay off the sex and hit the books! You finished third in the grade nine class behind Thura. I want you to get back to winning ways, give that little dandy a run for his money!" I smiled and thanked him. "Will you come back to Montego Bay to practice after law school?" he asked. "I heard you're planning on doing law."

"No…" I said, "I want to stay away from this place."

He passed a hand over his short stiff hair. "That's a shame, there are plenty of fine law offices opening all over the city. It's such a pity when a man feels the need to flee his homeland, but I know it all too well. I was only eight when my father had to flee Malaysia. A man's real place is with his family. Do you understand me, Chauncey? Family is everything… they know our secrets… they share our soul."

I said, "Tell me, Dr. Sotwae, which of your families knows your secrets and shares your soul? Your wife and children, or New Lots and those whores you chum with in the Red Room VIP lounge?"

He let out a soft laugh like a tyre losing air. "Careful of the questions you ask, boy; they might get you into trouble. But I like your straightforwardness. We'll pick up this conversation some other time."

He bustled me out of the office. "Now come, I have other patients waiting." Now, in full view of waiting patients, he held me in a half embrace. "Pick those grades up! Thura told me he's wiping the floor with you in Spanish, yet when I ask him to make orders over the phone to the Spanish restaurant he speaks gibberish. Here's my card."

"I already have it."

"No you don't." I took this card and looked at it. I felt as if I'd been handed a key but the door was mine to find. "Keep it in a safe place." I nodded and tucked it in my wallet. "I hear you have quite a memory, that you throw Harding's quotes back at him like a frisbee." I took the hint and memorised the card's number.

The next day as I sat in literature class, Harry passed a note to me. It read: *Nietzsche was right: God is dead. So is your dick.* I snickered and Master Harding said, without looking up from the register, "Glenn, Knuckle, quiet." Then he closed the register and said, "OK boys, let's pick up where we left off on Tuesday. Glenn, will you do us the honours."

Harry began reading, "Lor, Missis! Lizy's drawers is all open, and her things all lying every which way; and I believe she's done clared out!" He paused, then continued, "There was a great running and ejaculating –" then stopped altogether.

193

Harding looked up. "Glenn, what is it?"

"I'm sorry sir but I think this book needs some sex; it's too staid. My apologies to Miss Stowe, but I think she's done us a great injustice – not an inch of sex to be found, not even in the book margins, when we all know it was goin' on everywhere, at all times, in the big house, in the cabins, in the stables, in the fields."

Harding covered his mouth, but his eyes showed his amusement. "OK Harry, give it some sex."

Harry read, "Lor, Missis! Lizy's drawers is all open, and her cunt's all lying every which way –" The boys guffawed and jerked their desks. Harry continued reading as if nothing had happened, with a serious face. "There was a great fucking and ejaculating –" Now the uproar was too much and he had to stop. Harry stood and exhorted us with his hands. We clapped, he bowed and retook his seat.

In the lull that followed Stennett said, "Sir, why did they paint the school the colour of beef mince?"

We knocked the desks and shouted, "Here! Here! The minister has the floor!"

Stennett pressed his point. "It was supposed to be Chester red, not that contemptible shade.

"Sangria," said Thura. "It's called sangria red, Stennett."

"Thura just made up a word."

"I did not! It's a simple matter of nomenclature; the shade is named after the alcoholic punch of the same colour and is derived from the Spanish *sangria* which means –"

I cut him off. "Thura needs directions to the bathroom again, he's having verbal diarrhoea."

Master Harding said, "Stennett, take that up with the powers that be."

"But you're such a power, sir," said Mola. "You're our light, our sun, moon and stars."

We got out of our desks and went down on one knee and said, "A mighty fortress is our god, Oswald Harding." We heard Dr Leader coming down the corridor, muttering to himself as usual. Harding glared at us. "Get up, you numskulls! Right this minute!"

The fat boy Smitty said, "Sir, what you have on your hands is a dilemma. Either you provide us with an answer to this pressing question of shades, or we'll remain kneeling and Leader will discover your godhood." The footsteps were just upon us and Leader turned the corner on this scene. He glowered at us, then at Harding.

"Master Harding, what is all this? Why are these boys kneeling before you?" Harding stammered, then wet his lips as he did on the day he told us to take out our penis instead of our rulers. Thura jumped up and said, "Dr Leader, I can explain. You see sir, it has to do with a matter of a shade of paint wrongly classified as the colour of minced beef, or I should say…"

Dr Leader stared at him like a dog about to devour a plate of biscuits, the cane dancing behind his back. He growled, "Every-one except Sotwae, this brave soul, sit down. Sotwae continue, and if you don't make sense I'm going to tear the flesh from your rump so badly your father will have to upgrade his qualifications to fix it. I taught him chemistry, you know, they called him Loose Lips Sotwae. Like you he was a quick studier but never knew when to keep his mouth shut." He swivelled his head. "Harding, that includes you. Sit down you bloody fool!" Harding did so quickly, like a well trained pup.

CHAPTER 12 – MAN OVERBOARD.

Harry plopped down beside me one morning in the cafeteria with a big grin on his face. "We were right all along, my friend."

"What you talking 'bout?"

"Get this, now I know why Fatty left Munro."

Stennett had left Munro, he claimed, because a boy had reported him for sexual harassment. The story went that they were both in the bathroom when Stennett approached the boy and asked a "favour": he had tight foreskin and was wondering if the boy could help him retract it. This was supposedly a code that gay boys used to find others whom they suspected shared their persuasion. But Stennett had erred. The boy freaked out, ran and reported the incident to his form teacher, then his friends. Word spread. Armed and angry, boys began a manhunt for Stennett. They had to barricade him in the staffroom before campus security secreted him off campus. He never went back.

"He's in exile," Harry said, hardly containing his excitement. "The fucker's in exile." The glint in his eyes indicated he was planning some elaborate mischief.

"What you going to do?"

Harry was a master of psychological assault. I knew he would take his time to plan something special, to put on a true show of blackmail and torment.

But before Harry could sink his teeth into Stennett, our crisis erupted.

At the start of our final year, Tristan and I had been running a hustle. Usually, I wouldn't join his ventures, but I badly needed the money to pay off my debt to Russell for the computer. He was getting antsier about it; the interest was also piling up. I never understood why Tristan continued his small-scale ventures; these days, he appeared to have all the money he needed. He was working all the angles – meeting the smiling accountant types by

Carol's Wall Bridge, doing his internship with the Fire-Clappers Crew – both engagements increasingly less discreet, as if he didn't care what we or anyone else thought. But his petty hustling continued. It might have been ingrained into his personality, his way of holding on to some level of independence or even self-worth. It had occurred to me to ask him for a loan, but I felt that taking his money it would be seen as endorsing his lifestyle.

We bought boxes of fudge at the Crazy Jim Dairy Depot in the city and smuggled them onto campus to sell during recess by the Lower School. Usually, we bought them early in the morning before school began, and stashed the boxes (stacked with dry ice for preservation) by a bushy hillock behind the row of teachers' cottages, till the bell went at ten. It was the perfect hiding place, a bit of no man's land only inhabited by tall bush, lizards and stones. But a group of seventh graders had been watching us; they knew where we hid the boxes in the deep clumps of grass. One morning, just as recess began, we returned there to find the boxes gone. But I had a hunch. We soon found the culprits, a bunch of boys in 7-3, just about to enjoy the spoils of their loot, grinning and handing out fudgesicles. They were surprised to see us. Naturally, we had to punish them.

When they saw us, they retreated to the back of the classroom, their faces panic-stricken. Tristan told me to stand guard, but when I stepped outside, he locked the door so I couldn't get back in. Worried, I watched him through the window. He took a Cuban cutlass from his knapsack – like the one Spider had maimed Grantley with that day at the school's pavilion – and ordered the boys to line up along the walls. He did it proficiently, like a stick-up artist. What exactly was it the Fire-Clappers had him doing? Moving from boy to boy, he frisked them, taking their wallets and removing the money, saying, "Be quiet an' no one will get hurt." The boys were too frightened to resist. When he finished, he ordered them to lie on the ground, then knocked the boxes of fudge off the table. "Let's call this a fair exchange," he said. "An' if I hear anything 'bout this I know where to find all o' you."

Most of the boys still hadn't moved when he unlocked the door. When he stepped outside, he walked away quickly without acknowledging me, taking the route behind the eighth grade block.

As I jogged after him, I heard some of the boys saying his name with awe. "It was him," one of them said. "It was really him, Tristan."

I caught up with him near the edge of the block. We walked shoulder to shoulder. He tried handing me a wad of bills.

"I don't want it," I said.

"Suit yourself. You too good to take it?"

"I just don't want it."

He smiled like a parent humouring a naïve child. "You know, it's not really stealing, we just takin' back what is ours – in currency."

"So now you walk with a machete and rob people in broad daylight. What's next? Robbin' a bank?"

"Don't be dramatic. I'll understand if you want to drop out of the venture. I'll give you back your investment. Clean money, of course. For clean hands."

"Fuck you, Tristan. It's not about the money, you know that."

He stopped and faced me. "Then what's it about?" I'm sure all that was unsaid between us was written on our faces, he daring me to speak candidly, assured of my unwillingness to tear at the scab of old wounds. As usual, I backed off. I didn't take the money but I tried seeing things from his perspective. Maybe my indignation was overblown. Maybe. He saw the change in my attitude and responded.

"We can't keep doin' it this way," I said. "Someone else will steal from us."

"I agree. We need security."

"Security?" I said. "You mean bodyguards to watch the fudge?"

He laughed. "No *buh-buh*, I mean real security. You know… makin' our business legitimate."

"Legitimate?"

He drew patterns in the dirt with his finger, thinking or pretending to, then said, "I'm goin' to propose a deal to Raymond."

Raymond was the manager of the school's two cafeterias. They had been privatised years before for better management, since they had been losing money, and Raymond, a former hotel manager, had been brought in to balance the books. The quality of the food and service had improved, so business had picked up.

"Why would Raymond need a middleman?" I said. "If he wants to sell fudge he can buy it himself. It won't work."

"Have some faith."

However, there was something else at the bottom of my hesitation. "Even if he does agree, by the time we split the money, there'll hardly be any left for us."

He put his arm around my shoulder. "You have to think of it as an insurance premium, Chauncey, protection against theft. Every business has operational expenses. I'm afraid you'll just have to follow my lead on this one. Business was never your forte."

In my head I was screaming: *It's not worth it Tristan!* But instead I said: "I'll go with you when you make the proposal."

A look of hesitancy crossed his face. He saw that I noticed. "Sure," he said, sticking his hand out for a handshake. Even as I shook his hand, I knew he was lying. He knew that I did.

A few days later, things changed forever.

Tristan stormed into class with his shirt ripped and his mouth bleeding. He was in a temper, his eyes bloodshot and his chest heaving. It was the session before lunch. Ms. Ramsey, our form teacher, was as much startled by the sight as we were. Cursing and crying, he grabbed his knapsack and muttered through tears, "Mi go buss up him bumboclaat!" A sinking feeling sat in my stomach. He didn't seem to see or hear any of us. He was absorbed in his rage. When Mola said, "Tris, what happen?" and grabbed his arm, he flounced away and Mola's chair almost flipped over. He ran out of the class, one hand on the cutlass concealed in his bag.

We ran after him. Alfred Livermore, one of the gay masters, stopped him with a hand to his chest. "Woah woah, what's wrong?" Tristan cursed and tried to get past him but Livermore blocked him. "What's wrong, Petgrave? Answer me, boy." Tristan opened his mouth, but his anger overwhelmed him. He bit down on his fist and screamed, gritted his teeth and *grrred* and paced back and forth like a trapped rat. Livermore gripped his shoulders and said, "What does the sign outside my door say?"

Tristan struggled; Livermore held him fast. Tristan took deep long breaths and mumbled, "I have to live by the code inside my head else I will die."

"Say it again," said Livermore.

"I have to live –"

"Louder!"

"I have to live by the code inside my head else I will die!"

"Now keep your shoulders and your head up. Walk like a Chester man. This school is as much yours as any other boy's."

Ms. Ramsey intervened and Tristan seized the opportunity to escape. "I'll see about it, Ramsey," said Livermore, hurrying off after him. We made to follow, but Ms. Ramsey ordered us back to class. However it didn't take long for word to reach us. He'd been ganged up on and assaulted.

When the bell rang minutes later, we hurried down the steps and across the Upper School courtyard to the gazebo outside the student dormitory. There was a gathering. Jeffrey, a boy from 11-4, was holding court. When he saw us coming, he said to his friends, loud enough so we could hear, "See the rest of the aquarium here." There were snickers as boys turned to look at us. Stennett whispered, "Don't upset them… please." I had a firm grip on a T-square. Harry held a length of pipe behind his back that he'd got from the Industrial Arts Block and kept handy under his desk lid. Russell was in front, armed with diplomacy. We stopped just before them. Russell said, "What happened here?"

Jeffrey stared him down. "Who *you* to question anybody?"

A boy from the group said, "But you rude, man, don't you see you talkin' to the student body president."

They laughed.

Harry said to Jeffrey, "Keep your girls quiet."

One of the lackeys stepped forward, but Jeffrey held him back. Harry was fingering the pipe behind his back and tapping his foot. Boys en route to the cafeteria stopped to watch. "All right," Jeffrey said, "no harm, no foul. You want to know what happen out here? I'll tell you. Let's just say a little birdie tell us 'bout a little thing he witnessed yesterday evenin' after school, involvin' your friend and another party, so we had a little *chat* with him – your friend – to clear up some details, an' things kind of… *escalated*."

The one that had stepped to Harry rolled his eyes and sucked his teeth. "Fuckin' fish." 'Fish' being a slang term for homosexuals.

Harry sprang the pipe and got him clean across the head. The attack caught him by surprise and he only just blocked the second blow with his right arm while falling back, his left hand cupping his smashed ear. The pipe connected with his wrist, a dull thick sound; he howled in pain. I was meanwhile trying to break free from Jeffrey's grasp to place enough distance between us to land a blow with the T-square, but he pulled me forward and we rolled and tussled on the ground. Someone kicked me in the side of the head as I raised myself to strike him. Mola pulled me up by the collar from a tangle of arms and legs and we bolted for the South Gate by Bailey House, a hail of stones pursuing us. We took the shortcut by the Fuller back wall and came out on lower Orange Street, our hands and eyes searching our bodies for injuries, my head still aching from the blow.

We sat in silence in a patty shop on St James Street. I wondered where Tristan was and what had happened. Stennett finished eating and belched. Alvaranga stood up.

"Where you think you going?" I said.

"Back to school."

"We're not going back," I said. "An' you sure as hell can't go back without us."

"Nobody banishing me from my own school. I won't be bullied," he said.

"Sit down an' shut up," Mola said.

"No, leave him. Let him go," I said. "Mr. President… he won't make it past the gate."

"We shouldn't have run," Harry said. "Now we look like cowards."

"And what the fuck did Tristan do?" Stennett said, dusting patty crumbs from his trousers. "I swear, I'm not cut out for this kind of thing."

"You be quiet!" Harry shouted, glaring at Stennett. "I have a bone to pick with you, but not now. In the meantime just shut your trap! You should feel right at home running from mobs, Mr. Foreskin Fugitive."

Stennett's eyes popped, his lips quivered, he looked disbelieving, then just plain miserable. He opened his mouth to speak but the hostility on Harry's face was too much. He shifted in his chair, fuming in silence, drumming the Formica table with his fingers.

Russell, standing akimbo, looked out of the window. A woman with a cardboard plaque round her neck stating she was a deaf-mute sat on a stool across the street, clanging a bell at passers-by and pointing to a blue plastic basin at her feet, half-filled with coins and paper notes. "Well," Russell said, "we can't sit here all afternoon."

After ten minutes walking around town, we came across a gathering outside the courthouse on Regent Street. They seemed to be awaiting someone's arrival. DJ Bones had set up his equipment at the head of the gathering. He had on his customary wave cap and noise reduction headphones, and was warming up the crowd with a few teasing spins and scratches on the double turntables: *What kind of... what kind of... h-h-h-homicide!* We stopped to see who they were waiting for. A tall, distinguished-looking man in a well-tailored, knee-length parka standing beside us cast a stink-eye at the bums across the street. They were pestering the vendors to let them have the leftover newspapers so they could use it as toilet paper and to make paper bricks for burning night fires. "Look at them," this man said; "they wouldn't spare a glance at the front page to know what's happening in the world around them, they just want to wipe their asses with the news." He sighed. "They're the big stinking shitheap of this city, human refuse. The uptown sadists fuck them, the politicians use them as puppets to hold up banners and distribute flyers, though they don't know what's written on them. They serve no purpose. Who would miss them?"

The crowd was finally hushed, people craning their necks to see. Like everyone else we jostled to get a view. The smooth gestapo shoved a wheelchair-bound man aside, while removing a small notepad and pen from his parka. "Hey!" the man protested. "You think because I'm in a wheelchair you can just push me around?" The gestapo twitched his lips and smoothed down his pencil moustache: "Well... yes." Then DJ Bones did the record rewind sound effect and held the needle in place long enough to keep our tension taut till the beat dropped and our heads snapped in rhythmic response. *What kind of sick mind operates like that?!/I'm on my way... it's Tracy!... rat-tat-tat-tat-tat-tat-tat!/bullet hole that entered near the top of your vest! Brass knuckles won't help you when your hands ain't clean. And you ain't dressed for this affair... h-h-h-homicide/Jesus*

Sa-a-ves! People went nuts. The noise shook the street like a stadium packed with roaring hooligans. That's when we knew who the biggest star in the city was. "Jesus for mayor!" went up the cries, as Jesus Saves, emerging from the parking lot, like a heavyweight champ, stepped out of the shadows to stand on the curb wall. Now, an even bigger crowd stood before him, getting bigger by the minute, spreading onto the road. It was midday, but the sun retreated and the street grew dark. The neckline of Jesus Saves's yellow T-shirt was already dark with sweat; he seemed to be thinking, waiting, looking over the gathering.

Someone started clapping passionately, shouting, "Bravo, Good Teacher! Good for you!"

People whipped around to see who it was. It was a bum, wearing an old, red, chipped firefighter's helmet marked: Saving Lives and Protecting P——, an old man with a shrunken face, his clothes dark and stiff with dirt. He'd been skirting the edge of the crowd, picking up bottles and putting them to his mouth to empty them. When he realised he had an audience, he spoke even louder, "The octopuses are crawling all over this city. They don't use camouflage no more. The whole town is their playing field! They have cleats laced up on all eight limbs compared to our two, and they bleed black blood!"

Some people started chuckling, shaking their heads in pity at his senseless rant.

The bum, affronted, stepped into our midst and wagged his finger. "Mark my words, you have to play dirty to survive in this game, and you can't waste tears for innocents who get shafted!"

A man kicked at him. "Move your stinkin' self before I settle with you!" The old man jumped back and sheepishly pulled down the helmet's visor and drifted to the other side of the street.

Jesus Saves looked pointedly at the retreating tramp. He said to the gathering, "Friends, I wouldn't be foolish enough to ask any of you to try and change the world on your own. That's not what this campaign is about, but it's certainly what you do that will define you. The same questions we ask of our leaders, we must also ask of ourselves." His face was serious, his tone foreboding. "A change is coming and it will knock at your door whether you want it to or not. If you're unwilling to join the wave of transformation you will be cast aside, like the straggler in the ant trail, the column will go on without you. We *all* have to answer to God for the moral failure that landed us in this mess, not just the politicians. And beware, when the ball starts rolling, things will happen very fast. Make no mistake, this score will be settled in the streets where it began. The case of 'the Montego 36' is only one of the bitter fruits of the 'war' cooked up by the Parish Council, the so-called war the police use as a sheriff's badge to perpetrate brutality against the defenceless, like the teenaged gays, turned out of homes and communities, who live together, forming their own family, in the abandoned buildings on Weimar Road."

There were groans of disapproval. A man called out, "Careful now, Master, de battybwoy dem will hear an' get cocky." There was a clamour of approval.

Jesus Saves looked down at the man and spoke so his voice would carry. "My brother, remember Charleston Jones." This quietened most of the crowd; they looked at each other, then back at Jesus Saves with subdued faces.

Someone said, "But what business him have goin' to dancehall dressed like a woman and whining up pon man? Him call dung trouble pon himself."

A woman shook her head, steupsed and intoned, "Wha' dem do to dat poor bwoy was nutten short of a lynchin'. An' de dutty gal who sell him out have blood pon har hands… Mercy."

Another said, "No Mummy – is not de gal who blow him cover. Dat is only rumour. I was there. Is de mob who find him out. It was Hennessy Sunday. They drag him outside de bamboo lawn an' brace him 'gainst a wall an' say: 'Are you a man or a woman?' Then dem use a lantern to examine him feet an' conclude it too big to be a woman's feet. *Hehehe*. But even when dem find him out dey cut him loose. Yes. An' only sayin' 'Battybwoy! Battybwoy! Leggo 'bout yah!' An' him was almost home free."

"Home free…" someone echoed.

"But him blood too hot yah, man," the storyteller continued, as if anguished by Jones' recklessness. "Is like him did see a pretty coffin wha' him like. De idiot turn back an' dash weh him freedom – dash weh him life. Even when him other transgender friend pullin' him arm an' tellin' him, 'Walk wid me. Walk wid me.' Him turn right back roun' an' confront de man dem."

The teeth-sucking woman cried, "Dat was de voice of Jesus!"

The storyteller now had everybody's attention. "Then somebody pull him bra strap an' him run – de battybwoy run! – an' dem run him dung an' beat an' stab him an' shot him an' run him over wid dem car – twice!"

"That's jus' overdoin' a t'ing," said a sky-juice vendor languidly, who was sitting in a tree beside his cart, looking down at the street theatre.

"Two hours," said the storyteller, holding up two fingers. "Two hours dem beat him for, before dey drop a buildin' block on him head an' mercifully finish him." He finished with a voice that was a mixture of scorn and pathos, "But wha' him tink was goin' to happen? Who him tink him is, Daniel in de lion's den? Dyin' an' sayin' wid him final breaths: 'Diego Tobago see an' know…'

The sky-juice vendor was at a loss. "Why him never satisfy wid goin' to de underground gay parties?"

Jesus Saves shot back, "That's victim blaming."

Someone said, "Only de rich battybwoy dem go deh suh. Dey wouldn't let him in. Gays prejudice 'gainst gays. Yuh never know?"

"I say de real victims were de men he deceived when he was dancin' wid dem."

Jesus Saves addressed the storyteller: "Brother, were you part of the murderous mob?"

The storyteller made no comment.

DJ Bones chanted *Murderer! Blood is on yuh shoulder. Kill I today yuh cannot kill I tomorrow!*

Jesus Saves looked pleased, watching the talking continue in earnest. He had them where he wanted them, debating and thinking things over in an open forum. They'd got there themselves and after the talking petered out, people could be seen sifting through all that was said. Only the sky-juice vendor could be heard smacking his lips and slurping what was left in the bottom of the bag. Jesus Saves finally said, "Listen to me, everyone of yuh here. All de police are doin' is using their 'war' against these 'undesirables' as an excuse to half-ass the Charleston Jones investigation, just as they're doing now with the Montego 36."

String Bean joined him on the ledge. He waved a banner of a blown-up image of Dennis that had appeared in the papers. The crowd roared and cheered. A woman beside me clasped her hands and turned to me wide-eyed: "They drained the mud lake but they didn't find a single soul. He's alive. I can feel it. Can you feel it?" Dennis had been consecrated for the purpose of this moral campaign – and had entered the bloodstream of the city.

I wondered about the "change" that Jesus Saves spoke of? Could I be a part of it?

Someone called out, "Jesus, you started this movement. You first drew attention to this injustice, an' now they're profitin' from it."

Others sounded their agreement, though it wasn't clear to me who "they" were.

Jesus Saves raised a calming hand. "Friends, you've known me long enough to know I have no appetite for politics. I am only the voice crying in the wilderness." He pointed across the street, behind the crowd to where the old man who'd earlier been shooed away was lying on the pavement by a pool of vomit. Blackbirds had landed and picked at it. "Look at that," Jesus Saves said, shaking his head. He addressed the man who'd attacked the old man, "Brother, just now you shunned that poor defenceless man. But I tell you, in his own way he spoke truth, and the least you do to one such as himself, you do to me."

"Good Teacher," the man replied, "if you only knew who that man is, or was, you would cry shame. That is none other than Maurice Picknight, the great Picknight who used to own half the gas stations in Montego Bay. Now look at him, lyin' in filth, throw 'way him life an' business because of heroin. Now him don't have dry shit in his ass to call his own."

The crowd buzzed. Some thought they recognised him, had known the name when it was important.

"Yet he has a claim to the rights and freedoms we take for granted. He needs our help, not our scorn."

Another man asked, "But how can you help some o' dem when dem seem hellbent on destroyin' themselves?"

Jesus Saves considered the question. "All I know is that when the crows drink the vomit of that poor devil, we will all swallow the bitterness."

The sky jumped with lightning and thunder. Wind came and you could smell the rain coming. People dispersed. The smooth gestapo walked across the courthouse lawn to get into his radio car. He was, after all, one of the plainclothes officers tasked with monitoring Jesus Saves and his campaign.

That evening when we got home, we stopped by Tristan's house. Clare said he'd left, had packed some of his things and gone to his father's in Knockpatrick, out in the country. He had left a message on the table saying he'd stay for a week, so she shouldn't worry, though she thought it odd he'd gone at all, and so suddenly. He and his father weren't exactly on friendly terms. Luckily, she didn't question us.

The next day, when we returned to school, was tense. We spent most of the morning holed up at the Pav, armed to the teeth. But the fallout never came. Alvaranga came to school later than us, and brought his father with him to bring pressure to bear on Jeffrey and his lackeys. So they backed off, for now, anyway.

It was later that day that we heard the full story of what had allegedly taken place, that had caused the boys to assault Tristan. Apparently Marco, a boy from 11-4, had been walking by the cafeteria late that evening, when he heard strange sounds coming from Raymond's office. Upon investigation – silently prying and peeping through the office window – he saw Raymond and Tristan "doing the business". Naturally he was traumatised, but held his nerves to stay long enough to see the act through, then reported his discovery first thing the next day.

Tristan had football training on Wednesdays, so we'd left him behind. But there was more.

Later, as we sat having lunch outside the Lower Sixth study room, one of the security guards, short and thickset, with powdery sweat marks decorating his blue uniform shirt, shambled up the slope towards us, huffing with each step. He didn't introduce himself, didn't try to be friendly, so we kept on eating, waiting for him to speak. "Your friend came here dis mornin'," he said, "'bout half past ten. I was sittin' by de main gate. I said to him, 'Man, if I was you, I wouldn't set foot on dis property.'"

"Why you tell him that?" I said.

The guard's mouth fell open, his heavy jowls drooping in dark damp rings of fat round his neck. "You don't hear what dem boys settin' to do? Plannin' to lynch him on sight! They swearin' up an' down dat if him ever cross dat gate, they skin him clean. I told him so."

"What him do when you told him that?" Harry asked.

"He never say a word," the guard said. "Just give de place a good long look, then turn an' walk 'way. You boys should be careful. Trouble don't set like rain." He shambled back downhill to his post.

Indeed all eyes were now on us, boys all over the Upper School spoiling for confrontation. In the span of a few hours, we had gone from a state of simmering hostilities to a ceasefire to clear and present danger. But we stayed calm. For now, we were conditionally safe.

CHAPTER 13 – THE BAILEY HOUSE TRIAL

I felt as if I had failed Tristan again. As much as I didn't want to believe what I'd heard about him, I wouldn't have been surprised if it were true. I felt threatened by this new commotion, insecure and exposed. I was angry, too – irrational as I knew it was. I felt he'd done what he did – if the story was true – intentionally to hurt me. So far our search for him had been fruitless. He hadn't returned to school, and when I visited his father's house in Knockpatrick, Philpot was surprised to learn his son hadn't been to school, since he dressed in his uniform every morning and did his "bookwork" at the table every night. He didn't, though, appear overly concerned with his son's affairs. When he asked me what Tristan's favourite subject was and I told him it might be math or accounts, the look on Philpott's face said the question had been superficial, so I stopped talking.

With the heat on at school, we were spending more time off campus. We had lunch in the city everyday except Thursdays, when the cafeteria served callaloo loaves, their speciality.

One Wednesday, on my own, I ran into Jesus Saves at the delicatessen at the intersection of Union and St James Streets. He was sitting at the back of the shop, a confusion of papers spread before him, and odd boxes and bags at his feet. I bought lunch and slid silently into the seat before him. He didn't look up, just pushed a sheet of paper across the table. "What does this look like?"

I studied the sheet. "It looks like a comic strip."

"Exactly, a one-panel comic strip to be precise. This is Papa Boar, Mama Boar and the two boar children."

The Boar family were standing upright by the side of a road, dressed in camping clothes, boots, floppy hats and carrying fishing rods and creels. They were looking up at a sign that had the silhouette of a boar against a background of crosshairs. The sign read: **Hunting Season Is Now Open**. Mama Boar says: "I think I have some leftovers in the fridge."

"Well, what do you think?" he asked.

"Hmm… it needs work, but it has potential."

He puckered his lips. "You're right." Then he gave me his attention, peering into my face. "Young Garvey, what's troubling you?"

"What makes you think anything is wrong?"

"You're here by yourself, aren't you? I've never seen you without your friends."

"I just need some time alone, that's all."

He peered at me, knocking his pencil against his gold tooth, his stare like a doctor's probing a patient. "You know, when I was a boy, my mother took me with her to the fish market every Thursday and we would walk from stall to stall inspecting, trying to figure out which was actually that day's catch. She always said: 'James, the brighter the eyes, the fresher the fish,' over and over, like a mantra." He jabbed the pencil at me. "You, my friend, are no fresh fish. You weren't caught today. There's a strain in your eyes."

"I'm fine," I said. "How about this? Mama Boar says nothing. They're just standing there, well dressed and obviously civilised, feeling fully integrated into human society, and obviously out on the hunt themselves, looking up at the sign. Let the irony of the scenario be the punch line."

He considered this and grinned. "Of course. That's it! The picture is the punch line. How could I have missed it?"

Immediately he began his revisions, his head bowed.

I started eating. "Ugh, this croissant is terrible," swallowing with some difficulty.

"I know," Jesus Saves said. "It's like the fat woman round the back bakes them under her armpits."

I stifled a laugh. "What are you going to do with them? Your drawings – they're rather good."

"Oh, nothing noble like submitting them to the *Sun* or anything like that. Thank you by the way. It's just idle doodling to keep me occupied over the next forty days."

I stopped chewing. "What's happening over the next forty days?"

"You haven't heard? My wilderness experience starts today. There are forty days to go to Election Day. I'm going to use them to protest outside the Parish Council."

I stared at him in bewilderment. "You mean live like a bum?"

He stopped drawing and narrowed his eyes. "Tell me, Young Garvey, what do you think of the homeless, truthfully?"

I gulped. "I don't know that I *think* anything. I know they exist. I see them everyday. But I've never had occasion to consider their circumstance. They're just there, I guess, kinda like… background."

He stabbed the space between us with his pencil. "That's what I'm trying to change. We acknowledge their humanity only when their rights are abused, when their circumstance, as you say, impinges on our own in some way." He licked his thumb and rifled through the sheaf of papers, trying to find a clean sheet. It occurred to me that I always ran into him in various shops and restaurants, though I never saw him eating, and when vendors gave him food on the street, they never asked for money. "Mayor Gallimore is worse," he said. "To him they're just squashed dog mess. Now he's frantically trying to scrape the stink off his shoe."

A woman sitting near us said, "Some of us are eating here."

A man in a white apron behind the counter said, "Jesus, I was there for the crucifixion but I didn't stay for the burial."

The woman said, "Some of us like to take the Lord for a poppy show."

Jesus Saves said to the man, "Well, brother, as you can see, the grave couldn't hold me."

The man laughed. "Give 'em hell, brother. The whole a Montego Bay is behind you."

The woman said, "If that is the case, the whole city needs a straitjacket."

I said, "I was also at your crucifixion. Who left the Tyger to watch over the Lamb? William Blake, right?"

Jesus Saves winked at me. "No fooling the scholar is there?"

I smiled. "But let me ask you something; hasn't nature showed us that for the Tyger to devour the Lamb is the way of the world?"

Jesus Saves twiddled the pencil between his fingers. "The Taoists say nature is impartial, that it takes no sides, that rain falls on all fields and the tides rise regardless of who stands on the shore. We humans are agents of nature but also agents of conscience. I believe it's every man's duty to protect the defenceless from the passion of the predator. Mind you, the Tyger lurks in all of us, the impulse to take advantage of the weak and unprotected, which is why, as much as we decry the mayor's wrongdoing, we must also find it necessary to forgive him, to understand his motives without sympathising with them."

I wondered where this man, whom I'd never taken seriously before, found his depth of courage. I tried screwing up my own. "Can I tell you something?"

"I've been waiting."

But in the end, the furthest I got was telling him how we'd harassed Dennis that day at the beach. My burden wasn't lifted. My stomach was still in knots.

Jesus Saves was compassionate. "Everyone makes mistakes. Besides, you were just a child. I'm sure Dennis doesn't hold it against you. And it's your lucky day; your road to redemption starts here. Here, help me carry these bags up Union Street."

As we were leaving, the Chinese proprietor, a short elderly man, stringy-looking with nervous hands and a shy smile, emerged from the door behind the cashier's chair to hand Jesus Saves a bag of freshly baked loaves. He awkwardly fastened two pins with the shop's logo on Jesus's olive-green trench coat. It was a promotional deal, Jesus Saves later told me. As long as he wore the lapel pins, the proprietor would provide him with food for every day of his protest.

I wasn't prepared to see a crowd of eager spectators lining both sides of the street, waiting to catch a glimpse of their hero before he started his vigil. When he emerged, they broke into spirited cheering. He received the adulation impassively. I wished I could make myself smaller, holding up the black rucksack like a barrier between me and the crowd. A fat man with a heavy, shapeless, clean-shaven face shoved a black microcassette recorder towards Jesus Saves. "Jesus, what do you hope to achieve with your latest move?"

"The cause is the same," Jesus Saves replied. "I'm just following the people's mandate." His tone was clipped, as if the weight of his undertaking was beginning to sink in.

The reporter looked at me. "And who is your disciple?"

"This... this is Young Garvey, a fellow humanitarian."

"Hail, Young Garvey!" someone shouted. The refrain was picked up.

I smiled through my teeth, waving feebly. The reporter asked, "Young man, do you remember me?"

It took a while, but I finally did. He was the man who'd interviewed me that morning at the *Sun's* office, after I'd won my scholarship. He was a slimmer man then, with facial hair as I recalled. I said that I did. He shoved the tape recorder at me. "Are you here on your school's behalf?"

"I – I'm here for myself, just trying to do my part."

"And what part is that?"

I tried putting some heft into my voice. "To help my fellow men, regardless of their station in life." The applause was encouraging. "I don't think it's ever too early to start."

The reporter gave me a sly look; he smiled at his colleague. "No," he said, "I suppose not."

An old prostitute named Baby, once a beauty who'd grown scraggy and vinegar-faced, emerged from the crowd carrying a slice of watermelon and offered it to Jesus Saves. She said she couldn't afford a whole one, so she'd bought a slice with her few remaining coins. Jesus Saves was moved. He could hardly articulate his thanks. But many people grumbled, mostly the women. A man remarked, "She could have offered him much worse." This brought titters from the men. Jesus Saves gave the man a reproving stare and took a bite of the juicy pink flesh, then offered the fruit to Baby. She giggled foolishly and demurred, but Jesus Saves insisted. She pushed the lank hair from her face and cupped his hand, craning her neck forward to bite into the fruit, slurping, sucking, licking the juice from her lips and the corners of her mouth. An elderly man said warmly, "That's it ol' girl. Don't waste a drop." The performance of sharing the fruit was absorbing. No one could take their eyes off them.

The march on the Parish Council began. The people moved up the street singing: *We will follow King Jesus till we die!* Others began singing the Wailers: *"We're comin' in, comin' in, comin' in, comin' in, comin' in, comin' in, comin' in, comin' in from de co-o-old."*

I walked to the right of Jesus Saves. Baby was on his left. She locked arms with him, skipping and swaying the edge of her skirt. Strangers slapped my back and tugged at my shoulders. I'd never felt like a bigger fraud in my entire life.

The Wailers's song on the people's lips – IT'S YOU – IT'S YOU – IT'S YOU I'M TALKING TO! seemed insistently and oppressively accusing. I kept thinking: Yes, I am ready for my day of reckoning, ready for it to consume me from root to tip.

Returning to school, I took the back way through Fuller and climbed the cracked steps in front of Bailey House. I saw Stennett sitting by himself in the gazebo outside his dormitory building. He was hunched over, biting his nails and wobbling his big thighs together. When he saw me, he looked relieved, as if I'd rescued him from the torment of solitude. Since Harry's insinuation about his past at Munro, he'd been spending more time away from us, even taking his lunch by the dorm, which only strengthened our belief that the story was true. But our own troubles meant we had no time to pursue the matter further. Now he jumped up as I hurried past. "Chauncey, wait, can I talk to you?"

I slowed down, my back to him.

"Listen, I know I've been a bit scarce lately…" He laughed timidly. "Just trying to catch up with school work is all."

"Nothing wrong with beating the books," I said.

"Hell, we've all been busy right? It's not like –"

I turned to face him. "What is it you want, Stennett?"

"Chauncey, I just want you to know… I just want to say…"

"To say what? Spit it out, man!"

"I just want you to know that whatever you've been hearing about me, not a word of it is true. It's nothing more than a smear campaign. Just boys being mean. I admit I have enemies. But I have no secrets."

"If you have nothing to hide, then why spend all your time holed up in the dorm, eh? Why don't you just clear the air an' tell us what really happened. Because you can't tell us nothing happened. We're not fools. Nobody that mean to slander somebody without reason."

"Chauncey, you've always been reasonable. I always felt out of all the guys I could talk to you." His voice quavered. "I guess what I'm getting at is… even if something did happen, not that I'm saying anything did, it's no basis for you guys to judge me now. The Stennett that you know, the one standing before you, is the real deal. Your friendship and support mean everything to me."

I stepped back and smiled tauntingly. "So it is true!"

"No!" he shouted, shaking his head vigorously. "It wasn't like that. You have to believe me. I'd never do that! And if I caught anyone trying to do such a thing, I'd wring the nasty faggot's neck myself!"

"What's this – your self-hate phase?"

He looked miserable.

"Frankly, Stennett, I'm not trying to hear your woes right now. I have my own problems."

He was silent, hands in his pockets, staring at the pebbles he moved around on the ground, back and forth in an aimless way. "You know what it feels like to wake up every day and step out of my room? It's like stepping out of a plane without a fucking parachute. I'm tired of the suspense. I can't wait to hit the pavement and be done with it."

I was almost sorry for him. "Yea? Well I guess I overestimated you. Don't you see we all in free-fall now? Don't you see you have to find a way to survive? You think I have time to care what happens to you or anyone else?"

A kind of recklessness inflamed his eyes, the skin beneath his eyelids stretched tight. "You is a real sonofabitch, eh, Chauncey." His anger caught me by surprise. I'd never seen him so self-possessed. "Real hardhearted sonofabitch! Don't care, eh?" His voice flattened to a low threatening snarl. "Well, I'm going to make you care, mister. Just watch."

I walked away as if I hadn't heard him.

The trial took place that evening, in the circular ruins of the little amphitheatre in the basement of the burnt-out shell of Bailey House. Tristan was being tried in absentia for his alleged crimes against the "ethos" of the school community. We were to be witnesses. This was serious business, a Chester tradition dating back to the founding years.

The stage was set. Boys from the Upper School sat on the crumbling concrete steps that formed a semicircle round the old performance pit, the rows of seats going up for eight levels; on the opposite end of the amphitheatre, to the right of the seating area, was the witness box, an old disused lectern that stood on a dais raised two and a half feet off the floor, with a tall wooden stool behind it. There were no jurors, only judges: a delegation of New Lots members, nine in all, seated to the right of the witness box on a long mahogany bench on a decrepit stage platform about five feet higher than the witness box. The New Lots Society was Chester College's secret fraternity, almost as old as the school itself, and definitely the oldest fraternity in Jamaica. Past members included the pick of the elite, from the first Jamaican ambassador to the UN to Mayor Gallimore himself. None of this, of course, was public knowledge; you got wind of it through snatches of conversation picked up across campus.

It was past six, the sky flushed dark pink, with smudges of vermillion from a fading sunset; in the belly of the beast it was even darker. The New Lotters were dressed in full academic garb: school blazers, ties, graduation gowns and graduation caps, the tassels sweeping their faces. Weak light from an overhead bulb illuminated the witness box; an electricity line had been run across the yard from the pantry; another bulb dimly illuminated the judges, though their faces remained obscure. Only the head judge who sat in the middle, the bulb dangling directly over his head, was recognisable: it was the Beer Kaiser. He had returned as the former leader of the Society to sit in on the case. The other eight judges were most likely Upper Sixth form boys, whose identities were kept secret; each was to be formally addressed as Brother Leader Justice, with the collective body titled Brother Leaders Justice. The Beer Kaiser bore the title of Supreme Brother Leader Justice, his frog face sour below a powdered wig, his distinguishing feature. A scribe sat to their left behind a worm-eaten desk at a typewriter, waiting to start his transcript. As witnesses, we sat in the front row, on the lowest rung of steps.

Mumbling sounds above our heads rose and fell, swelled and subsided, like the wings of a gigantic fly. When the Beer Kaiser banged his gavel, a hush followed, terrible in its suddenness. I was the first witness summoned. Walking over slowly to the witness box, I took my place behind the lectern. The scribe, from his elevated seat to my right, said: "Good Citizen, state your full name for the record, please."

"My name is Chauncey Fritz Knuckle."

Someone in the crowd said, "Now if that's not the name of a queer then I –"

"SILENCE!" The Beer Kaiser's baritone boomed.

"Place your right hand on the school's handbook before you, and raise your left. Do you swear to tell the absolute truth so help you, God?"

"I do."

"Take your seat."

The questions from the judges were questions I had anticipated, but feigned effort in answering. Almost every judge asked a variation of the same question: if we'd noticed anything "untoward", "problematic" or "unseemly" in Tristan's behaviour, anything inconsistent with Chester's "ethos" (this word was their favourite), before the reputed incident at the cafeteria. We had all agreed to say no, because to say otherwise would mean trouble; they would have asked us why we hadn't come forward before or taken action in some way; it would mean that we'd been complicit. We had to make sure that everyone understood this.

After my examination, it was Mola's turn, then Harry's; the final one to take the stand was Alvaranga. Things were proceeding relatively smoothly.

Then they summoned Marco.

"When did you witness the incident in question?"

"7:18 p.m. on Wednesday of last week."

"You seem pretty sure of the time."

"It could have been later but definitely not sooner, Brother Leader Justice. I know this because I'd just finished cadet training at 7:10 p.m."

"What business did you have passing by the back of the cafeteria? Surely that's out of your regular route?"

"I was taking a shortcut back to the dormitory."

"Are you a boarder?"

"Yes, Brother Leader Justice."

Beside me Harry fumed. "He's a liar!" he whispered. He made to rise from his seat but Alvaranga grabbed him. "Are you mad? They'll eat us alive if we challenge them. Keep your ass quiet and stop being selfish!" That's when it struck me. They didn't care whether Tristan was innocent or guilty; that wasn't the point of the trial: all they wanted was a sacrifice, to make an example of him, to keep the other boys in line. New Lots was notorious for staging witch hunts and sham trials, picking "offenders" as if by lottery, or from hearsay, then convicting them to instill control and fear into the school body, to purge any impurities from young impressionable minds.

One of the New Lots judges noticed the commotion. "Good citizen, is there something you wish to say? Do you wish to approach the box? Have you remembered something you'd like to share with the court?"

Alvaranga pinned Harry firmly down into his seat. "No Brother Leader Justice! Sir!"

"Very well... Shall we proceed with the testimony? Now, Cadet, describe for us the events of that evening."

Marco did so in graphic detail.

"As you were witnessing this... lewdness, did you take any measures to safeguard your own purity?"

Marco considered the question. "Many times, Brother Leader Justice, whenever the lewdness, as you say, got too intense for me to carry on looking. Once it got so disgusting, I had to say, 'No homo', repeatedly."

Some of the boys snickered at Marco's earnestness; he spoke as if he believed this charm actually worked. He was brain dead, we all knew, a dullard who tried to prove how much of a Chesterite he was by burdening himself with extracurricular activities to justify his scholastic failings. Pity was the only thing he deserved.

"Did it ever occur to you, cadet, that you could just have easily looked away than to submit yourself to something so obviously upsetting?" This was from the Beer Kaiser.

The question caught Marco off guard. After a few minutes, he muttered in a pathetic, broken voice, "I'm no faggot..."

After Marco's testimony, the judges went to chambers, the old dilapidated dressing rooms behind the stage, frowsy with termites and all kinds of vermin. It was shabby and ridiculous, like children playing house, but with real people's lives. I was briefly filled with indignation, but it didn't stay with me.

They came back after five minutes with the verdict. Tristan was banned from ever setting foot on campus – tried, convicted and expelled by his peers, without need, it seemed, for intervention from the school's administration. As for us, we were placed on probation, to be monitored by the school community for any "untoward", "problematic", or "unseemly" behaviour, and would suffer banishment if ever we were seen in the accused's company. Sounds of approval rumbled through the stands.

The Beer Kaiser looked at us. "Do any of you have any final statements? Anything to say, perhaps, in your defence?"

Stennett jumped to his feet. There was a commotion. The judges conferred, perhaps telling the Kaiser who Stennett was. Checking his transcript, the Kaiser said, "The chair recognises Brubeck Stennett, the transfer scum that came to us from the cesspool of Munro College." The Kaiser allowed himself a smile. "And who has blossomed into a slightly more tolerable eyesore." The boys laughed and the tension of the proceedings ebbed away.

Stennett had the floor. We could only hope he wouldn't sink us further by saying something foolish. He cleared his throat, "Supreme Brother Leader Justice, honourable members of the Brotherhood, let me come straight to the point. What Tristan has done is a tragedy, but may I implore the Brotherhood to show him mercy. Yes, he's strayed from the fold, violated the natural laws of society and nature. What he needs is not only reproof and correction, but, if I may so venture, mercy. For who among us hasn't, at some point, fallen short of the standards set before us?"

There were disgruntled murmurs from the students. But the Kaiser motioned him to continue.

"Brothers, as we've seen from the scandal surrounding the despicable treatment of the homeless citizens of St James, our society isn't perfect. There's much room for improvement in our attitude towards our underprivileged fellow humans, who through unfortunate circumstances, indolence, or moral weakness, have fallen into a disadvantaged life. Their humanity is too often overlooked, but, as is evident in the spirit of charity sweeping the land, their condition is not beyond rehabilitation. This is the same charity I'm suggesting we show to our fallen brother, the same benevolence I was humbled and grateful to receive as a stranger joining this dignified company from distant shores."

Murmurs peaked again. The Kaiser raised a hand.

"Don't get me wrong," Stennett added. "I'm not seeking to undermine our stance against homosexuality. It should not be confused with the human rights debate unfolding around us, for it is *not* a human rights issue."

"Here, here!" Stennett was finally making sense. One boy said, "But de battyman dem saying if gay rights aren't human rights, then gay people aren't human."

"Rubbish!" Stennett said. "What they need is a course in logic. Their logic is flawed: human beings have human rights, gay people are human beings so therefore gay people have gay rights. No. Gay people do have the same human rights as the rest of us. They do not have gay rights, for those don't exist. Do they want extra rights? More rights than the rest of us? The more sinister among them would have us believe we're being tyrannical, but it's their lobby which is tyrannous, as it seeks to legitimise their lifestyle, impose their brand of morality on the rest of us. Here is the logical argument, brothers: human beings have human rights. Gay rights are not human rights. Therefore human beings do not have gay rights. Their misunderstanding underscores our duty as the educated minority of the country to address these flawed ways of thinking before its corrupting influence spreads."

The applause was deafening. Harry was shocked. "Maybe he's not gay after all." I wasn't convinced. "Maybe he's a quick learner."

"But then, brothers, you'd expect people who spend their lives trying to fit square pegs into wrong holes would be devoid of logic." Laughter. He was on a roll, a contortionist who'd executed a complex aerial manoeuvre and landed on his feet. Even the usually taciturn Brotherhoods Justice laughed openly. They might have given him perfect tens for his performance. I watched Stennett exchange a look with the Beer Kaiser; it seemed a cryptic understanding of each other's motives, a sly acknowledgement. So Stennett, in one brilliantly timed move, achieved the acceptance he had always sought and saved himself. Brimming with confidence, he continued, "So all I'm asking for brothers, out of concern for a regrettably confused soul, is leniency, a chance to reconcile him to the benefits of our collective wisdom, to show him the error of his ways. Why kick a man when he's down? Matter of fact, why kick him at all? We are not, after all, like the hoodlums outside these gates who make their point through violence."

One of the Brother Leaders Justice asked: "And what about you, fatman? How do you stand with the ladies?"

Stennett laughed. "Me, Brother Leader Justice? Let's just say that in the land of snatch, I'm a one-eyed king. My cock is like a monster that needs to be put down."

The Beer Kaiser had to bang his gavel to quell the guffawing. "All right, fatman, we've heard you out and we'll take your request into consideration. But I'd warn against harbouring false hope. The rulings of this court usually stand. Nevertheless" – and the Kaiser's eyes twinkled as he said this – "you've impressed us. That's the courage and brotherliness we like to see our charges display."

Raymond, the other party recognised in the "lewd" act, wasn't brought up on any charges, mock or real, nor was his name even mentioned in the proceedings. He was a benefactor of the Brotherhood and therefore an untouchable.

The lights suddenly went out. The janitors, having finished their cleaning rounds, were closing the main buildings and had thrown the main switch at the Pantry. Panic erupted, boys scurried up the steps towards the main exit like blind rats, bumping into each other. I made it out, breathing the open air deeply. The world had felt strangely compressed, as if reduced to the surface of my skin.

When I arrived home, Girlie was sitting at the kitchen table with her face cupped in her hands. She got up immediately and called, "Mama."

I heard Mama answer from the bathroom, "Dat him, Girlie?"

"Yes ma'am he jus' come. Chauncey where you been? You couldn't call, bwoy? You had us worried sick." I said nothing, dropped my knapsack on the floor and sat at the table. Aunt Girlie saw something was troubling me and she didn't press for a response, didn't even tell me to go wash my hands. She had prepared my favourite meal: yam, green bananas, dumplings and pickled mackerel and she put the plate into the microwave. I didn't have the heart to tell her I had no appetite. She came back with the plate. "You want to eat in the dining room?"

"No thanks, here is fine."

She set it down and sat before me, but I didn't look up, I didn't want to meet her eyes. I poked the fork into the soft yellow yam and steam spurted. Aunt Girlie was speaking, but I didn't reply. She gave up the effort of conversation and got up from the chair. The arch of her back told me my silence made her uneasy and she was waiting for me to speak, but I kept ramming the food down my throat. I looked up and my aunt's attractiveness held my gaze. I watched as she took a scrunchie from the top of the fridge and pulled her hair into a tight ponytail before washing the dishes, her neck small and slender. I felt sharply possessive towards her.

"You enjoying it?" she asked, pouring soap over the sponge.

"Yes," I said, "it's very lovely." I was thinking of her not the food which I couldn't really taste. "You were saying something before, while you sat at the table."

She darted her head around, her beauty stronger in her anger. *What man could deserve this?*

"Is now you feel like talkin?" she said irritably. "I said you didn't wish me a happy birthday. It was las' Saturday."

"Ah! Mi figet! The sixth, me remember, man, jus' forget on de day. Happy belated birthday." I got up and went over and hugged and kissed her. She didn't hug me back but I didn't let her go. I kissed her lips and she pulled her head back, slightly surprised, with a look of amused enquiry. She tried to pull away but I held her fast. She seemed to realise my desperation, or perhaps just gave in to my strength. Now she put her arms around my waist, keeping her soapy hands free, rubbing her wrists against my sides, trying to soothe me.

Girlie, you got all of Mama's beauty but none of her strength.

"Your birthday is my bank code, you know." I recited the series of numbers.

"That's not my birthday," she said sharply, breaking my embrace and turning back to the sink.

222

It was the number on Dr. Sotwae's card. I had been back to see him and we had discussed this business of "family" and "loyalties" in more depth. Looking back now, I see this was the beginning of a separation from all those I loved but couldn't help betraying. I would always carry them somewhere inside me, in the world that was reduced to the surface of my skin that night at Bailey House. That world was the only place where I knew I would be safe from the onslaught to follow. I sat back down to eat. I ate rapidly now without even tasting the pepper on the pickled mackerel. I washed everything down with a glass of water.

Aunt Girlie couldn't help herself; she asked with a forced casualness that didn't fool me. "What number is that by the way?"

"Oh, probably just some exam code," I lied.

"You're doing mock exams now, right?"

"Yes," I said quickly. "That's what held me up today, I was with my study group and lost track of time."

"You're not yourself these days... ever since Tristan moved out. It must be hard not havin' him around for the first time ever in your life." I remembered Papa had once said the same thing, while I'd been thinking about having seen Tristan by Carol's Wall Bridge.

I wiped my mouth with the napkin. "Is that a question?" I corrected myself and continued in a softer tone, "Tristan moved out a long time ago, before he left here, he has long had a new family. Perhaps it's time I move on too, start making new connections."

"Yuh temperature all over de place, eh? One minute yuh hot, de next yuh cold; this second yuh lovey-dovey an' de next yuh tetchy an' thin-skinned." I dropped my eyes, not wanting to meet her questioning stare. I wished Mama would come out of the bathroom and change the course of the conversation. "This edginess of yours... I don't like it. Perhaps you should get a checkup."

"I'm fine, Aunt Girlie. I've been to the doctor; he already gave me advice."

She sighed. "It will pain us all when you finally leave here to go off to school. You've been in my arms since you were a baby, ever since your mother died. I can't have any of my own, an' though I never had any milk in me breasts, I still put them in your mouth come night, an' you suck them till you fall asleep. You remember my birthday on the sixth? I remember the day you born every day because I was there in the room pushin' with Jean, right till yuh come out."

Jean, oh Jean. What exactly did you push out of your vagina?

She made a low, sad laugh.

I brought my plate to the sink. Standing beside her, watching the water beat her bony hands, the light swimming in the shallow saucers between her collarbones and shoulders, I felt I couldn't do without her, the way I knew I would feel about Mama in the days before departure. She looked at me from her eye corner with the smile that made taxi-men jump out of their cars filled with passengers and offer to carry her groceries to the gate.

"You goin' to help me finish these dishes?"

"No – that smile ain't goin' to work tonight."

She huffed good-naturedly. "You goin' to jus' stand there an' stare at me?" She looked disappointed and tightmouthed, the look she'd give me as a boy when, after piggybacking me by the side of the house, she'd feel my hard dick pressing her back. She would set me down and look at me till I felt ashamed for something I couldn't control. *Girlie please, one more ride. No! Playtime is over.* Now she said reprovingly, "You can't have me, Chauncey. You can never have me. Don't look at me like that."

I dropped my head and bit my lip. I said. "You remember that time… you cut off all your hair so low it looked like a man's."

She cackled and glanced at me, then sighed. "Yes… you were about six. An' when you came home from school an' came to my room door an' saw me, you bawled like a baby."

"That's because I thought it would never grow back."

"You refused to have supper that night, an' cried yourself to sleep."

"Why did you do it? Cut your hair?"

"I don't remember, Chauncey; it was so long ago."

"Try, yuh mus' remember, man."

"Why yuh insistin' suh?" She seemed intrigued at the challenge. "Oh yes… I was dating this boy then, an' he refused to let me alone, so I cut off my hair, thinkin' he would dislike it an' finally call it quits."

"Why couldn't you jus' break up with him?"

"He wasn't havin' it. Young men can be that way, Chaunce. They fight to keep something even if they don't really want it. They have to make it ragged first, have their fill, then chuck it, or chaw it like a dawg on a bone tryin' to suck all de juice."

"Well?"

"Well… you have to choose de dawg carefully, an' avoid too many careless fucks. You have to preserve your juice, especially when you're young."

"That's not what I mean," I said. I didn't like it when she talked like this. The bitterness caught me by surprise.

She measured me with her wry smile. "That's exactly what you mean, even if you're pretendin' you don't know. Look at you, all grown up, pawin' bones an' suckin' juice, droppin' careless fucks."

I snorted and looked away.

She laughed at me. "I'm sorry, sweetie… I mean careless toothmarks on bones – didn't mean to upset your sensibilities."

My frustration with her playful crudeness, her denial of the hallowed image of her she knew I cherished, was something that pleased her.

"Well?" I said.

"Well what, bwoy?"

"Did he leave you alone?"

"No more questions, Chauncey. An' here, make yourself useful. Take this rag an' clean de stove top. An' make sure you remove de burners firs' before you clean it. Now, I have a question for you. What did Harding say to you that day on de verandah he kept lookin' at me an' grinning like an ass?"

"You remember that, eh. He said…" But her expression wasn't one that was eager for an answer, just plain, plain placidness. It made me want to know what, if anything, she did take pleasure in. She could sometimes appear angry on the street when a man complimented her looks, or she saw that it had caught his eye. I said, "He said he didn't like that you had put your hair up, that it looked like a bird's nest."

She sniggered softly and lowered her head. "He said that…?"

"God's truth. He said he'd come all the way to my house and had wasted his time."

"You can't always have what you want."

"What do you want, Girlie?"

She set the wet glass carefully into the rack. "I want a baby, Chauncey. I want a baby of my own so bad. Somet'ing to show for all de cock an' cum I keep tekkin. An' all de abuse, too. Things keep goin' inside me, but nothing worthwhile ever comes out."

I felt as if I'd been slapped, and turned away.

She cocked her head. "Yuh askin'… so I tellin.' Look at me, bwoy; does your aunt still look like a juicy bone?" She held my chin with her wet fingers and jerked my face to focus on her. "Look at me!" I stiffened and pulled away from her clasp. "What yuh cryin' fo'? Yuh have tears to waste? OK… say I leave Reds, which I know you an' everybody dyin' to see, say I leave Reds, you think the good master Harding, even if he was of a marryin' mind, would marry me when he knows I cyan mek baby?" Another tear slipped down my face. She stamped her foot. "Stop yuh bloodclaat cryin'! Dis fuckin' pity-party everybody willin' to lavish on me like a baby shower!" She laughed dryly again. "Don't cry, mi bwoy, dat is life. Maybe Harding will chaw the bone a bit yes, suck some more juice – Lawd knows I don't have a lot left – but will he keep it? Will he wrap it in a bow an' keep it? For what? He ain't stupid."

I wiped under my eyes with my thumb and middle finger. If I had looked at her face, stark in its frankness, the tears would've flowed again, so I didn't look.

"Reds has been gnawin' dis fuckin' useless bone so long now he might as well finish it. He's earned it. He bad but he ain't bad as all dat. He ain't as bad as they all mek him out to be. So what if they talkin' bout girl pregnant for him? Who to say it's his? De licks hurt yes… but even bad dawgs have to eat."

She finished washing up as if nothing had happened. Through the window the night was black and quiet, save for the black-masked bird's singing. "Tell me something nice, Chauncey, woo your aunty with the beauty of your words."

She bit her pink full lip, the way Marzipan always did when she orgasmed. I said, "That yellowthroat is going to sing till it swallows a mouthful of the darkness, then another mouthful, and yet another, till it swallows the dark trees and the wood, and the seas, till it sucks the whole earth under its skin. And swallows your sadness too." She turned off the tap and looked hard at me as if wondering where the words had come from. Then the bathroom door clicked open and both of us became self-conscious. I knew Mama was heading straight for the kitchen, and knew I had only minutes to tell Girlie all that she meant to me.

"I remember when I was small and Clare would call Tristan home and I was left lonely, I always went to Sheila first, but he'd tell me he was too tired and I should play with my toys from America, but whenever I came to you, you always put down your novel and played with me till it was time for dinner."

Now she smiled with such genuine happiness it restored something of my good feeling. "Yes, you owe me big time for all those books brought back to the library too late. What you gettin' me for my birthday?"

I looked down the open armpit of her dress to her breasts with their short, crusty nipples. "A bra," I said.

She cackled and covered her mouth, then splashed the suds at my face. I ached for her. Behind me Mama said, first to Girlie, with that power of hers that reminded me no secret was safe, "Yes, a man is a man, an' beer is beer, even if yuh pour it in a dirty boot an' drink it, but that's de bitterness of life, drinkin' beer from a dirty boot." Girlie ignored her. Then Mama said to me, "An' you – comin' home all hours a night these days, an' you don't know who is who in dark taxi, who is good, bad or in between. I want to know if you t'ink 'bout all dat. Giddy like nutten ever since you have house key jigglin' in your pocket. But you watch dat giddiness. Fire deh a mus-mus tail him t'ink a cool breeze."

CHAPTER 14 – THE CONFRONTATION

Tristan had surfaced. The story making the rounds was that he'd been spotted driving around in Colors's black and yellow Nissan Pathfinder. Apparently, he was working at a mall in the city, running a video game arcade operated by the Fire-Clappers crew.

Colors was Montego Bay's most famous motorcycle stuntman and racecar driver; he also happened to be its most celebrated philandering homosexual. He would throw lavish parties on Labour Day and Christmas, would get Ronny McKnight to host his annual bike-a-thons, then on New Year's Eve it was his "All White Party" aboard his yacht by Pier One, attended by the who's who of Montego Bay, from the mayor to the archbishop. Come September there was the "Back to School" fundraiser, where he gave away books and pencils and hugs to needy children. He was a hero, plain and simple, a philanthropist and the greatest rally racer "Team MoBay" had ever known, and Montegonians live and die by their motor sports. To malign him in some areas of the Bay was to court death. All things considered, it was a non-issue that he was homosexual, that he was notorious for sleeping with schoolboys (sometimes, allegedly, with the consent of impoverished parents whom he paid off). I had witnessed grown men who, out of pure bravado, had sworn to chop Colors limb from limb if he walked too close to them on the street, grabbing his hand, kissing it and giggling like schoolgirls at the Caribbean Rally Championships in Ironshore, after he had led Team Jamaica to victory.

In a similar vein, discussion of a cafeteria boycott, feeble to begin with, had petered out. Raymond hardly attracted so much as a bad comment. The cafeteria still prospered. He had eyes and ears among us, too.

We, on the other hand, were relegated to the status of school scum. Alvaranga's prospects of being elected head boy plummeted. Saul Christie won in a landslide, without even campaigning.

Immature pranks followed: oversized dicks drawn on our chair seats; forming a "shame circle" around us at morning assembly; or falling out of the cafeteria line as soon as we stepped in. The janitors were even paid to hose down the concrete outside the Lower Sixth study room where we had lunch. We were outcasts, without recourse to teachers or the administration. Perhaps the biggest change in our circumstances was Stennett's desertion. Soon after his bravura performance at the Bailey House trial, he took leave of our company, and now moved in an elite circle. Mola reported, "You hear he's been approached by New Lots right?" The induction ceremony traditionally took the form of a marriage, complete with the inductee, the bride, wearing a white gown and tying the knot in Bailey House's decrepit chapel, symbolically being married to the brotherhood. It was a members' only affair, of course. And as much as boys scoffed at its ironic, homoerotic tone, most would have given their little fingers to walk down the aisle carrying the bridal bouquet. "The fucker," Harry said. "He saved himself and left us in the shit."

"You'd have done the same," Alvaranga said. "You just didn't think of it first."

We took the shortcut through St. Helena's cemetery on our way to the arcade to see Tristan.

We had been anxious all day, the prospect of seeing him after so long made us strangely awkward with each other. "I wouldn't believe Marco's story for a minute," said Mola. "Tristan could have any girl him want over by Helena's. Could even fuck the nuns."

"Fine time to talk," said Harry. "Why you never speak up at Bailey House?"

"But what reason Marco have to lie?" I said.

"Maybe him holdin' a grudge 'gainst Tristan," Mola replied. "Maybe somebody pay him to do it. The way Tristan carryin' on these days him bound to make enemies."

"I don't know," Russell said, "I just don't know…"

We went down St Helena's hill and crossed the pedestrian walk by the clock tower over to Kent Avenue & Fort. On the stonewall below the cannon, the gigolo's credo was written in black spray paint: *By the sweat of your balls you shall eat bread.* Harry chuckled. "You remember that Wednesday Tristan scored the winning goal 'gainst Mannings, an' the Helena girls get on like hooligans when him throw him jersey at them after the game?"

Mola nodded. "Even the *stoosh* ones who wouldn't spit in your mouth if you're thirsty. Even if he's guilty of what Marco said – God forbid – is it right for the school to treat him the way they did an' demand we do the same?"

"Sanjay, you're missing the point," said Alvaranga. "We don't get to evaluate what's right and what's wrong."

Sanjay said, "Tristan is the one-armed swordsman."

"Like Fang Kang?" asked Harry.

"Yeah."

"How you figure?"

"When the swordsman lost his arm, what was the first thing all the toughs wanted to do?"

"Pick on him," I said.

"Because…?"

"Because his vulnerability was plain."

Harry said, "I see where you're goin' with this… No I don't see where you're goin' with this."

Sanjay said, "And when he lost his arm, what was the first thing Fang Kang thought to do?"

"To place himself in self-imposed exile, to run away," I said.

"Exactly, because he thought he was less of a man, that he was no longer fit for the sword school, the only world he knew. But he was wrong wasn't he?"

"Now I see where you're goin' with this," said Harry. "The half-burnt manual that taught him left-hand swordplay was enough to make him a complete swordsman, more powerful even than if he had trained ambidextrously at the sword school."

Sanjay said, "Yeah, but Xiao Man's love makes him realise an even more powerful truth, that he was a complete man all along, with or without both arms, and with or without the mastery of the sword. In fact the discovery of the sword manual only reimposes limitation on his life. At the end when he disavows the swordsman's life and chooses a simple life with Xiao Man – the only non-judgmental person he's ever come across – he chooses freedom."

"Are you saying Tristan's banishment is his freedom?" asked Harry.

"I'm saying the philosophy of the sword school is irrelevant when the embattled swordsman realises he's the only one who can put limitations on himself by accepting the limitations of his society. But sometimes he needs a watershed, or a Xiao Man, or both to realise this."

"Well, that's just fine and dandy," Russell said, "but this isn't the movies. We live in a society. We live in a culture. We have to live within that culture. I don't want to try to change the culture because I can't. It's too big. That's what Stennett figured out and that's why he's not with us anymore."

We turned into a narrow lane and passed some hardhats working on a light pole. Their flagman, an old retired pick-pocket named Bawn-a-Bay – so named because of his perpetual boast that no matter how loathsome he was, he was a Montegonian born and bred – was sitting on the curb, drowsy and half drunk in the afternoon. He ignored us until he saw our Chester epaulettes, then stood up and doffed his hardhat.

"Young sirs."

We returned the nod and passed. Mola said, "There's no lout as idle as the flagman is there?"

"Idleness begins and ends with them, Sanjay," said Harry.

Bawn-a-Bay overheard these remarks and released a spate of obscenities so foul we looked at each other with frozen grins. Then he beat his bony chest like a drum, shouting, "I'm a Montegonian, jus' like all a yuh! I bawn up a Cornwall Regional hospital an' yuh can check me buth sutificate if yuh don't believe. I bawn a Bay! An' who can tek dat from me? Not a livin' soul! I don't go to no fancy school. I don't get no education – an' nobody go drive me outta Bay. I cyan tell a nex' man how to wear him pants, an' I don't want nobody try tell me how to wear mine! Mi nah go draw up meself or live under rock-stone fe please none a oonuh! Nobody nuh more dan mi!" He beat his chest again. "See me yah! Big dutty stinkin' Bawn-a-Bay! Tek it or leave it – but I nah seek nuh buyer. Remember dat!" He took very slow steps back to the curb and sat back down.

Harry walked over and touched his shoulder. "Bawn-a-Bay,

sorry man. Why yuh carryin' on suh? We didn't mean any disrespect."

He made a bitter face and waved Harry off. "Go yuh ways, schoolbwoy; leave me in peace."

Harry took out his wallet and dropped fifty dollars into Bawn-a-Bay's hardhat. We all walked over and dropped money into his hat. When Bawn-a-Bay saw how much was there, he released a short choking sob, then lost control and wept. We walked away, silent for a long stretch. Then Harry said, "You know he goin' to buy rum this very minute. Let him drink."

Sanjay said, "I feel like I jus' throw flowers on a casket."

I said, "You know Bawn-a-Bay goin' to get de biggest funeral yet. De whole Bay goin' to show up."

"Fuck all a dem," said Sanjay. "They force him to crawl on his belly his whole life. When he go rum bar they scorn him so much they serve him in a cup wid his name on it. If he walk by City Centre or de tourist zone, police drive him back wid blows. So wha' they showin' up for? Bawn-a-Bay is right. If they didn't love you in life, they nah go love yuh in death."

Russell appeared deep in thought. Then he said, "Marco is a damn liar. There's no doubt in my mind. But at the same time I feel there's something at the bottom of it, an' Tristan's hands ain't clean."

"Well you gettin' the perfect opportunity to ask him face to face," I said.

We said nothing more. Somehow we all knew we weren't heading for a friendly reunion.

When we got to the mall, we climbed the stairs up to the games arcade, thought about going inside – already teeming with school-boys who'd cut school to stack up on tokens and sit round their favourite games all afternoon – then decided to send word instead by one of the two grim-faced men sitting outside to inform Tristan we'd come to see him.

He had changed. He had gained weight; fat in his face had softened his sharp features and made his eyes look small and sleepy; he had also grown out his hair into a frizzy, bleached-bronze Afro.

"Tristan!" Harry exclaimed, making a fist and stepping forward for a friendly dap. Tristan stepped back. Harry blinked in surprise, his arm hovering before falling limply to his side.

Tristan was unsmiling and unfriendly. "What you want?"

Mola was eying the two security thugs. He said to Tristan, "Can we speak in private?"

Tristan bit down on the toothpick dangling between his teeth.

One of the thugs said, "Dem botherin' you, Tristan?"

"No Stumpy, everyt'ing cool." He said this in an easy way, showing us he had clout, then walked over to the balcony rail and jammed his foot against the bars, levelling a cold gaze that took us all in, then looked over our heads dismissively. "Say what you come to say an' leave. I can't stand out here all day."

We stalled. Then Mola said, "Tristan listen, we know you had it rough these past days but –"

"Wrong," he interrupted. "You don't know a fuckin' thing. But who you-all think you be, eh? What you think would happen when you come here today? 'Bout you *know*. What you know, eh, Sanjay? Tell me?"

Mola shrugged, looking around as if to say he'd given it a shot and now it was someone else's turn.

"We're not your enemies, Tristan," Harry said. "You know that. We're on your side."

Tristan laughed bitterly. "An' what side is that? You not afraid they turn you outta school, too? I hear they have you all on probation. What if they hear 'bout this little meeting? Plenty Chester boys inside, you know. You not afraid they see you an' report it? You sure you want to be on *my* side?" I could see he wasn't angry, as I'd thought. He was enjoying himself.

Something ruptured inside me. Things were going too easy for him, and all wrong for us. This was not what we'd come for. I felt the sudden urge to hurt him, because he was hurting us – me. But it was more than that. My feelings of guilt were rising so thickly it felt like a wave of nausea. To avoid the sickness, I focused my anger on him.

I stepped forward. He braced up off the rail and stood erect, his feet apart and his shoulders up. He had been eying me ever since we came, waiting for me to speak, and now he looked as if he anticipated an attack. The security thugs stood up.

"How dare you?" I said. "How could *you* do this to us? Do you know the hell you've put us through these past days? An' yet you stand here actin' like we owe you something. You're the coward who ran, while we stayed at school shovellin' shit, takin' all the heat and fightin' your battles. Havin' people scorn us and treat us like dogs when we didn't do shit to them. So don't stand there actin' self-righteous an' smug like we owe you something, because we don't! We didn't tell you to go suck some man's dick for lunch money."

He launched, catching me flatfooted. He used the back of his hand, slightly cupped, to raise his knuckles and bring them in contact with my nose bridge, the tips of his fingers extending up to my eyes. An acute pain shot through my face; water sprang to my eyes. The move was calculated. It was what a stronger person does to a weaker one, to establish dominance, more so than to inflict pain. What a father might do to a son, or a man to a girlfriend or wife, an alpha-male to a weakling. The way he did it in public, too, standing there relaxed, waiting for retaliation, welcoming it, was a challenge that, if I walked away from, would once and for all define our relationship. I leaned over to steady myself, tears blurring my vision. I thought briefly of charging into his stomach and taking him down. The commotion had attracted an audience gathering outside the shop, Chester boys among them, watching the whole thing with relish.

I stood upright. He stared into my face; his small, flesh-enclosed eyes had lost their sleepiness and were bright with aggression. He stepped past me and approached Mola, knocking the Trapper Keeper from his hand; it crashed to the floor, spilling its contents. Tristan reached down and picked up the compass that had clattered out of the geometry set. Mola grabbed him and he jerked his arm loose. He walked back to me with tight-jawed determination, raising the compass to my eyes.

Harry said weakly, "Tristan…" My heartbeat pounded. I couldn't have moved if I'd wanted to.

"You see this?" Tristan said. "If you so much as set foot outside this shop again, I go ram it straight in your spine. Then you won't able to move, an' you can stay here as long as you like, since you seem to always want to hang on to my tail. Try me."

I slapped his hand away and shoved him. He went reeling back but quickly righted himself and came at me, clenching the compass, but one of the security thugs stepped between us. "All-you schoolers leave dis place," the guard shouted. "Now!"

Tristan was spitting with rage behind him; his eyes never left my face. I started moving back, still facing him, gripping my bag straps to hide my trembling hands. Just before I turned to go I said to his face, "Battyman, shit-dick, sodomite, faggot."

He slapped his chest and shrieked; both guards had to hold him back. "Yes, Chauncey!" he cried. "You should know!"

I didn't look back. "Don't waste your breath," I said. "You're as good as dead to me."

CHAPTER 15 – THE RIOTS

On the third day of the mayoral election riots, we were at school sitting in an agricultural science class when a sixth-form student ran to the doorway and beckoned Ms. Ramsey. Their conversation went on for some time. Master Gordon-Marsh, the form teacher from next door, abandoned his class to join the conversation. He kept darting looks around, especially in the direction of the pantry across the yard, as if he saw something that caused alarm. Their voices were low and disquiet broke out in the class because we couldn't hear what they were saying. Behind me a boy discreetly tuned in a transistor radio. A reporter's voice said, "...*Spontaneous roadblocks, looting and burning of debris have already shut down sections of the city and persons are being asked to exercise extreme caution if travelling on foot. Motorists should be on the lookout for unruly demonstrators extorting passage fees along main thoroughfares. Businesses and schools are being advised...*"

"Turn off that radio!" Ms. Ramsey shouted. Her voice was shaky. The conversation at the door continued in earnest. That there was rioting in the city wasn't news to us. We were all concerned, yet secretly excited. Gordon-Marsh called out, "There!" pointing toward the grassland beyond the pantry and row of teachers' cottages. "There goes one of them!"

Senior, a boy who'd gone out on a bathroom break, came back. He too kept looking around him as if being chased by phantoms. The doorway assembly quizzed him. A boy said, "Jus' like Senior to go all the way to the city to take a shit." Then someone mimicked Ini Kamoze: "*Call de police, police, police, po-lice. Senior went to take a shi-it.*" Ms Ramsey was still standing in the doorway with her arms crossed, biting her lip. Master Gordon-Marsh said loudly enough for us to hear, "Ramsey, I would advise you to bolt the door and close the windows." We looked at each other. He and the sixth form student left. Ms. Ramsey pushed Senior inside.

Now it was her turn to look anxiously across the yard. Senior took his seat but said nothing and looked at no one. He was normally quiet, but now we couldn't bear his reticence. No matter how much we badgered him, he just sat rigidly, his face blank. The radio crackled to life again. "*Commuters are being forced to walk long distances as bus drivers and taxi operators have abandoned their routes to join the protest. Sections of the Marzouca Sugar Estate have been set ablaze. Several private vehicles have also reportedly been set on fire, and members of the Fire Brigade have allegedly been stoned while trying to put out the blaze. This last report, however, has not been confirmed. The police…*" The radio sputtered and fell silent. Ms. Ramsey closed the door. She looked helpless standing before us, and her inexperience worried us. Fresh out of college, she was the youngest teacher on staff, petite, cheerful, with a short gamine haircut, large ears and an elfin grin. Now her indecisiveness made her appear even more childlike. If things took a turn for the worse, we were prepared to take charge. Yet none of us knew what was happening. There was rioting in the city. That was all we knew. Before, the news had thrilled us, now it was beginning to make us tense. A boy sitting beside the open decorative blocks on the other side of the classroom suddenly pulled his chair back from the wall. We whipped our heads around, startled by the screech. "Somebody's outside!" he whispered. "In plain clothes, with a bandana covering his face." Ms. Ramsey instructed us to close the windows. "Miss, I think you should tell us what you know," Alvaranga said. Another boy, peeking through the decorative blocks, said, "I see two o' them! They crouchin' outside the chemistry lab! One has a bottle torch!"

Senior finally spoke. "The Fullerites," he cried. "The Fullerites are here!" He grabbed his head between his hands. "The school is under attack!"

The news numbed us. We wasted precious time sitting in collective stupefaction. The fight had come to us. It was just as Jesus Saves had said: "The change will knock at your door, whether you want it to or not." Fleeting shadows moved outside. Boys jumped back from the open-block wall. We heard footsteps trampling the rose plants hedging the building. We were being surrounded. We had to act quickly. Ms. Ramsey remembered she hadn't locked the door. When she tried, she realised the deadbolt was faulty. The door could only be locked from outside. She started moving her desk for a barricade. We helped her. "Come away from there!" she whispered to the ones regrouping by the decorative blocks. "Is there anything here we could use to screen that wall?" she asked. We shook our heads. Senior started crying.

Alvaranga stood up. "Miss, I think you should leave the class."

Ms. Ramsey stared at him. "Why is that, Russell?"

"It's not safe, Miss. Especially for a woman. If they really want to get inside, nothing will stop them. As a matter of fact, none of us should stay. We're sitting ducks. We don't know what's happening outside."

"And that's exactly why we should stay where we are," said Ms. Ramsey. But in the end, she relented. We opened the door cautiously, stepping out in a tight circle with Ms. Ramsey in the middle. A small group broke off and escorted her to the main staffroom.

Outside, boys watching us from nearby classroom windows slowly started coming out, too. We heard a commotion at the end of the block. We approached cautiously to investigate. In front of the dormitory, behind a low wall, a group of tenth graders were hurling rocks in the direction of Bailey House to keep a pack of Fullerites at bay. The Fullerites were moving furtively through the crumbling building. Some wore bandanas below their eyes, like train robbers in old Westerns, but many were barefaced and armed with stones, steel pipes, machetes and slingshots. They seemed intent on entering the teachers' cottages beyond the dormitory. They moved in a wide arc from Bailey House down to the pantry, but the steady hail of rocks was making their progress slow. If they got to the cottages, they knew we'd be hesitant to throw rocks, mindful of the glass windows. We had to stop them.

Some boys ran down the slope to defend the chemistry labs while the rest bolstered the dormitory squad, hurling whatever stones they could find. But we had little to aim at. Our targets were well organised, their movements cunning. We had no kind of strategy, only our numerical advantage. Our arsenal running low, a boy scaled the wall to gather rocks in what had become a no man's land. A stone hit him in the face. We heard the dull sickening sound of his jaw crack. Grabbing his face, he went to ground, screaming and squirming. As we made frenzied attempts to haul him back behind the wall, two Fullerites sprinted across the grassland to take up positions just a few yards in front of us. One of them was Pap Smear, the poetical pickpocket who'd mugged us. Wielding machetes, he and the other man kicked at the door to the teacher's flat, but when the door finally gave, it clanged against a burglar bar inside. All the houses were built like this. Pap Smear was at a loss; he hacked the door with his cutlass and cursed. They were stranded. They couldn't go inside and it was impossible to move back to Bailey House. We took careful aim, ready to slaughter them both with the stones we had. We felt desperate to destroy them. The injured boy was dragged off moaning to the sickbay. A standoff ensued. Then a lower schooler came running up and told us what was really happening. The Upper School attack was a decoy. The majority of the Fullerites had all this time been by the Lower School. The whole lower campus, including their cafeteria and tuck shop, was under siege, with one of the guards being captured and held hostage.

No one knew how to proceed. We couldn't abandon the Upper School, as much as we wanted to help the younger boys. The Fullerites appeared patient, waiting for us to make up our minds. Then we heard a heavy rumble passing the school gate. A few of us scurried to the fence. A military tanker was rolling down the street, with two military jeeps behind it and two squad cars in front. The soldiers in the jeeps dangled their legs outside the vehicles, and had machine guns spread across their laps. The squad cars drove into the schoolyard. The tanker and jeeps headed to the city.

When the Fullerites heard the sirens, they retreated. Pap Smear and his friend escaped. Now boys ran en masse to the Lower School. Our group was about to follow them, but Harry stopped us. "I've had enough," he said. "No one at this school cares about us, anyway. What's the point?"

We left by the eastern gate.

Now we saw the rioting in the city, firsthand. At Lower St James Street, an armed mob streamed past the courthouse. They stopped at the KFC restaurant on Harbour Street Plaza, barged into the building, frightening off the lone security guard. The mob helped themselves to food and sat down to dine. Those who weren't hungry commandeered the cash registers. When a cashier stood stubbornly at her machine, a rioter reasoned with her. "Lady, don't be foolish. Colonel Sanders ain't you poopa. Now step aside before I burn de ugliness off your face with this pot o' fryin' oil."

Outside, rioters flagged down a white Nissan Hiace bus, carrying tourists from the direction of Falmouth. When the driver seemed determined not to stop, they moved to the centre of the street. The bus swerved to avoid hitting them. It climbed a grassy verge and screeched to a stop. The driver refused to open the doors. The men began beating the sides of the bus with their hands. The bus tilted. Tourists screamed. Some snapped pictures. The driver, an elderly man, finally came out brandishing a tire iron, waving it at the swarm of angry faces. The mob backed off, but they saw that his hand was trembling.

"What all-you want?" the driver said.

The ringleader stepped forward. "We want foreign currency."

The driver looked incredulous. "Wha'? Does this look like a fuckin' cambio to you?"

The ringleader wasn't laughing. "Nobody have to get hurt, Daddy," he said. "Jus' stay calm."

Someone smashed a bottle at the driver's feet. The theme of the riot so far could be summed up thus: don't sacrifice yourself needlessly in protecting someone else's interests. The driver seemed to have understood this. He stepped back. The rioters appreciated his cooperation. They cheered him. They set upon the van in good spirits, sliding back the doors. The more eager ones tried climbing through the windows. A plump tourist woman, wearing a low-cut blouse tight around her bosom, realised they'd been abandoned. She stared after the driver in shock. "Lennie! How could you?" The driver sat on the verge looking lost. The other tourists did what they could, beating the intruders back with *Welcome to Jamaica* pamphlets and roadmaps.

A shaggy brown dog ran through our midst, wagging its tail and looking about, but no one paid it mind. It was Harry who recognised it. "That dog," he said.

"What?" Alvaranga said.

240

"That dog… It's Dennis's dog."

It darted after a man running past us, dragging an empty noose behind him and chanting: "Tally the ballots and hang the crooks. We not afraid o' they dirty looks!" He was stripped to the waist, his arms and upper body smeared with black grease; he wore black trousers cut off at the knees, and his head was covered in a makeshift executioner's mask, which showed only his eyes and mouth. He looked fearsome, like a masquerader in *Jonkanoo*. But his voice, when he spoke, cracked like a whip, high-strung and comical. He kept glancing over his shoulder. When the dog was close to catching him, he sped on, lifting his knees theatrically. "Trouble coming!" he shouted, pointing at the dog. "People, look and save yourselves!" We ran after him. When he saw us giving chase he ran faster.

"Dennis!" Mola shouted.

He began playing a game with us, ducking behind buildings or turning suddenly into side streets, baiting us as he did the dog. He turned into a lane where looters had just kicked in the showcase glass of the Winners Sports Centre at the Jumbo Mart Depot. They were grabbing armfuls of expensive-looking trophies, cricket bats, balls and other things. We saw the broom vendor, who sold outside the Civic Centre, hurry past us with his peculiar gait, easing down on the shorter leg, then tipping up on the longer one, a fluid motion like a little dance. The spirit of the riots had transformed him. He had grabbed a cricket helmet. "Howzat?" he said, pointing to the helmet. "Signed by the great Sir Garry Sobers." Then Gassan Aziz, looking great and terrible, came tumbling down his office steps, with four armed guards behind him, and made after the scrambling looters. "TIPPY!" Gassan Aziz roared. At the sound of his name, the broom vendor yelped and glanced over his shoulder and scrambled away like an injured crab, the helmet bobbling on his head.

Still in pursuit of Dennis, we came out on the other end of the lane, just a few yards shy of Sam Sharpe Square, though had it not been for the monuments, we'd have hardly recognised the place. It billowed with black smoke. The choking smell drove us back. People were wetting their shirts in the fountain and tying them over their mouths and noses. Others shouting, "Down with

Gallimore!" stoned motorists trying to get past the barricades of flaming debris dotting the street.

"It's too dangerous," Mola shouted above the din. "We have to turn back!" We caught sight of Dennis on the other side of the street. He lured us through the maze of wooden stalls and carts of the fish market. All the vendors had fled, abandoning their fish, spread out on blue tarpaulins, with large chunks of ice packed tightly around them. Oily fish-smelling water puddled in the trash-choked gutter. The dog stopped and sniffed. Dennis stopped too, waiting, watchful. The dog licked its chops, preparing to eat. Dennis called out, "Come, Trouble. Come, bwoy." The dog didn't move. It set down on its haunches to emphasise its intentions. Dennis got angry. Holding the noose open, he moved forward threateningly.

Mola stepped forward. "Dennis, we know it's you."

Dennis said nothing, watching the dog eat.

"And… we're sorry for how we treated you before," Harry said.

"Dennis, you remember how you saved Tristan that day at the beach?" I said.

Dennis peered at me through the holes of the mask. His eyes seemed to soften with concern.

"Yes," I said. "I know you remember. Tristan's in trouble again, Dennis. I wish you could help us, tell us what to do…"

Dennis stared at me, then returned his attention to the dog. "Come, Trouble," he said, but the dog ignored him; now it lay on its belly and stretched out its forelegs. Dennis dropped the rope. The game was at an end. When he turned and walked up the street, we didn't follow.

Russell accompanied Mola back to his family's shop at City Centre. Harry and I took a shortcut home through Fairfield by the old disused train tracks. A thought told me to retrieve the rope Dennis had left behind.

CHAPTER 16 – END GAME

Two weeks after the riots, on the eve of Tristan's birthday, I returned to his father's house in Knockpatrick. We were on the roof, with nine other boys about our age and younger, all of them strangers to me. They weren't city boys – doubtless the rural chapter of the Fire-Clappers, with Tristan, the outsider, their de facto leader. They knew I was nervous of their company and constantly gave me hard, confrontational looks, trying to intimidate me with their body language, as a kind of running joke. Tristan stayed close to me, though his own body language remained calculatedly aloof. We were both mindful of what had happened the last time we met, but we didn't say anything about it. Instead, we sat with our backs to a low wall partially surrounding the roof and talked – at least I talked – about random things, about school. I told him about my anxiety over my final exams, about the Fullerite invasion, about seeing Dennis during the riots. He didn't say anything, didn't reach out or jest as he usually would, just looked and listened in an unfocused way, puffing on a chillum that had been changing hands among the group. When he finally spoke, it was of the chillum he was turning over in his hands, admiringly. "You know it take me five days to build this? Part clay, part wood, part glass an' part rubber." He gripped the drawtube and took a long deep draw, sucking in his cheeks and holding in the smoke with his eyes half-closed before exhaling. "It became a hobby… like pottery class or something." He smiled placidly.

I gave him a wan smile. "Congrats."

He took another pull. "When I smoke it, I bubble like Saturday soup, bwoy." He was mellow, and immensely pleased with himself.

He handed it to me. I palmed the glass bottom, feeling the pressure of the water gurgling in the filtration chamber; I sucked the smoke slowly up the drawtube and held it, giving it time to cool before inhaling. I convulsed with a bout of coughing. As soon as I pulled the smoke into my lungs, my head went heavy. "Where you get this man?" I said. "It's the strongest weed I've ever tasted."

Tristan beamed proudly. "High-grade skunk, bwoy, straight from Westmoreland. Not like the bush weed they sellin' downtown."

"You sellin' weed now?"

"You really want to know?"

I shrugged. "Just askin.' You give any thought to comin' back to school, possibly repeatin' form five? I mean, it's not like you were expelled you know. Your case is special."

He rested his head against the wall. "Yes, my case is special all right."

"You know what I mean."

He playfully shoved my knee. "Chauncey, relax, man. You not here fifteen minutes good, an' already tryin' to rehabilitate me, eh. Great friend that you are."

I ignored the sarcasm. But I was uneasy. I thought that my being here might be just another of his ploys to always keep me dangling, to always be in control of the situation, that he had invited me here just to taunt me. I watched him from the corner of my eyes – so always at ease with himself. I tried to fight down the malice creeping into my thoughts. We smoked some more and drank into the night. He started talking more. As time passed, it got easier for us to fall back into old ways. He asked about my family. I told him Sheila had full control of the farm, that Papa had left a portion of it to him in his will. I said, "You hear what happen to Fish Tea? That he's back in lockup?"

He nodded, his eyes watery from the stinging smoke. "You remember that time people told the constable they see Fish Tea stealin' marl from Lime Quay, an' the constable went to his shack that night to get him, an' Fish Tea said, 'Constable, what you want? I gone to my bed!'"

The laughter bubbled in my throat and I finished the story. "An' when the constable kick open the door and pull off the bedspread, he see Fish Tea's soles caked with marl an' ask him: 'Gone to bed with feet like that?'" We burst out laughing and recited Fish Tea's catchphrase whenever he sallied through the neighbourhood scavenging: "Im come from outta Spanish Town Jamaica… Fish Tea sweeter than your mornin' coffee! Nah take tea nor nuh talk from nobody…easy!", though when I thought of how precarious and absurd Fish Tea's life was my amusement died. I waited for Tristan to stop laughing, then said, "So this is it, Tris, this is how you plan to live?"

He closed his eyes and sighed. "Chauncey, seriously, stop bein' so fuckin' grim, man."

I said nothing.

"Damn funny thing," he said, "I never felt more in control of my life. You just have to shoulder each day as it comes, earn your way a little at a time an' keep your goals in mind. That is what I say." He looked at me, as if to see the effect of his declaration.

"If you say so, boss."

This agitated him. Perhaps he felt he had to make himself better understood. "You remember how I lose my temper that day at Sugar Navel? Part of it was because I was afraid. I saw too much of myself in that girl an' couldn't face it. But the only enemy to defeat is your own self-pity. That's how it starts. Then you stick it out; you do what you have to do till you can call your own shots."

I looked at him. "So that's what this is about, trying to beat them at their own game?"

He smiled at me pityingly. "Do you believe I was with Raymond that evening in the cafeteria?"

The question caught me off guard. He noticed my discomfort. "I don't know," I said.

"Well, don't you *want* to know?"

"I don't care. What does it matter?"

The smile widened. "Yes, the writer, always watching from a safe distance."

I sighed and dropped my head between my legs. "Here we go again… always makin' yourself into a fuckin' martyr."

He continued as if not hearing me, "The way you watched from the door of the woodwork shop that day, lingering long enough to get your kicks. The way you watched at the whore-house. I gave you your performance – I gave you your pleasure." He leaned closer; his voice rasped with emotion. "All that material for your precious little stories, though you only wrote lies – too scared to face the truth – that no one corrupted you, that *you* were always rotten to your core!"

I jumped up and grabbed the front of his shirt, hauling him to his feet and holding him against the wall, his back leaning over the ledge. He giggled like the Green Goblin and I giggled right back, ghoul to ghoul, our minds in sync.

"Truth or dare?"

"Truth."

"You see, Peter Parker," he snarled, "the spider didn't turn you into a creepy crawly thing. You! – you were always a creepy crawly critter to begin with… the spider bite was only a stimulus. Hahaha!"

"Truth or dare."

"Dare."

"I dare you to let me go."

I did let him go and his eyes bulged with panic and his hands flew up to grab my wrists. The other boys moved to intervene but I held him steady and released him. He was embarrassed, but losing his initial shock, his expression hardened and he glared at me. I wasn't intimidated, just sick of all his bullshit. The boys observed us a while longer, then returned to their own affairs, smoking and talking. "Lovers' quarrel," one of them said; the group chuckled.

In the past, whenever I'd fought with him, I'd felt miserable. But now, when my temper subsided, so did my need to struggle with him anymore. I think I accepted our irreconcilability with relief. I knew I'd lost him, that our relationship was too altered by exposed feelings and disenchantment to ever go back to an uncomplicated friendship. I said to him evenly, "So I guess your excuse is that you were corrupted, and you had no choice. But what can you really accuse me of? Of running away that day? Fine, go ahead. But we've both suffered. You know that. But that part of our lives is over. We're not children, anymore. At some point you have to start taking responsibility for yourself. I suggest you start before it's too late."

He studied my face with a questioning look. When he spoke, his voice was remote and detached and I found myself without the urge to listen. "So I should take responsibility and become a model citizen like you've become, eh. That's all right. I don't have to lie to myself. I know what I am. An' contrary to what you think, I'm no slave. My will is mine alone to break. An' you're wrong, it's different for me in a way you'll never understand."

After that, it truly felt as if there was nothing left to be said. Later, the radio on the downstairs terrace announced midnight. He pulled a gun from his waistband and fired three rounds into the air. The boys blew finger whistles and popped champagne, wishing him happy birthday and playing music on the component set up on the roof. He was happy. It was good to see him that way. We'd been drinking and the alcohol started taking effect, making it easier to forget our conflict. The warmth of blood rushing to my face was like the warmth of old feelings I knew I'd never recapture with him. It dawned on me that I'd heard no sound downstairs, except the radio, that the house was empty. Then the sound of a car pulling up outside the gate broke our revelry, catching everyone off guard. We were all of us alert, pulling back from the edge of the roof. But Tristan was composed.

I'm jumping forward a bit here to tell what I've come to understand happened that night. The police had picked up two men in the city, colleagues of Tristan's, on a tip earlier that evening. The police knew they were to meet with him in Knockpatrick to deliver guns. So they coerced the men into taking them to the meeting place. All along, Tristan had been the object of a special operation.

The car was still throttling downstairs, one of the long-body black ones with gull-wing doors they called Street Scavengers. One of the men came out and yelled: "Tristan. Is Swarmy. We get de ting dem." When Tristan walked out to the front side of the roof, the police released a spray of bullets; one punctured his lung, one grazed his neck, another clipped his collarbone, pushing him back. It happened so fast. They were on the roof, six of them – the ones they called Acid Squad – in black boots, dark-blue uniforms, black helmets and Kevlar vests, shouting and pointing their assault rifles, kicking us to the floor and jamming our faces onto the concrete, telling us to spread our arms and legs else they

247

would shoot, then walking around us, kicking our feet apart and stooping to perform quick searches.

I lay directly across from Tristan. He was on his back, attempting to raise his head, breathing raggedly through his nose, his chest moving up and down steadily, and clutching his neck, the blood leaking between his fingers. The squad leader walked over and knelt beside him, raising his helmet to look down into his face. He said in a steady, almost bored tone: "Tristan Petgrave?"

Tristan managed to raise his head, forcing short bursts of breath through his mouth. I could see the outline of his gun gleaming on the concrete, within reach of his hand. "Yes," he answered, "but don't kill me."

The policeman had seen the gun, too. Pointing to it, he said, "Pick it up."

Tristan looked momentarily baffled, but then understood.

The officer smiled crookedly, and said again, "Pick it up, birthday bwoy," then pressed his thumb into the wound on Tristan's collarbone.

Tristan yelled and started crying. It sounded like the panicky sounds of a child who wakes up in the dark and realises he's alone. He snivelled and coughed. "Please, me a beg you."

It was the ease with which the policeman pulled his piece and pressed it to Tristan's temple and fired that made me sink into a protective nothingness. I was only brought back by the residual twang of another bullet hitting the concrete. I opened my eyes, pressing my cheek to the cold ground, just to feel if I were alive. I felt an exhilarating joy, but that high didn't last. It was replaced by exhaustion and bewildering shame. When I looked over at Tristan, his head was a mess. The policeman took up the gun, placed it in Tristan's palm and folded his fingers over it with a graceful, deliberate motion that was almost like affection, a final rite. Then he stood up and signalled to his colleagues. One of them shouted: "On your feet! All-you sleeping a jail tonight. Every single one o' you! You lucky we don't blow your bulbs right here. You set o' nastiness." They took more guns from the other boys, who seemed grateful to be relieved of them, almost happy to be going to jail, to have had their lives spared. They dragged me to my feet, but I had no legs to walk on. For a while I thought they would shoot me for insubordination. I had a perverse urge to run to Tristan's corpse and unclench his fist, to tell him it was all right, that he didn't have to fight anymore. It was then that one of the squad lifted his helmet and I saw that it was Leanhead, a boy who'd graduated Chester two years before. He looked into my face and called out to the squad leader, "Sarge, I know this one." The squad leader looked at me, then walked down the steps at the side of the house. They rode me down in the jeep, but didn't put me in handcuffs like the others, and dropped me off in the city by the Rapid Sheffield store. When the van was out of sight, I leaned against the building and vomited till my stomach was raw and tight and hurting.

I told my family all that had happened when I got home. Sheila ran over to Clare's house. I soon heard the wailing break out. Lights started jumping everywhere but I went to bed and tried to sleep. The darkness in the room felt bottomless. I closed my eyes to stop the sensation. My room was next to the kitchen and the tap was dripping with a loud persistent *drip drip drip* on the hard surface of the sink, with a rhythm so regular that even when I plugged my ears I could tell when the next drip was coming. Then I was on the roof again. I rolled over and there he was beside me, as plain as day. His body was whole; there were no signs of his wounds. But a stream of dirt, fine as hourglass sand, was pouring steadily from his nostrils, like a dark nosebleed; I could see it was the very essence of life leaving him, that he was going back to dust. Terrified, he grabbed me around the waist and wrapped his cooling body around mine, digging his fingernails deep into my arms, then into my back. "I don't want to die, Chauncey. Please don't let me die!" It was all I could do to free myself, to pull away and dig his cold fingers from my flesh. I cursed him and finally managed to get up. I ran to the kitchen and splashed water on my face until the tightness in my chest receded. "It's only a panic attack," I muttered. "*It's only a panic attack.*" I breathed more evenly. My tension ebbed. When I came back and saw the crumpled sheet, my first thought was to cast it aside. But I lay down instead, passing the sheet through my fingers, passing it over my body, feeling the fine texture of his pain, until I shivered and ejaculated his ghost, then went soundly to sleep.

In the morning I woke with a renewed will to live, a longing to cleanse myself of the stale breath of his memory, to return fully to the embrace of life. I had survived; he had not. I gathered up the sheet, carried it out to the yard and dumped it, along with the clothes I'd slept in. I felt his anger rekindle, wherever he was, for it was another abandonment. But I remained unrepentant. I had survived; he had not.

CHAPTER 17 – FINAL MOVEMENT

It was the heart of the rainy season when we said farewell to Tristan. Steady, pouring rain. Bouquets battered on graves, their petals embedded in the soil's sodden blackness or floating on the film of muddy water swelling across the grounds. Our party was one of a handful in Pye River Cemetery that Sunday afternoon. I took a last look at him, dressed in a dark suit, wine-coloured shirt and silver bow-tie, his hair cut in the way he'd always worn it, the powder on his face forming thick white swirls of sediment below his nostrils, his skin unnaturally dark from the bullets' poison. My thoughts retreated to where he'd been happiest, the beach – painful to accept that the blue light of the sea would never again fill his eyes, that I'd never again smell the raw scent of his sandy sunburned body, that the soles of his feet, soft and white like sea foam after swimming, had taken their last steps. As they lowered the mahogany-and-elm casket into the vault, the choir sang louder to cover the mounting sounds of grief. When I saw his mother crying, I remembered when Brother Mac had said: "You coulda cry till your tears touch the sea." Standing between Russell and Harry, my eyes waywardly followed the tracks of crabs gone into hiding across the cemetery. By nightfall, many would be part of some gleeful crab-hunter's catch. When Pastor intoned the final prayers, I found myself wiping tears away with the heel of my hand, murmuring the childish benediction for a crab's wasted beauty, *Come butter come fat*, wishing them Godspeed in their retreats, hoping the tide would turn in their favour for once and they'd find their way back through the marshlands out to the estuary, safe from the hunter's hands. But it took a stubborn imagination to sympathise with a crab's seasonal sacrifice, especially when the outpouring of grief around you was constant.

Clare threw the first rose on the casket and we followed suit, then we left, trying to avoid the sinking mud. *Shalom.*

★

A few weeks after attending Tristan's funeral, I went to see Leanhead, the police who'd recognised me that night on the roof.

I had taped the report on the evening news the day after Tristan's death. The sergeant, a man named Fowler, told the reporter: "A police van patrolling the Knockpatrick area came under heavy gunfire where Tom Redcam Avenue intersects Collins Drive. We returned the fire and later a man was found suffering from gunshot wounds in nearby bushes, and was pronounced dead on arrival at hospital." Never mind the "nearby bushes" bit, Tom Redcam doesn't even intersect Collins Drive, but ends in a gully opposite the old rubber factory, about two miles away. This was no surprise – the standard script they read for most police killings, with little variation in plot.

Leanhead had an awkward, sloping-shaped head – the source of his nickname. He had enjoyed a reputation as a prankster back at Chester, a real lout for the most disgusting practical jokes; his party piece had been saturating tissue with urine and throwing it up to stick to the ceiling of a bathroom stall and drip on unsuspecting boys. However, he was never mean-spirited, and even after Tristan's death, I found it hard to hold a grudge against him.

I went to see him at the No: 14 Police Station on Barnett Street where he was stationed. He was surprised by the visit, but understood why I'd want to talk. We went out into the courtyard to sit on blue plastic chairs, our backs to a high, barbed-wire wall, which separated the administrative buildings from the jail barracks. He sucked on half an orange and hurled playful insults at passing colleagues. He looked bigger, more muscular than I remembered, though with the poor light on the roof and in the van I really hadn't got a good look at him. His face still had an easy open look that could be taken for friendliness, but it wasn't friendliness; now it seemed the blank contentment of a closed-minded man, resigned to his duties. I kept thinking of how he had shared jokes with us back at Chester, had gambled with Tristan by the Pav, and borrowed money from Mola. Yet inside two years out of school, he could execute his duties without hesitation and consideration for former friendships. Yes, he had intervened on my behalf that night, but the tone in which he'd spoken, the empty look he'd given me, was not that of the person I'd known. I wondered what side of himself he would show to me now.

Leanhead spoke first, leaning back in his chair and folding his arms: "The way I heard it, Tristan just got up one day, dusted off the seat of his pants like Job and said: 'I going to the hills,' and that's how everything started.

"He was rising quickly in the ranks of the Fire-Clappers, but he wasn't satisfied. He was running the sweepstakes scam, in collaboration with Colors – you know the one where they call unsuspecting people in the States, usually old retired folks, and tell them in a fake Yankee accent that they just won a million dollars in the so and so sweepstakes, but in order to clear their winnings they have to send a processing fee, and the people so fool-fool and greedy they believe them. They send US $100, $300, $600 day after day through Western Union to 'offshore subsidiaries', to clear the big cheque, but never receiving a cent. Well, Tristan had that one pat; ran it like the Red Cross. Business was good, with call centres all over St James, as far as Negril. From what I hear, they were making upwards of three million dollars a month. Plus he was helping out with the arms distribution leg of the gang. But still he hated the city and everyone in it: good, bad straight and queer. He started siphoning off guns to stock his own stash, selling to anyone – random people, rival gangs. Started arming the bush. Building his own ragtag outfit of barefoot illiterates – those same boys on the roof that night in Knockpatrick. They weren't Fire-Clappers material, they weren't gangsters, just hungry-belly earthworms. But the Jacket Man caught wind of his treachery and ordered Spider to liquidate him." Leanhead took a look around before speaking discreetly. "They paid Fowler to do the deed, so it would look good for Gallimore – a poster scalp for the fight against organised crime. Plus Tristan's own father co-operated readily with our operation. When we tell him what his boy was getting up to, the man was speechless. But it was the filth, Chauncey, not so much the gangsterism, that punctured him. It hurt and shamed him. You should have seen his face. We all felt a bit sorry for him. That's never a pleasant thing for a man to hear 'bout his own blood from strangers. He disowned him. Became a ready accomplice. We called him in advance that day and told him to leave the house, on the pretext, of course, we were only going to arrest Tristan."

Leanhead paused, looking into my face and waiting for me to say something. When he tired of waiting he said, "I hear them faggots say he had a dong like a toddler's arm. That he could choke you with and do much worse besides." He leaned forward, staring at his hands dropped between his knees. "He was too dangerous to live, Chauncey. Plus he was crippling the criminal muscle of this entire town. They wouldn't let him get 'way with that. God knows I didn't want to go that night; it went against my natural feeling. When I think 'bout him cold and lifeless…" He shook his head. "Man, it cut me up. For days I don't eat. But is it right for us to blame ourselves? I mean, what Tristan think was going to happen?" He sounded hurt, and again looked insistently at me.

"I guess he just didn't care anymore," I said.

He sat back and folded his arms, his anguish melting and the look of cruel contentment returning to his heavy, razor-bump scarred face. "But don't you see what's happening, Chauncey?" he said, picking the remains of the orange from his teeth with his grimy-nailed fingers. "We're practically the victims now, the *new faggots*. These newfangled gays are the aggressors. Soon they'll have the swinging dicks and we the gaping cunts. They already control half this town, and the means of production. We're at war, and we losing, but I'll tell you as Joshua told the Israelites – choose you this day who you will serve. As for me and my house…" He patted the service pistol on his hip and smiled savagely. "I'd rather put this piece to my head than take a hard one up the ass. I don't even need God as my witness. He has forsaken this place." He stood abruptly to signal our meeting was over and stuck out his hand. I got up and shook it without looking at his face, wondering at the religious zeal with which he'd spoken at the end.

My grandfather always said the best way to season boiled snapper was to stuff the okra pod down its throat; that way the flavour explodes inside the fish's belly while cooking and the slime stays permanently in the flesh. He called it his culinary doctrine. As I left the station, I thought of the bullets piercing Tristan's flesh that night as entrenching Leanhead's doctrine. His remorse was shallow; no doubt he'd discharged his duties assured of the righteousness of his cause, perhaps even with fervency. As long as he believed he was at war, and war naturally claimed casualties, then his conscience was clear. Yet as much as I despised his fanaticism, I couldn't dismiss him as deluded to his face. As a rookie cop, the war he'd spoken of was real insofar as he could see and feel its consequences. And his tone seemed to suggest that my nonalignment would sooner or later bring me up against it, or at the very least, in the interim, produce frustration.

But there was no war between gays and straights. It was propaganda sold to the public, a construct of the police fed by a smouldering jealousy against the power of those few gays who'd circled their wagons and whom they didn't dare touch, and at whose beck and call these same 'lawmen' were, if the right strings were pulled in the right places, and the bribe was tempting enough.

It was the last day of examinations and the most important. Math Paper II. I had studied "professionally" with the help of Harry's father as a tutor, and had aced Paper I, the multiple choice section, back in mid May, but Paper II was a whole different kettle of fish, even so, by my own estimation I'd been doing well so far, had even managed to keep my calculator, pens and pencils dry, free of nervous sweat. But then came a question that stumped me. I began to feel faint and must have blacked out. In this state I heard a strange noise, looked up and saw Tristan. I was trying to speak to him but he shrugged and walked off and waved goodbye.

When I came to, they were standing over me in the sick bay. Master Harding bent and peered into my face and said, "Knuckle, *full well* or *fully well*, which usage is correct?" I rubbed my forehead and answered, "In modern English, adverbs modify adverbs so the phrase *fully well* is standard. But the phrase *full well* is a surviving usage of *full* as an adverb, and is more common than *fully well* which is sometimes considered incorrect but is in fact a hypercorrection." Harding said to Dr Sangster, "He seems fine to me. But you're the physician." Sangster gave me a quick checkup and said, "Exam stress probably triggered it."

Master Harding drove me home and in the car he said, "So Dr. Sotwae told me he's been discussing this business of family with you…"

The next day I was allowed to finish the exam in Master Laird's office. I aced it. Boom! I had the habit of taking at least twenty minutes to memorise the questions on a math question sheet before moving my brain muscles to do anything else, before even lifting my pen; it was part laziness and part stubborn instinct. I would slowly commit the selected questions to memory, my lips moving silently, and allow my mind to swallow all the details it could. I worked faster that way when I finally began writing, mentally working not only the question I was doing but anticipating others to follow. I'd done this since a student at prep school and I had memorised what I could of the chosen questions on paper two and practised them that night and slept on them and went the next day more than prepared.

One Friday, after Mola and Harry left work, and Russell and I left school, we met up. The four of us played a few rounds of pool before wandering out to the Hip Strip after nightfall, passing a bottle of Stone's Ginger Wine between us. Harry said, "Jesus… you always hear them before you see them. The white socks…" A group of young Americans approached. One said, "Caleb, let's stop by that jerk cart below the neon lights across the street and get some jerk beef." Caleb said, "Nah dude, Jamaicans don't jerk beef. Whatever you do never ask a jerk man for jerk beef – chicken and pork only – else they'll give you the crazy eyes or make that *tchat!* sound through their teeth." The one with the jerk craving said, "Makes no sense though…"

"Says the foreigner," piped Harry, glaring at the group.

Caleb said, "Do we know you, bro?"

"Listen Cable," said Harry, "you're this close to having your first really awkward vacation encounter. I'd suggest you keep walking."

"Who are you to tell me what to do?"

"Who are you to tell us what makes sense? Try walking with the handbook next time instead of your hubris."

"I'm not going to dignify that with a response."

"You just did."

Further down the strip we saw a very dark, leggy hooker on the sidewalk, in glitter lipstick and eyeliner and a tight shimmering dress and heels, waving down taxis heading into Mobay proper. Mola said, with his mouth open, "What a tall drink o' Sprite…!"

Russell hugged Mola round his neck and wagged his face. "Sanjay, you don't like black women, but you like black cunt whenever we buy pussy. You notice he never buys the Indian whores, Chauncey? Always chooses the blackest ones?"

I laughed and said, "I think we're entitled to be offended, Russ, but then Sanjay was always a peculiar fish."

Mola said, "Chauncey, how we goin' to get along wid dis one?"

"Swimmingly," said Harry and took the lead. He pitched his cigarette and opened his arms as if to embrace her and said with a big smile, "What a way you pretty like snow-cone." The girl laughed shallowly at his corniness and said, "Harry, is like every street I turn pon I see yuh, all hours a night. Yuh nuh have a yawd, bwoy?" Then she walked with us, sharing our liquor and jokes.

Harry said to Russell, "Russ, take off de damn sixth-form tie. School's out; is like yuh sleep in de damn thing." Russell took it off and hung it round the hooker's neck and kissed her on the lips and her glitter came off on his mouth.

She said, "I see you before… drivin' dat two-door Mercedes to school… cool cool."

"Careful, Russ," said Harry, lighting the hooker's cigarette, "she has pretty car eyes."

Russell pulled her closer. "She has pretty eyes, period," and whispered something that made the girl pull back and say, "Huh?" in a loud exaggerated voice as she laughingly coaxed the bottle from him. He could never handle liquor and was already red-eyed and slurring his words. Russell shouted in her face, "I said I want to see that glitter lipstick on my cock!" Passers-by turned to look. I took off my sixth-form tie and stuffed it into my pants pocket. The woman laughed coquettishly and covered Alvaranga's mouth: "Shh! Keep your voice down! All in due time, dear…"

Russell hugged Harry and said, "A glittery cock!"

"A shimmery cock!" responded Harry. Then he hugged me and sang, "A sparkly cock!"

"A candy cane!" I sang back.

Then he hugged Sanjay: "A bejewelled cock!"

"A Rolex cock!" said Sanjay. Then we hugged each other and trapped the girl in our midst and shouted: "That's all we want for Christmas!" We persuaded her to accommodate us at Pier One, a private beach further down the strip where hookers fucked tourists by the stone reef. We had to scale the tall fence, since the venue was closed. "Ladies first," Harry said. So she hitched up her skirt, stepped into his meshed fingers and prepared to climb. But just then we heard voices approaching us from the other side, a mishmash of accents. Harry motioned us back into the darkness behind the low stonewall. When they entered the pool of light before the fence we saw five of them, two white, two black, and a top-heavy hooker with narrow hips and big calves. We guessed that two were North American, one Barbadian and the other we couldn't place. They'd been out scuba diving by Jack Tar Village and had come into town for "group therapy". The hooker told them to go ahead, she had dropped something and was looking for it under the street lamp by the gate.

Harry said, "Nobody move! I have a plan."

As the men climbed over, one said with a frat boy's glee, "Man… that was bedder than the Negril spring break pussy… whooh!" Another: "Jamaican punany irie mon."

Harry whispered, "You hear that beautiful chime boys… that's the sound of satisfied customers." When the men had climbed over the fence, and the hooker finally mounted the gate and was perched at the top, Harry emerged and jounced the fence slightly.

The hooker drew a sharp breath: "Who de fuck is you? Listen to mi yuh redskin dawg! Nuh fuck roun' mi nerves tonight, yuh hear!"

Harry said, "Throw down all yuh money. Me nah guh ask a secon' time. Take a look down, is a good twelve foot drop an' yuh boun' to bruk a bone. We goin' to leave yuh right here an' tek de money anyways."

"Harry!" said Sanjay.

"Sanjay, be quiet!" Harry said. "An' go look if anyone comin'."

Sanjay whispered, "Harry, yuh askin' for trouble! Why yuh think they call de red light district de red ants nest?"

"Shut up!" said Harry.

The whore hissed, "Dutty jancro! Cum nyam out mi pussy when mi red!"

Harry jounced the fence harder and she screamed and slipped; her leg dangled and a shoe fell. Harry showed his teeth to the whore: "Livin' on a man's eyelash... when him blink yuh boun' to... finish it for me."

"Fuck you!" said the hooker and spat. We dodged the spittle and Harry prepared to give the fence a big push when the girl with us lurched towards him with tears on her face and grabbed him from behind. "No, Harry baby, don't dweet..."

"Awrite" said the one perched at the top, "I comin' down." Russell emptied the bottle and tossed it in the bush and put his hands on his hips and laughed, "But this almost melodramatic!"

The woman threw down the money from her handbag and Harry began picking it up. But when she prepared to climb down, he said, "Not so fast. Throw down the handbag."

"Fe wha'? Me already give yuh de money!"

"Throw it down! If I find a cent in it I go bruk yuh up meself."

She heaved a sigh and threw down the bag and Harry turned it out, then threw it aside. His face, his voice, his whole manner had changed into something that made Mola and me feel uncomfortable. As the girl climbed down, Mola said, "Harry, give her back de money." Harry ignored him, whistling and counting the bills. Mola shoved him. "Now!"

Harry only laughed. When the girl finally stood before us, seething, Harry said, "Dis is all of it?"

The girl screwed up her lips and cut her eyes.

"Don't make me ask yuh again!"

"Yes! That's all of it!"

Harry said, "Take off de wig."

Her eyes widened. Before she could move Harry dragged off the wig, swift as a gull standing atop an Old Joe's head and plucking fish from its open beak, and tore off her stocking cap and snatched the wad of cash falling from her head. She fell on her knees crying, "Wooiie! 'Zaas Chris' mi money! Mi bloodclaat money! Mi money wah me wuk so hawd for! Tamarind Sue, wha' yuh go do? How yuh fe go home wid two long han' to yuh pitney dem, an' go look ina dem face when dem nuh have nutten fe eat? When yuh not even have soap a yuh yawd fe wash yuh pussy fe guh back a wuk tumorrow!"

"Shut yuh mout' an' get up! Wha' yuh tryin' to do? Call down crowd? Get up! Cuz I promise yuh a bruk up!"

The woman stood whimpering, "'Zaas Chris' mi money…" then stiffened and prepared for her licks. When they didn't come, she dried her eyes and retrieved her shoe and tightened her shoe straps. Her eyes threatened a beating for the other hooker, even though this girl had intervened to save her. Harry threw some bills at her. "I go spare yuh dis time."

She scrambled to the ground, took them up and counted them. She turned to the girl with us and said, "Dutty gal, remember seh yuh tek food outta me pitney dem mout' tonight." Then she tramped off, her narrow hips moving angrily.

"She's always droppin' something eh," Harry said, bending to retrieve her lipstick. He opened it, looked at it and said, "I wonder if my father would like this shade?" Then he tried some on. "It suit me?" He grabbed the girl. "Give us a kiss." She cringed and shook her head. He pushed her away. "You too? Start walking!" She hesitated. He feinted at her. "Get!" She shook her head and made to go to Russell, but he had fallen asleep on the low stonewall. She gave us a miserable look and walked off slowly, pulling her dress down, wary that the other woman was waiting.

Harry caught the anger in my face. "What? You have something to say? You of all people? Out with it!" Then he said, looking like an angry clown with lipstick smudged all over his lips, "This is what I'm goin' to do someday. I'm goin' to be a pimp. I'm goin' to open an establishment to make Sugar Navel look like a nunnery. Look pon me face good."

I chuckled despite myself and said, "I lookin' boss, now yuh only need a little eyeliner." He clenched his fist and looked like having a go at me.

"Yuh think I jokin? An' don't think I goin' anywhere else. I openin' it right here. Is just like Bawn-a-Bay say, they coulda cry shame some more, let dem; is their tears wasting." He beat his chest. "A yah me bawn, a yah me live, no bwoy cyan run me weh, else a big big worries." He whistled to the girl who was still dawdling and she ran to him. She took his arm and they walked out of the dark long narrow lane towards the bright lights and traffic noise of the main street. When they were out of sight we heard a bottle smash, screams, sharp braking and honking of horns. Sanjay made to go to help, but I held his arm. "He's on his own."

"You OK, Chaunce? Too much excitement for me, tonight. I'm gone." Sanjay gave me a hug, and headed home to the family shop. I wondered when I would see him again, what we'd still have in common.

I shrugged Russell awake and he jumped up as if fighting phantoms in his sleep: "Wha? Eh!… Ugh…" He rubbed his hand over his face and slurred, "She'll be all right… the night is young… Chauncey, call a cab at the pay phone. I too mash up fe walk, star."

I walked back from the payphone, waited for a cab to arrive and bundled Russell into it. I looked about. No sign of Harry. I needed to clear my head and went to sit on a bench.

A gigolo, hugging a fiftyish white woman, stopped in front of me. She had her hand on his big bare chest, giggled and said, "…the man I met was a college man…" I tried to listen to what they were saying, but could only catch snatches. She was blonde and pretty. The gigolo tipped the bottle to his head then put it to her mouth but she refused. She looked admiringly into his face and bit her lip. He kissed her and whispered something; she cackled like my aunt with her head thrown back and said, "…because you care about your children's feelings…"

The words, "her beauty made me blush", suddenly came into my head, oddly, because the gigolo was singing the gibberish of a lewd calypso – *Pumpokopeeno, pumpokonaano.* He clutched her buttocks and gyrated against her crotch. She pushed him off, sat on a cut-stone wall and pushed her hair from her face: "I'm tired Patrick… and you're drunk…" She took off a sandy slipper and rubbed her toes as he tried to pull her up. "I'm tired of walking… Let's go back to the hotel…"

I felt miles apart. Worlds away. Why had that phrase popped into my head? I knew it was for a reason, my mind trying to show me something, give value to an experience I'd considered unimportant, and that I should never ignore it. Where had I heard the phrase? It was a conversation with Master Harding. He'd seen me reading Faulkner and had said: "You copy the teacher till you know his technique, till the technique swims in your blood." I'd asked him what came after that. "Then… well, think about the first time you saw Marzie, Knuckle. What happened?"

"Her beauty made me blush."

"To them any wedding is better than no wedding and a big wedding with a villain preferable to a small one with a saint."

I knew that was *Absalom, Absalom*.

"I wonder if she makes you blush the way the colour just rose in your cheeks at my challenge?"

I asked him what he was driving at, and he'd said, "Knuckle, the day you discovered your gift, you became your own master. Don't ever worry about 'then what'. For someone like you it's immaterial."

But was I content to be what I had become? Was it enough to observe, to record, to tell the truth? What had I become? Was there any way I could repair what I had done to Marzie? I had broken and thrown away the Red Dragon, had felt sick when I looked at that story again, but could I pretend I had lost my urge to hurt women? Where had that come from? It was easy to say it had come from school. Chester had taken me out of my parochial shell, shown me some of the possibilities of a life removed from the norms and limited expectations of Anchovy. But what had I allowed it to teach me? To walk a certain way, to laugh a certain way at certain jokes, to be one of the boys. And I had been a great copier. To my own detriment. Without giving thought to all the toxic, misogynistic indulgences.

And how did that fit with the two women I loved, who'd cared for me? I'd quarrelled with them when I felt they were getting at me, but I'd always respected them, hadn't I? I replayed a conversation with Aunt Girlie complaining about my bad habit of leaving clothes all over the floor. I was writing and ignored her; she'd told me to "stop tappin' that damn computer!" That I wasn't a child anymore for her to clean up after me. I'd tapped the same computer key repeatedly in tightly wound anger, told her I could hardly find time to write, that Saturday was mine. She'd exploded, "Ho-oh, is who yuh tellin'? You goin' have to do a lot better than that boy… a lot better!" Then I'd made the mistake of referring to myself as a man. She laughed, quietly, sardonically: "Man? A man knows he has to do better for himself an' for those countin' on him. A *man* does things he don't like for people he loves – you listenin'? You think I naggin' you eh… disturbin' you for spite…? Better is very hard to come by, boy…an' we have high expectations of you, not only 'bout bookwork but character, so start by showin' some respect to yourself an' those who deserve it."

Yam, bananas, mackerel, a glass of sparkling water. Prayers before bed. Words without rhyme or meter. What had a boy like me been raised on but love? The pride of loving tormented women who spoiled as much as they fed. And they'd fed me a sound education. I'd grumble at Mama and Aunt Girlie, but I could never dream of hurting them. I knew in my heart they were right, though I knew I never much thought about them when I was with my friends.

With them, I'd thought of myself as being at one remove, the observer, the thinker, but could I claim to be any better? I was as much seduced by the sweet pleasures of the trash talk that invariably had women as its butt – or gay men.

But what did I owe this place and its unchallenged cruelty? Not challenged, at least, by me. I knew what Harding was telling me, that a man like me could have only one true concern, cruel as it may sound, and that was to push my talent to its limit. But was that enough? Was the world what it is, as my hero Naipaul claimed? Could it be better? I was confused – that, I knew. Guilt was an inconsistent presence in my brain. Sometimes I thought that only the writing mattered, that it didn't matter how well or badly the writer behaved. Sometimes I had felt oppressed by the orthodoxies of a "privileged education", the bars of convention that Tristan never broke through but died beating his hands bloodily against, but I knew it had given me all my skills and certain strengths. How much had I delighted in jousting quotations with Master Harding, in setting out to impress him? I liked to think I was my own man, different from my friends, but I also knew too well the temptations that Harry confessed when he said to me, "Chauncey, I feel like I gettin' too wild in this place, no joke, like I tryin' to paint this town red with my own blood, with no other reason than to see how much I can get away with, an' prove to everyone else how much I can carry on."

I'd come to depend on Harry's happiness at my successes, academic or otherwise, and accepted his support without a second thought. He'd always had the exasperating ability of not knowing how to hold a grudge – which had made it impossible to fall out with him while we were growing up. Yet what I'd seen of Harry this night had made me deeply uncomfortable about my own excesses. I didn't want to emulate his guilelessness, his lack of restraint and his lack of ambition. Part of me felt this made him inferior to me, despite my own flaws. Part of me felt ashamed to think this. But my flaws defined me, as his defined him, and I was secretly happy to be leaving him, and the others, behind, thinking – knowing, that if I stayed in Montego Bay we'd sink together. I saw him as part of my predicament, a potential encumbrance, yet knew that thinking this was unfair, a cop-out.

But Tristan – he was my greatest failure, though I knew that what came with all the pain of having watched him suffer at the hands of the school's cruelty, which I'd taken part in willingly, was part of my self-discovery, the mixed-up emotions and self-deception included. But Tristan, Tristan… I had loved him and it hurt that I could never tell him what I felt.

A bottle crashed to the ground and smashed. A drunk stopped in front of me, glaring at me.

"Mi Bawn-a-Bay. Big dutty stinkin' Bawn-a-Bay! Tek it or leave it – but I nah seek nuh buyer. Remember dat!"

There was a message there. I stumbled to my feet and headed home.

ABOUT THE AUTHOR

Dwight Thompson is a Jamaican working in Japan as an English teacher. His work has appeared in the *Montego Bay Western Mirror*, *Pepperpot: Best New Stories from the Caribbean* and *The Caribbean Writer* where he won the Charlotte and Isidor Paiewonsky Prize. One of his stories was also shortlisted for a prize in the 2012 *Small Axe* Literary Competition.